Slow Coming Dark

A Novel of the Age of Clinton

H. A. Covington

D1227581

Writers Club Press
San Jose New York Lincoln Shanghai

Slow Coming Dark
A Novel of the Age of Clinton

Writers Club Press
an imprint of iUniverse.com, Inc.

For information address:
iUniverse.com, Inc.
620 North 48th Street, Suite 201
Lincoln, NE   68504-3467
www.iuniverse.com

ISBN: 0-595-12523-9

Printed in the United States of America

This book is dedicated to all the victims of Bill and Hillary Clinton, from Juanita Broaddrick and Jerry Parks and the many others whose names and stories are known, to the massacred innocents of Waco, to the nameless and forgotten children murdered in the bombing of Belgrade. On behalf of the real America, in anguish and humility, I apologize for what we have done to you all through our cowardice, our sloth, and our apathetic acceptance of tyranny and atrocity. Some day, however tardily, I honestly do believe that we will give you justice. When that day comes I hope and pray that you will, in turn, grant us forgiveness. —*HAC*

Contents

1   He to the Appointed Place 1

2   Enter First and Second Murderers 12

3   Enter Three Musketeers 31

4   She to the Appointed Place...38

5   The Stage Is Set..41

6   The Song of the Lavender Canary 65

7   Enter the Ingenue 77

8   Welcome to the Hotel California 100

9   Enter Sam Peckinpah 123

10 Sicilian Defense 154

11 Nightblood...209

12 The Empire Strikes Back 223

13 The Ides of October...252

14 Slow Coming Dark...271

About the Author 273

The Clintons are real. This story is fiction.

1

He to the Appointed Place

It was well past midnight when the telephone rang beside the bedside of Agent Matthew Redmond of the North Carolina State Bureau of Investigation. Redmond, a compact and muscular man well into middle age, turned over sleepily and sighed, running his hand over his slightly itchy scalp. Beside him his wife's head lay on the pillow, her silky yellow hair foaming over the quilt. The central air conditioning rumbled soothingly in the darkened bedroom. Outside the house on Boundary Street, in the hot August night, thunder rumbled far away in the muggy darkness. Matt refused for a moment to acknowledge the irritating fact that his phone was ringing, and then muttered, "Damn!"

"Let the machine get it," said Heather, her voice muffled.

"It's for me," he replied with a yawn. "Probably a murder here in Chapel Hill or over in Carrboro, if they're calling me in at this time of night. Just what I need right now, leaving a nice warm bed to look at a dead body."

"You don't know that until you hear who it is!" protested his wife, but he started to get up even as the answering machine kicked in and Heather's voice filled the room, chirpy and cheerful. "Hi! You've reached the Heather house! Also Tori's occasional rest and refueling stop, the den of the mighty Trumpeldor, and last but not least, the secret, cigar-smoke filled headquarters of the Southern Sherlock Holmes himself, Two-Gun Matt! Leave a message at the sound of the tone, unless you're one of the bad guys, and if you are...watch out!"

"Playing with the answering machine again, Watson? You really think a bad guy is going to leave a message?" asked Matt, chuckling as the answering machine beeped.

"Hey dere!" came a voice. "Dis is one of de bad guys."

"Is that your buddy Cowboy screwing around?" asked Heather, looking over a slender bare shoulder at him and the phone.

"Don't think so," replied Matt with a frown.

"Redmond, you dere?" came the voice, in a thick Bronx accent. "Dis is Eddie DeMarco. You remember me, dontcha? From when you was a Fed? Eddie Miami?"

Matt snatched up the phone. "Eddie Miami?" he demanded incredulously.

"Yeah, it's me," came the man's voice, the recorder still rolling, his voice filling the bedroom. "Surprised ta hear from me, aintcha?"

"Not at all, Ed," said Redmond, fully awake now. "I get a lot of Mafia hoods calling me up after midnight to chat. How the hell did you get my number?" Heather sat up in bed, surprised and alert, her hair tumbling down over her nightgown.

"I got a secret source of information, dis lady who tells me dese tings. She's called directory assistance. Look, Redmond, I ain't just calling to bat da breeze. I'm out here at da airport, Raleigh-Durham. Just got in from Miami. I want to turn myself in. To you."

"What for?" asked Redmond.

"I was kind of in da wrong place at da wrong time," said Eddie cautiously.

"Yeah? Not an unheard of predicament in your profession, Ed. How wrong a place and how wrong a time?"

"Bad wrong, man. Bad wrong." Matt almost thought he could hear the man shiver. "Some *babania,* some stiffs, some real stone killers. It happened on a boat out of Key Biscayne. Dis guy's yacht. A guy you would know his name, know whaddum sayin'? It ain't just da killing. Dat happens all de time when you're dealing *babania.* Hey, you know how it goes. But dese were some really important people. *Pezzonovante,* big shots. Connected up in Washington and New York. I was going to go somewhere and let da heat cool off, but I think been spotted. They're after me now. I'm a loose end, and dese rat bastards are looking to tie me up. Dis is way outta my league, Redmond. I want ta come in from the cold."

"Wait a minute, you're telling me a drug deal on a boat in Florida went bad and some people got killed?" demanded Redmond, grabbing up a pen and taking notes on a pad by the bed. "What was the name of the boat and where is it now?"

"Nevvah mind dat. I'll tell you da whole story once we work out an immunity deal, but you got ta come get me and arrange for protection first."

"Eddie, I don't make plea bargains, the prosecutor does, and it sounds to me like you're talking Federal jurisdiction anyway. Or at least Florida state. I haven't been DEA for almost nine years now, and I haven't been Federal at all since 1993. I resigned after Waco and came back home to be a state cop. Why are you calling me and not the DEA or FBI if you want to turn yourself in?"

"Because they're da ones dat did the killing. Feds! Rat bastard Feds!" There was dead silence for a time. "I came here to North Carolina because you're here. I remember you from when you was a Fed. You was an okay guy, for a cop. I also heard you got your own reasons for knowing dat Feds can get really bent. I figure you to be da only cop I know who'll make sure I make it into da courtroom alive, not get shot trying to escape or get my ass shanked in da shower in jail by some bullpen nigger dey slipped a carton of cigarettes to whack me. I want you to come and pick me up."

"Matt, it's a trap!" urged Heather fearfully. "They're finally coming after us because of what happened with Bennett!" *[See "Fire and Rain"—Author]*

Matt put his hand over the phone. "I'm way ahead of you, honey. I've got to go, it's my job, but don't worry, I'm taking the cavalry." He removed his hand and spoke into the phone. "Eddie, I'll come and see you, and if you tell me you have knowledge of a crime I'll take you into custody. But I'm a North Carolina state investigator now. Florida and drugs aren't my jurisdiction any more. If you're involved in something in Florida you'll be sent back there. If it's a Federal offense you'll be transferred to the Federal system. I can't stop that."

"Hey, dontcha tink I know how da system works?" asked Eddie impatiently. "Who better? I been beatin' it since I was ten years old. But I want you to hear my story and I want you to be the one to call the Feds once you've heard it. I heard what happened with that asshole Bennett. Good riddance to dat motherfucker, forget about it! I knew him, no loss at all there. Once the FBI knows you're involved and I'm not da only one who knows what's going on, dat's gonna make me a lot less expendable."

"And by the same token make me a lot *more* expendable" returned Matt sourly. "Gee, thanks, Eddie! Of all the guys you could have chosen to tell whatever the hell your little secret is, you picked me! What a pal!"

"Look, for fuck's sake, Redmond, I don't have time ta screw around! I know dey're after me! If you're not gonna help me, den I gotta disappear. Now are you coming for me?" demanded Eddie, his voice tinged with hysteria. It struck Matt that the man was genuinely afraid. *Maybe there's really something going on,* he reflected.

"Where are you, exactly?"

"Hang on, a plane's taking off." Matt could hear the roar and beating shriek of a jet engine, and DeMarco started shouting to make himself heard. "I'm at a phone booth just outside Terminal C here, down by da first parking lot! I'm gonna hang up and go to da little coffee shop just off de lobby in Terminal C, right by the U. S. Air desk! Nice public place where everybody can see. When can you get over here and get me?"

"I live in Chapel Hill, which is within spitting distance of RDU. I can be there in half an hour, but I'm bringing airport security and my SBI partner with me," said Matt, speaking loudly to be heard over the jet engines.

"Good," said Heather. "Wake Cowboy's ass up for a change."

"Bring Billyboy wit you for all I care. No, no, on second thought, definitely do *not* bring Billyboy," DeMarco concluded with a shaky laugh. "Okay, I guess you remember what I look like. You still wear dat funky hat?"

"Wouldn't leave home without it."

"Okay. I'll spot you den…*Sweet Jesus, no!*" he suddenly screamed. A quick succession of titanic explosions, so loud they drowned out the jumbo jet and rattled the answering machine and hurt Matt's eardrum through the phone receiver. Then the sound of the jet died away. There was a slight rattle as someone picked up the phone on the other end.

"Hello! Eddie?" shouted Redmond. There was a giggle on the line, light and airy and evil. It could have been a man or a woman. Then the phone was hung up.

Matt turned to his wife. Heather's face was slack with horror. "Shotguns," he said.

✳✳✳

Matt stood beside the corpse in the damp, steaming night, his trademark brown fedora pulled over his brow, and his hands in the pockets of his windbreaker. The air pulsed with whirling blue police lights and crackled with bits and pieces of radio chatter. The dark sky was still flickering with distant lightning and muttering with thunder, but it wasn't raining yet. The SBI crime scene unit was laboring to get everything done before a downpour washed away any evidence. One technician was dusting the telephone receiver for prints in the forlorn hope that some killers had not yet learned the rudimentary work skill of wearing gloves. Beside Matt stood his boss, the director of the SBI. "Hope you don't mind my calling you out, Phil," said Matt apologetically, pulling out a long Dominican cigar and cutting the end with a pocket cutter. "But you'll admit, this one's kind of unusual."

"Yeah, we don't get many mob hits in North Carolina," said Phil, a grizzled older man in a rumpled suit and hooded raincoat. "Not too many of our home-grown corpses wear silk suits. Dammit, gimme one of them thangs, you gone get me out here at two in the morning." Matt handed the director the cigar he had cut and cut another one for himself, then lit them both with a Bic. Fragrant smoke drifted through the air. The dead man lay sprawled on his back on the sidewalk. He had been small and thin. The shotguns at point blank range had obliterated his face and almost cut him in half. He lay in a pool of blood that steamed slightly warmer than the humid August night. Blood and brain matter were splattered all over a white concrete pillar fifteen feet away. "You say you were talking to this mope on the phone when he was blown away? Why was he calling you?" Matt held up the answering machine tape.

"You'll hear for yourself. He was gibbering about politicians and celebrities getting killed in a dope deal gone bad on some boat in Key Biscayne. He came all the way up here to turn himself in to me because he figured anybody who whacks out assistant directors of the FBI can't be all bad, even a peckerwood state cop."

"Shit," said Phil.

"My sentiments exactly. I was pissed off at first when the government suppressed that incident, but then I was glad. I just wish they'd done a better job. Every damned Federal suit, every damned tabloid reporter, and now it looks like every damned hood on the street knows about it. You know Heather and I still get calls from fringe reporters? Matt Drudge left a couple of messages on our machine last week."

Phil shook his head. "Matt, after that bad craziness back in October '96 I still don't understand why you didn't take your ladies and that damned cat and light out for parts unknown. You're branded, my friend. An Enemy of the People, and we all know *what* people."

"You gotten any pressure from above to fire me?" asked Matt.

"No, and that's what's scary," said Phil grimly. "It's like the régime wants you where they can keep an eye on you, and lay hands on you real quick. People don't just get fired in the Age of Clinton any more, Matt. They end up…well, you see how they end up," he said, gesturing to the mortal remains of Edward DeMarco.

"Eddie said some kind of Federals were out to whack him because of some killings on a boat down in Key Biscayne, Florida," said Matt. "He said there's big names involved."

"You figure he was on the level?" asked Phil.

Matt shrugged. "Jesus, Phil, who knows nowadays?"

"Tell me about it. Even as recently as ten years ago I would have said he was a lying hood trying to jerk our chain," Phil continued. "Today, I have no trouble at all taking it as a working hypothesis that this man was murdered by Federal agents to cover up some new scandal in this unspeakable administration." A tall, rangy man with a drooping gray handlebar moustache and wearing a Stetson hat materialized out of the darkness, dressed in jeans and a sport shirt, badge and a .45 Colt Peacemaker hanging from his belt. Arthur Garza was an affirmative action import from Texas, a retired San Antonio police detective who had been offered the moon and the stars to come into the North Carolina SBI as the agency's first allegedly Hispanic operative. This came after a Federal personnel audit had criticized the SBI's lack of Hispanics, and the Janet Reno Justice Department had threatened to file a Federal lawsuit. In an episode that still angered him, the director had been approached by a highly paid and well connected Washington D.C. "diversity consultant" who advised him that Reno only wanted a few Hispanic names on the payroll to be satisfied and a gesture of "good faith", such as hiring the consultant for a $100,000 fee. The suit later admitted, after a convivial evening of Jack Daniels in a expensive downtown Raleigh hotel suite, that half this sum would be kicked back to the Democratic National Committee.

Still, buying the DOJ off was less expensive and time-consuming than a lawsuit. Phil managed to get by with hiring a few Americanized Mexican and Cuban clerical workers with names ending in "ez", as well as a blond, blue-eyed woman from Chile who was in fact doing a superb job running the SBI's LAN computer system. But there had to be at least one Hispanic agent, and again they had lucked out in Arthur "Cowboy" Garza. Fifty years old but as vigorous as a young man, street-smart and motivated by a passionate loathing for crime and criminals in every form, highly competent and well liked, Garza had only one drawback. He was a brown-haired, blue-eyed Caucasian descended on his mother's side from the German colonization of Texas which took place in the nineteenth century, while his father was descended from a grandee who had been one of the first Spanish settlers of Texas on foot of a grant from the King of Spain in the eighteenth century. Garza had another ancestor who had been a general in the Confederate Army. He didn't speak a word of the Spanish language; his grandfather had been the last of his family even to so much as visit south of the border. But he had that precious Hispanic surname that brought him in at the level of senior investigator with a salary to match, and he filled the DOJ's diversity requirement. So Garza had been paired with the impeccably Anglo-Saxon Matt Redmond, who spoke a fluent Colombian dialect from his years as a DEA agent, and when it was necessary to deal with Spanish speakers on a case it was the gringo who hablayed the Español. "Any luck on the security cameras?" Matt asked his partner.

"SOL there, I'm afraid," replied Garza. "The cameras are the swivel type, always moving. The killers timed it so they hit the guy when the camera was pointed down the lot."

"And when a jet was going overhead to muffle the noise of the scatterguns," pointed out Matt. "Cool hands. How do we know there was more than one?"

"We got a couple of distant eyewitnesses, a cabbie doing a drop-off, a baggage handler on a smoke break, a couple of people in the parking lot. Looks like two guys in a pickup truck. They pull up, driver and passenger both get out with their weapons, driver pulls down on the vic over the hood of the truck and the passenger fires from the hip, badda-bing, badda-boom. One of them slides over and hangs up the phone just to be neat, I guess, then back into the truck and they're easing on outta here. Nobody was close enough to get a license number or even give us a make on the truck, except it was light blue and kind of battered. They think. The actors were probably back out on Interstate 40 before you had your shoes on, Matt."

"I thought Mafia torpedoes drove long black limousines," said Phil.

"They picked the kind of transportation best suited to the time and place to be inconspicuous," said Matt. "Yeah, we're definitely talking pro on this one. My guess is they got on 40 East and somewhere between here and Benson they changed vehicles. We need to put out a call on any abandoned trucks. We'll probably find it in the parking lot of a K-Mart somewhere. Maybe they left something behind for forensics."

"Why 40 East?" asked Garza. "Why not head west for Greensboro?"

"Because they'll want to get on I-95 at Benson and head for either New York or back to Florida," explained Matt. "That's where this comes from. The late Mr. DeMarco, aka Eddie Miami, was a button man in the Genovese crime family. My information is about ten years old, admittedly, but as I recall he was in Dominic LaBrasca's crew working out of the Dolce Vita Social Club in Bensonhurst. Eddie also had a lot of action down in Florida, hence his name. Back in the eighties he was the henchman of a guy named Tommy Rossi. Tommy the Terrible, they called him. Tommy was the Genoveses' man in Florida, and he and Eddie worked out of the Casablanca Club in Fort Lauderdale. I busted him a couple of times on drug raps. He and Rossi and about twenty other players were all involved in a big drug indictment, one of those cases that goes on and on and on for years, like wrestling an octopus, with hearings and motions and delays of every kind imaginable, and then one day you hear it's all been dismissed on some stupid technicality, some i you didn't dot or t you didn't cross four years before."

"Henchman," chuckled Phil, puffing on his cigar. "I haven't heard that term in years."

"More of a gopher, really. Eddie never really made it big in the Mob. Small potatoes all his life. He was dependable, but he was dumb. Not managerial caliber, you might say. But he seems to have gotten involved in something heavy on some upper crud yacht down there and he became a loose end that had to be tied up, as he himself put it."

"Tommy Rossi," mused Garza. "That name rings a bell. Didn't he turn up floating in an oil drum off the coast of Miami a few years ago?"

"That's the guy. He was about to be questioned by a Senate committee on some gun running and dope activities in South America. CIA-connected stuff. They used Tommy as a subcontractor and I guess the Company thought he was a loose end to be tied up. Eddie didn't want to follow suit."

"Any connection, you figure?" wondered Garza.

"Could be." Matt turned to Phil. "Are you giving this one to me and Art?"

"This yay-hoo was killed while he was on the phone to you, Matt. Sounds like the fickle finger of fate to me. I guess it's yours," said the director.

"I guess it is," agreed Matt. "Probably won't involve too much skull sweat or any arrest where I can display my dashing derring do. Doubt if I'll get to plug any more FBI bureaucrats or CIA hit men. Damn! The actors will be out of state by sunrise, guaranteed, and if we get lucky and make a case against somebody, some other department will pick them up in Florida or New York for extradition back here. Or Federals. I'll be in early and start making calls to the FBI and the locals down in Biscayne, see if we can figure out what this alleged drug boat homicide is about. That will give us a starting point. Eddie didn't have the imagination to make things up, so there's a boat with some bodies out there somewhere if we can find it and it hasn't been scuttled in the Bermuda Triangle. If there's anything political or drug-heavy to it the Feds will be in here on the double and grab the case from us. Especially if it does involve anybody who could embarrass the administration any further."

"Which means it will all disappear from the light of day," growled Garza angrily.

"The joys of living in a one-party state," said Matt with a shrug.

"Hey, guys, no grousing, now. The people spoke in '96," quipped Phil bitterly. "The Chinese people, that is."

"You guys realize in a couple of years I'll have to arrest you if I see you with those cigars?" added Garza. "For the sake of the children, of course."

11

Enter First and Second Murderers

The small park in the Hamptons was warm, but not overly hot; the morning was overcast but not actually threatening rain. By a small lake, a dumpy old man sat on a park bench, feeding the ducks that swam about in front of him with pieces of bread that he tore from a long, stale Italian loaf. He was dressed in slacks and a rumpled shirt. An incongruous Alpine hat with a small feather was on his head; beneath the hat he was bald as an egg. His blotched hands rent the bread and flicked it at the ducks, who fought over it. A slow burning, cheap cigar was clenched between his teeth. The old man never removed it from his mouth, and the ash fell onto his shirt.

At a discreet distance behind the old man, two other men lounged beside a long black Cadillac with illegally tinted windows. The license plate of the Caddy was known to local police, and it was never stopped, for the windows or anything else. The old man was very generous in his support of the underpaid and overworked law enforcement personnel of Long Island. One of the men standing by the car was about sixty years old, swarthy and powerfully built beneath his suit, his hair still speckled liberally with black. He wore aviator sunglasses, and his jacket bulged from the gun he carried in his shoulder holster. It was one of the most expensive legally licensed, privately owned handguns in New York, the permit having cost $30,000 slipped under the table to a judge of the state Supreme Court. The second person leaning insouciantly on the

Cadillac was a handsome young man in a subdued but expensive sports jacket and tie, a teenaged Frank Sinatra with sparkling blue eyes. A blue Bonneville with rental plates drove slowly down the asphalt road into the park and pulled over about twenty yards from the bench where the old man sat, who gave no sign that he noticed. The two men at the Cadillac shifted their weight and eyed the car. The driver sat behind the wheel. "That the guy?" asked the younger man.

"Yeah," said the older man. "Just wait and don't do nothin'. He's checking everything out." The driver of the car got out, a tall man of indeterminate age, dressed in a dark conservative business suit. He walked up to the old man and sat down beside him on the bench.

"So that's him!" breathed the younger man. "So that's Five o'Clock Johnny!"

"Okay, you know that name," said the older man. "Everybody knows that name. But you don't call him that. Not ever. You call him Mr. Visconti to his face and Johnny Vee to friends of ours. When you gotta say his name at all, which ain't a good idea."

"You're telling me! Talk about a rep! I've seen guys with a dozen hits under their belt damned near crap in their pants at the very mention of him! Like he was the fucking devil or something. Come on, Vin, he's that good? Really?" asked the young man, fascinated.

"He's that bad. Really." said the older man.

***

"Hello, John," said the old man on the bench, smiling. "How are you?" The man in the suit was lean and well muscled beneath the silk fabric, his blue chin shaven smooth, his coiffed black hair shot through with the slightest touch of distinguished gray. He leaned over and without the slightest embarrassment kissed the old man formally on both cheeks in a Continental gesture.

"Hello, *padrone.* I'm well indeed, now that I see you," he said. "It's been too long."

"Good flight from Seattle?"

"Yes. How can I help you, Dom?" Visconti knew from long experience that there would be no small talk, and he waited to see what the old man wanted of him. Whatever it was, he was eager to perform the service, for he needed only one look at the man's pasty face and to hear his heavy, labored breathing to know that he was not long for the world, and it would be the last service he would ever render. Tears welled in the old man's eyes.

"Joey's dead, Johnny," he quavered. "Shit. I still can't believe it. My last child on earth. My youngest. Joey's dead. Those rat bastards killed him."

Visconti scowled, enraged at the pain someone had caused the old man. "Jesus! Dom, I didn't know. I haven't heard anything. When? What happened?"

"Five days ago. They got him on a goddamned politician asshole's yacht, down in Key Biscayne," said Dom.

"Who got him, Dom? Who killed Joey?" asked the younger man gently.

"Suits. Fucking Fed suits. FBI or Justice or somebody working for the Fed suits."

"Christ! How the hell did Joey get involved with Uncle Slime that heavy? Why didn't they just indict him or something?" asked Visconti sharply.

"I'm not really sure myself, John," said the old man wearily. "He told me some of what he was doing and I warned him against getting in too deep, but kids never listen to their old man. Joey was working some angles with Eddie Miami, and he was making money hand over fist. I didn't complain maybe as loud as I should've, because he was kicking me back a percentage. Dope and gambling and orgy junkets on the boat, all these damned Senators and Congressmen and TV network big shots and CEOs and whatnot going down to the islands to do shit they don't dare let anybody see 'em doing here in this country. Big fucking mansions on some of the small islands down there owned by major multinational bloodsucking bastard corporations with stacks of money and cocaine lying around and private armies of security guards all over the place, secret meetings between motherfucking heads of state, everybody sitting around planning on how they was gonna split up everybody else's pie and fuck the whole world up the ass. These cocksuckers are bigger crooks and killers than any of us ever thought of being!"

"You got that right," said Visconti with a nod.

"And when they got through conspiring, Joey would bring in the whores and the bugger boys and the booze and the dope and the roulette wheels and the nose candy, and they'd all get butt nekkid and fuck everything with a pulse and stick every kind of dope in the world into their veins or up their nose. You know how they act. Joey wasn't exactly a priest, but he told me some of the things these big shots got up to made him want to puke. There was some things Joey wouldn't do for them, like get them really little kids. A lot of those fucks like itty bitty titty, ya know. Or little boys. Anyway, some big names got involved. I mean really big names, *pezzonovante*. I guess it was only a matter of time before Joey found out something he shouldn't or saw something he shouldn't, and so they whacked him out."

"What about Eddie Miami? What does he have to say?"

"The rat bastards got Eddie, too. Got him in North Carolina, of all places. No idea what the fuck he was doing down there, why he didn't call me, why he didn't tell me what happened to Joey. Maybe he was in on it, but I don't think so. Eddie was always a dumb fuck, but I don't think he was dumb enough to put the finger on my kid. They blew him away right in the middle of Raleigh-Durham airport. How's that for balls? Gotta be Feds, John. They know they're gonna get away with it. I always told Joey to leave those scumbag Washington fucks alone. Out of our league. He should stick with our own kind of people, forget about it. But Joey always was a high flyer, ya know? Thought we was good enough to do business with any white bread Episcopalian asshole, any fucking movie star, hey, they ain't no better than us, forget about it! They want what we got, so we give it to them. We give them their dope and their broads and their dirty videos and their bugger boys, and we launder their fucking junk bond money and settle their union problems and hide their money from the IRS, whatever, and we wet our beak just like we do everywhere else. Plus he liked hanging out with that kind of people, ya know? The kid had class. He was always sophisticated, like. Not a street bum like his old man. He wasn't really into the street side of the business. Joey was an upmarket kind of guy. Yeah, dat's de woid, upmarket. I used to hear about him doing parties down in Washington with all the big politicos, out in Hollywood doing movie deals, balling actresses, putting on the glitz, having a great time. Kind of envied him, ya know? When I was his age I was doing twelve to twenty in Leavenworth. I never really got to kick up my heels, sow my wild oats, ya know? I gotta admit, I was proud of him, John. Kinda re-livin' my lost yoot through him? Can ya unnerstand?"

"I understand, Dom," said Visconti, his hand on the rambling old man's shoulder.

The old man turned to him, tears streaming down his face. "Teresa ain't taking it good, Johnny. Not good at all. Our last child. It ain't right. A man shouldn't outlive all his children. A mother shouldn't have to bury her last baby in the dirt, and my doctor tells me in a year or so, maybe less, it's gonna be me. I got de cancer, prostate. Teresa's gonna be all alone when I'm gone. Them yellow so-called bosses on the Commission says it's too big for Our Thing, we don't dare strike back, against cops or Feds, they tell me not to do nothin', but I can't do that, Johnny, I can't walk away from it. I can't die knowing my son's blood ain't been avenged. The earth of my grave would reject me as *infamita*, a dishonored man, and I couldn't get no rest. It ain't right they should do this and get away with it, just because they're big shot white bread *pez-zonovante*. You know what I was once, John. You remember me when I was on the street. Once men walked in fear of the very name of Dominic LaBrasca. Twenty ago I would have said to hell with the Commission, I would have gone down there to Washington and found out who did this, and I would have cut their hearts out and drank a glass of their blood right on the fucking Capitol steps. But I ain't that man no more, John. I'm old and sick and weak and tired of living. You know what I want from you, John. Will you? For old times' sake?"

"It's done, *padrone*," said Visconti, quietly, without hesitation. "Whoever they are, Dominic, however high they sit among the *pezzonovante*, I give you my word. It's done."

✱✱✱

"He was a kid on the street in the Bronx, maybe ten years old," the older man said to the younger one. "I dunno how it happened, somebody told me once your uncle Buddy caught Johnny breaking into his car, smashing the window wid a brick, and he grabbed the kid and told him no, dis is how ya do it, showed him how to pick a car door lock. Anyway, Buddy took the kid under his wing kinda, ya know. Back in dem days Buddy was running a crew out of that bar we had down on the Ave, what the fuck was it called? Maxie's. Yeah, Maxie's. He let Johnny sleep on a mattress in the back room and gave him odd jobs to do around the place, sweeping up, washing dishes and glasses, running out for cigarettes and coffee and canolis, dat kinda stuff. Then he started using him for numbers pickups, lookout on some warehouse heists some of the crew did, running around the neighborhood selling little bits and pieces of hot stuff to the housewives and the old folks, cigarettes and hamburger and baby clothes. You get the picture? The kid grew up in Our Thing."

"I get the picture, Vinnie," said the young man. "I gather that was Buddy's style, all right. I don't remember him, but I've heard a lot about him."

"He was a damned good man, your uncle Buddy," said Vinnie with feeling. "Woulda made a damned good boss! Anyway, when Johnny Vee is about fourteen, Buddy has a beef with this half-assed Jew wiseguy over in Brownsville. Name was Benny Klassen. They called him Bedbug Benny because he was fucking crazy, always talking to himself, teeing off on guys for no reason. They also called him Benny Buttfuck because he was a sissy fag, always got young boys hanging around and you knew what dey was dere for. He had a club called Otto's Hole and he had kind of a half-assed crew, bunch of junkies and freaks, trashed-out car thieves and stickup artists nobody else would work with, forget about it! Had porno in the back room, little bugger boy whores upstairs, really sick degenerate operation, know what I mean? He started ripping off some of our guys, jumping our numbers runners and shylock collectors with about ten of his creeps at a time for their day's take, stuck up a crap game Buddy was running, bullshit like that. He's talking about how he's gonna take the whole Family down, take over New York, how he's gonna start by raping Buddy up the ass, crazy shit like that. De guy had delusions of grandeur. Thought he was a human bein' or something. Obviously, we gotta take action.

"So one day we're sitting around in a war council in the back room of Maxie's, talking about how we can get this motherfucker out in the open, take him out, get his mooks and take them down too, so forth and so on. Johnny's serving drinks and cleaning the ashtrays, and he hears dis what we're talking about. He asks Buddy if he can have the afternoon off. Buddy says yeah, we're busy, don't none of us think nothing more about it. Six o'clock or so that night, Johnny comes back. We're still back in the back talking up all these plans and ideas for hits, not getting nowhere, and John walks in. He goes to Buddy and says 'You don't have to worry about Bedbug Benny any more.' Buddy says 'Yeah? How's that? He left town to join the circus?' We all laugh. And the kid says, 'No, Benny and his main man Leo and that creep Willie just got whacked out over at Otto's Hole'. So we perk up our ears. We figure the kid's heard the news on the radio or something. 'You're shitting me!' says Buddy. 'Who the hell did that?' And this kid Johnny just looks at him and says, 'I did.' Then he looks at me and says, 'Vinnie, I took one of those guns out of your stash, a .38, and about half a box of hollow points. They're all in the East River now, after I used them. You'll want to dock my pay for whatever you figure they was worth.' Sure enough. The kid takes one of my guns from the stash, rides the bus over to Brownsville, walks right into Klassen's joint and clips all three of these guys, cold. Just three shots, each one right to the head, badda-bing, badda-boom. Then walks out, ditches the piece in the river, comes back to Maxie's, and starts serving up the drinks and the espresso again."

"Jeez!" whistled the younger man admiringly. "Fourteen, you say? I was an old geezer of eighteen when I first made my bones! What did Buddy do?"

"After we check it out and we learn the kid isn't bullshitting us, Buddy calls him back in the back. I was there. He hands the kid an envelope. Fifteen grand. He says, 'You do a man's work, you get a man's pay.' Then Buddy reaches over and grabs Johnny Vee by the collar with both hands, shakes him good, gets right in his face, and says 'Now you listen to me and listen good! You *never, ever* do anything like this again without somebody in the family, a man of respect, tells you to do it! We live by rules, and if we break them we die by those rules. Okay, it's partly down to me. I should have told you the rules and told you about Our Thing before this. I think maybe you've got a future in This Thing Of Ours, but the first thing you learn is you obey the rules and you don't go off doing cowboy shit like this all on your own. From now on you do what I tell you, no more, no less, and some day you will be a great man in This Thing. You fuck up and I swear I will kill you myself! *Capiche?*' And Johnny takes it all quiet and respectful, and he just says '*Io capiche, padrone*.'"

✳✳✳

"Whoever has done this to you will pay," said Visconti. "But I need to know as much as you know, *padrone*. You know this is true. Please, put your trust in me, and hold nothing back. Now, you say Joey was supplying what by way of goods and services to these government and Hollywood people. *Babania?* Gambling? Women? Catamites? That puzzles me. These things are so common in government and corporate upper echelons these days that no one gives a damn any more. You sure he wasn't involved in anything else? Something political?"

"John, I just don't know. I can tell you this: Joey's clientele was on a very elevated level."

"How elevated?" asked Visconti.

"To the very top. Fucking El Presidente Billyboy himself, he said. Joey claimed he was sending five kilos of top grade coke a month to the White House through some flunky on Clinton's staff and it was all for Billyboy himself. Can you believe dat?" said the old man, shaking his head in wonder and disgust.

"*Five kilos* a month?" exclaimed Visconti, stunned. "*Minchia*, Billyboy's nasal passages must be as slick as an ice rink! He must be barely *compos mentis* most of the time! This drug addict is running the country? Beautiful!"

"Apparently Hillary is actually running the country, as much as anybody is," said Dom. "Hillary and Janet Reno. Hillary is supposed to be the one who actually gave the military orders to bomb Serbia. Joey heard a lot of those things at some of these events he organized for the *pezzonovante*. He passed them on to me, and the Family was able to profit off some of this information. That fucking ugly-ass bull dyke Reno doesn't bother us at all, as you know. When she was appointed Attorney General we let her know we had some information on some carpet munching she did in Florida, ones where the girls were prisoners in jail and she forced them, others where the women got so sick of what she made them do that they committed suicide. Kind of like the same hold we used to have over J. Edgar Hoover, except he was a fag and Janet's a dyke. We haven't had any real trouble from DOJ since then, except for what they did to Chin Gigante, and that case was left over from Bush."

"So why *do* you think Joey was killed, Dom?" asked Visconti. "The whole country knows Bill Clinton uses drugs and women, and they don't care. He survived impeachment, and everyone seems to accept him for what he is. Anything Joey had to say, if ever he had talked, would simply have been twisted around by the White House spin machine and made out to be just one more part of the vast right-wing conspiracy."

The old man breathed deeply. "I think you're right. I think Joey found out something. Something political. Something they couldn't allow to come out. Something so bad it would blow Billyboy out of the water, even as switched-off and hardened to all his bullshit as people are today. Or it may be that it was about Hillary. You know that bitch may be our next Senator? Jesus, give me Al D'Amato any day. Joey hinted as much during his last phone call to me."

"God, what could it have been?" wondered Visconti. "The bastard sold nuclear technology to China for campaign contributions and everyone gave him a pass on *that!* What else did Joey tell you the last time you spoke with him, Dom?"

"He said he was taking a party out on a yacht, a yacht belonging to a Senator."

"What Senator?" asked Visconti.

"The drunk."

"Which drunk?" asked Visconti.

"Kennedy. Teddy wasn't there, though, he just let Joey use his boat. I don't know if he's involved or not. They found the yacht floating in the sea. Eight dead people besides Joey himself and two missing. One of the missing was some fucking movie starlet Joey said was supposed to be the main attraction. The other was Eddie Miami. The stiffs were some high-class hookers, a couple of ship's crew, a couple of dead suits who were corporate assholes of some kind, and two government big shots. Plus Joey. Shotgun at close range. There wasn't nothing left of Joey's face. We had to bury him in a closed coffin."

★★★

"So how'd he get the name Five o'Clock Johnny?" asked Tony admiringly.

"You remember how your uncle died?" asked Vinnie.

"Yeah, I remember. Some kid Buddy slapped around came back with a gun and shot him."

"The kid was a punk who was selling dope to school kids in the neighborhood. He thought he could get away with it because his father was a precinct captain and his uncle was a bookie. Buddy took his responsibilities as a *capo* seriously, and besides, he didn't want dope in the neighborhood because dope brings heat. Buddy and me and Pete the Polack worked the punk over and told him to never show his face in the neighborhood again. We thought that was enough. We was wrong. *Dio*, we should have put him in the trunk! A week later we're standing on the sidewalk outside Maxie's batting the breeze. It's rush hour, five o'clock, lot of cars and a lot of people on the sidewalk and we just don't see this cocksucker until he's right at arm's length. He shoves a gun in Buddy's face and shoots him right between the eyes, shoots me in the gut, and then runs off into traffic. We didn't say nothing to the cops, of course, but some citizens on the street ID him and they arrest the asshole. Of course, everybody assumes this guy will last about twenty-four hours in Riker's Island before he gets a shank in his eye in the shower. But do you remember who was our so-called Boss of Bosses back in dem days?"

"Castellano."

"Yeah, Big Paul," said Vinnie sourly. "Big fucking big shot businessman live-in-a-big-white-mansion-on-the-hill fuck-the-street-guys Paul. Paul says we don't take him out, it would bring down too much heat. This fuck Paul actually says he don't want us the get bad PR, as he puts it. Since when has the fucking Mob ever gotten *good* PR? *Minchia!* No, he says, let the law take its course. Can you imagine dat? A so-called boss saying let the law take its course?"

"Forget about it!" said Tony vehemently.

"Well, we knew damned well Dom wasn't going to take that lying down, and we were about ready to go to the mattresses with the Gambinos. Chin Gigante was going batshit because he knew even he couldn't call off

Dom from avenging his oldest son, and Dom was going to put us Genoveses in the position of defying Paul. Paul couldn't lose face like that, and there'd be a big fucking war. We were scared Chin was going to hit Dom just to stop him from killing this fucking punk and to prevent a war between us and Paul. But dis kid Johnny took it all into his own hands. One day they're transferring this punk into a prison van down at the courthouse, to take him back to Riker's, and badda bing, badda boom! One shot from a high powered rifle by a sniper on the roof, right between the eyes! At five o'clock exactly, the very time Buddy died."

"Hence Five o'Clock Johnny," said Tony.

"Oh, it gets better," continued Vinnie, lighting a cigar and reminiscing. "The punk's father and uncle run crying to Paul, screaming that Dom did it. The next day the precinct captain is walking down the street and he gets an ice-pick through his ear into his brain, collapses on the sidewalk, nobody sees nothing because it's five o'clock, the rush hour, and the sidewalk is jammed with people. The evening after, the uncle who's the bookie is stuck in traffic on the Verrazano Bridge at five o'clock and a guy in a hat and dark glasses walks up beside his car and gives him a head full of .22 hollow points, then walks off down through the traffic jam. Walking, on the fucking Verrazano Bridge at rush hour, and he gets away, and nobody to this day has idea one how he managed *that*."

"Sounds like a warning to Paul," said Tony. "Pretty gutsy for a teenaged kid to be warning off the *capo di tutti capi*. Or pretty suicidal."

"No, it wasn't even that," said Vinnie, shaking his head. "You see, the killings continued over the next five or six weeks. We knew it was Johnny, but he'd vanished and nobody could find him, and believe me, every guy we could get on the street was looking for him, to call him off or kill him if we had to, to stop the slaughter. We're talking fucking Sicilian vendetta here. Every male member of that punk's family over the age of twelve got hit, just like they did it in the old country for centuries. Shot. Stabbed. Garrotted. One guy got blown to kingdom come by a remote control bomb in his car. Another got thrown off the Empire

State Building, and that's another one we got no fucking idea on earth how he pulled it off, how he got the guy up there. They found a thirteen year old cousin hanging from a tree in Central Park. They tried to run, they tried to hide, but he got them all. Brothers, uncles, cousins. A college boy was found drowned in a fountain on campus. One guy was fished out of the bottom of Niagara Falls with more .22s in his brain pan, another guy was found in a dumpster in New Jersey. Fourteen corpses all told. And every one of them at five o'clock in the afternoon. Medical examiner even put the time of death on the kid they found hanging at five P. M. This is a sixteen year-old kid doing all this, bear in mind. I tell you, there was something goddamned supernatural about it. We was in fucking awe."

"Jesus!" said Tony, awe-struck himself. "So what happened after this Sicilian Kid Rambo ran out of targets?"

"One day he walks back into Maxie's, goes behind the bar, puts on his apron and starts serving drinks again. I went up to him and I said, 'Are you fucking crazy? Paul's got an open contract out on you. I'm supposed to be blowing you away right this fucking minute!' And he looks at me with those eyes of his, which I hope to God you never see like dat, and he just says, 'Do what you gotta do, Vin. I did.'"

"So what did you do?" asked Tony, fascinated.

"Obviously I didn't blow him away. In the first place, we all loved Buddy and we thought Paul was a lame piece of shit. In the second place, I gotta admit something. I was scared of him. I still am, and you'd better be too if you've got two brain cells to rub together. This guy is the coldest stone killer I have ever known, and lemme tell ya, I known 'em all. Hell, I started out under Albert Anastasia, but this Johnny could make Albert shit in his pants. I wasn't going to find out what he'd do if he seriously thought I was going to clip him. I suspect if I'd tried I wouldn't be standing here talking to you today."

"So what happened?" asked Tony.

"Castellano was in a rage, but Dom went to him and got down on his goddamn knees and begged for Johnny's life. And you know what Paul did? He graciously allowed Johnny to live, for a price. Dom paid him off. Bought Johnny's life from Paul for cold cash. Nobody knows how much, it was a hell of a lot of money, but that was Paul for you. He had green eyes."

"Hey, Buddy was my uncle and all that, but that wasn't right. A don who allows somebody to ignore his orders and then lets his punishment be bought off?" said Tony, shaking his head. "You can't do things like that. Your own guys lose respect, and when they lose respect…"

"Your green-eyed don ends up like Paulie did in front of Sparks Steak House. Badda bing, badda boom," said Vinnie with an eloquent shrug.

"Badda bing, badda boom," agreed Tony.

✳✳✳

"I'll start in Florida, then work my way up to Washington, if that's where it leads," said Visconti. "Dom, how exactly did Joey operate? What names and fronts did he use? I may have to backtrack whatever it was he was working on that got him into trouble. Who else was Joey with down there? Wiseguys? Guys who would know his business?"

"He worked a lot out of his own place, Chez Joey's in Palm Beach. Most of his customers came through Palm Beach crowd, Kennedies and those fucks. Joey had about a dozen companies going at any one time to cover his junkets and juggle his money around, hide it from the IRS," said Dom. "Lessee…shit, what were some of them? Hi Life Entertainment, Jet Set Escorts, Angel's Escorts, Palm Beach Modeling Agency for the girls, plus he had a liquor wholesaler called Quality Beverage Distributors. That one was more or less legit, that way he got his own booze wholesale, and the liquor dealership and Chez Joey's were what he put on his tax returns for the IRS. For moving cash and cleaning cash there was Everglades Investments, Sunshine State Credit Union and Palco Financial Services. Sunshine State even issued its own Visa cards, can you beat dat? Joey had a real estate company as well that holds a lot of property in blind trusts, you know, for big shots who want to stash a little sweetie in a luxury condo in Florida or keep a nice secluded mansion for private business of whatever kind, and have nobody know who owns it. What the fuck was the name of that one? Oh, yeah, South Florida Escrow Corporation." Dom rubbed his jaw. "Now as to people who might be able to help, Lew Lefkowitz and Joey were real tight," said Dom. "Lew got Joey a lot of his hookers and his porn."

"I know Lew," said Visconti.

"His *babania* and his coke he got from all over, wherever he could get the best price, Cubans, Colombians, Jamaicans, hell, you know everybody in south Florida is a dealer. Pills and speed he got from a biker type named Jimmy Jesus, used to ride with the Pagans, I think. I don't think any of his suppliers would know what went on during his junkets, though. Eddie Miami was his number two man, and they whacked him too, so either he knew something or the rat bastards thought he did. I know who you can talk to down there, though. Didja ever heard of a faggot con man in Miami named Ian McKinney? *Minchia,* he even has a faggy name. Ian. Sounds like a fucking pig squealing. Runs a kind of badger game. Rips off big business types who are secret queers, gets pictures of them getting their dick sucked by a man and scams money out of them in some business deal, then threatens to expose them if they go to the cops. Anyway, this queer also does a line in general blackmail besides his own deals, so he likes to dig out the dirt, any kind of dirt, the higher up the better. So he knows just about everything that goes on in South Florida. You might try him."

"I know Ian," said Visconti with a smile. "I've had some dealings with him. You're right, he's very well informed. I'm sure he'll tell me anything he can."

"My guess would be that Joey got whacked because of something political or something to do with his junkets. Maybe some big shot politician or chairman of the board stepped on his dick bad, snuffed a hooker during a sex game or Joey caught him taking a suitcase full of cash from fucking Arabs to give them our latest H-bomb, something like that. So the rat bastards killed him." Dom started to weep again, then pulled himself together. "John, I have one more request. This is Family business, but it's also family business, if you get my drift. I want you to take somebody from the family with you on this job."

"No can do. I work alone, Dom. You know that," replied Visconti firmly, shaking his head. "There are only a few men in the entire country I will involve in my work in any way, all of them specialists who can do things I can't, all of them proven men."

"Hear me out, John," Dominic indicated the two men at the Cadillac with a jerk of his head. "That kid there. That's my grandson. Lucy's boy, Tony Stop. He's twenty-one years old and he's already a better earner than some wiseguys I know who have been in Our Thing all their lives. Runs a couple of numbers books and a lotta shylock volume, a coupla restaurants and bars, and he's got his own Teamsters local. Every one of them earning, no problems, the kid's a money machine. He's a worker, too. He made his bones three years ago, got straightened out when he was twenty, and he's done three more jobs of work since, all on his own with no backup. Like you, John. Badda-bing, badda-boom. No muss, no fuss, no bother, no repercussions, the cops are stymied at the starting gate, always seamless and professional.

"John, I ain't saying this just because he's my grandkid. Tony is good. He's *damned* good, John! You know what kind of human crap Our Thing is getting these days, these so-called soldiers we've got now. Druggies, crazies, washed-out bozos like Eddie Miami who wouldn't have shined a button man's shoes in the old days. This Thing of Ours has been going down the tubes for years, John, but I think Tony might be the guy who can change that, someday after I'm gone, when he gets some years on him. Tony will become a true *uomo di rispetto*, John. He's smart as a fucking whip, cool as an iceboig when de heat comes on, he's a street guy but he can pass for Joe College, he shows respect for the old ways, he thinks with something besides his dick or his greed. I ain't saying this to kiss your ass,

John, you know I don't kiss nobody's ass, but Tony reminds me of you, when you was young. No shit. But if he's going to be de guy who turns Our Thing around, then he's got a lot to learn. I want him to learn from the best, John. That's you. I ain't asking this for me, John, or even for Tony. I'm asking this for the future of Our Thing. Tony has to learn from the best, so some day he can *be* the best. Otherwise the goddamned Colombians and Russians and Triads and Yakuza are going to put us in the ground. John, please…this is important."

Visconti thought for a while, then sighed. "This is going to be a complex job. I admit I could use an extra set of hands and eyes and ears, and your recommendation for any man is good enough for me. But Dom, no favoritism. Your grandson or not, he comes with me he does what he's told and he does it right, the first time. If he puts one foot wrong, he comes back to you. No argument, no explanations, no bullshit. If I just don't *feel* right about him, he comes back to you. I apologize for dictating conditions like this to you, *padrone,* but this is my work now, and this is how it must be."

"Agreed. Absolutely. But you watch. I tell you, the kid is good," Dom motioned. The two men standing by got into the Cadillac, started the engine, and drove slowly over to the bench and parked. They got out, and Tony approached. "Tony, do you know who dis is?" Dom asked him.

"This is Johnny Vee," replied Tony, his face calm and expressionless, his voice respectful.

"Wrong!" snapped Dom. He took the burned out cigar from his mouth and stabbed it at the younger man for emphasis. "From dis moment on, as far as you're concerned, dis man is Jesus fucking Christ and all twelve Apostles rolled into one! When you are with him on dis job, I ain't your boss nor your grandfather no more. Dis man is your boss. You will do what he tells you to do, when he tells you to do it, and exactly how he tells you to do it, nothing more and nothing less. You will not give him word one of bullshit. When John says jump, you say how high? When John says run, you say how far? You got all dis, kid?"

"*Io capiche, padrone,*" said Tony calmly.

"Get your suitcase and put it in John's car." Tony went to the Caddy and pulled out the suitcase out of the trunk. "He's yours, John," said Dom, holding out his hand. "The honor of the family is in your hands. Oh, one more thing." He snapped his fingers and Vinnie stepped forward, pulling a manila envelope from his jacket. "We ain't talked about money, but you know it ain't no object. Hell, what am I gonna spend it on these days? There's a hundred grand in there, and there will be more when the job is done."

"This will be more than adequate," said Visconti, putting the envelope in his jacket pocket. He stood up, Dom stood up, and the two men embraced in farewell.

Without being told to do so, Tony got behind the wheel of the Bonneville and drove, an act of deference on his part to the older man demanded by Mob protocol. Without asking he got on the Long Island Expressway heading back to the city. Visconti stared out the window, chewing his thumbnail meditatively. As they entered the borough of Queens Tony finally spoke. "LaGuardia or JFK, John?" he asked. "I'll need to get off at the right exit."

Visconti smiled. "LaGuardia. We're going to Florida."

"I figured that."

"When we get to the terminal, I'll turn the car in. You go to the Delta desk and cop us two tickets on the next shuttle flight to Miami."

"First class?" asked Tony.

"The only way to fly, kid. I'll give you a credit card."

"I got a whole wallet full of my own plastic, gold Mastercards, American Express, you name it. None of 'em hot, all of 'em on legitimate businesses. But why not pay cash?" Tony's sharp eyes had not missed the manila envelope. "Plastic leaves a paper trail."

"Yeah, so you make sure the paper trail doesn't lead anywhere. Ticket counter clerks are gonna remember somebody who plunks down a couple of grand in greenbacks for two first class seats. Two guys in business suits with a credit card, they forget as soon as you leave the counter. You're not strapped, are you? Not in your suitcase?"

"No, I never pack unless I'm working."

"Good. When we get to Florida I'll get us tooled up."

They drove on in silence until Tony got off at the northbound exit off I-495 leading to LaGuardia airport. Then he spoke again. "John, I'm with you all the way on this, you know that, but how high do we take it?"

"As high as it leads, kid. Everyone who had a hand in your uncle's death goes. No ifs, ands, buts, or maybes."

"Like with Buddy?" asked Tony, daringly. He didn't know if the death of his older uncle was a taboo subject.

"Like with Buddy," said Visconti.

"What if it goes all the way up to Billyboy himself?" demanded Tony.

"Then Billyboy goes. Your grandfather knows that. That's why he reached out for me. We whacked a president once before. We'll do it again if need be. You want out, kid?"

"Hey, not me," said Tony, shaking his head. "I dig a wild and crazy ride."

"I think I can promise you that," said Visconti.

III

Enter Three Musketeers

Karen Martin sat on a table, smoking a cigarette and drinking a bottle of Michelob, her long tan legs crossed. She was wearing cut-off blue jeans and a tank top t-shirt over her statuesque torso. Her toenails and fingernails were polished bright neon blue. Her long hair was a luscious, mellow brown, a rare return to her natural color. Her thirty-something face was chiseled, sharp, Scotch-Irish craggy and hard yet handsome and sexy, a map of Ulster via the Appalachians and Broken Bow, Oklahoma. A snub-nosed .38-caliber revolver in a nylon holster hung off the wide leather belt around her slender, muscular waist, but the real danger was the switchblade carried in her bra. She had killed eight men and three women with it. It was impossible for any man to look at Karen Martin without experiencing a mad desire to throw her on her back; she was one of those women, she knew it, and she used it to destroy men. At age fifteen she had been the most sought-after hooker in New Orleans, no mean accomplishment in a town renowned since the eighteenth century for its belles of the Oldest Profession. Once she had singlehandedly entertained the entire crew of a Gulf oil rig over a Labor Day weekend, leaving on a supply boat that Tuesday morning with every dollar on board in her shoulder bag and every man on the rig knowing he'd gotten his money's worth.

She was dressed in tackies now, but from her huge wardrobe closet in Little Rock she could produce, and wear convincingly as the occasion demanded, a $25,000 Dior evening gown; a stylish executive business suit for glass ceiling-smashing, feminist boardroom wear complete with matching briefcase containing recording gear and weaponry; a black leather dominatrix's outfit including whips and chains; a maxi-dress with hippie love beads and head scarf with matching accessories such as granny glasses and New Age crystal pendant; a nun's habit; police-women's uniforms from New Orleans, Houston, Miami, Little Rock and Atlanta, complete with regulation-issue belts, sidearm, and equipment; and a complete ski outfit including skis which she could handle at com-petition level on the hardest slopes at Aspen and Vail. Karen Martin was the first of the legendary hit team called the Three Musketeers.

Across the living room of the expensive Palm Beach hotel suite, the second Musketeer was talking on the telephone. Bob Blanchette was blond, balding, thin, as nondescript as a grocery store manager, and as lethal as a cobra. A Cajun from Thibodeaux, he was the deadliest pro-fessional killer the Dixie Mafia had ever produced. South of the Mason-Dixon line his grisly reputation rivaled John Visconti's in the north and on the West Coast.

Blanchette once organized a riot in the Louisiana state prison at Angola as a cover for his escape, killing two guards in the process. When black criminals in Biloxi, Mississippi had demanded from the cracker mob what amounted to an affirmative action program in the gambling and prostitu-tion businesses along the Gulfport Avenue strip, Bob Blanchette settled their demands with a .45 Browning pistol and a chain saw. The resulting dumping of mangled black flesh offshore had produced an influx of sharks so noticeable that marine biologists wrote learned papers on the baffling subject to this day, being ignorant of the true cause.

A Federally protected witness was within days of testifying against the Bandidos motorcycle gang's methamphetamine chemists and put-ting them all away. Blanchette penetrated a government safe house, killed the informer under the noses of the Witness Protection Service Marshalls, decapitated the corpse and Fed-exed the head to the United States Attorney in Houston. When the Italians tried to move in on the three billion-dollar annual South Carolina video poker business, some well-dressed and well-coiffed Baptist businessmen in Atlanta and Greenville retained the services of Bob Blanchette. To the present day, police in South Carolina still found the charred and gutted remains of Cadillacs with New York and Pennsylvania license plates parked on lonely fire roads and sunk into cypress swamps, their skeletal occupants burned black with lead pellets rattling in shattered skulls. Interestingly, the paths of Bob Blanchette and John Visconti had almost crossed during this period. Representations were about to be made to Dominic LaBrasca to bring in Johnny Vee for a true celebrity death match, but a combination of Federal indictments and other unrelated factors had caused the New York and Philadelphia Cosa Nostra families to put South Carolina on the back burner for the time being. Then in 1992, Bob Blanchette found a new and more powerful employer.

Karen Martin respected Bob Blanchette not only for his skills, his organizing ability, his ruthlessness and his business acumen, but because he was the only man she had ever met whom she had been unable to seduce. Bob had married a small dark Creole girl from the bayous many years before, when he was seventeen and she thirteen, although for the purposes of the license Anne-Marie gave her age as the minimum legal fourteen. They now had six children in a colonial mansion outside Baton Rouge; Anne-Marie was as slim and dark and enigmatically beautiful as she had been on their wedding day twenty-seven years before. So far as anyone in the underworld knew, Bob Blanchette had never touched another woman since his wedding night. When Karen routinely tried to put the moves on him the first time, Blanchette had told her, "No, I don't play that." When she tried the second time he'd said, "I said no. Try it again and I'll kill you." She had believed him, and he had thereby become the only person on earth she respected as a human being rather than as a skilled criminal. A man who was faithful to his wife was an romantic anachronism who fascinated her.

The third man in the room sat on the couch, reading a comic book, and spitting occasional wads of tobacco juice into a Waterford crystal fruit bowl he had appropriated for a spittoon. Luther Lambert stood six feet nine inches and weighed about three hundred and fifty pounds, all of it muscle. His beard was golden and cascaded down his chest almost to his waist, where he tied it into two forks. His yellow hair hung down his back in a ponytail. Elaborate blue and red and yellow and green tattoos curled up his arms and covered his shoulders, snakes and skulls and dragons and naked warrior maidens in horned helmets. Beneath the matted hair on his chest was a beautiful reproduction of Botticelli's Venus. On his back was a magnificently wrought tattoo of Jesus Christ, arms outstretched in benediction, marred by a huge penile erection protruding through the Savior's white robes. Tattooed tears ran down his cheeks from his eyes into his beard. His brain was roughly the size of a walnut.

The third Musketeer was an Ozark hillbilly who had dropped out of school in Eureka Springs, Arkansas as soon as he turned sixteen years of age, thus terminating his third run at graduating from the sixth grade. He built his body by doing weight-lifting exercises with a Volkswagen. Luther had once done a couple of seasons as a strong man in a circus, where he performed tugs of war with camels and buffalo and the smaller elephants, and won. A bison once became enraged and charged him, and Luther killed it with a single punch. He had one talent that seemed to be some kind of natural compensation for his stupidity. Unable to read or write beyond the most rudimentary level, unable to understand the most basic principles of science or engineering, Luther Lambert was a genius with automotive engines. He gained entrée into crime through this skill; he could rebuild a Honda Civic with an engine that could outrun the most powerful Highway Patrol pursuit vehicle, which had put his services in high demand with the backwoods moonshine and drug runners.

But Luther's first love was mayhem. He was utterly fearless, because he was too stupid to be afraid of anything. Since teaming up with Bob Blanchette, Luther had been shot and stabbed more than twenty times, the result of Blanchette's habit of using him as a human battering ram and shield in dangerous situations, but Luther never complained. He assumed that's what his large carcass was there for, to provide cover for Bob and Karen. Lambert's body was a mass of scars, but he was for all practical purposes invincible. Two barrels of double-ought buckshot, a full clip from an AK-47, and a whaling harpoon fired from a cannon had all failed to kill Luther Lambert, while the wielders of these weapons had died. Luther tore them to pieces with his bare hands. He could use a gun if he had to, but considered them crass and unsporting. When the time came to get physical, he preferred an axe. Better yet two, one in each hand.

Luther was uniquely qualified for his work by virtue of being a psychopathic sadist. He enjoyed torturing people in order to hear them scream, especially women, all of whom he hated unto death. The one exception to his misogyny was Karen Martin, who was Luther's queen and goddess because she never laughed at him and bought him regular gifts of comic books, Jolly Rancher candies, Red Man chewing tobacco, Whoppers and Big Macs, which latter burgers he devoured ten at a time. He chewed the tobacco and sucked on a dozen of the fruit-flavored Jolly Ranchers at the same time; he liked the taste, and as a result of this practice his expectorations were a bizarre technicolor. Bob Blanchette's role in Luther's primitive *weltanschaung* was simpler still. Bob Blanchette was God.

Now Blanchette was speaking. "She got away, Doofus. Hey, it happen sometime. We ain't none of us poifect. Don't worry, we take cay of it. We took cay of that Eye-tie greaseball and we'll take cay of dis Hollywood bitch for you. She's a gawd damned star, Doofus, she cain't just drop out of sight!" Blanchette's accent sometimes caused his employer to confuse him with one of his Cajun advisers. Doofus mumbled something on the phone. "Yeah, yeah, hey, Doofus, you know it ain't that, I respect de hell out of you, you de man, you *mon brave*, you know?" said Blanchette tiredly. "Hey, you know this phone might be tapped. You want us to call you by you real name, huh? Doofus is kind of you code name, so nobody will know what a truly great and powahful man our boss be. Kinda like you de top secret agent. Okay?"

"Tell Doofus that's my code name for his goddamned crooked dick!" yelled Karen. "Worst piece of meat I ever sucked! You ever tried to give a blow job at a right angle?"

"Can't say as I have," replied Blanchette dryly. "What's that?" he said into the phone. "Oh, Slideen say hello. I sholy calculate you made a big impression on her. Yeah, she keep talking about you, she say you a real man. Hey, you man enough to take care of Slideen you man enough in my book. Sho, de whole country know you got the manpowah, Doofus. Ever woman in America want to give it to you, you oughta know that by now. Look, it'll be taken cay of, Doof. Have we ever let you down? We took cay of Parks and Foster and all them others, hey? Now you just quit worrying youself. There ain't gonna be no problem." He hung up the telephone. "Damn fool. He fucked up. His ass be in total eclipse," said Blanchette in disgust. "He musta stuck Colombia up his nose."

"This shit's getting pretty deep, Bob," said Karen quietly. "Every time we pull his flabby ass out of one hole, he digs himself a deeper one. I don't like it. You saw him on TV that time last year, supposed be apologizing to the whole damned nation for getting a few blow jobs from that JAP in his office. He was coked up to his eyeballs right there on the air. We're working for a fucking junkie, and that's stupid business, Bob. You know damned well if he was anybody else we wouldn't touch him with a ten-foot pole. That bitch wife of his hates our guts, and she is gonna send bull dyke Reno and her Feds after us if she gets half a chance. I bet you dollars fer donuts she's working on him now, trying to convince him we know too much and we're a loose end."

"I know it," agreed Blanchette grimly, "But we got to clean this last one up. Then we disappear. We got enough money now, but that Hollywood bitch has to go. We don't know how much that dago DeMarco done told her, and we don't know why the hell he tipped her the wink. He ain't a problem no more, but she still is. We can't leave her running loose, Slideen. Maybe she even knows our names. It ain't just Doofus we're protecting, it's us. We got to finish this thang."

"Ah seen her in the movies," said Luther, sending a cascade of green and purple juice into the Waterford crystal. "She's purty. When we catch her, kin ah make her sing and wiggle some?"

"You can make her do the hootchie-kootchie with your little blow-torch, Luther," promised Karen. "You can toast her up nice and crisp and we'll give the sharks a nice hot meal for a change."

"I like feeding the sharks," said Luther with a sigh, before returning to his comic.

10

She to the Appointed Place

Again, a telephone rang on a bedside table at a little past midnight. This time it was in an elegantly furnished, valeted apartment on the fourteenth floor of a high rise building in Rosslyn, Virginia, just across the Potomac from Washington, D.C. The woman who lived there was not asleep. She was lying in bed in a nightgown reading the hardback book version of *Schindler's List*. A stainless steel 9-millimeter automatic pistol lay by the telephone, with a customized grip to fit a smaller feminine hand. She picked up the cell phone; it was only used for Bureau business and only her Bureau colleagues had the number. "Yes?"

"Special Agent Weinmann?" came a strong, authoritative woman's voice.

"Yes, this is she."

"This is the Attorney General of the United States. I apologize for calling you this late."

Andrea Weinmann had already recognized the caller's voice. "It's no problem, Ms. Reno. I was still up. How can I help you?"

"Ms. Weinmann, something has come up, a problem which requires very deft and professional handling. I have spoken to the First Lady and she has recommended that I ask you to deal with this problem. She tells me that you have handled sensitive matters before with success and discretion."

Political bullshit, thought Andrea. *Wonder who's got caught with their fingers in the cookie jar now? Why the hell can't He get any decent help?* "I'm flattered the First Lady recommended me, Ms. Reno. I pride myself in my professionalism."

"The administration appreciates that, Ms. Weinmann, and I think you won't find us ungrateful to those who stand by us and our progressive principles during this time when we are under siege by this malicious right-wing conspiracy to destroy our President. There is one thing I want to ask you before I definitely bring you in on this, though, and it's a bit personal, but I'm afraid it's necessary."

"Yes?" asked Andrea politely. *No, I will not go to bed with you, you revolting old cow.*

"I am informed that you were something of a protegé of the late Assistant Director Charles Bennett. Is that correct?"

"He was one of my rabbis at the Bureau for a time, yes," replied Andrea cautiously. "We were personally involved as well for about a year until I got the departmental training courses and assignment track I wanted, then we got back on a purely professional basis. I'm sure you were told that, Ms. Reno." *An adequate lover, but I've had better. A clever man in his own limited way, but venal, materialistic, not a very interesting man in the final analysis. That's the one thing I could never forgive in a man, not being interesting. Are there any interesting men left, other than Him? Chuck Bennett was bent as a pretzel, and I'm sure you know that too, Ms. Attorney General.* "I hope that I haven't been unduly frank, ma'am, but you asked me a question and I answered it as honestly as I could," said Andrea.

"I understand the practical considerations of being a woman in a man's workplace, Ms. Weinmann, especially in a macho male group like the FBI," said Reno diplomatically. "We all have choices we have to make, and sometimes we choose to play the game in order eventually to reach positions of power where we can change the rules and grab onto the ball. Or grab their balls," she added with a coarse chuckle. "The reason I asked is that this assignment involves your traveling down to Raleigh, North Carolina, to assist the local law enforcement authorities, and you will have to work there alongside a certain individual. A North Carolina State Bureau of Investigation agent named Matthew Redmond." Reno almost spat the name like an obscenity. "You are aware that while Assistant Director Bennett 's death was officially ruled a suicide, there is, how shall I put it, another version of the events surrounding his demise?"

"That this man Redmond was responsible for Chuck's death? Yes, I heard that," said Andrea. "I take it from the lack of any retaliatory action that the administration prefers at this time to consider the official verdict on Chuck the correct one?"

"We do. For the time being. That may change in the future."

"There will be no problem in my working with Mr. Redmond, Ms. Reno. Frankly, my relationship with AD Bennett simply didn't leave that much feeling behind it. It was a career move, as you've indicated you understand." *This Redmond, however, does sound like an interesting man. You neglect to add that he's also supposed to have driven the late Congresswoman Margaret Mears to genuine suicide, a personal friend of both you and Hillary Clinton. I'd like to meet him, just out of curiosity. Maybe fuck him before I kill him, since I presume that's what Ms. Horse-face is leading up to. Is he handsome? Surely the Bureau must have a file on him. I'll check before I go down there.*

"Yes, I understand, but I had to ask. Could we get together tomorrow morning at ten o'clock and we'll discuss it? Not my office at the Department. Go to the Executive Office Building across from the White House and tell the Secret Service guard at the desk you have an appointment in Room 200. He will be notified that you are expected."

"Certainly, Ms. Reno." *The Bunker itself? Gevalt! This must be more than just another bimbo eruption*, she thought to herself as she hung up. *I wonder if He will be there…how I long to meet Him close up, not just at official functions. I remember that one day at that stupid meeting, in the conference room. He noticed me. I know He did.*

That night Andrea Weinmann dreamed of Him, and she awoke wet and covered with sweat, her heart pounding, crying out His name.

0

The Stage Is Set

"The lady from the FBI will be here in a few minutes," said the director to Matt and Cowboy. "She called from the airport and said she's taking a cab directly here. I hope she can fill in some blanks for us. Matt, what have you come up with thus far?"

The three men were sitting in a conference room in the old SBI building on West Morgan Street in Raleigh. The director had declined to move his personal office and records out to the new extension in Garner which housed the laboratory and the bulk of the department, as well as his violently feminist assistant director who constantly intrigued to get his job and fulminated against his cigar-smoking. A *modus vivendi* had been reached where Phil and his team of agents operating out of the massive granite building on Morgan Street actually tracked down Tar Heel criminals, and Betty Springer had her own little politically correct empire dedicated to stamping out racism, male chauvinism, and the use of tobacco in any form within the confides of the Garner Road Extension building. She also constantly fought to keep her PC peons in the Extension itself. Phil's desk was always piled high with memos and letters from his employees pleading for a transfer back to Morgan Street in any capacity, a file clerk, a janitor, a night watchman, anything.

An air conditioner rumbled in the window, keeping out the muggy August heat. Even so the men's jackets were off, draped over the back of their chairs, and their ties were loosened. Matt's Colt Python .357 Magnum with the six inch barrel hung under his left armpit in a chamois leather and velcro shoulder holster rig; his fedora and his use of this non-regulation weapon was the source of a whole file of memos from Betty Springer, all of which Matt ignored. Cowboy Garza was now following suit with his Stetson and his ivory-handled Peacemaker, which caused Ms. Springer to blow a gasket on a regular basis. His 100% clearance rate covered a multitude of sins, but Matt had a sinking feeling his winning streak was about to come to an end. *Mob hits are almost impossible to solve and convict on,* he reflected glumly. He consulted a file full of reports and faxes and printed e-mails in front of him. "I think it's pretty obvious that the murder boat Eddie was talking about was the *Jolie Madame,* out of Palm Beach, last known port of call Key Biscayne," he replied to the director's question. "That's the only reported incident which seems to match what he was babbling about on the phone. The vessel was recovered drifting by the Coast Guard twenty-two miles south of Marathon. An oceanographic research ship actually found the derelict vessel. Nine corpses on board, all homicides."

"Senator Teddy Kennedy's private yacht," muttered Phil in disgust. "The media has been doing some babbling of their own. The whole country knows about it. CNN is spinning it like a top, scared shitless it's going to turn out to be some new Democrat scandal."

"Nine dead bodies on a Senator's yacht can fill up an awful lot of air time," chuckled Matt. "Actually, it was only one of Kennedy's three Florida yachts. He has three more in Massachusetts waters. Teddy's time seems pretty well accounted for. He left his office in Washington on Friday afternoon, took the shuttle to Boston, was picked up by his chauffeur at Logan International. By then he was probably too drunk to drive. He spent the whole weekend in Hyannisport, and whatever he may have been doing there it looks like his alibi is solid. Besides, he may dunk his car in a pond while he's smashed and leave a girl to drown, but I can't see Teddy blowing away nine people with shotguns, much less hacking them to death with an axe. That's a bit rambunctious even for the Kennedies. His generation of Kennedies, anyway. Bobby or John I would have had second thoughts about; they were hard motherfuckers, and those Skakel kids were psychos, but Teddy is too soft for this kind of action. I will try to get an interview with him, but I doubt it will help much. According to his press office he is totally shocked by the whole thing, blah blah. They may be right, for once."

"Shotguns? Any possible ballistics match on DeMarco?" asked Garza.

"Very occasionally a shotgun wound can be matched to the weapon through some peculiarity in the barrel or the ammo, but not often," replied Matt. "Smoothbore. But it's the same M.O. I think it's clear in a general way what happened, now that we know Joey LaBrasca was involved. Eddie Miami was a known associate of LaBrasca's. Somebody wanted LaBrasca taken out, bad. It must have been important. They wanted him gone so fast that they didn't care who they massacred to get at him. Eddie was either on the hit parade himself, or else he was in on the hit, possibly as a finger man. That would make sense. He said he was a loose end; once he'd set LaBrasca up and the hit was carried out, he was an inconvenient witness."

"So he comes all the way to North Carolina and tells you it's some kind of Federal thing?" asked Garza skeptically.

"He wanted to surrender himself to me," pointed out Matt. "If he was involved in multiple homicide even as an accessory, he was going to prison for a long time. He knew that. He preferred to come here and give himself up rather than risk whatever was waiting for him out there. Guys like Eddie survive by figuring the odds at all times. Eddie figured his odds for survival were better in a North Carolina jail than anywhere else in the world. What does that tell you?"

"The fact that he ended up with his brains splattered all over the facade of Terminal C tells me both he and you are right," said Garza with a wry smile.

"What about the vics on the boat?" asked Phil. "What have we got on them? Any North Carolina connections? Any possibility they might have been the intended targets?"

"It could be," admitted Matt. "Four of them were fairly high up in the corridors of power. The kind of gray flannel suits who actually run things as opposed to the suits the television cameras focus on, if you understand. No Tar Heel connections that we know of, and the only one of these we've got any jurisdiction on is DeMarco. There are times when I miss being a Fed and being able to cross state lines." Matt read from the file. "Fred Carlson, aged 40. Captain of the yacht. Shotgun to the head. Burton Frierson, aged 23, crewman. Shotgun to the head. Kristin Manning, aged 20, and Cynthia Morrison, aged 21, both employed, if that's the word, by Angel's Escorts, a known prostitution front run by Joey LaBrasca. Both sodomized, tortured by burning with what the medical examiner thinks was a propane or welding torch, then ankles and wrists bound with electrician's tape and hanged naked from the foremast with several doubled lengths of heavy test fishing line. Cause of death, slow strangulation. Their dangling bodies were what caught the attention of a passing oceanographic research vessel, who radioed the Coast Guard.

"Victims five and six, Robert W. Sipple, aged 36, vice president of international marketing for DuPont out of Wilmington, Delaware and Don Federer, aged 32, attorney for the Wall Street law firm of Skadden, Arps & Co. Stabbed to death by a very sharp knife or ice pick through the eye, testicles bruised and ruptured by extreme pressure, possible manual. Federer was also sodomized before death, but this may have been voluntary; condition of decedent's colonic wall and sphincter muscles showed evidence of stretching and tearing and elongation, as well as several reconstructive surgeries common among long term passive homosexuals. Genitals of both men severed and missing. Coming in at seven and eight, Congressman Karl Zimmer, six-term Democrat from Minnesota, and United States Attorney Kent Hansen from Miami, both dead from blood loss and trauma consequent to being dismembered by a heavy bladed instrument, probably an axe. Bits and pieces of them were scattered all over the boat and some body parts are missing, presumably thrown overboard and eaten by sharks, along with Sipple and Federer's private parts. Finally, Guiseppe Gianpaolo LaBrasca, age 32. Known Cosa Nostra associate, son of Genovese crime family capo Dominic LaBrasca. Shotgun to the head."

"Holy Jesus!" whispered Phil, shaking his head. "What on earth kind of savages are we dealing with here?"

"With the kind who enjoy their work," said Matt. "The kind who are so monstrous that even a lifelong Cosa Nostra hoodlum like Eddie Miami was sickened and terrified."

"Feds?" asked Cowboy.

"Maybe. Look, guys, you know there's nothing sweet between me and the Federal government, but let's remember Eddie DeMarco was a thief and a liar and a numbskull. As much as I despise Billyboy and his scurvy crew, I'm not inclined to take the word of a Mafia mope without some kind of corroboration. Some of those Italian gentlemen in silk suits like to get down and dirty as well, you know." The phone rang. Phil answered it.

"Send her up," he said into the phone. "The FBI gal is here. I asked her to bring down what she could on the *Jolie Madame* and also their profile on LaBrasca and DeMarco."

"Good," said Matt. "My information is almost ten years old and I'd like to find out what our boy Eddie has been up to in the days since he was smuggling coke."

"Knock knock," said a woman from the open door, suiting the action to the word. Cowboy Garza's jaw dropped in open and unabashed admiration; he barely restrained himself from giving a wolf whistle which would have gotten him fired. She looked like a Cosmopolitan model for Best Dressed Businesswoman of the year, tan suit with matching jacket and shoes, stylish alligator handbag over one shoulder and black briefcase of tooled leather in one hand, flawlessly permed jet-black hair at collar length, pearl earrings, understated makeup so expertly applied she appeared to be wearing none, and a Lady Rolex watch on her wrist. Phil rose. "Come on in, ma'am. Have a seat. I'm Philip Hightower, director of the SBI. These are agents Redmond and Garza. They're working on the DeMarco homicide."

The woman nodded politely to Phil, set her briefcase and handbag down on the table. She took out her badge case and opened it to display her ID, then walked directly to Matt, her hand out. "Special Agent Andrea Weinmann, FBI," she said in a cool contralto, a faint smile playing on her lips. "I see the fedora on the table, but I only see one gun."

"Don't believe everything you see on tabloid television, ma'am," replied Matt with a resigned smile. "That Two Gun Matt nickname is based on one incident in Mexico which would never have happened if I'd been as sharp and on the ball as I'm supposed to be. My rep is greatly exaggerated, believe me."

"I don't know. You left quite a legend behind you at DEA and Justice as well," replied Andrea. "If we get some time I'd like to talk to you about some of your cases. I'm always interested in learning from other law enforcement professionals." *And learning how you are between the sheets,* she thought. *A bit long in the tooth, according to the DOB in your file, but you sure don't look it. Oh, yes, definitely between the sheets material here.*

"Can I get you a soft drink or something?" asked Phil. "Too damned hot for coffee."

"No, thank you. I'd like to get right to business," said Andrea, sitting down in a smooth motion and opening the briefcase. "Gentlemen, I'm here to share information with you and I'd also like to get what you have on the DeMarco angle. The Bureau concurs that Mr. DeMarco was involved in some way in the multiple homicide that took place on the yacht *Jolie Madame.* The Department of Justice has assumed full jurisdiction over that case."

"How is that, ma'am?" asked Matt. "Narcotics? I talked to a guy I know from my DEA days down in Florida and he tells me they had enough cocaine, Ecstasy and pills on that yacht to set up a dealer in business. None of it was removed by the killers, which is a significant clue. Rival dopers would have cleaned out the stash and carried it off to add to their own inventory. But wouldn't that drug angle give DEA first crack at it?"

"Since the murders appear to have been committed on the high seas, we are treating it as a case of piracy, which makes it FBI jurisdiction."

"Yo, ho, ho, and a bottle of 'luudes,'" said Matt. "That's stretching it a bit, ma'am. You guys must really want this one bad."

"We do, for reasons I will explain in a moment. Florida local law enforcement is no longer involved, but as yet the jurisdictional issues in the killing of DeMarco aren't clear. We'll probably want this one too because of the likely interstate flight aspect. Agent Redmond, do I understand correctly that DeMarco was actually speaking to you on the telephone when he was killed, and you recorded the conversation?"

"That's right," said Matt. He held up a cassette tape. "I already made you a copy of my answering machine tape. You want to hear it now?"

"Please," she asked. Matt slid the tape into a recorder on the table and played it, including Heather's initial chirpy greeting. Andrea showed no emotion as the shotguns went off and a man died, but frowned lightly at the little laugh as one of the killers hung up the phone.

"That's the bit that makes my flesh crawl every time I hear it," said Cowboy with a scowl.

"First question. Who or what is Trumpeldor?" asked Andrea. Matt laughed.

"A very large orange cat who will eat anything that is not nailed down, but who will attack and maul a human in order to get at cheese, his favorite being sharp cheddar. Heather is my wife. Tori is my adopted daughter, aged nineteen, a rising sophomore at UNC this fall, education major. She wants to be a teacher."

"Good for her," laughed Andrea. "Our public schools need all the dedicated professionals they can get. Second question. Do you gentlemen believe this line DeMarco was handing you about Federal agents of some kind being involved in these killings? If so I'd like you to be honest with me. I'd like to know where I stand."

There was a brief silence. "I have an open mind on the subject," Matt finally said. "You have to admit that some very long strings have been pulled in the past where Senator Edward Kennedy was concerned, although it doesn't look to me like he's involved in this. Yet. Suppose you tell us what you have on the Florida boat thing? I know it's not our jurisdiction, but we need to know anything which may be relevant to a crime committed in North Carolina."

"In other words you don't know yet whether I'm not down here to cover it all up," said Andrea with a wintry smile. "Fair enough. What with all the X-files type paranoia about government conspiracies these days, I don't blame you."

"It's not all paranoia," said Matt quietly.

"No. No, it isn't," said Andrea, looking him in the eyes. "I know more or less what happened to you three years ago, Agent Redmond, or let's say I know what the rumor mill says happened to you and your family. All I can say is that I wasn't involved in it, and not all FBI agents are corrupt. Please give me the benefit of the doubt."

"All right," said Matt. "So what's the story on the *Jolie Madame?*"

"I'll start by telling you that there is another aspect to this case which hasn't gotten any publicity yet, one which has some ramifications."

"Political ramifications?" grunted Phil. "Teddy again?"

"No, not really. But it may become an even more high profile case that it is now, which is why the Bureau wants to handle it," she said. "There was a tenth passenger on the boat, or who should have been on the boat. A well-known actress. She's missing."

"What well known actress?" asked Cowboy.

"Alice Silverman," said Andrea.

"Who?" asked Phil. "Sorry, I don't keep up with the latest Hollywood output. Too much violence and pointless sex fer me. I watch the old movies on American Movie Classics. Give me Jimmy Stewart and the Duke and Maureen O'Hara any day."

"Alice Silverman...let's see, she's that hot little teenaged blonde number, pardon the chauvinist political incorrectness," mused Matt. "I've seen a couple of her movies. Got her start on MTV when she was about fourteen, I believe. Doing rock music videos?"

"That's right," agreed Andrea. "She was earning a million dollars a year by the time she was sixteen and she left MTV for the big screen. She's not a teenager any more, she's twenty-three years old and she's got her own production company now. After the videos she started out with some light comedy. Her first big box office hit was *Nancy Drew,* where she played the title role, then...oh, I forget all the titles myself."

"Yeah, she's done about eight or ten major movies in the past few years," mused Matt. "Tori likes her; she's *got Nancy Drew* in her video collection and a couple of others. You'd know her face if you saw it, Phil."

"There was that comedy she did about the dog, the Great Dane...*Marmaduke, The Movie,* yeah," mused Cowboy. "That was pretty funny, if you like dog flicks. Then the one where she got chased by dinosaurs. *Clones.* Not as good as *Jurassic Park,* but great special effects."

"Oh, yeah, wait a minute, didn't she do that one about the air-head Valley Girl in Beverly Hills? *Hopeless?*" asked Phil. "Yeah, I think I did see that one. Okay, I know who you're all talking about now."

"And she was Wonder Girl, and in her latest she starred with Schwarzenegger in that one where he invades Cuba and blows up Castro...Jesus, you say she was supposed to be on that yacht?" demanded Matt. "How do you know?"

"Jacob Shapiro, her agent, called us in a wild panic when he heard the yacht had been found," replied Andrea. "She flew out from Los Angeles to Miami the day before on a corporate Lear jet from DuPont. One of the other victims, Robert Sipple, sent it for her. She landed at Miami and was met by a hired limousine that drove away in the direction of Key Biscayne, where the yacht was docked, and that was the last seen of her. The limo was found abandoned on a back street in Delray Beach the next day. Her personal assistant, a woman named Carla Renfrew, and her nanny, a woman named Serafina Flores, were with her. So was her two month old infant son, William Silverman. They are all missing as well."

"Oh, shit," muttered Phil. "Pardon my language, ma'am."

"Oh, shit indeed," said Andrea with a grim smile. "At our request Alice's agent and her entourage are keeping quiet, but Hollywood is the world's biggest rumor mill after Washington itself, and I suspect in a few days the word is going to get out that she's missing. The Bureau is claiming jurisdiction on the theory that she might have been kidnapped, but there has been no ransom demand. I just hope we can somehow find them alive."

"Ma'am…you realize if these women were on that yacht, there's a good chance they were killed as well, and their bodies thrown into the sea?" asked Cowboy.

"Mmmmm…don't know about that, Cowboy," ruminated Matt. "That doesn't really play. Why throw a couple or four bodies overboard and leave the rest lying around rotting in the sun? Come to that, why not sink the whole ship, burn it or blow it up or scuttle it in some way, to cover up the crime and delay its discovery? It's almost like these people *wanted* their handiwork to be found. But why? Who were they sending a message to?"

"It also revives the question of who the hell was the real target of all this?" said Phil. "We've been proceeding on the assumption that LaBrasca was the target and all the others got in the way. There's the Mob connection; whatever else they may get involved in, corporate big shots and Congressmen and U. S. Attorneys don't usually get whacked out like gangsters. But could it part of a plot to kidnap or kill this actress?"

"It's a can of worms," admitted Andrea. "There does seem to be a Mafia connection through your Eddie Miami. My first reaction would be that target of the hit was Joey LaBrasca and the whole thing was Cosa Nostra, but frankly the time and the place puzzles me. It looks like overkill to me, pardon the expression. If LaBrasca offended the Mob in some way and they meant to execute him, why not wait until they got him alone in his club or his apartment in Palm Beach? Or gun him down in the street with machine guns in the classic Chicago style if they wanted to make some kind of Mafia point? Look at the way they took out Eddie Miami, quick and clean and professionally. The Mob doesn't generally slaughter innocent bystanders; it's bad for business and it brings heat, like it's doing in this case. They generally confine their violence to their own kind."

"Maybe these others weren't so innocent as they seem," commented Cowboy.

"Maybe not the dead people on the boat, no," replied Andrea. "But this disappearance of Alice Silverman and her employees and her baby puzzles me. It doesn't seem to fit into any meaningful pattern. Alice Silverman wasn't connected in any way with organized crime that we know of. She is a wealthy and successful young woman, but she actually seems pretty strait-laced by Hollywood standards."

"She's got an illegitimate child, and that's strait-laced?" asked Phil skeptically.

"She kept the child, she didn't abort it, and although she has a nanny her people in Hollywood tell me she cares for the baby herself as much as she can given her work schedule, and she dotes on him. She doesn't do drugs at all and everyone swears she doesn't hang out with dealers or hoodlums like some of the Tinseltown crowd do. You won't find her on the front page of the tabloids in your grocery store checkout lines. Alice doesn't get drunk and smash up restaurants or run down pedestrians with her sports car, she's about the only actress of her generation who hasn't slapped Leonardo DiCaprio in public, nor has she been sued for lesbian palimony. No lesbian relationships at all, apparently. By Hollywood standards that's downright puritanical. The Bureau has teams looking into the past of Congressman Zimmer and Mr. Hansen, any cases Hansen was handling, so forth and so on, but frankly I think that's a dead end. Hansen dealt with anti-trust actions and handled DOJ's anti-Microsoft campaign in South Florida, but if Bill Gates did this it's the first time he's resorted to violence. We're looking into that possibility, of course, but as Agent

Redmond said, it just doesn't resonate. Gates has enough money to play the game our way, with lawyers and PR and lobbyists, and besides, I think he's too geeky to hire hit men."

"You're forgetting that Eddie DeMarco stated when he was talking to me on that tape that Feds did it," pointed out Matt.

Andrea shrugged. "I don't know what to say to that, Mr. Redmond, except that I can assure you the Bureau's desire to locate Alice Silverman and her child and to track down the killers of a Congressman and a U. S. Attorney is quite genuine. Believe me, my brief on this came from the highest level. I will be going down to Florida after I finish here to help the team of agents assigned to solve this case and find Alice Silverman, and that's what I intend to do. I would not be party to any cover-up or any violation of the law." *How seriously do you take that wedding ring on your finger?* she almost asked out loud.

"Fair enough," said Matt in a conciliatory tone. "Frankly, ma'am, this is unlikely to be much of our baby. The SBI is only concerned with DeMarco, and I would be amazed if his killers are still in the state of North Carolina. We have a couple of very sketchy eyewitness accounts of what happened, all from people who were too far away to recognize anyone or get a license number. We were hoping to find the pickup truck the killers used, but even that has eluded us. They must have stashed it good. Hell, if they were real pros they've had it compacted into a square of steel scrap by now, or maybe sunk it in a swamp somewhere down east off I-95. If we do find it I'll let you know what our forensics people come up with, or better yet we'll let your FBI technicians work it over. As to who did it, all I can say is that I've got an open mind about it, but there is a definite Cosa Nostra connection and that's where I'd start if I was Federal still and the primary on this case. I have reason to be paranoid about Federals, ma'am, as you know, but that doesn't mean I believe everything some hood tells me."

"Well, if it will set your mind at rest, there is some indication that it was done by one of the other Mob families," replied Andrea.

"What indication is that, ma'am?" asked Phil.

"Old man LaBrasca seems to know something about it, and he's out for blood," replied Andrea grimly.

"Dom the Butcher? Jesus, is he still alive?" asked Matt.

"Need I ask why he's called Dom the Butcher?" asked Cowboy in a wry voice.

"Actually, it's because he owns a string of meat-packing companies," replied Matt. "But the name is definitely appropriate in the other sense as well. The old man is a stone killer. How do you know he's gotten involved, Agent Weinmann?"

She pulled a cassette from her briefcase and popped it into the recorder. "Listen to this. It's an excerpt from a Title Three wiretap we picked up yesterday. One of the men on the phone is a Genovese soldier named Albert Molinari, aka Al Jones, aka Al the Horse. Like many such mob monikers, no one calls him that to his face. The other is a Gambino associate named James Cagolitti, aka Jimmy Skins because of his predeliction for hijacking fur shipments in his younger days. These wiseguys always talk in a kind of code on the phone, as I'm sure you recall, Agent Redmond, but they were sufficiently excited by this incident to slip briefly into a state almost approaching intelligibility." She hit the play button.

"You wanna keep things cool," came a rough Brooklynese voice from the speaker. "That's Cagolitti," said Andrea.

"Dis is hot as bubbling cheese, betcha dere's Feds swarming all over south Florida rattling everybody's cage now," the voice on the tape continued. "Any idea who done it, Al? You know I wouldn't axe dat normally, in Our Thing when one of our friends goes away curiosity ain't fucking recommended, forget about it, but anybody who's dat *upazzi* I'd kind of like to steer clear of. It ain't smart doin' business wit people who leave nine stiffs lying around out on a boat, man."

"I don't know nuttin', but I know whoever da fuck it is, dey're in a world of hurt," said Molinari. "Dey got something comin' to 'em dey ain't gonna like."

"Yeah?" Cagolitti sounded interested.

"Yeah. You know who Dom has reached out for?" Molinari's voice dropped to a whisper. *"De Five o'Clock guy."*

"Jesus, Mary and Joseph!" replied Jimmy Skins. "You're shittin' me!"

"I ain't," replied Molinari.

"Jeez. I gotta go. Forget I axed. I don't even like *thinking* about dat guy. It's bad luck."

"It's worse luck for whoever killed Joey," said Molinari. "Gives you goose bumps, ya know? Dead men walking around out dere who don't know dey're dead yet. Meet me tonight at da cab stand, eight o'clock. I got somethin' for you."

"Okay." Cagolitti hung up.

Matt whistled. "I'd say you got your work cut out for you, lady. You FBI guys don't find whoever did this before Johnny Vee does, you won't find anything but a greasy spot."

"Who's Johnny Vee?" asked Phil.

"One of the few criminals I know of whom I wouldn't care to go up against unless I had to," said Matt grimly. "John Visconti, aka Johnny Vee, aka Five o'Clock Johnny. The most ruthless, dangerous and efficient hit man in the entire history of the American Mafia. What's John been up to lately, Agent Weinmann?"

"He lives in Seattle now and runs a few Mob controlled businesses by way of a steady income, but two or three times a year he is called out to handle the most sensitive and urgent assassination contracts," said Andrea, laying a file before them. Matt leafed through it while the others looked over their shoulder. "He is believed to have carried out murders in Italy, Spain, Great Britain, South America, and Jamaica, as well as all over the United States and several in Canada. He specializes in what I suppose you'd call job lots."

"He takes out entire crews if the Mob bosses think it has to be done," explained Matt.

"Any chance he did the killings on the boat?" asked Cowboy.

"If so, why would LaBrasca be calling him in apparently to find the killers and avenge his son?" asked Andrea.

"Could he have done DeMarco?" asked Phil.

"Possibly, although I believe he usually works alone," mused Matt. "Dominic LaBrasca is his official godfather or rabbi or whatever. Other families have to go through Dom the Butcher if they want Johnny on a job, and Dom gets a commission. LaBrasca may indeed have ordered DeMarco hit if he thought Eddie was involved in his son's death. Joey was Dom's last son. All of them dead either in Mob wars or other causes. Who's the Genovese heir apparent now?"

"Looks like it's one of LaBrasca's grandsons, an up and coming young thug named Anthony Stoppaglia, mob moniker Tony Stop and/or Little Blue Eyes, because he supposedly looks like a kid Frank Sinatra," replied Andrea. "I can't see it myself, but these are admittedly mug shots. Maybe Tony doesn't look his best." She handed them another file. "Our Bureau office in New York brought Dominic LaBrasca in and questioned him for three hours, until his attorney showed up and raised hell, but LaBrasca said nothing. Our New York contacts can't seem to find Tony Stop to question him, but LaBrasca may have him hidden away somewhere until the danger to his family is past, if that's what's going on. The kid probably doesn't know anything anyway. There is a hell of a lot we don't know about this case."

"You say you'll be going down to Florida to follow up?" asked Matt. "I almost envy you. God, I'd love to be able to sink my teeth into this case, instead of nibble around the edges on this DeMarco sideshow! Almost wish I was Federal again!" he added with a chuckle.

"Why don't you come back?" suggested Andrea. "Not the Bureau, for obvious reasons, but I'm sure the DEA or Marshalls Service would jump at the chance to have you."

"I resigned after Waco, ma'am," replied Matt in a level voice. "If I was a Federal agent again I'd love to be on this case and track these monsters down. But the next case I got might demand that I fabricate evidence against some old coot out in the woods who isn't harming anybody, but some suit decides they don't like his political views. Or I might be called upon to burn a group of religious people alive in their church, or shoot down a mother with her baby in her arms, or destroy the life of some security guard whose sole crime is to be white, male, and overweight. I'd really like to work on this with you, Agent Weinmann, but I also like being able to look at myself in the mirror every morning and not loathe what I see."

"*Whoooo!*" said Andrea archly. "That's telling *me!*" *Would you be that strong in bed?* she wondered. *Would you throw me down on my back and tear my panties as you ripped them off me, you're so eager to possess me? Do you have any idea what I would do for such a man?*

"Nothing personal, ma'am. If you really are straight then my hat is off to you, and some day you will find, as I did, that you cannot serve this government and keep a clear conscience. Would you like for me to write all that last spiel out for you, so you won't have to paraphrase it for your report to Janet Reno?"

"I'd like it better if you take me to lunch and let me convince you that you're wrong, about me, anyway," said Andrea.

"Why not? Let me wind things up here and I'll meet you downstairs in five minutes," replied Matt easily.

After she left Cowboy chuckled. "Hey, *compadre,* she's really coming on to you!" he said. "It was like me and Phil wasn't even in the same room!"

"I noticed," replied Matt in a dry voice.

"Matt…" Phil said softly. "Careful, okay? That woman is one of these overeducated Yankee bitches who thinks all Southern white men are stupid barbarians and beneath contempt. I sensed it in her every word and move in here just now, and so did you. So why is she trying to stroke you?"

"I know," said Matt soberly. "Phil, maybe this is it. Maybe they've decided it's payback time for Bennett and they're planning some kind of convoluted revenge. Hell, maybe they even set up this whole goddamned DeMarco thing, although the business on the boat seems to be a bit over the top, even for Clinton. Or maybe she's just some sexually repressed New Yahk JAP who's looking for a bit of rough and finds a redneck who blasted an Assistant Director of the Bureau into kingdom come to be some kind of kinky erotic turn-on. I've got to find out whether or not she's harmless."

"Harmless, my friend, is one thing that there lady ain't!" said Phil with finality.

Five minutes later Matt was escorting Andrea towards his Taurus in the underground parking lot. "Any kind of cuisine in particular in mind?" he asked. "Chinese? Greek? Good old Southern grease? Raleigh has some first class restaurants."

"I've got plenty of time," she said. "My flight from RDU down to Miami doesn't leave until seven tonight. Chapel Hill is only about forty minutes away. Do you mind? I haven't seen the UNC campus in years, and I really would like to check out the Rathskeller again. After that, any chance I could meet the mighty Trumpeldor?"

At Chapel Hill's famous Rathskeller, Matt seated her and excused himself. He called his wife on her cell phone. Much to the surprise of both of them, she had retained her accounting job at the University of North Carolina campus across Franklin Street, even after having been involved in the high profile arrest and imprisonment of her extremely politically correct department head almost three years earlier. "Hey, Watson," he said. "You available for lunch at the Rat? I'm over here with an FBI agent, someone I want you to meet."

"Hopefully he's an improvement over the last FBI agent we ran across," said Heather.

"It's a she, and she's a real knockout. Kind of a Jewish Agent Scully. I need a chaperone. Half the people in here know you and me, and by two o'clock this afternoon you will have heard the latest rumor that I'm stepping out on you. Seriously, Heather, I want you to scope this lady and give me your opinion."

"Give me fifteen minutes."

Matt returned to the table. "I gave my wife a ring and asked her to join us. I hope you don't mind," he told Andrea.

"I understand," said Andrea with a chuckle. "You need a chaperone to protect you from my wily Levantine charms."

"This is a small town. People do talk," said Matt, a little unnerved by her perception.

"Will your wife object if we talk shop?"

"She and I talk shop a lot. I keep after her to take some criminal justice courses and change careers. Heather's a damned good detective herself. I have had a couple of cases since we met that she's really been helpful on. Okay, now, no BS, what is your take on this situation and what is the party line in Washington? You will note those are two separate questions."

"There isn't a party line yet, as you put it," Andrea told him. "Honest Injun, Matt, so far as I could tell nobody up there has any idea what the hell this is all about, and that bothers them. They don't like surprises. They've had enough of them with this administration. Obviously, any time a Congressman and a Mafioso end up dead on the same boat, there are political implications and there has to be political damage control, especially if the dead Congressman is a Democrat. My job is to find out exactly what damage we have to control, and to find Alice Silverman if she's alive. Not necessarily in that order, Matt. If she is alive I'd like to bring her home. That's the kind of thing I joined the Bureau for. Is the pizza here still as good as it was ten years ago?"

"It varies, but this seems to be a vintage year. Do you eat pizza? Mixing milchig and fleischig and all that?"

"I devour it wholesale, and every time I do my highly observant grand-parents all roll in their graves, I'm sure," laughed Andrea. *A bit anti-Semitic are you, nu?* she thought. *Better and better! Nazi rape fantasy here we come!* "Mind if I save us some time and answer what I suspect is your unspoken question? The answer is no, this isn't about Chuck Bennett. I think they've decided that incident needs to be interred with his bones, so to speak."

"Pardon my polite skepticism, but fair enough," said Matt. "I'm sorry if I sounded a bit rough on you before, Ms. Weinmann, but you have to concede, I have reason to be paranoid."

"Just because you're paranoid doesn't mean they're not out to get you?" laughed Andrea. "Any chance I could persuade you to call me Andrea, by the way?"

"OK," chuckled Matt. "Now what do you yourself think this is all about? Please, feel free to speculate."

"I haven't really got any ideas yet, Matt. Not enough data. This Alice Silverman connection bugs the hell out of me. The only thing I can figure is it was a kidnaping gone wrong."

"So nine people were slaughtered Friday the Thirteenth style and left floating on the high seas in a boat full of drugs in a botched kidnaping?" asked Matt, arching his eyebrows.

"I admit there are a lot of unanswered questions," said Andrea, sipping her iced tea. "So what's your take on it?"

"You're right, we just don't have enough data yet. But we know there are some very vicious and very efficient pros involved, and we know that kind of talent doesn't work for peanuts and they don't work for just anybody. Somewhere in all this there is a secret, a secret that someone very rich and powerful wants kept at any price, and it isn't just about drugs and whores. Thanks to that ridge running bush ape in the White House, nobody cares enough about drugs and whores nowadays to kill over them." Andrea's face twitched quickly. "Ooops, sorry, did I touch a nerve there? You a Clintonista? Of course, you would be."

"I believe that Mr. and Mrs. Clinton have done a lot of good for the country despite his personal issues, and that we should respect the office whatever we may think of the man, yes," she said quietly. "I also know that if it were not for programs like affirmative action I would not be sitting here carrying an FBI badge. The last person to get anywhere in the FBI wearing a dress was J. Edgar Hoover. I don't want you to feel that you have to walk on eggs around me, Matt, and I understand why you have some negative attitudes in view of what happened to you, but I think I'd best make my politics and my views on the President clear from the start."

"Okay, I'll cool it," replied Matt. "I'll even try to say president instead of Billyboy when you're in earshot. It's not walking on eggs, Andrea, it's just being polite. I am of the last generation of Southern men who grew up in the old ways, among which was a rule that one did not deliberately offend a lady."

"I can live with that," she said with a smile.

"Getting back to the case, my suggestion is that you start with the Congressman and work your way through his corporate contacts like Sipple and Federer. Men like that do not take vacations. They weren't on that boat by accident."

"We're way ahead of you, but what about Alice Silverman and her party?" asked Andrea. "Where do they fit in?"

"Since she hasn't shown up, and we have no body yet, she and her child and the other two women have either been murdered elsewhere and their bodies concealed, or else they have been kidnaped, or else they escaped the massacre somehow and they're in hiding, understandably enough. I'm dubious on the kidnaping theory. If she was as clean as you say, and not involved in the drug culture, the only reason for snatching her would be for ransom, and we have no ransom demand so far as we know. Would this agent of hers tell you if he had received such a demand?"

"Mmm, I think so. We made it very clear that we would frown on any independent negotiations with anyone who contacted him, and we're having him discreetly watched and his phone tapped just in case."

"Ah, here comes Heather," said Matt. He rose, but Andrea was up before him, extending her hand to Heather.

"Special Agent Andrea Weinmann, FBI," she said with a smile. "I heard your voice on that answering machine tape, and I'm glad I could meet you in person." *So this is my competition?* thought Andrea. *This skinny piece of shiksa white bread?*

"Heather Redmond," said Heather, returning the handshake. "Also known as Watson to the Southern Sherlock Holmes. I hope you can catch the people who killed Mr. DeMarco. I know he was a hoodlum, but I heard that man die, and whatever he was, he didn't deserve that." *You want him, don't you, Agent Scully?* thought Heather to herself. *Oh, yes. Well, slaver away in envy, lady, because I got him and you sure as hell ain't getting him!*

"Okay, what's the verdict?" asked Matt when he got home that night.

"First off, she wants to do you," said Heather, handing him a capuccino.

"I'll spare you the smutty macho rejoinders. I got that vibe off her as well, and that could be a problem. Are you sure your feminine intuition is on target there?" asked Matt quietly.

"Yes. Don't let your male ego get too inflated, but yes. Believe me, Matt, women know these things, especially where their own men are concerned. Probably some instinctual throwback to the primordial caves when we had to fight off rivals for Ug's affection with tooth and claw."

"Need any re-assuring?" he asked.

"None whatsoever. If there is one thing I have learned about you, Matt, it's that you are a man of honor. I know that if you were stranded on a desert island with Andrea Weinmann, that wedding ring on your finger would ensure that you never touched her beyond whatever was necessary to save her from sharks and cannibals."

"So it would be," agreed Matt.

"Not to mention the fact that you declined the country charms of the luscious Darlene down in Lumberton. Yes, I know about that, we won't get into how, except to say that when I learned about that episode it was…well, it was one of the best things that's ever happened to me, and if it was possible for me to love you more than a hundred per cent, that day you got a hundred and ten."

"Damn! Heather, I should have told you!" said Matt with a sigh.

"You should have done no such thing. It wasn't important to that case then, and it's not important now. The main question is, what is Andrea Weinmann really after in all this? What are her orders from Janet Reno, really? I can't read her, and that in itself somewhat disturbs me. Her lust for your middle-aged yet still delectable carcass attests to her good taste in men, but it says nothing about her fundamental honesty. I find it very difficult to believe that those political gangsters in Washington have just decided to write off Charles Bennett as one of those things, and I am even less convinced that Hillary Clinton has decided to forgive and forget over that vile bitch Margaret Mears."

"I'll call up a guy in Washington I know with the Bureau who might be willing to talk to me about her, if he knows anything," said Matt. "Frank Hardesty. Damned fine cop who ended up on the wrong end of the politics, so he's in Records now or something while he counts off his days to retirement, but he still has his ear to the ground. Anyway, Ms. Andrea is now winging her way south and will be chasing non-political gangsters down in Florida, so I'm not sure how I might get dragged into anything hinky. Eddie Miami's demise up here is pretty much a sideshow. The real problem is Alice Silverman. Where the hell is she? Did they kill her? What about the secretary and the nanny and the baby? Damn, I wish I had been able to talk to Eddie and hear his story!" The front door slammed.

"Hi Mom, hi Dad!" said a tall, willowy young beauty with honey-brown hair and crystal green eyes who poked her head into the kitchen. "Bye Mom, bye Dad!"

"Where are you off to tonight?" asked Heather.

"Tennis practice with Sheri and Tina and Bobbi," said their daughter Tori, who was on UNC's women's tennis team.

"Not a date? Ain't you gots you no boyfriend *yet?*" laughed Matt teasingly. "Jesus, what's wrong with the college guys in this town? In my ancient day they would have been all over you."

"They're mostly immature dweebs with their caps on backwards" said Tori. "I'm supposed to go all swoony over Beavis and Butthead? Give me a break! Besides, soon after they hit town the guys all hear about your gruesome reputation, and they back off. I'm kind of a latter day Chapel Hill Lorna Doone. I need to find a guy who's willing to take you on in a gunfight if need be. Hey, look, Dad, there are freshmen girls who are already shacking up before they've finished registering for the first semester. Be glad I've decided to look over the merchandise for a bit before I buy. I keep asking you to introduce me to some of your younger cop friends, but you won't do it."

"You're not going to turn into a cop groupie, are you?" asked Matt in half serious concern. "That's a good way to end up with some steroid freak thug who will abuse you and beat on you, Tori. There are good cops, but an awful lot of bad ones as well."

"I'm a *man* groupie, Dad. Don't worry, I'm not dumb enough to fall for some Neanderthal in a uniform, but if there's anything under the uniform worth knowing I'd be interested," she replied, grabbing a Diet Coke from the fridge. "Dilbert doesn't cut it with this girl. The way I figure it, the last real men in this society are going to gravitate to the police and the army, in the mistaken impression they will be doing something worth while."

"Matt, have you been poisoning her mind with your reactionary polemics again?" laughed Heather. "I even heard her refer to the president as Billyboy the other day!"

"No, no, she's smart enough to figure things out on her own!" insisted Matt with a grin.

"You know, honey, you really could do a lot worse than Dilbert," said her mother. "Kind of limiting your choices in a university town, aren't you?"

"Hey, you got lucky here. Why can't I?" asked Tori. "Gotta run!" After she bounced out Heather looked at her husband.

"We both got lucky here," she said softly.

"What a coincidence," replied Matt. "So did I." He leaned over the table and kissed her, crushing her long soft hair in his hand. "How fast can you get naked from the time Tori slams the door on her way out?" he whispered.

"Got a stopwatch?" she asked.

01

The Song of the Lavender Canary

John Visconti and Tony Stoppaglia checked into a suite at the Palm Beach Hilton. The first thing Visconti did was to make a long distance call to Seattle. "We'll be getting a package by special courier, overnight delivery," he told Tony. "A heavy package addressed to Donald Robinson, who is me. That's our armament. When it comes, if I'm not here, you sign for it. Remember, in this hotel you're Frank Martin, that's how you sign for the package. Don't open the package until I get back from wherever I've gone to."

They quickly turned up a lead. The Florida underworld had already gotten the word down from New York: everyone was to cooperate fully with Johnny Vee and tell him anything and everything he wanted to know. Sudden unavailability or reluctance to speak would be regarded as obstruction of Dominic LaBrasca's justice for his murdered son, and with Five o'Clock Johnny on the scene, it was clearly understood that this would be hazardous to one's health. They started by going down the list of Joey LaBrasca's former business associates. Lew Lefkowitz was a pudgy, cigar-chomping Jewish criminal entrepeneur who made the most of his Mob connections and who liked to pose as a tough guy, a slob who brutally bullied and abused his prostitutes and subordinates. He came up to the hotel suite voluntarily in a cold sweat of fear, and practically fell all over himself blubbering everything he could think of that he knew or had ever known about Joey LaBrasca's operation. It didn't help that Visconti had asked him to stop by at five o'clock. When it appeared that he knew nothing useful, John dismissed him with a quiet word, and Lefkowitz practically collapsed in the elevator on the way down to the lobby in relief that he wasn't on the spot.

The ex-biker Jimmy Jesus also came in voluntarily. He was a hulking, tattooed, bearded man with a ponytail, still brawny in his forties, a brute who had killed half a dozen men himself, including two in prison brawls. He was wary but respectful of Visconti and understood that it was in his interest to be candid and truthful, but he knew nothing that could be of any help. Before he left, Visconti slipped him an envelope of cash. "That's for your time, and also for you to keep your ears, open, Jim," he said. "As a favor to Dominic. You give us something solid on this one and it's worth a good deal more."

"You got it, Mr. Vee," said the biker. He didn't collapse in relief on his way back down, but he did stop for a stiff drink in the hotel bar. Killer though he himself was, the icy Visconti stare had unnerved him.

"Now what?" asked Tony.

"We need to speak to a faggot named Ian McKinney," said Visconti. "There's no point in calling him up here. If he knows I'm looking for him, he'll run and hide, and I don't want to have to chase the little cocksucker down. Let me see if I can find out where he's set up shop these days." On his cell phone Visconti called a mob-connected businessman who owned a string of gay bars and bathhouses throughout Miami and Fort Lauderdale. Half an hour later the man called back and spoke briefly with Visconti. "He's in a fag bar called the Mousetrap, in Delray Beach," said John. "He'll probably be there most of the evening. It's where he holds court and does his business. Blackmail and information. Let's go."

"How do you want talk to the guy, John?" asked Tony as they drove through the dark warm night with the surf pounding on their left and the lights from beach homes and Cuban hot food takeaway stands on their right. "I mean, how heavy should I get?"

"You don't get heavy with him at all, you let me do that. Just make sure Ian and I aren't interrupted while we have our little chat."

"We ain't got any guns."

"We will when that package gets here from Seattle, but this isn't a gun situation, kid. We're not out to whack anybody or raise a commotion, not yet, anyway. All we want to know is what the word is on the street about what went down on board that yacht. Besides, if you can't handle a bunch of bugger boys without a gun, you ain't gonna be much use to me, eh?" Visconti found the gay bar and had Tony cruise around the block. "When you go into a place you don't know, always give it the once over," he told. "But only once. Go around twice and you get noticed. What you look for is two things: entrances and exits, and the immediate street layout so you'll know where to go if you have to make a fast break. You don't want to end up turning into a blind alley with somebody after you. Now park here," he said.

"We're a block away from the joint!" protested Tony. "Suppose something does go sour and we need the car in a hurry?"

"Then you look to be in good enough shape to do a little running. Always park some distance away, not a half a mile away, but not right in front of the place you're going into, either. You want as few people as possible to see what you're driving, and that includes any muscle men who might have hostile ideas. You don't want to come out and find your tires slashed or your windshield busted. Let's go."

"Do you know this McKinney faggot by sight?" asked Tony as they walked toward the Mousetrap in the muggy night heat. The pounding ocean surf was audible even over the 70s retro disco music from inside the bar.

"Oh, yeah, and he knows me," said Visconti grimly. "He tried to put the arm on a friend of ours once, with some pictures he had of a couple of homos doing filthy things. One of the homos was a college boy, the son of a don. Pardon me if I don't tell you which one. McKinney was hooked up with some Cuban wannabe wiseguys down here, and he was dumb enough to think they could protect him from Our Thing. Wrong. I got the negatives and all the prints off Ian when I showed up at his apartment carrying the head of the biggest Cuban with me in a bowling bag. He saw the light, real fast. He not only gave up the film and the negatives, he gave up the don's son, told me where he was hiding. I snatched the kid and took him back to New York to his father."

"Gee, a boss's son turned fag? I'm surprised the boss didn't tell you to just kill him," said Tony, shaking his head.

"I took him back so the boss could kill the boy himself, which he did, right in the basement of the family home. The old man stuck a .357 Magnum up the kid's ass while he screamed for mercy, and then he pulled the trigger."

"*Yow!* Dat's gotta hoit!" exclaimed Tony. "But you didn't kill this blackmailing fag McKinney as well? Why not?"

"The don had a better idea, make Mr. McKinney a living warning as to what happens when you try to blackmail a friend of ours," said Visconti with a grim smile. "After I got the pictures and the kid's address, I cut McKinney's balls off. The don still has them in his den, in a jar of alcohol."

"And you think this guy is just gonna tell you what you wanna know, after you cut his balls off?" laughed Tony incredulously.

"There's still his cock," said Visconti. Tony was about to laugh again, then he realized that Visconti was not smiling.

The inside of the bar was garish pink and maroon leather, potted palms, thick carpet and the stink of cheap perfume and male sweat. On the dance floor a dozen male couples, in various costumes ranging from leather to a full floor-length evening gown to a simple jock strap, writhed and cavorted to the Village People chanting about wanting them as new recruits for the Navy. A mightily muscled bouncer dressed in tight white slacks and a tank top T-shirt, his receding hairline giving away his certain steroid usage, eyed them lasciviously. "Well, hey, guys!" he simpered. "You're new here. What's that, the Wall Street look?" He sidled up to Visconti. "Wow, aren't you the lucky one, dearie! Your boyfriend is a *doll!* Are you two like, monogamous?"

A single look from Visconti silenced Tony's imminent explosion. "We've just stopped in to look for a friend. Ah, I see him now." Visconti motioned Tony to accompany him and they moved across the room towards a corner table where a thin, gray-headed, limp-wristed homosexual personage of the kind generally described as "screaming" was sitting with a pretty young man, twittering animatedly and caressing him on the cheek. He was wearing a Hawaiian shirt and his fingers sparkled with rings. Then McKinney looked up and saw Visconti approaching. He shrieked like a woman in terror, leaped up and ran for the rear exit. Visconti and Tony pelted after him, flinging the dancers aside and knocking over a waiter with a tray of drinks. They caught him in the rear alley. Visconti slammed McKinney up against the wall. "Tony, keep an eye out," he ordered.

"God please don't, John, please, oh please, my God don't do it, John, I didn't know it was going to happen, I didn't know, please, please..." sobbed McKinney in utter terror. Visconti punched him in the belly. McKinney keeled over, retching.

"Didn't know what was going to happen?" demanded Visconti. "Didn't know Joey and all those others were going to get whacked? Whacked by who?"

"He...he came to me, just wanted some information about Joey's boat parties," quavered McKinney. "And he wanted to know when they were going down to the Bahamas again. Joey ran those junkets regular, like clockwork, Tuesdays and Saturdays. I didn't figure there was any harm, hell, everybody in town knew, and he gave me five grand to bring him and Joey together. Said he had an extra special friend he wanted to bring on the trip. I didn't know until afterwards when her and Eddie came to me...but Jesus, I should have known, with a rep like his..."

"You give me a name *now*, motherfucker, or I will cut your tongue out and send it up to New York to go in the same jar with your stones," hissed Visconti.

"Blanchette!" screamed McKinney in terror. *"It was Bob Blanchette!"*

"Hey, I know dat name," said Tony. "Ain't he dat heavy hitter wit the Dixie mob?"

Suddenly a huge shadow loomed in the pale overhead light of the alley. The bouncer from the Mousetrap was padding toward them, biceps and pecs rippling, eyes rolling, balled fists like hams raised in menace. "Oh, no, no, dearie, can't have that, no no no I mean a little leather work is one thing, but we can't have you bothering our patrons in such a rude and uncouth manner. I must chastise you, dearie, really I must," he gibbered. Tony Stop struck like a bolt of lightning. A kick to the groin, two jug ears grasped and a face pounded into an upraised knee, the heel of a right palm smashing a cheekbone to powder, a stomp that crushed the instep of the big man's foot and sent him crashing and screaming to the ground, then kick and kick and kick and kick, one to the kidneys that made the urine splash into the white trousers, one to the solar plexus, one that audibly snapped a rib, then finally one to the temple that made the pile of meat on the alley floor collapse and shudder into unconsciousness.

"Fuck you, dearie," said Tony. He hadn't even broken a sweat.

"Now, you were telling us about Bob Blanchette?" said Johnny to McKinney, who was staring at the pulverized bouncer on the reeking alley floor, about to faint. "Blanchette came to you and asked you to put him in with Joey for one of these degenerate parties, okay, we've gotten that far. But Blanchette isn't a party animal, from what I've heard. He works for hire, Ian. Who hired him to kill Joey LaBrasca?"

"I don't know, in God's name I don't know!" moaned McKinney. "Sweet Jesus, do you think he'd tell me something like that? But it wasn't Joey they were after. It was this chick. This actress. Alice Silverman. She was the mark," whispered McKinney. "Her and her baby."

"What?" demanded Visconti sharply. "Give it to me, Ian! All of it!"

"Eddie Miami brings her to my place, the morning after it happened," he moaned. "She was supposed to be on the boat. They tell me that Blanchette and a real nasty bitch named Karen Martin and some crazy giant biker are after her. He wants me to stash her and the baby and two other chicks, women who work for Alice, while he goes up to North Carolina and hooks up with some former DEA guy he knows. Eddie says he can trust this guy to do the right thing. Says he can't trust any other cops because Blanchette was doing the contract for the Feds. DeMarco didn't know I was the guy who had steered Blanchette in their direction, so I kinda felt responsible, you know…"

"So Dom was right," growled Tony. "It was stinking rat bastard Feds! Wait a minute. Alice Silverman, I know her. She's the actress who did that movie about the big dog, and the other one where she gets chased by dinosaurs. Why the hell do Feds want to kill her and not my uncle Joey?"

"Her and the baby," said McKinney. "Eddie and Alice were both sure on that. The baby had to go as well."

"Why?" demanded Visconti.

"They didn't tell me, John! They just asked me for a place to hide while Eddie went up to North Carolina!" insisted McKinney. "And this Silverman chick gave me a check for ten grand! So I took them out to this beach house I have access to up in Fort Pierce. The owner is a friend of mine, he's in Europe. Then I hear Eddie got whacked right in the middle of Raleigh Durham airport, and I get spooked, so I…"

"Go on, Ian," said Visconti dangerously.

"So I call the Fort Pierce place. I get no answer. I go out there and…and I see…" He looked at them in horror. "John, I don't know how they found the place. As God is my witness I didn't tell them anything…"

"Dead?" demanded Visconti.

"The other two women were dead. All over the house in bits and pieces. Somebody must have chopped them up with an ax or a chain saw. Sweet Jesus, the place was a slaughterhouse! I puked all over the floor when I saw it. But as near as I could tell from what I saw, they didn't get the Silverman woman, or the baby. Or if they did, they took them away."

"How much did Blanchette pay you for the information?" asked Visconti gently. To emphasize his point he reached and with incredible speed and force grasped McKinney's left ear and ripped it off his skull as if it was paper, blood spurting from the hole in his head. McKinney screamed like a dying animal in terror and agony. Visconti studied him. "How did you contact Blanchette to tell him about the beach house, Ian? Or do you want both ears off?"

"*Little Rock! 501-239-0045!*" shrieked McKinney in agony. "It's an answering service! You leave a message and a number for Mr. Wilson, and he calls you! That's all I know, John, I swear on my mother's grave that's all I know!"

"501-239-0045," said Tony. "Got it."

"Okay, Ian, just one more little thing, and then I'll let you get back to sucking dicks and blackmailing people. Let's get back to Eddie Miami. Who was this cop he was going to for protection, this ex-DEA guy?"

"That hotshot they call Two Gun Matt," sobbed the broken wretch before them. "You know, the one they did those TV shows about, he was in *People* magazine. He used to be DEA, but he's some kind of North Carolina county mountie now. What the fuck is his name? I can't remember. Please don't hurt me any more. John, I can't stand it…"

"Redmond," said Visconti dryly. "Matt Redmond."

"Who's Redmond" asked Tony.

"One of the few police officers I know of whom I wouldn't care to go up against if I could avoid it," replied Visconti. He let McKinney slump down into the alley, throwing the ear down at him. "Go to a hospital and get that sewed back on if you want. Let's get out of here. Tony. I don't like the smell."

"Uh…" John looked up and saw Tony glance at the sobbing wreck of McKinney on the alley floor and make a quick slash across his throat, a question in his eyes. Visconti shook his head and beckoned for them to go.

On the drive back up to Palm Beach, Tony asked, "Uh, John, I thought everybody who was involved with Uncle Joey's death had to go? So why didn't we ice that fruit fly? He set Joey and the others up for the hit."

"Don't worry, he'll get his," chuckled Visconti. "But Ian still has one thing left he needs to do for us. Think about it a bit."

They drove on in silence for a while. "So it was this cracker hit man Blanchette who whacked Uncle Joey?" said Tony.

"That makes sense," said Visconti, chewing his thumb thoughtfully while he wiped his hands and his jacket sleeve of McKinney's blood with a handkerchief. "He usually teams with two other workers, a really hard bitch named Karen Martin and a big hillbilly muscle man named Luther Lambert. They call themselves the Three Musketeers, and they don't just work for the cracker mob, they specialize in serving the needs of corporate America, so to speak. They've done jobs for a lot of the big multi-nationals, AT & T and General Motors and Chase Manhattan. I heard a rumor that they were also Billyboy's main muscle in Arkansas when he was governor, and after he became president as well. Blanchette is the brains. The street talk is that he did Jerry Parks and Vince Foster and arranged for Jim McDougal to be slipped a fatal dose of digitalis in prison. If they're involved then this is something big for sure, and it's also going to be rough sledding for us. These people are pros, the best. They don't work cheap, they're damned good at what they do, and when we go after them we don't fuck around. Make no mistake, kid, if we don't get them first, they'll get us."

"They can't be that good," said Tony.

"Oh? So what makes you think so?"

"They was stupid enough to kill a Sicilian," replied Tony darkly. "Not just any Sicilian, but a LaBrasca. They knew who'd be coming after them."

"Apparently they were paid enough to disregard my rather grim reputation," said Visconti with some amusement.

"Wit all due respect, *padrone,* I wasn't talking about you. I was talking about me. So what do we do now?"

"We need to locate Blanchette and his team, and we need to find Alice Silverman, if she's still alive," said Visconti. "She can tell us some things perhaps even Blanchette himself couldn't tell us. Who hired him? Why was she marked for death? She can tell us *why* all this was done, and that's vitally important. Once we know the why, we will know the who."

"So how do we find Blanchette? Call that number?" asked Tony.

"No, he'd spot anything we tried to set up that way in a heartbeat. I tell you again, kid, this man is no fool. Have you figured out yet why we left candyass Ian alive and bleeding and pissed off with my habit of excising bits and pieces of his anatomy? What do you think he's going to do now?"

"*He's* gonna call that number and tell Blanchette we're after him!" exclaimed Tony in admiration, suddenly seeing the light.

"Exactly. Why waste time trying to hunt Blanchette down? Let him come to us. And what do you think Blanchette is going to do with a loose end like Ian?"

"Ice de fruit fly!" exclaimed Tony.

"Yeah, probably have that Lambert ape of his go to work on what's left of Ian with his chain saw. Don't worry, Tony, everybody goes, like I said. But this is going to be really tricky, kid. That's why I want to find the Silverman woman before they do. She might be able to fill in the gaps for us. We're making a list, kid, and I want to make sure everybody who belongs on it is there before we take it into the next phase."

"And then we start killing?" demanded Tony.

"Then we start killing," confirmed Visconti grimly.

✶✶✶

The next morning Matt Redmond came into his office and found a note on his desk. "Contact the Director, private cellular number." Matt dialed the number. "Yes, Phil?" he asked.

"Matt, I'm at Senator Helms' house." said Hightower. He sounded haggard. "His private home, not his office. Please come over here right away and tell no one where you are going."

Twenty minutes later Matt pulled into a graveled driveway on a shady, tree-lined street in one of Raleigh's inner city neighborhoods, up to an unpretentious but spacious and well kept two story home of nineteenth century vintage. He knocked on the door and was astounded when the door was opened by United States Senator Jesse Helms himself, a slightly built, dignified old man leaning on a cane, a humorous glint in his eye behind thick spectacles. "You must be Matt Redmond," he said, extending his hand that gripped Matt's firmly despite his years. "I remember those fedoras, used to wear one myself when I was your age. Glad to meet you, son! I've heard a hell of a lot about all them darin' exploits of yours!"

"It's an honor to meet you, sir," said Matt, flustered. "Ah, I got a message from SBI Director Hightower…?"

"He's in the parlor," said Helms, beckoning Matt inside. "Come on in. Matt, we got a hellacious problem we're gonna need your help with." He opened the door to the living room. Matt saw Hightower sitting in an armchair. Then he heard a baby give a short cry. He turned and a stunningly beautiful young woman in a pale beige pants suit rose from the sofa, holding a bundled infant in her arms. Her hair was long and blond, her eyes crystalline blue, and her face was a frozen mask of haunted pain and fear. She looked like she was about to turn and flee out the French doors. The first thing that hit Matt was that this woman was terrified out of her wits. Then he recognized her. "You're Alice Silverman," he said.

"You're Matt Redmond?" she whispered.

"Yes, ma'am," he said quietly, taking off his hat. "How may I be of service to you?"

"You can save my life," she said dismally. "They killed Carla and Serafina. I heard their terrible screams as they died, while I was running away with my child in my arms. Now they're trying to kill me, and kill my baby."

"Who?" asked Matt urgently. It was as if Hightower and Helms weren't even in the room. "Who is trying to kill you?"

"Bill Clinton," she whispered. "He wants me dead. He wants my baby dead!"

"Why?" asked Matt gently. She looked up at him in anguish. "I know Clinton and his works, ma'am. You needn't fear you won't be believed. Why is he trying you kill you, and why does he want to kill the baby?"

Her eyes and her voice were dead with utter misery. "Eleven months ago, Bill Clinton raped me. After he was through, Hillary Clinton raped me." She held up the wiggling bundle. "This is Bill Clinton's son. Now he wants us both dead. I have come to you because you are the only lawman in the country who will believe me, and who has shown that he has the courage to stand up to them. If you don't help, then my child and I will die. Will you help us?"

"Yes," said Matt.

011

Enter the Ingenue

"Matt, before this goes any further, can we have a word in private?" spoke up Senator Helms. "You'll excuse us, please, Miss Silverman?"

"Don't worry, I'll still be here when you get back," said Alice with a wry smile. "I have no place else to go."

Matt followed the Senator and Hightower into Helms' carpeted, book-lined study. As soon as the door closed behind them he said, "With all due respect, gentlemen, what the *hell* is going on here? How did she get here, and why is she here at all? Has she told you anything about who killed DeMarco or what happened on the yacht?"

"She was never on the yacht," said Hightower. He seemed to have aged ten years. "She'll tell you in a bit what happened, and it will blow your mind. Matt, this is big. It is beyond anything I have ever come across."

"As to how she got here, at four o'clock this morning I was awakened by someone pounding on my door," said Helms. "By the way, Matt, I believe I heard you are a cigar smoker? Try one of these."

"Uh…rolled Havanas, sir?" asked Matt, his eyebrows arching.

"There a *few* things about Cuba I like," chuckled Helms, his eyes twinkling as he and Matt both lit up. "Anyhoo, like I was saying, I get woke up at four this morning and I find this lovely Hollywood movie star and her baby standing on my porch, with a very incredible story to tell. An incredible credible story, if you follow. A story that I believe, Matt."

"And what will you do with that story, Senator?" asked Matt bleakly. "Impeachment failed. Sir, let me be blunt. I know that you personally did everything you could and I don't fault you at all, but your colleagues in the Senate had the chance to rid our country of this sick, drug addicted tyrant and they dropped the ball. We're stuck with him now."

"And the United States Senate shall carry that disgrace throughout its future history," agreed Helms. "As to what I intend to do with her story, that's easily told. I intend to make one of the final acts of my lengthy life on this earth the thwarting of William Jefferson Clinton, at least in this one small matter. Maybe that's a petty reaction, but there it is. There is nothing at all that we can do with Alice Silverman politically. The people of this country have rendered their verdict and that verdict is that Bill Clinton gets a pass, whatever he does. With rage and bitterness in my heart, I have come to accept that. God will judge America for this. I will no longer try. But I still believe that truth and right and justice have enough power and strength to do one thing, and that is *keep that girl and that baby alive.* I can't undo the past eight years, Matt. I can do nothing to bring back those nuclear secrets from China or restore the presidency of the United States to some kind of dignity, nor can I bring Vince Foster or Admiral Boorda or Jim McDougal or any one of a dozen others back to life. But I can damned well make sure that two more deaths aren't added to Clinton's total body count. Those two lives in there are lives that Bill Clinton will not take. I have sworn that to her."

"How?" demanded Matt. "How will you keep that promise, Senator, when every other attempt over the past eight years to restrain Clinton from any act, no matter how murderous or treasonous, has failed? I think you both know I will do whatever I must, but how can you keep her and that baby alive if the most powerful man in the world wants them dead?"

"I haven't lived on Capitol Hill for almost thirty years without learning a trick or two," said Helms grimly. "Matt, let me tell you exactly what I am asking of you. I want you to keep Alice Silverman and her baby safe while I negotiate with that yellow dog piece of hillbilly white trash in the White House for her life. I'm flying back to Washington tonight, and tomorrow I am going to ask for a private appointment with the president, ask in such terms that he will be sure to see me. I am going to say some things to him that I believe will convince him that it is best for him and for those whom he serves to accommodate me in this little matter of Alice Silverman's life. I want you to keep them alive while I do this."

"I will, or die myself in the attempt," replied Matt quietly.

"From what I hear, you will." replied Helms. "Son, I wish to God we had ten thousand more like you in this country. Then maybe we'd have a chance."

"Matt, you of all people know what you are committing yourself to," said Hightower. "I don't mean just Clinton's gunmen. You heard what that woman from the FBI said about the Mob sending that character Visconti in on this, the one you said you wouldn't want to go up against unless you had to? Sounds like you may have to if you get in this deep. You sure about this, Matt? What about Heather and Tori?"

"They will understand and expect nothing less of me," replied Matt. "I want to ask one thing of you both. I want to call my partner Cowboy Garza and have him in on this, and I want to call my wife and have her here when we hear Alice Silverman's story. I cannot do this without both of them."

"Do you think you have the right to involve your family?" asked Helms.

"Yes, and neither of them would ever forgive me if I did not involve them. Gawd, let Tori miss a chance of meeting Alice Silverman? She'd rend me in twain! OK on clearing Cowboy's case load for this, Phil?" Hightower nodded.

"Son, you do what you have to do," said Helms. "Just make sure that just this once, the good guys win one. This old bull still has enough horn left on him to be of some use. I'll back your play all the way."

Matt took out his cell phone and dialed his wife's work number. She answered. "It's me. Heather, it's happening again. You walked through the fire with me once, Watson. Will you do it again? Are you with me?"

"All the way, Holmes," she said with out hesitation.

"Then beg off work somehow and come to Raleigh, right now," he said. "I'll give you the address and tell you how to get here. I want you in on this from the ground up. We beat them once before, Watson. Now we're going to beat them again."

✳✳✳

They sat in Jesse Helms' parlor, coffee cups before them, Helms and Hightower and Matt and Cowboy Garza and Heather Redmond. Heather took the baby from Alice Silverman and quietly fed him a bottle, followed by a muddy concoction of Gerber plums, burping him while the actress sat miserably in an armchair, staring at the floor, speaking in a low monotone.

"It was a Democratic fund raiser at the Beverly Hills Hilton," she said. "Everyone was there, Streisand and Ted Danson and Mary Steenburgen and Whoopi Goldberg and Woody Harrelson and Susan Sarandon and...well, you know, the whole crowd. Everybody who is anybody in Hollywood, not just show people but the finance and media people, you get the idea. It was one of those gigs where my agent told me I had to show my face, see and be seen, let everybody know I'm on the side of the PC angels, all that crap. Jesus, I have to do about one of those a week, even when I'm working. They're a damned nuisance. I have to get a new gown for each one just to show off for the paparazzi. The only thing unusual about this one was that Bill and Hillary were both there. I guess you know they don't do too many public gigs together since Monica, so that attracted a lot of spin, another reason Jake Shapiro told me I needed to be there, to make sure I got noticed. Nothing happened during the dinner and the speeches, I had a shoot at nine the next morning, and I wanted to go home. I'd already called for my limo driver. Then...oh *shit*, I don't know why I was so stupid!" she moaned. "I mean, Jesus Christ, it's not like the whole world doesn't know about him! What the *hell* was I thinking?"

"You got the summons to a hotel room?" asked Matt gently. "That's usually how he works. Who brought the summons? A Secret Service agent?"

"An LAPD cop," said Alice. "A black guy, a captain of detectives. Look, I know damned well I was an idiot to go, I think I knew it at the time. After Paula Jones and Juanita Broaddrick, no woman has any excuses any more for pretending they don't know what that so-called invitation means. But my God, *he is the President of the United States! The President!* How, how can you say no…and I thought if his wife was with him, I mean, surely I'd be safe…? Oh, God, I know I brought it on myself…"

Heather looked up sharply, her face angry, her voice ringing out like steel. *"No!"* she almost shouted. "No, Alice! That's bullshit! Let's get one thing straight right now! No woman *ever* brings rape on herself! Never!"

"Thank you," Alice said with a wan smile. "My mind knows that. It's just my heart that won't ever quite be convinced."

"I understand," said Heather, turning away, her eyes misting.

"Go on, please, ma'am," prompted Phil Hightower.

"I went up to the room, I spoke to the Secret Service agent on guard outside, he let me in, it was their best suite, of course. Bill and Hillary were both there, and so I relaxed, I figured it was OK if she was there. I mean, like, what's he going to do with his wife watching? They offered me a drink, which I accepted, and then they offered me a line of coke, which I didn't. I don't do drugs. We sat and talked for a while about general stuff, the movie business and politics. I noticed they were both snorting pretty heavy. Hillary keeps her coke in a compact in her purse, and Bill has a little leather case with a mirror and his works in pockets inside. Then all of a sudden they…" She fell silent.

"Yes?" prodded Matt softly.

"You won't believe me. No one will." said Alice Silverman, in her voice the despair of all the world's end.

"Please continue, ma'am," said Matt.

"She pulled a gun on me," said Alice. "Hillary Clinton pulled out a pistol and pointed it at my head and told me to take off my clothes."

"*What?*" shouted Cowboy, stunned.

Alice Silverman's body shook like a leaf in a breeze. She was almost convulsive she was trembling so terribly at the memory. "I started to say something, Hillary kicked me to the floor, and Bill ripped a $17,000 Versace gown off me. By then I knew they were serious, I knew they were sky high and they might kill me, and if they did I'd end up lying in park somewhere as a so-called suicide. So I took off my bra and my panties by myself. It was like some kind of nightmare, like I wasn't really there, like I was outside my body watching. The bra and the panties were intact afterwards, but the Versace gown was a shredded mess. Then when I was naked they fucked me," she said lightly, in a giddy voice. "Both of them. Hillary held the gun on me while Bill fucked me, and got me pregnant, and then Bill held the gun on me while Hillary and me…oh God, I can't speak of that. I can't. Let's just put it this way, she's not a normal lesbian and she likes to do some really weird stuff, and we did it all. I don't know who was having more fun, her or Bill. He was watching and…making comments and suggestions the whole time." She leaned back in her chair, staring at the ceiling, her eyes half insane, tears coursing down her cheeks. "*Hath no man's dagger here a point for me?*" she whispered. "That's from 'Much Ado About Nothing', you know." She looked at the horrified Redmond. "Matt, I don't suppose I could persuade you to pull that famous .357 Magnum out and put a bullet in my head? Right now I want to be dead so bad I can taste it."

"And what will happen to William if you die?" asked Heather, openly weeping.

"I know," Alice replied.

"Why didn't you abort the child?" asked Matt. "Our wonderful liberal democracy gives you the right to do that."

"Look, I'm not a very good person," said Alice. "In Hollywood sex is a tool and a weapon. I'm not going to sit here and tell you I haven't been on the casting couch. It took a dirty weekend in Tijuana doing a *menage à trois* with a producer and his wife for me to get *Nancy Drew,* and I got

Clones by blowing Sid Kaplan in the sauna in his office on no less than four occasions. I'm up for a major part, the female lead in Steven Spielberg's next film, but to land it I have to get a certain woman executive producer in my corner, and before all this other came up I had already arranged to spend a weekend at her place on Catalina where I would have given her voluntarily what Hillary Clinton took by force. That's one thing, that's just business, nothing a good long hot bath can't take care of. But killing a baby, a human life that moves inside you, that's something else. You're normal people and I know you think I'm glitterati trash, and I am, but I'm not baby murdering trash. It wasn't my baby's fault that his father is a rapist and a son of a bitch. And once he was born, once I saw his little face and held him in my arms and felt him wiggling and heard him chirping, I knew that something good had come of that terrible night. That's what has kept me sane and kept the razor blade off my wrists. That's why I continued to say nothing, even after the fear wore off for a while. God, you wouldn't *believe* all the gossip in Hollywood about who his father is supposed to be!" she laughed in genuine merriment through her tears. "Everybody in pants from Bill Gates to Marlon Brando. If only they knew! He is mine, he's not Bill Clinton's. I thought he would be mine forever. But now his father is trying to take him away from me..."

Arthur Garza then made a gesture that endeared him to Heather forever. He rose in silence, walked over to the wretched woman sitting in the armchair, took her hand, bent low, and kissed it. Then he returned to his seat, without uttering a word. "Did you tell President Clinton that the child was his?" asked Helms.

"He wouldn't take my phone calls. When William was born I wrote him a letter and sent it to the White House, and as far as I was concerned that was the end of it. I told him I never wanted him to come near the baby, that he was a disease and his wife was a monster and I wanted nothing to do with either of them ever again."

"Which did wonders for his ego, I'm sure," muttered Hightower.

"That letter may well have been your death warrant. Hillary has to have that New York Senate seat. As bad as it must steam her to have to wait for four year while Al Gore keeps her seat warm, she can't just go leaping into the presidency without any formal experience in office, and she knows it. Did you get any answer from him?" asked Matt.

"Not then. Eventually I got an answer of a sort, yeah. The Coast Guard found his answer floating on the ocean in that yacht," she said, shuddering. "They were after me," she whispered in horror, staring at them. "I didn't believe it, but that little guy Eddie, he told me all about it. He said they were going to kill us all on that boat, just to get my baby and me. Make it look like I got caught up in a drug deal gone bad, maybe blame it on Columbians or the mob. They killed all those people anyway. I don't know why."

"How did you come to meet a gangster mook like Eddie DeMarco, Alice? How did you come to be mixed up with that business on the yacht at all?" asked Matt.

"I never heard anything from Clinton, time went by, and I thought it was all over. A guy named Bob Sipple who was big wheel with DuPont told me he had some heavy investment lined up for my production company, which is something I need. I want to be able to make my own pictures without having to rely on the usual Hollywood sources of financing, not to mention avoiding the casting couch. I was supposed to meet these people on the yacht during a cruise down to the Bahamas. Sipple sent a private jet for me, and as a kind of insurance I took along my secretary Carla Renfrew, and Serafina, who was William's nanny, and the baby himself. Understand, I wasn't worried about anything violent, I just wanted to make sure it wasn't some kind of orgy some corporate big shots were planning with me as the star attraction. I get a lot of that kind of shit, and the presence of a baby with a nanny and a big battle-axe secretary hovering in the background kind of tends to dampen executive ardor, if you get my drift. So we get to Miami and everything looks cool, Bob sends a limo for us to take us down to Key

Biscayne, and this guy Eddie is in the back. Say's he's the social director for another guy named Joey LaBrassy or something, I didn't catch the name, who caters for executive retreats and whatnot. On the ride down he was playing with the baby and talking with Serafina, who was young and kind of sweet, and then…oh, I guess he must have had an attack of conscience or something."

"Eddie Miami had a conscience?" asked Matt skeptically.

"Look, Matt, I know everyone tells me Eddie was a hoodlum, and I guess he was, but he saved my life and my child's life, and he never asked me for a cent!" returned Alice with some spirit.

"If he really was able to do a decent thing like that, after the life he led, and he came here to North Carolina only to be murdered for that one righteous act, then North Carolina owes him justice," replied Matt grimly. "Go on, please, ma'am."

"We get to Key Biscayne and park at the marina, and he sends the driver off to do something, then before we even get out of the limo he jumps in the driver's seat and starts the engine and we're roaring back out of town. We didn't know what the hell was going on, I thought maybe I was being kidnaped, but Eddie gets a few miles out of town and pulls over onto the beach, and then he gets back in the back and he says, 'Look, ladies, I gotta tell you. I'm a real scumbag, and I always figured there was nothing I wouldn't do for money, but I can't do dis thing. I can't be a part of dis. I mean that's a *baby*, for fuck's sake! Dis whole thing is a setup, Alice. Dey're going to kill you and dat baby. Bill Clinton has sentenced both of you to death.' Those were his exact words. Then he told me. And I believed him, because it made sense. He didn't know why, but he knew that Bill Clinton wanted my baby and me dead. That's why it made sense to me, why I knew he was telling the truth."

"What did he tell you, ma'am?" asked Matt urgently.

"When the yacht got out to sea we were to be intercepted by a speedboat, and three people were going to board the yacht and kill us all, with the help of Eddie and this guy Joey LaBrassy. They weren't supposed to kill LaBrassy, he and Eddie were supposed to go back in the speedboat with an alibi all set up, but Eddie didn't trust them. Okay, maybe that's why he helped us, because he sensed they were going to kill him as well, but he was right, you all know what happened. Only they killed LaBrassy too, probably because I wasn't there and they figured he'd double crossed them."

"Did he give you any names on these three assassins?" demanded Cowboy.

"Yeah. He said the leader was a guy named Bob Blanchard."

Bob Blanchette?" shouted Matt and Phil Hightower at the same time.

"Yes, that was the name," replied Alice, nodding.

"Who's Blanchette?" asked Helms. "You both seem to recognize the name."

"A murdering psychopath," hissed Phil. "A world class hired assassin from what we call the Dixie Mafia. That son of a bitch has killed at least four people in North Carolina that we know of, Senator, but we've never been able to lay a finger on him! For years I have wanted Bob Blanchette's ass in that Green Room down at Central Prison so bad I could taste it!"

"The Three Musketeers!" exclaimed Cowboy Garza. "Hell, we've heard of them in San Antonio! We know they did a couple of jobs in Texas as well, real smooth hits, not a fragment of evidence we could work into any kind of real case. They cut off the head of some Federally protected witness down in Houston and sent the head to the DA. The Texas Rangers use Bob Blanchette's picture as a target on the pistol range. Matt, I'll bet you dollars to donuts they did the DeMarco killing! It's their style, all right."

"I won't take that bet, Cowboy, because I think so too," said Matt with satisfaction. "Alice, let me guess. The other two were a killer slut named Karen Martin and a big mountain muscleman named Luther Lambert. Am I right?"

"You got it," replied Alice.

"So what happened after Eddie Miami had his conscience attack?" Matt pressed her.

"I was pretty freaked, and so were Carla and Serafina. Carla wanted to go to the police, but what could any Florida cop do against the President of the United States? Eddie asked us if we would trust him. I said yes, what else could I do? I could hardly think straight. He said he would arrange for us to hide in a safe place while he contacted you, Mr. Redmond. I knew your name, I saw that article about you in *People* magazine when I was a teenager and I also saw those stories they did on you on TV. He told me this weird story about you being the best cop in the whole country and the only one who wasn't afraid of Clinton, how you were supposed to have had this big gunfight with some big FBI honcho and a team of assassins from the CIA and killed them all and gotten away with it. Sounds almost like a screenplay. Is that story true?"

"More or less," admitted Matt, exchanging a rueful smile with his wife Heather. *[See "Fire and Rain"—Author]* "That's a long story and not germane to the present situation, but I'll tell you about it when time permits. What happened next?"

"Eddie put us up in a cheap motel that night, and then the next day he took us to meet this gay guy he knew, a man named McKinney. He didn't want to use any of his regular contacts because he didn't know who he could trust, he said this McKinney was the best of a bad lot. McKinney wanted money, I wasn't too impressed with him, but I was scared and I figured I kind of better go with the flow. I gave him ten thousand dollars, and he took us to this beach house in Fort Pierce, a nice place, where he said no one would be able to find us. Eddie said he was going to come up here and tell you what was going on, Mr. Redmond. The next morning we hear that the boat was found with on the ocean with all the people on board dead, and when I heard that I was willing to go along with anything Eddie said, I was so scared. Eddie was scared too. He came up here, and then the morning after that we heard on the news that he had been killed as well." Alice was shaking in terror. "Look, have any of you got a cigarette?" Heather quietly took a pack of Virginia Slims out of her purse and handed it to her along with a Bic.

"Sure you can spare them?" asked Matt with a chuckle.

"I'm down to five of these butts a day, and look who's talking with those big Dominican stinkers of yours!" she said.

"And how many does Tori sneak out of your pack per day?" asked Matt.

"Two or three," she said with a smile. "Our daughter is of legal age now and she could buy her own, but she knows we don't approve so she still acts like a teenager," Heather explained to an amused Helms. "She's a big fan of yours, Alice, and before all of this you're going to have to meet her or she'll never forgive us."

Alice lit the cigarette. "I'm like Mark Twain. I can quit any time I want, I know because I've done it a hundred times," she said.

"What happened after you heard DeMarco had been murdered, ma'am?" prodded Phil.

"That night, when we were about ready to say to hell with it and catch a plane back to LA and try and sort it all out from home, Serafina comes in and says there is a car in the driveway," said Alice, tears starting to course down her cheeks again. "Somehow, I don't know how, we all knew that, that...that it was *them*. Carla and Serafina thrust William into my arms and tell me to run. I'm confused, then all of a sudden the front door just crashes in and this..." Her hand was shaking and her whole body trembling again. "This *thing* comes through, this giant with a forked beard and tattoos of tears running down his face into his beard and he's carrying two axes, one in each hand. I am going to see that face in my dreams for the rest of my life. He was Death, and I knew it. I just ran, God forgive me, I left my friends there to die, oh, please dear God, forgive me, I left them there to die, and I ran out through a basement door with William, and as I ran away I heard them screaming, oh God those terrible screams..." She broke down and sobbed for a time.

"That would have been Luther Lambert. He's a two-axe man, if I recall correctly. Do you remember the address of the house, ma'am?" asked Matt softly.

"5930 Indian River Parkway," whispered Alice in agony.

"I'll call the police in Fort Pierce," said Phil, quietly taking out his cell phone.

"How do you think they found you, Alice?" asked Cowboy Garza.

"I guess McKinney sold us out. He was a bit too pleased about that ten grand I gave him. I guess he wanted more and he got it. Anyway, there's not much more to tell. I got to an ATM and drew my max amount on three or four of my credit cards, so I had some money and I could buy some bottles and formula for William and all, but I was scared to book a flight because they might trace me through the airline. I ended up coming here to Raleigh on a Greyhound bus, a twenty-six hour trip because the bus seemed to stop at every little town in the Okeefenokee and wandered through half South Carolina to get here. I was looking for you, Mr. Redmond, but I didn't know where to find you. I ended up in the Raleigh bus station at four in the morning with my baby in my arms, and the only North Carolina person I could think of who might know where to find you was Senator Helms, so I looked you up in the phone book at the bus station, Senator, and I took a cab here and pounded on your door until I woke you up."

"And thus by sheer luck you came to three of the few men in this country who have the balls to stand up to Clinton," said Cowboy. "You're a lucky lady."

"Three, Cowboy?" asked Matt pointedly. "You in on this? If you'd rather not, there will be no hard feelings, buddy. I mean that."

"I don't like rapists, and I don't like men who kill people, and I damned sure don't like men who try to kill babies," said Cowboy shortly. "I'm in, Matt."

"Good man," said Helms approvingly.

"McKinney will be our first lead…oh, shit, I keep forgetting I'm not a Fed any more!" snapped Matt. "I'm a pissant North Carolina gumshoe! No offense, Phil."

"None taken," said Phil. He spoke into the phone. "Hello? Who is this? Detective Lozano? Detective, this is Philip Hightower. I am the director of the North Carolina State Bureau of Investigation, calling from Raleigh. I have a report from a CI that indicates there may be a double homicide down there on your turf. You need to check out an address at 5930 Indian River Parkway, Fort Pierce."

"What's a CI?" asked Alice.

"Confidential informant," said Heather. "See, Holmes, I have picked up a thing or two hanging around you."

"Ah, Heather, I thought your husband's name was Matt?" asked Alice curiously.

"He's the Southern Sherlock Holmes, according to the tabloid media, and so I ended up as Watson," explained Heather.

"A real Watson," said Matt. He turned to Helms. "She figured out why there were no dead bodies in a car we pulled out of Quarry Lake in Chapel Hill before I did, and that time down in Lumberton Heather realized who Mr. Bones was before I did. She's not here just for decoration, Senator, believe me." Hightower finished his conversation and clicked his phone shut.

"The Fort Pierce cops are on their way to that house," he said. "Okay, Matt, what do we do now? First question, do we tell that fine thang from the FBI that we have Alice Silverman and her baby on ice? My gut says no."

"My gut and yours are in agreement, Phil, but my mental jury is still out on Agent Weinmann. If she's straight she could be of immense help. If she's bent, letting her know about this could be a fatal mistake."

"Who's Agent Weinmann?" asked Alice.

"An FBI Special Agent assigned by Washington to find you," said Matt. "Kind of a real life Agent Scully, very smart and very efficient. She was here yesterday, now she's down in Florida looking for you. When the Fort Pierce cops find the house and…possibly find your secretary and your nanny, although maybe they were able to get away…"

"Carla and Serafina are dead," said Alice dismally, hanging her head.

"I hope you're wrong, but in any case, Special Agent Andrea Weinmann and her team will be on that place like white on rice, and they will pick up your trail to Raleigh very quickly. If for no other reason, they will guess you're here because Mr. Hightower reported the beach house to the Fort Pierce police. They will find this character McKinney, and they will squeeze him dry of every ounce of information. The FBI are sons and daughters of bitches, but they are very good at what they do when they put their minds to it. Alice, this is your life and your baby's life we're talking about. I do not recommend that you involve Agent Weinmann at this time, but I may be wrong about that. I honestly don't know whether she can be trusted or not."

"If she is with the FBI then Janet Reno is her boss, and Bill Clinton is Janet Reno's boss, and Hillary is Bill Clinton's boss," said Alice. "I know that much. No. No FBI until Senator Helms talks to the…talks to that man."

"So what do we do?" asked Phil. "Our SBI budget doesn't run to safe houses."

"Keep them here," said Helms immediately. "Even Clinton and Reno's thugs will think twice about trying any rough stuff in my home."

"With all due respect, sir, you are wrong," said Matt firmly. "If Weinmann is bent, then her orders are to kill Alice and the baby, or else set her up for the Three Musketeers. They will know we have gotten ahead of them because we knew about the Fort Pierce beach house, and when you see the president about this they will know you are involved. Again, with all due respect, sir, I have doubts about whether you will be able to call off Clinton and his dogs. My guess is that thirty minutes after you leave Clinton's office this house will be visited, by Weinmann and her crew with a warrant if you're lucky, and by the Three Musketeers with their axes if you're not. I think I know you well enough to know that you understand the risk to yourself…"

Helms waved it aside. "I'm an old man, Matt. I've pretty much done what I come here to do, and I can't think of any more honorable way to make my exit than resisting the Clintons' evil. I don't think they'd dare, but if I'm wrong, I was still right, if you get my meaning. But the same holds true for you, you know. They know DeMarco was coming to you before he was killed, and now they can figure out that it was to make a deal over Alice and the baby. When this Weinmann woman tracks her back up here to North Carolina, she'll come to you after she comes to me."

"We got to stash them," said Cowboy. "But where?"

"You need to stay in the state, Matt, to make sure you still have jurisdiction and legal authority as a law enforcement officer," said Phil.

"The Purloined Letter," said Matt. "Where is the best place to hide something? Right under the noses of the people who are searching."

"So where do we stash the Purloined Movie Star and little William?" asked Heather, cradling the sleeping baby's head on her shoulder.

"The RDU Sheraton," said Matt. "Practically within sight of where Eddie DeMarco was killed. The manager owes me a rather large favor, since I pretended to believe he was unaware of the fact that one of his accountants was robbing the Sheraton chain blind and he wasn't looking the other way in exchange for evenings of illicit passion with the woman in question in the Executive Suite. Couldn't have proved a damned thing anyway. He will look the other way for us as well, while we all register under false names, and he can arrange for one room to be cleaned and changed by Heather and me with no nosy maids coming in. Alice, I hope you like daytime TV and room service meals, because you're going to be getting a lot of both. Either myself or Cowboy here will be with you, 24 hours per day, strapped and loaded for bear."

"They come for you, they gonna have to get past me first," said Garza. "I been a cop for thirty years, ma'am, and ain't nobody got past me yet."

"All this sound kosher to you, Alice?" asked Matt.

"How long?" asked Alice directly. "How long must I hide? How long *can* I hide? You know, it's not like I'm unknown. I've already missed a promo shoot for the Schwarzenegger film I did, *Thunder Over Havana*, and I've missed an appearance on Tinseltown Talk. I'm sure the word is already going through the Hollywood grapevine that I've disappeared, and I know Jake Shapiro, my agent, is going absolutely batshit."

"He is the one who brought in the FBI," said Matt. "Alice, you must not have any contact with him at all. He hears from you, he'll contact Weinmann."

Alice looked at Helms, "Senator, please, you have to tell me. What if you can't persuade him to leave us alone? How are you going to call off Clinton and his assassins?"

"I must confess, sir, I am rather interested in how you intend to do that myself," put in Matt.

Helms sighed. "You know I'm the chairman of the Foreign Relations Committee. Some months ago we acquired proof that Clinton personally approved the sale of some very dangerous technology to the Red Chinese in exchange for five million dollars siphoned through assorted fronts into his personal legal defense fund."

"And you did nothing with this evidence of treason?" demanded Hightower angrily.

"Actually, Mr. Hightower, we were going to take a second run at impeachment, if you can believe that," said Helms wearily. "Then the original source for the material was found dead in his apartment. Someone hacked him to death with an ax. Two days later the woman who was our secondary source pulled up to a stoplight in Arlington, Virginia. A car pulled up next to her and someone in that car shot the woman through the head with a .410 shotgun slug. The police are treating it as an attempted carjacking. We got the message." Helms looked up at them. "Miss Silverman, I believe that Bill Clinton's goal right now is to ride out the last of his term with no more scandals, which is probably why he is coming after you and your baby. We can no longer threaten him with impeachment over this little matter of betraying the United States to a foreign power. But one word from me to Rush Limbaugh and Matt Drudge and the Washington *Times* and a few others, and it could sure as hell wreck Hillary's Senate chances in New York. I think he'll see reason. For your sake, I hope so."

"And what if he refuses?" asked Alice, her face white with fear. "Or what if he promises to leave us alone and then keeps on trying to kill us...?"

"You have one ultimate weapon, Alice," said Heather. "You can go public. Go to the media and tell your story."

"And lose everything I have?" said Alice bitterly. "And never work in Hollywood again? And be lucky if I can get a part in summer stock or dinner theater in Fresno? And probably end up working in a laundromat in San Jose to keep myself and William fed and clothed and keep a roof over our heads? And be viciously slimed like all the others, Gennifer Flowers and Juanita Broaddrick and Kathleen Willey...oh, damn him! *God damn him! God damn them both!*" she cried, weeping, beating her hands helplessly on the armchair.

"Alice, I can't promise you that you won't end up in that laundromat," said Matt. "That is beyond my power. I can only promise you that you and your baby will be alive to meet whatever the future brings you."

"Fair enough," she said, standing up, her face calm. "Let's get on with it."

✳✳✳

Some hours later, in Fort Pierce, Florida, Andrea Weinmann stood on the beach looking out to sea. The wind ruffled her raven hair and billowed her skirt against her knees. A storm was building in the distance, thick towering black clouds soaring high in the sky over the Bahamas. A man in a suit materialized at her side. "Yes, Fred?" she said.

"Alice Silverman got away," Agent Frederickson told her. "She made four withdrawals totaling $1,200 on her credit cards at a Bank of America ATM in the Ocean Spray Mall at 8:12 PM, night before last. The bank security cameras in the ATM booth confirm it was her, and she was carrying the baby. I'm running an airline check on flights to Los Angeles."

"She didn't go to L. A.," said Andrea. "She went to North Carolina. Who the hell do you think that redneck Hightower's so called confidential informant was? Those cracker Keystone cops up in Raleigh have her, damn them! Check the airlines for flights to RDU, and then send a local field agent to check the bus terminal for buses to Raleigh or to Chapel Hill. Someone will recognize her from her photos, especially if she had a baby with her. But we're not going to wait. Leave Morrison here to liase with the locals and clean up that mess in that house back there. Call the Attorney General's pilot in Miami and tell him to get the jet up here to pick up the rest of us. We're going up to North Carolina."

After the FBI agent left she kept on staring out at the restless, pounding sea. *Damn you, Matt! You beat me to her! Just sitting up there in North Carolina with nothing but your little shitty peckerwood badge and you still beat me to her. Oh, Matt, what will it be? God, you turn me on! And now that we're after the same prize you turn me on even more. I want your body next to mine so bad…when I make my move, surely you will see that I am the one for you, not that skinny blonde WASP bag you're married to? What could we not do together, Matt? What could we not achieve? What incredible things we could accomplish as a team, if only you would accept me and accept Him? Do I love you? I don't know, but I must have you. Please don't reject me, Matt. Please don't make me kill you…*

★★★

In a luxury condominium some miles away, Bob Blanchette stood over the bleeding, dead piece of meat that moments before had been Ian McKinney. In revenge for his ear, Ian had indeed been foolish enough to dial a Little Rock answering service and try to make some more money out of a very bad situation. Blanchette leaned against a kitchen counter, idly poking one of McKinney's severed arms with his toe. His face was expressionless, carved in stone. "Viscawnti. Oh, dat be jus' fucking wondrous. Now we got Jawn Viscawnti on our tail. Oh, dat be jus' *c'est* fucking *magnifique*! Hey, thanks a *lot*, Doofus!"

"Johnny Vee," said Karen Martin. "Hooooo, boy! Now, that is really *all* we need! Bob, you know we're going to have to kill Visconti now as well? There's no breaking with this shit scene until we do. We could move to the fucking South Pole, and Visconti would still find us there. Plus it looks like this goddamned Redmond character is in on it now."

"I know it," said Blanchette, his voice pure ice. "Toss up which of them sons of bitches be woice fo' us."

"Somebody done cut his balls off," said Luther, pointing to the carcass.

"Yeah, Viscawnti done dat," said Blanchette. "I hoid dat story."

"This here Visconti cain't be all that goddamned good," said Lambert.

"Why you say dat, Luther?" asked Blanchette.

"He din't kill this faggot," pointed out Luther. "Left him alive to rat him out to us. Fucking sloppy work if you ast me."

"No, no, I wouldn't say dat. Luther. I wouldn't say dat at all. Jus' lazy is what it is. Mister Vee wants us to come to him, is what it is. He knew dis fag would call us. Sumbitch."

"Yeah? Well, why don't we just oblige the feller? I kinder got me a hankerin' to meet big bad Mister Vee. Bob, I know I ain't got no smarts, cain't do it myself, but what say you bring me and this bad-ass Eye-tie Visconti together and less see who got the manpower, OK?"

"I think we may jus' do dat lil ole thang, Luther," said Blanchette. "But I got a haunch about dis. Less go."

"Go where?" asked Karen.

"Back to Nawth Carolina," said Blanchette. "I got a feelin' heah. Dass where she be. Her and dat baby. Nawth Carolina."

✦✦✦

Tony Stoppaglia watched in fascination while John Visconti opened the big, heavy carton marked "Personal Computer System" which had arrived from Seattle, and laid a deadly array of guns and ammunition out on the hotel room bed. "Jeez, I wish I had my own collection here," he said dreamily. "I got some real beauties. I got a couple of Glocks and a really sweet little Beretta I like to carry, and a derringer, and a fucking full auto Uzi and AK-47, and a Mannlicher 8-mil deer rifle with a telescopic sight I can drive nails with at four hundred yards. No disrespect, John, but those look like junk guns, fucking Saturday Night Specials!"

"These are, yes," said Visconti, pointing to eight small pistols in a row. "Mostly 22s, a couple of .32s, a .380 and one .25. That's exactly what they are, Tony, junk guns you couldn't hit the broad side of a barn with. They're working guns, kid. Throwaways. Tell me, what's the first thing you do after a hit, eh?"

"Get rid of the piece!" answered Tony, suddenly understanding.

"Exactly. These are disposable. You have to get in close, where you can see the guy's brains and make sure, but after you use it you toss it, and what are you out? A hundred bucks? Do you really want to whack a guy with one of your thousand dollar Glocks and then have to toss it in the river? It's a sin to waste a beautiful piece of craftsmanship like that, a Glock or that Colt Python Mr. Redmond carries. When we start getting down and dirty with whoever it is we're after, if at all possible we take them out with these weapons and then toss 'em. However, we may have to do some real cowboy shit, especially now that we know Blanchette and his crew are involved. OK Corral stuff, a proper firefight." Visconti took out several more metal items wrapped up in newspaper. He unwrapped one, weighed it in his hand, and then fished around in the box until he came up with another parcel, which he also unwrapped. "This is yours for the duration, kid. It's a Charter Arms .44 caliber Bulldog, three inch barrel. Son of Sam Special. Here's a shoulder holster rig and a box of .44 ammo, Devastator rounds with a mercury fulminate primer cap embedded in the hollow point slug. This is about as close to an artillery piece as you can carry in your pocket. It will blow a hole in a guy the size of a telephone book. After we're through, if you use it well and honorably in the Family service, it's yours."

"Thank you, *padrone*," said Tony, pressing the barrel to his lips. "May I axe what you will be carrying? I'm just curious."

"A Czech manufactured Makarov automatic, 7.65 millimeter," said Visconti, holding it up. "But when time and place shall serve, I intend to do this in the old way." He took out several long newspaper wrapped parcels, opened them, and assembled a slender and deadly contraption. Tony's eyes widened and he whistled in admiration.

"A *lupara!*" he said. "Jeez, Dom would really love see that!"

"It's not just traditional, Tony. The sawed-off shotgun is the deadliest personal weapon ever invented for close in work," said Visconti, hefting the double-barreled 12-gauge. "This one isn't even illegal. It has a 20-inch barrel and the stock is still on it."

"You don't coat your bullets with garlic, do you, John?" asked Tony.

"I'm not quite *that* old country, no," replied Visconti with a smile. The phone by the bedside rang. Visconti picked it up and listened for a bit. "Thank you, Jim. Give me an address for Fed-Ex. You got five grand coming." He noted down the address and then hung up. "That was Jimmy Jesus. The Fort Pierce cops found the house with the two dead women in it. They were chopped up like *calamari,* so that sounds like our Three Musketeers all right. Jimmy has a friend in the Fort Pierce police department who gave him the straight skinny. The call came from North Carolina, some state cop up there. We know Eddie Miami was running to this guy Redmond to make a deal of some kind. He presumably told the Silverman woman where he was going. It seems obvious that Ms. Silverman escaped the attack on the Fort Pierce beach house and she must have made her way to North Carolina to seek out Redmond."

"So we go to North Carolina?"

"Yes. Problem is, we will have to drive up there. That will lose us precious hours, but I can't risk trying to get all these weapons on board an airplane, and I don't want to screw around with the paperwork on a long distance rental." He pulled out the envelope of cash that Dominic LaBrasca had given him and tossed it to Tony. "It's still early. Get a cab to one of the downtown dealerships and buy us a car. Not a Caddy, but something late model and functional and inconspicuous, a Nissan Ultima or something like that. You got a Florida license?"

Tony flipped through his wallet. "Ah, no, no Florida, but I got three New York, two New Jersey, and a Connecticut."

"Use one you're not too attached to. You'll have to get rid of it after you make the buy. Just make sure you don't use your real one. By the by, we have another problem. Jimmy's contact informs him we have some competition. Some Jew bimbo FBI agent has a whole platoon of suits down here looking for Alice Silverman, and they all just took off for Raleigh Durham airport on a government Lear jet. Looks like someone up in Washington wants this cleaned up. Don't haggle on that car, just pay whatever the dealer wants for the vehicle and the plate and get your ass back here with some wheels. We have to find Alice Silverman before this FBI bitch does."

"How do we find her?" asked Tony.

"We find Matt Redmond," said Visconti.

0111

Welcome to
the Hotel California

"Andrea Weinmann wants to meet with me," Matt told the other people in the hotel suite. "I just checked my messages on my voice mail at work, and also at home. She's back in Raleigh and she left messages for me on both. I think we can assume she knows you're up here in North Carolina somewhere, Alice."

"No word yet from Senator Helms?" asked Alice, in the middle of changing the mewling wriggling baby's diaper on the king-sized hotel bed.

"Not yet. Give him time. He's working his way through the maze up there to the big rat with all the cheese, but it's a Byzantine world he has to do this in, and there will be some twists and turns and delays while Billyboy tries to slither out of this one like he's slithered out of everything else."

"Ms. Weinmann sure moves fast," commented Heather. "Pay attention, Tori, you're going to have to do that yourself some day," she commanded her daughter.

"Not for a while, I hope," laughed Tori. "I don't even have a boyfriend yet, remember? Never mind a husband. Oops, sorry, ah, no offense, Alice."

"None taken," said Alice with a smile. "I'm not a conservative, I can't be in Hollywood, but you're right, really. This isn't the way these things should be done. In a way I envy you, Tori. You've actually got more of a chance of finding a decent man than someone like me."

"We were talking about that the other day," said Heather. "She says she doesn't want Dilbert, she wants someone who will take her father on in a gunfight if need be."

"Well, you know what I meant, Mom," said Tori. "I just don't want to end up with a nerd I can't rely on in a pinch, and that's what most guys my age seem to be, or else preppy jerks or dumb jocks. I suppose I may have to end up settling for a dumb jock."

"Don't *settle* for anything, Tori," said Alice. "There are still some good men out there. I mean, jeez, there must be, somewhere. Children need fathers, real ones, and God knows if I'll ever be able to swing that, find a real man who is willing to be a real father. Not in Hollywood, for sure. John Wayne is dead and buried, worse luck. I had a chance to marry Leonardo DiCaprio, our agents set up the deal, he would have claimed to be William's father, plus he's a Catholic, which would have pleased my parents."

"Uh, I thought from your name that you were Jewish?" said Heather.

"No, my real name's Sobieski. My dad's Polish and my mom is Lithuanian. When I first got in with Jake Shapiro he advised me to change my stage name to something Jewish-sounding as a career move. Anyway, I passed on that show biz marriage with Leo. Aside from the fact that he's a narcissistic asshole, he wanted the lead in at least two of my coming pictures, which I could have gone with because the jerk is still a hot item since *Titanic,* but he also wanted creative control and that's a sure fire recipe for a bomb. Leonardo's got all the artistic inspiration of an orang-outang. William's a baby now, but I'm really worried about what it's going to be like for him when he grows older and I'm never around for him, always leaving him with nannies and later on governesses and tutors and private schools and so on. God knows what kind of drugged out psycho Beavis he'd turn into. I've decided that if I get out of this mess, and I'm still marketable, I'm going to make as much money as I can for the next three years, and then cut way back, only one picture every two years or so, so I can be with him as much as

I can when he starts to develop his mind and his personality and he really needs me. I love my career, it's what I always wanted and I will hate to downshift it, but he's more important."

"You got it right, lady," said Cowboy with a smile. "Speaking of career women, Matt, what are you going to do about Agent Weinmann? Dodge her?"

"If I dodge her she'll come looking for me, and I don't want her looking," said Matt grimly. "I have to meet with her, if only to find out what she's up to, but I also want to make sure she doesn't have any nasty surprises planned. This ain't gonna be pizza at the Rat."

"Meet her at Morgan Street, like before," said Cowboy. "I mean Jesus, even Clinton's people ain't gonna try an attack right in the SBI offices! If for no other reason than the fact that it's full of gun-packing Southern boys!"

"One step ahead of you, Art," said Matt. He picked up the hotel room phone and then put it down. "Nope, on second thought I better use my cellular." He dialed. "Agent Weinmann? Matt Redmond here. Looks like we're playing phone tag, guess you aren't in, but if you want to call me back my cell number is…" Andrea's voice was audible in the room. "Ah, there you are! Yeah, I apologize for the delay in getting back to you. I'm out in the field on a case. No, nothing major, just some Jamaicans over here in Greensboro peddling coke in the projects, nothing I can't let ride for a bit. You wanted to speak with me? Meet? Well, yeah, I'll be checking in at the office before I go home tonight. How about…no, no need for you to waste time on a trip to Greensboro, I'll meet you at Morgan Street at four o'clock. How's that? Sorry, got to go, I have a Greensboro PD team here I need to get with. See you at four in Raleigh, OK? OK."

He closed the phone and motioned Heather and Cowboy out onto the balcony into the blast furnace-like heat of the August day, leaving Tori and Alice powdering and tickling the baby to make him smile. "Just before I came up I talked to Frank Hardesty of the FBI," he told them. "He told me something disturbing. It seems that several years ago, our

Agent Scully wannabe Andrea and Assistant Director Chuck Bennett were an item. He says it wasn't anything serious. Andrea has a reputation for sleeping her way to the top, and she's gotten it on with a number of other senior men at the Bureau to get on the fast track, then dumped them when she got whatever she wanted from them by way of career enhancement. But she's also allegedly done some very hush hush wet work for unspecified big wheels up there in La Cesspool Grande, nothing Frank could pin down for me, just rumors. I can't shake this unhealthy suspicion that she does not have Alice and William Silverman's welfare exactly to heart."

"One more scandal and Hillary can forget about that Senate seat," commented Heather.

"And without that New York Senate seat she can forget about a run for president in 2004," said Cowboy. "Matt, that Mafia mope on the wiretap tape said it. This thing is hot as bubbling cheese. Both the Clintons *have* to silence that girl in there, at all costs!"

"I know. Art, could you ask Tori to step out here, please?" Garza went back inside.

"Be careful, Matt," said Heather quietly. "Losing you now would kill me and Tori as well. She's just gotten used to having a father in her life again, after all those years without one. I'm scared if you're not here she really will end up with some bum who uses her for a fucking block and beats her, just so she can have a strong male of some kind in her life. I live in terror that she is going to have to go through what I went through with my own Bill."

"I really do think she has better sense than that, but don't worry, we won't have to find out," he replied. "I intend to stick around for a while." Tori stepped out onto the balcony.

"You guys talking about me again?" she asked. "My ears were burning."

"In a way," said Matt with a sigh. "There's something I'd like to ask of you. Tori, when I get back this evening, I want you to go on home and hold down the fort there. When your mom and I started more or less collaborating on some of my cases we deliberately decided that we weren't going to keep you in the dark, but we've never made any secret of the fact that this kind of thing isn't what we want for you. I'm nervous about this situation, honey. Three years ago when we first met, you almost got killed when you got caught up in my scene, and that's a bad scare neither Heather nor I have ever gotten over. There are some very nasty sharks circling in the water here, and if they get a whiff of Alice and William they're going to move in for the kill. Quite literally. I don't want you around when they do, and before you ask, I don't really want your mother around either, except for the fact that she'd cut me off at the knees if I tried to leave her out and besides I really can use her help. I knew you'd want the chance to meet Alice, and we've kept up our end of the bargain by keeping you clued in. I know you're an adult now and we can't tell you what to do any more, but I'd really take it as a favor if you'd get out of the line of fire."

"I second all of the above," said Heather. "Matt's right, honey, you're an adult now and that's a request, not an order. But it's a request I hope you'll honor."

Tori's face was blank. "Sure, if that's what you want." She turned and went back inside.

"That hurt her feelings, hurt her bad," said Heather bitterly.

"I know. But consider the alternative. Do you want her around when Luther Lambert rocks up doing his Paul Bunyan impersonation?" asked Matt.

"Oh, Christ, no! We did the right thing, I just hope she can understand that."

"Any chance I could persuade you to toddle on home as well?" asked Matt.

"Where, in your opinion, might I do the most good?" asked Heather bluntly.

"Here. Keeping that girl's courage up and giving her another woman to be with and talk to and lean on. There is no doubt about that."

"Then here it is."

"You strapped?" Heather opened her purse and pulled out her .38 snub-nosed revolver, the one she had pulled on Matt the first day they met.

"Got my concealed carry permit as well," she said.

"Can you use it if need be?" asked Matt.

"If some monster tries to hurt either of those children in there? I'll put one of these hollow points in his eyeball. Really."

"Gee, what happened to that liberal lady from Seattle I met back on that autumn day in '96, who came after me with a gun she didn't even know wasn't loaded?" chuckled Matt.

"She met a man who taught her how to keep her powder dry, Holmes."

✳✳✳

Andrea closed her cellular phone and turned to Agent Frederickson, who was holding a bulky electronic device. "He says he's in Greensboro," she said.

"Bullshit," said Frederickson. "He's in the Durham area. His call came through the com tower at Raleigh-Durham airport."

"He's got her stashed in one of those big hotels around the airport, or else in some little no-tell motel out in the piney woods." said Andrea. She turned to a second hovering suit. "Computer hack on the registrations in all the hotels within twenty miles of RDU. Use the IDC-212 back door that Mr. Gates has so kindly provided us with after his heart to heart talk with Ms. Reno a while back. When you get the data, concentrate on the really big ones first, Governor's Inn, Holiday Inn, Sheraton, Hampton Inn and Hilton. Run the registration info on all registered guests, drivers' licenses and plates and credit cards. If you don't find anything likely there we'll have to do door to door at the backwoods fleabags, but my guess is that a star like Alice Silverman is going to want to hide first class. When we locate the two primary targets, Fred, do your double agent thing and tip off our three secondary targets. Remember, we have to terminate all five in order to bring this assignment to a successful conclusion, which I want to do in a single operation. We need kill all these birds with one stone, so to speak. If they show themselves, kill them, but otherwise do not, repeat, do not move until I have met with Redmond and spoken to him. There is a chance he may be willing to co-operate with the Bureau voluntarily, and I want to give him that chance."

✶✶✶

"So how do we find this cop Redmond now we're here?" asked Tony as he and Visconti rolled into Chapel Hill from I-40 in their Nissan Ultima.

"According to directory assistance, Mr. Redmond lives on Boundary Street," said Visconti. "Stop at a gas station, Tony. I want to get a map."

They cruised the leafy length of Boundary Street and quickly spotted Matt and Heather's house. "Nobody home," said Tony. "No cars in the driveway, anyway."

"Christ! If he has Alice Silverman on ice he could have hidden her anywhere in this whole state!" muttered Visconti. "Park up on this side street, kid. We're going to do a B & E."

"In broad daylight?" asked Tony.

"Burglars don't wear thousand dollar suits. We're going to go up to the front door and walk right in. Try to look like a cop on official business." They parked and sauntered up to the front door of the Redmond home. Visconti withdrew from his pocket an odd tool with many extensions, and within twenty seconds he had the front door lock open. He stepped inside, whipped out a small multi-meter with two leads, turned it on, and touched one lead to the # sign and one to the 4 on Matt and Heather's alarm system. The light on the alarm quivered red and then blinked green. "Always carry one of these, kid," said Visconti, placing the meter in his pocket. "You never know when you're going to have to disarm one of these shitty things. Now before we take one step further in, you put on these," he said, drawing from his pocket two packets of disposable surgical gloves.

"Got my own," said Tony, pulling a similar pack out of his pocket and opening it, pulling the gloves over his hands. "What exactly are we looking for, John? Besides that monster cat on the kitchen table?"

"I am not precisely sure. I'll know if and when we find it. Anything which looks out of place. Anything which may indicate contact between Alice Silverman and Redmond. Something like this," he said, picking up a cash register receipt from the kitchen table. Trumpeldor lazily rolled over and batted at the piece of paper in the Mafioso's hand; Visconti picked him up and put him on the floor, where he stretched and stalked away. "Redmond and his wife are both in their forties, I believe. They are a bit too old to have infant children, I should think. So why, one wonders, did Mrs. Redmond or someone in this house buy a large economy bag of Pampers at the local Wal-Mart?"

"You think it's Alice Silverman?" asked Tony.

"I'll find out," said Visconti. "They paid by credit card. I have a dummy corporation in Seattle that has an online Equifax account." Visconti made a quick call on his cellular phone. Three minutes later he closed it. "This purchase was made on Alice Silverman's Bank of America Gold Mastercard. Redmond has her, all right. But where? *Where?*"

"The Raleigh-Durham Airport Sheraton," said Tony.

"Eh? How do you know that?" asked Visconti.

"I read the handwriting on the wall," said Tony.

"Huh? You ain't going flaky on me now, are you kid?" demanded Visconti suspiciously.

Tony grinned and pointed to a blackboard on the kitchen wall. On it, Heather Redmond had written in green chalk, "Dear Tennis Bum: Leave Trumpeldor a couple of days' worth of dry food, water in his bowl, and as much cheese as your conscience will allow, and then meet Dad and me at the RDU Sheraton, Room 304. The Southern Sherlock Holmes and Nancy Drew are going into partnership."

✳✳✳

Bob Blanchette hung up the phone in the government-owned North Raleigh luxury condo where he and his fellow Musketeers had installed themselves. "OK. Looks like ouah Miss Silverman be in de RDU Sheraton hotel. Redmond is guarding her."

"How do we know that?" asked Karen.

"Doofus got a man on the FBI team that's tracking her, and he left a message on my Little Rock answering service. It's Janet Reno's people, look like Janet done switched complete to Hillary now she on de way in and Doof on de way out, and they ain't telling Doofus what's what, but he got one guy in de inside. Hillary wants that Silverman bitch dead even wuss than Doofus do. Really screw up her chance for that Senate seat in New York if she talk. Guess Hillary don't know Doofus got us on de job, the right hand don' know what the fucking left hand be doin', as per usual wid government woik. Got some Jew bitch FBI agent looking fo' Miss Alice and Sweet Pea now. They in town now and they just found out where she is theyselves."

"How far ahead of us are they?" asked Karen.

"Too damned far. We cain't jus' hear that glitterati bitch dead, we need to *see* her dead."

"Less go git her!" cried Lambert enthusiastically.

"We will, Luther, but this is going to be a mite tricksy. Big hotel full of witnesses, this got to be done right. We got to get in, do de deed, and get out. Slideen, you got a clean credit card? Good. Run over to the nearest mall, cop youself some yuppie threads and some luggage. Then take a cab out to the airport and rent a car. I'm sending you in foist. Check in and eyeball the scene. Businesswoman, reporter, tourist, play it by ear. You suss the layout and find out where the hell she is, exactly, what room she's in. I don' need to tell you how important this is."

"Do I go in strapped?" asked Karen.

"No. Jus' you blade. We don't know what kind of security Redmond has set up. For all we know he may have luggage searches and metal detectors and sniffer dogs or something. When was the last time you was mugged?"

"Not since I was nineteen, on a murder rap in New Orleans, so they won't have anything recent," said Karen.

"Okay, Redmond won't know you, then. Those bastards in Houston busted me in '90 when I did that job for the Bandidos, even though they had to let me go, and Luther's kind of conspicuous at the best of times, so we'll have to slide in under the door once you put the finger on Miss Movie Star and Sweet Pea. I'll rustle us up some camouflage and a clean vehicle. Don' get creative, just locate the bitch, then we all go in and we take cay of business. Luther, you might want to sharpen up them axes of yours for when we meet Mister Redmond."

✶✶✶

Matt parked his Taurus on the New Bern Avenue extension and walked towards the SBI offices. The day had grown cloudy and perceptibly cooler; in just a few hours the odd time of August known in Carolina as False Fall had descended upon the state, the air warm yet not hot, still yet tense. To his disquiet, Andrea Weinmann intercepted him at the door. She was wearing a light cotton summer dress and high-heeled sandals, cut close enough to accentuate a lithe yet voluptuous figure. A broad milk-white expanse of back and front was showing, with the slightest shadow of cleavage and one bra strap visible. Still professional, but just barely, and Matt would have been less than a man had he not wondered what it would be like to slide that strap off her soft shoulder and see the brassiere drop. She carried a large purse with a shoulder strap; Matt knew her gun and badge were in it and wondered if there was any bugging equipment as well. He wondered if she was alone or if they were being surveilled by her colleagues. "Hi," she said, nodding across the street at the old state capitol surrounded by leafy green oaks and statues of the long dead white males who had created and served North Carolina and America. "I wouldn't sitting on mind one of those benches while we talk, instead of some stuffy cubbyhole in there."

"The pigeons may do a number on your dress, not to mention your hair," said Matt with a chuckle. "Besides, on one side you'll have Andy Jackson staring down on you and on the other side our Confederate war memorial. Not a very PC atmosphere."

"Well, you're not a very PC kind of guy, are you?" laughed Andrea.

"No," he agreed, escorting her across the street. They seated themselves on a bench. Andrea drew the wrapped remnants of a submarine sandwich from her purse and began tearing off small chunks of bread, tossing them to the squadrons of pigeons who immediately descended to the ground to grab the food.

"Pigeons on the grass, alas!" she said. "Gertrude Stein."

"Pigeons in the air, despair!" returned Matt. "Father Gassalasca Jape. How can I help you, Agent Weinmann?"

"Call me Andrea, and you know perfectly well how you can help me, Matt. I have budgeted the first ten minutes of this discussion for fencing while you deny that you have Alice Silverman, and I try to make you admit that you do. Are we going to need the ten minutes?"

"No," said Matt with a smile. "You can get right to the threats if you like. Tell me all about how you'll charge me with obstructing justice and all that crap. Which you won't, because the last thing on earth Janet Reno and The Man From Hope want is for any of this to be on paper and in a public courtroom. Except for the FISA court, we haven't quite reached the point of secret tribunals in America yet, although I suspect it's coming."

"I believe that Senator Schumer is presently working on a draft bill for use in national security and domestic terrorism cases, yes," said Andrea. She looked off in the distance. "It doesn't have to be this way, Matt."

"I'm afraid it does, ma'am," he replied gently. "I still don't know what kind of a person you are, Andrea. A good person and a good cop, I hope. But the fact is that you and I serve different ideals, different gods if you will. How much do you know about exactly why that unspeakable slaughter on the *Jolie Madame* happened?"

"I know Alice Silverman was involved and may still be involved in a scheme to blackmail the President of the United States," said Andrea. "I have just been informed from Washington that Senator Jesse Helms is also involved, which makes it even more disgraceful."

"Do you really believe that's the way it is, Andrea?" asked Matt, his voice still gentle. "I won't try to argue with you if you do, but I'm curious to know if you really do believe it. If you have made yourself believe it."

"I don't think about it in those terms, Matt. I'm not a Marxist, but the Marxists have a few good concepts, and one of them is that there is such a thing as objective truth, a political and social truth which can be greater and more morally imperative than any mere state of factuality."

"Yes, back during the Monicazeit I recall our Fearless Leader's dialectic contortions over what is 'is'?" said Matt in a dry voice.

"Sometimes is isn't, Matt. I understand how cynical and depraved that sounds, but it's an accurate assessment. The objective truth here is that Bill and Hillary Clinton have been the best presidents in this century. They have presided over a period of prosperity and progress without parallel at any previous time in this country's history. The Clintons have defeated inflation and Serbian fascism, and we have come as close to defeating poverty as it may be possible to come. We have also come as close to genuine social and racial equality, true diversity, and an inclusive society as anyone on earth has ever come. It's possible we may be able to achieve an inclusive and diverse, multi-cultural world of prosperity and equality for all time, if the Clintons are allowed to continue in office, or rather if Hillary Clinton can become President in 2004. But she has to win that Senate seat in New York and build her political base and show the people her vision for America, while Al Gore keeps the chair in the Oval Office warm for her for this next four years. I know you don't share these values, Matt, and I am sorry for you in a way, but in a way not. You are among the last of your kind, and I have to admit, I find your courage and your own obvious commitment to your ancient way of life to be noble and incredibly attractive. But Matt, your world and Jesse Helms' world is dying, hell, it's dead already. There can never be any going back, only forward. Matt, you're young enough to change. You're young enough to have some part in this brave new world to come, and it really *will* be a brave new world."

"And the price of my entrée into this brave new world is to hand over a young woman and a baby to be murdered?" asked Matt sadly. "You don't know me very well, do you?"

"Oh, Matt, we're not going to kill Alice and her baby!" snapped Andrea. "We want to question her about those murders on the boat! You know, the crime the FBI is investigating? Yes, it's also true that during the process of investigation I hope we will be able to persuade Ms. Silverman to abandon any idea she may have of embarrassing the president or Mrs. Clinton, but we're not executioners or thugs. I told you, I'm not like Chuck Bennett."

"Not like your former lover, Chuck Bennett," corrected Matt.

"I see you still have your ear to the ground in the Bureau," she said with a rueful smile. "Matt, I last slept with Chuck Bennett four years ago. I gave him a hell of a farewell orgy if I do say so myself. But when I walked out of his apartment next morning it was all business between us from then on, and he knew that and accepted it. I never carried a torch for him, I always knew he was corrupt and dangerous, and as far as I am concerned you did what you had to do. That's the truth, I swear it. I repeat, I am not an executioner or an assassin."

"But the Three Musketeers are," pointed out Matt.

"I am *not* in any way involved with that crew, Matt, and dammit, I really *do* mean that!" she insisted. "Rather the reverse. I have strong reason to believe that Mr. Blanchette and Ms. Martin and Mr. Lambert are involved in these multiple homicides. They will be apprehended and if they resist they will be dealt with."

"Ahhh…comes the dawn! So that's it!" asked Matt, suddenly comprehending. "That's what you're doing, eh? Tying up a very ugly loose end for Bill and Hillary before he leaves office? A little termination with extreme prejudice? Or is that truth too objective for you?"

"It's right on the money," replied Andrea grimly. "I should think as a law enforcement officer you would be glad to see the end of those three and you wouldn't be too squeamish about the politically hygenic aspect."

"Hey, Andrea, no kidding, you catch those three anywhere in North Carolina where I've got jurisdiction, let me know and I'll be there with bells on, two guns at the ready. Bob Blanchette is a notch I definitely want to put on this Python of mine."

"I'll do that. From what I've heard of Blanchette and Lambert, we will need all the help we can get. Now, do we get Alice Silverman?"

"No," said Matt. "But you've been frank with me, so I'll tell you this much. Alice Silverman is not involved in any plot to embarrass or blackmail Bill or Hillary Clinton. Quite the opposite. She wants one thing and one thing only, and that is to be left the hell alone to raise her child and never again be reminded that Bill and Hillary Clinton exist, or as close to that state of affairs as possible. She is safe with us. Don't worry about her. You don't need her testimony for what you're going to do, since this is never going into a courtroom and we both know it. Let us handle the Silverman end of things for you while you hunt down the Three Musketeers. If you're as sharp as I give you credit for being, you can get to them before John Visconti does. You can even make things cleaner still by blaming the dead Musketeers on Visconti and then wasting him in turn, if you can catch him. There is an old saying that the law is supposed to be a shield and not a sword, but that's horse shit and we both know it. I am not naive or idealistic, Andrea; I lost any illusions I had about the law long ago. As far as I am concerned you can stack Blanchette and Visconti and a hundred dead hoods up like cordwood. I'll give you my applause, and like I just said, I'll even give you a hand if it comes down here in the Old North State. But Alice Silverman is not a hood. She is a scared young woman with a baby who has the right to live her life without the constant shadow of Luther Lambert's axe or your kind of persuasion. Your leader has given you a mission, Andrea. Do it and go back to Washington."

"I can't do it like that, Matt. I think you know that."

"Then we'll just have to see how it plays out," said Matt, rising from the bench.

"If we come for her, are you going to shoot?" asked Andrea directly.

"I don't know. For God's sake, Andrea, don't bring it to that! Aside from anything else, it would be almost impossible to keep it quiet. We have one thing in common, all of us, you and me and Alice and your superiors in Washington, we all want this settled without any sound and fury. Let's start from that common ground and see where it goes. Now, have your people had enough time to find my car and plant the homing device yet?"

Andrea laughed. "I'm here alone, Matt, but by all means, get yourself dirty crawling under your car looking for a tracker if you want. By the by, there's something else. I realize this isn't the most auspicious time to bring up the subject, but once this messy case is over, if we're still on speaking terms at all, any chance of you and me getting together for a long weekend in a nice, dark hotel room? I imagine your contact at the Bureau has already told you, for the chosen few I'm a garden of delights."

"I don't doubt it a bit, ma'am," said Matt. "And no jive, I'm honored you would offer me a stroll through the garden." He held up his left hand. "Do you know what the ancient custom of the wedding ring symbolizes, Andrea? It symbolizes a chain, a binding together of a man and a woman. The other day you met the woman who wears the other half of that chain. She and I are bound together in spirit, so that even when she is not present in body, she is always there in my heart and in my thoughts. A while back, in the wedding chapel down in Dillon, South Carolina, I made to Heather the most sacred promise that any man can make. My name isn't Bill Clinton, and I am not part of your brave new world, ma'am. That promise I meant, and that promise I will keep. Always. Until death do us part, and in Heather's case, I think if ever I lost her I would keep that promise until death reunited us again. One day, if you are fortunate, some man will wear the other half of your ring and will feel the same way about you. I wish that good fortune upon you with all my heart, Andrea, and that's the truth."

"That's the best thing any man has ever said to me, Matt," she replied quietly. "Thank you." She watched him walk away through the trees and the still, gray air. *It will be you,* she thought. *It will be my ring on that finger of yours one day. I don't know how, but I will make you love me as you love her. I know now that it has to be. It's you, Matt, only you.*

Matt Redmond paused briefly on his way back to his car. He looked up at the large statue of the three U. S. presidents born in North Carolina, Polk and Andrew Johnson and above them all on his horse, the chiseled Ulster granite face of Old Hickory himself, the soldier and statesman Andrew Jackson. *The house you once honored with your wisdom and your strength is defiled,* he thought. *There is a darkness descending on the land, a slow coming dark. A toad is sitting in your chair, and he is sending villains and bitches to murder women and children. But you have sons who have not forgotten, Mr. President. We will fight on.*

✦✦✦

"So do you know this Matt Redmond guy by sight?" asked Tony as he and Visconti sat in the Sheraton's coffee shop, munching grossly overpriced cheeseburgers.

"No, not really, I just remember some vague blurry pictures in *People* magazine some years back. He likes to wear a fedora, looks kind of like a redneck Albert Anastasia except he's a cop. On the other hand he may well know me and maybe even you from mug shots and FBI circulars. We need to be wary around here, kid. This is not our turf."

"So what do we do now?" asked Tony. "Go knock on the door of 304?"

"No. There's law around. We take a slow, careful look over this whole hotel. She's gonna be stashed in one of the rooms, maybe 304, maybe another. Redmond and his wife would appear to be in 304, and I assume she's come along to help with the baby and give Alice some female company. But we don't just assume that the Silverman girl is there. We don't know how many men Redmond has on guard duty or what his game plan is, or even why he's hiding her here. She must know something important and he must know that somebody's after her. He may even be guarding her from us. We take this slow and easy."

"Why did you axe for rooms on the second floor, John?" inquired Tony.

"If Redmond is on the third floor I don't want him between us and the ground, I want us between him and the ground. That's SOP whenever you have to work a big hotel like this, kid. Stay as close to the ground floor and as near an exit as you can. You never know when you may have to make a fast break, even go out a window. I repeat, we take our time here until we scope the layout. I don't want to go nosing around the front desk because that will trip an alarm somewhere and they'll be onto us. We stay off the third floor until the very last, but we go up and down the corridors and we check out every other floor and every room, looking for any signs of police presence, any rooms that have any funny comings and goings, and above all any signs of a baby. Check the garbage out back for used diapers and empty Gerber jars, look for any guys who seem to be just hanging around and who have bulges under their jackets, anything that looks out of place. We got to be circumspect about this, because remember, Redmond and whoever he's got here are going to be on the lookout in turn, on the lookout for guys who are doing just what we're going to be doing. Are you strapped?"

"No, that .44 you gave me is in my room."

"Good. I'm packing myself in case we get jumped. I have an Interpol Special Courier's permit, which may or may not help depending on whether any of these bumpkin local cops know what the hell it is. The Federal government recognizes such permits, but Deputy Barney Fife down here may not. You don't strap until I tell you to. I want to be very sure of my ground here before we make our move."

"And when we do find her?" asked Tony.

"Then we figure out some way to get in to see her and talk with her. Just talk, Tony. No heavy stuff, no ear pulling. I don't get the feel she's actually involved in Joey's death, although she was the proximate cause. She's a public figure and we can't lean on her without bringing unnecessary heat. That's all we want to do, just have a friendly talk and find out what the fuck is going on with all this and why the hell it's happening."

Across from them, at the front desk, a handsome and stylishly dressed thirty-something woman with a suitcase, makeup case, and briefcase was checking in. They could hear the desk clerk, a young Hispanic woman, across the lobby. "I'm terribly sorry, but we just can't find your reservation, Ms. Augusta."

"Nothing at all for a Livia Augusta from the Microsoft head office in Seattle?" laughed the woman merrily. "Oh, wow! Chalk up another one for Human Resources. And they say Bill Gates wants to rule the world?"

"But we do have an available room we can give you," said the clerk. "509, with a balcony over the rear garden."

"Oh, thank you, that would be super!" gushed the new guest.

"You want another tip from my vast wellspring of experience, kid?" asked Visconti, not waiting for an answer. "Don't have a sense of humor where your work is concerned. It can trip you up when you least expect it if you ain't careful."

"Huh?" asked Tony. "Uh, I don't follow."

"Ever read *The Twelve Caesars* by Suetonius? Never mind. Livia Augusta was the wife of Caesar Augustus. She also was one of history's greatest murderesses. She poisoned almost his whole family so her worthless son Tiberius could ascend the throne. When she died the Roman Senate proclaimed her to be a divine goddess." Tony stared at the woman who was now entering the elevator, a bellhop carrying her bags. "I have never seen that woman before in my life," said Visconti, "But I will bet you what's left in that envelope Dom gave me, that ain't no goddamned Roman goddess. That is Karen Martin."

"So they're here!" breathed Tony in excitement. "How the hell did they find us? Or find Redmond and Alice Silverman?"

"If we can pick up a trail, so can they. They're looking for not only Redmond and Silverman, but us as well, after their little talk with that faggot McKinney, which I assume he did not survive. We can assume that as well as Two Gun Matt, Bob Blanchette and his buddy Jethro Beaudine are in the neighborhood somewhere. Keep your eyes and your ears open and stay on your toes, kid."

"We gonna take 'em out here?" asked Tony.

"Yes, once we finger them, but I want to talk with Miss Silverman first before we unleash *il furio sangue,* because we're gonna have to make it hot and fast and then un-ass this area. I have to admit, she is beautiful, and I will regret mangling that magnificent body with the *lupara.*"

"Uh, you gonna use the *lupara* on a woman, John?" queried Tony. "I never done a woman before, but I always understood that when we gotta, it's our tradition to use the rope or a pillow or something that doesn't actually spill her blood, because it's bad luck. Using a shotgun on a woman don't really sound *omertà* to me."

Visconti smiled. "You know, Tony, in all my life in Our Thing I have only known two other American men who used that word *omertà* correctly. Those were your grandfather, and your uncle Buddy. Dom has indeed taught you well."

"Yeah, Dom explained that to me when I got straightened out," said Tony. "Most guys think it just means keeping your mouth shut to the cops, and that's a big part of it, but it's a lot more. It really means manliness."

"Manly honor, yes. Just like the word *mafioso* really means strong and proud and spirited, although you'd never know it looking at some of the bums we got in Our Thing nowadays. To answer your question, that lady there is a lot more *mafiosa* than most made men I know. She's doing a man's work in a man's world, and I will show her the respect of giving her a man's death. This is starting to get interesting," chuckled Visconti.

A tall girl with green eyes and soft flowing hair of dark honey strode across the lobby and through the coffee shop. She was wearing a light swirling summer dress, and her walk was a lissome and wholly unconscious ballet of youth and beauty that would have melted stone, could stone have seen her. "Yeah," whispered Tony, following her with his eyes, his jaw hanging slack in astonishment. "Very interesting. *Dio mio,* who is that?"

"Don't go off chasing skirts on me now, kid," growled Visconti.

"That is one skirt I will not chase. That is one I will catch." Visconti looked at him sharply. "What was it they used to call it in the old country? The Thunderbolt?"

"Bullshit!" said Visconti succinctly.

"Look, gimme five minutes, John! I just want to get her name and phone number."

"You're going to walk up to a total stranger and get her name and phone number in five minutes?" asked Visconti with amused skepticism.

"Of course," said Tony puzzled. "I'm an Italian."

Visconti suddenly relaxed and laughed. "Hey, I'll give you a whole hour, maybe more. I have to find a phone booth and make some calls, especially a call to Dom in New York and bring him up to date on how far we've gotten. By now he probably thinks we've dropped off the face of the earth. It's going to take some time for him to get to a secure phone, plus it's probably not a bad idea for us to split up. Two guys together stand out more than one when someone is watching." He leaned over. "Okay, all work and no play makes Jack a dull boy and all that. Fair enough. I'll give you the evening off. You can suss this place out a lot more inconspicuously if you've got some sweet young thing in tow, that way anybody who sees you knows what you've got on your mind, and they lose interest. But don't wander off. Stay in the hotel or the bar or the restaurant. You got that pager I gave you? Good. You keep it with you and you *don't* turn it off! If that thing goes off it means you come running, and I don't care if it goes off when you're on the down-stroke. This is a business trip, kid. Remember that. *Capiche?*"

"*Capiche, padrone.*" And Tony was off like a greyhound after a rabbit.

Tori stepped out onto the veranda of the hotel by the swimming pool, trying not to weep. *I love them, I admire them both more than any-one, all I want is to be with them in this adventure and they treat me like this?* she thought. *They still think I'm a kid, or maybe they just think I'm a nuisance. Why? Why do they shut me out? What must I do so they will let me in?* She fumbled for a cigarette from her purse, stolen from Heather's pack, and stuck it in her mouth, then remembered she had no lighter. She finally found a bedraggled pack of paper matches in the bottom of her purse which she pulled out, finding one single battered match within, which she tried to strike and which promptly went out in the mild breeze. It was the last straw. "Oh *shit!*" she moaned. She was going to cry now and make a fool of herself.

A silver Zippo flicked open and burst into flame before her face, lighting the cigarette before a surprised Tori could even draw on it. She looked up into the sparkling blue eyes of a lean, handsome young man, poised and sharp and elegant. "What a Continental gesture," she said, surprising herself with how calm and casual she sounded.

"Hey, I'm a Continental kind of guy," said Tony Stop.

✳✳✳

Later on, in the darkness, Karen Martin heard the lock in her door turn as she lay in bed. She slid the switchblade out from under her pil-low and clicked it open. The man slid into the dark room, paused briefly, and then moved towards the bed. When he came within reach Karen rolled forward and slashed upward in a lethal disemboweling stroke, but he was there before her, catching her wrist and twisting it, his knee down in her solar plexus. The knife dropped softly onto the carpet. His other hand was at her throat, cupping her larynx, caressing her windpipe, his iron fingers ready to crush. She recognized the grip as deadly and lay still. "Do you always sleep naked?" he asked softly.

"Sure do. Never know who's gone drop in."

"Do you know who I am?"

"Reckon I do," said Karen. "You here for killing or fucking?"

"Which would you prefer?" he said.

"You kill me now, you don't get to do me, unless you get off on doing it with dead chicks. But if you screw me, you better leave me dead on this bed, because if you don't, come tomorrow I gone kill you."

The man chuckled. "Think you can?"

"Know I can."

He rolled her over and quickly handcuffed her wrists behind her back. "For the next hour, I say it and you do it. At the end of that hour, I decide whether or not you're worth the *lupara*."

"One hour with me, mister, and you'll give me your loopy whatever and the keys to your guinea Caddy and any other goddamn thing I ast fer, so maybe you can get some more someday, which you ain't gonna, because this time tomorrow you gone be dead. Bring it on, my man."

For the next hour, he said it and she did it. At the end of the hour she lay on the bed, still pinioned, her body glistening with sweat in the faint light of the hotel parking lot lamps through the balcony curtains, watching him dress. "So what's the verdict? No noose is good news."

"You really should watch that sense of humor," he said. "That Livia Augusta bit gave you away this afternoon. The prospect of death doesn't frighten you?" he asked.

"When I was twelve years old, I understood how I'm going to die someday. If it's gonna be you, and it's gonna be tonight, then let's get on with it. A gun's too noisy, but my blade down there on the floor is nice and sharp, or you can use your necktie for the old Italian rope trick before you put it back on. I ain't scared. I dished it out enough, and I can take it."

"No. You gave me a bravura performance, and you are beautiful even in this dim light. Tomorrow, in the daylight."

"You understand, I wasn't kidding?" she said. "I see you tomorrow, you're dead meat."

"*Capiche, bellisima.*" He leaned over and placed a handcuff key in one of her pinioned palms. "I assume in your youth you acquired the basic art of getting out of cuffs?" he asked.

"Used to could do it in thirty seconds," said Karen, manipulating the key in her right hand. "Been a long time since I had to, probably take me a full minute now."

"I will be gone by then."

"You'd damned well better be." He moved towards the door. "Hey? Johnny?"

"Yes?" he said.

"Thanks. I ain't had a workout like that in a good long while. I enjoyed it."

"Remember it in hell, *bellisima.*"

IX

Enter Sam Peckinpah

In the gray light of early morning, Matt Redmond hung up the telephone. His face was dead white. He stepped out onto the balcony and stared into the dawn. Heather followed him. Behind them, Alice Silverman slept on the king-sized bed, her child beside her on a pillow. Cowboy Garza dozed in a chair, a 12-gauge shotgun across his lap. "What did Senator Helms say? Did he meet with the president?" demanded Heather in a whisper.

"Yes," said Matt. He went on in a conversational voice, "Apparently the leader of the free world is not only vicious and corrupt, he is quite insane. I gathered from Senator Helms that Billyboy was none too coherent, probably under the influence of narcotics, but the upshot of it is that if Alice Silverman breathes a word of what happened to her, or if Helms attempts to use his information on Clinton's treason, he intends to provoke an incident with Red China over Taiwan and launch a Cruise missile attack on the Chinese mainland. Clinton having spent the past seven years selling the Chinese the whole array of military technology we have, plus what they have stolen through the usual kind of espionage, there is no doubt that this would result in retaliatory missile strikes against the continental United States, and in pretty short order one side or the other would attach a nuclear warhead to one of their missiles. We let him get away with rape and murder or he brings Armageddon on us all. Oh, dear God, Heather, what am I going to do? How am I going to tell that girl in their that she and her baby are going to die, and there is nothing we can do about it?"

"What is Helms doing?" asked Heather urgently.

"He's getting the Republican leadership and some of the better Democrats together as soon as he can, some time today. He's going to tell them what's going on and see if he can get some kind of movement together to get a grip on Clinton somehow, see if there's any way he could be legally committed or something. He admitted it was a hopeless cause. If this political establishment had any will to get a grip on Clinton it would have happened a long time ago."

"What are you going to do?" demanded Heather.

"My duty, as a police officer and as a man. When the slow coming dark finally falls, when the servants of Bill Clinton's evil come for Alice and her baby, they will find me waiting. But this time it will be sanctioned. Not like with Bennett. This time it is sanctioned from the very top. You understand what that means?" he said dismally.

"Yes," she sobbed quietly.

"I love you," he said.

"And I you. Matt, please take me with you, whatever happens! If you have to go, let me come with you! I know that's selfish and it will almost destroy Tori, but I can't bear to be left here alone without you!"

"And I know it is selfish and weak for me to let you come with me, but I can't help it," he said dully. "I pray to God that some day Tori will forgive us." He went inside, shook Garza and woke him gently. "Cowboy, I just got off the phone with Jesse Helms. We have to talk." Garza got up and followed him back out on to the balcony and listened while Matt told him what Clinton's word had been. "I haven't known you long, *compadre,* but I think enough of you to give you a chance to bail," said Matt.

"No chance," said Garza.

"In God's name, man, *think!* What will…"

"No," said Garza. "Do you think for a moment that I could ever live with myself if I turned tail and left her and the baby for those carrion crows of Clinton's? Stop talking shit, Matt, and let's figure out what we gotta do."

"The first thing we do is to wake that girl up in there and tell her that her appeal has been rejected and her death sentence stands," said Matt. "And may God cause Bill Clinton to burn in hell for making me do something like that."

Alice Silverman heard the news and sank down into one of the balcony chairs. "I'm not surprised. I've been expecting it. OK, it's pretty obvious what I've got to do. I'm going home. I'm going to call the airlines and book a flight back to L. A. As far as I am concerned all of you and I never met. I'm the one he wants. Keep your mouths shut and maybe he'll let you slide. I'm going home to Beverly Hills and I will wait there for the end."

"And William?" asked Heather.

"There's a lawyer I know in Hollywood. He specializes in very quick and discreet adoptions for infants who appear at inconvenient times and places in the movie community. Within 48 hours after I get back, William will have a new name and a new mother and father."

"How could you possibly even contemplate such a thing?" demanded Heather. "How can you just give up your child and sit there in some mansion waiting for these three demons to come and take from you everything that you have?" Alice smiled, and spoke.

"Doth not death fright me?
Who would be afraid on't
Knowing to meet such excellent company
In the other world?"

"That's from John Webster, *The Duchess of Malfy*. I didn't plan on dying this young, Heather, but in a weird kind of way it's a relief. I don't have to worry about much of anything now, as facile as that sounds."

"So this murdering raping bastard Billyboy wins again?" asked Cowboy bitterly. "So you're just going to lie down and take it?"

"Of course he wins, Cowboy. He's Bill Clinton, and Bill Clinton always wins. It's in the script," explained Alice. "You may not like the ending, but you always follow the script. Men and women far more powerful than any I ever dealt with in Hollywood wrote this particular script, and it says Bill Clinton always wins. Look, guys, don't think I am coming on all heroic. I'm not. Right now I'm so scared I can barely refrain from shitting in my pants. But do you understand what this man Clinton is threatening? A possible *nuclear war* in which millions of human beings will die and civilization will be destroyed, if there is any final attempt to hold him responsible for his behavior? In a way, I've had a great privilege bestowed on me. I get to give up my own life in order to prevent that. God, what a movie this would make! I'm going to think of it as a performance from now on, and I am going to follow my own script, just like I'd like to have my last days and hours portrayed in the movie, and try to forget the fact that when the closing credits roll I'm really going to be dead. Er, Heather, any chance I could bum another cigarette?" Heather lit it for her; Alice's hands were trembling too badly to even flick a Bic.

"Alice, will you give me a week?" asked Matt. "Will you stay here with us, and do what I ask of you, for one week more?"

"What for?" asked Alice.

"I want to do a re-write," said Matt. "Let's flesh this script out a little. Give it some plot depth to go with the tragedy, some action to go with the introspection, a few unexpected twists. Who knows, maybe even a little comic relief? Make a much better flick. You can still do your dramatic death scene at the end if that's the way it plays out."

"And how many of your friends and your family does your re-write kill off?" asked Alice.

"As many as God shall decide to be the price of righteousness," said Matt.

"Matt, I'm not worth it. Really, I'm not. I'm a Hollywood whore. The week after you save me from all this I am going to be going down on Sid Kaplan again if it's necessary to get something I want. You have real lives, I have plastic, and it's not a fair trade just for me to make a real life movie. I don't deserve such a sacrifice," said Alice calmly.

"Obviously we all disagree, ma'am," said Cowboy Garza.

"One week?" asked Matt.

"On one condition," said Alice gravely.

"Name it," said Matt.

"If any of you make it, when the time comes for them to make a real movie out of my death, do what you can to make sure I am *not* played by Christina Ricci," she said. "Christina's a fine actress, don't get me wrong, but she takes herself too damned seriously, and that's not me. She's all Method, and I never was. I want Kirsten Dunst."

***

On the second floor below them, Tori Redmond watched the dawn lightening the windows of the room. She lay under a single sheet, her head cradled on Tony's chest, and he stroked her hair tenderly, kissing her now and then. Finally he spoke. "You OK? I didn't know it was gonna be your first time," he said.

"I'm OK," she said sleepily. "It was wonderful, Tony. It will be a good memory. Thank you. Now comes the part where you walk out the door. That's cool. I understood that last night. But you were what I needed at this moment in my life. Don't worry, I'll be fine."

"Suppose I don't want to walk out the door?" he said, staring at the ceiling.

"That would be even better, but I don't expect it. You're on a business trip down here and when you go back to New York you can tell all your friends in the restaurant supply business over a few drinks in the bar how you picked up this really hot college chick down in Carolina. It was restaurant supply, wasn't it?"

"Yeah, I got a piece of one of the biggest restaurant supply businesses in New York and Connecticut. Catering, too. We specialize in bar mitzvahs. I got other business interests as well. You might say I'm kinda diversified."

"A capitalist at twenty-one? That explains the snazzy wardrobe. Sure makes a change from these punk guys at school who wear T-shirts and backwards baseball caps and they're twenty two or twenty three and never even had a job."

"But what you said, Tori, you don't have to worry about that. I will never tell anyone any such dirty thing about you," he said calmly. "That would be disrespectful, you ain't no whore, to me you're a *madonna*. A lady."

"You know, I think I believe that. Thanks."

"Tori, I mean it. Don't axe me how I know, but you're special. I can't stay with you now, but it ain't because I'm being a bum and brushing you off after a one-night stand. Please don't think that. I really do have business here, serious business. My boss is in the next room. In a little while I've got to go back to him, and from then on I can't say where I'll be headed or how long it will be before I can get back down here. But I'm gonna come back, Tori. If you want me to."

"That depends. Are you willing to take on my Dad in a gunfight?" said Tori with a smile.

"*What?*" exclaimed Tony, sitting up.

"It's kind of an inside joke me and my parents have going. My Dad's a state police detective here and he has this gnarly reputation as a gunslinger. Kind of a Matt Dillon type. In fact, his name really is Matt."

"Yeah?" said Tony, his blood running cold. "Hey, babe, I meant to ask you last night, do you play tennis?"

"Mmm hmm. I'm on the UNC women's team. Why?"

"I just figured with those legs you had to be either a tennis player or a dancer. Beautiful," he said, shaking his head. "Just beautiful."

"Hey, Valentino, you've already had your way with me, no need to keep up the compliments," teased Tori.

"I'll still be complimenting you when you're seventy," he told her.

She sat up in bed and looked at him. "You're serious?" she asked.

With a mixture of horror and wonderment, Tony then knew that he was. "Yes," he told her. "I don't blame you if you don't believe me, and like I said, I got a lot on my plate right now and I can't stay around and prove it to you. Just give me your number, Tori, and wait. One day I'm going to call you. For true. That is if your Dad doesn't shoot me first." *Or I don't shoot him,* thought Tony. *Cristo mio! Suppose it does come to that?*

"Actually, he and my mom are here in this hotel," said Tori. "They're kind of busy too, but who knows? If you can stick around another day maybe you can meet them."

"That would be great," said Tony. "Uh, what are they doing here?"

"Oh, they're kind of helping out a friend who's staying upstairs. It's a long story." Tori giggled. "You know, they're in the next room from the friend I told you about, that's 304, and this is 204, right? They think I went back to Chapel Hill last night, but all the while I was in the room right below them losing my virginity. By the by, actually, I'd better be the one who walks out. I need to get home and change clothes. I'll come back and try to meet them for breakfast, but if Mom sees me in the same dress she might get the idea I haven't been home. In fact, they may have been trying to call me, and they'll be worried." She leaned over and picked up the phone and dialed. "Hi," she said when Heather answered. Tony could hear her mother's voice on the phone.

"Tori, I called the house last night. We were starting to get concerned."

"I'm OK. Mom, you won't believe it, but as I was leaving the hotel last night I met somebody, and we struck up a conversation, and I ended up going out on a real honest to God date. So you and Dad can relax a bit, seems like I'm not a total wallflower." She listened to her mother's reply and said, "Oh, he's from up north, not too much older than me but he wears a suit and he actually has a job. He works for his family business. Mom! Do you think I'd let some total stranger pick me up? No, I just got home late and I guess I didn't hear the phone. You guys available for breakfast over there at the Sheraton? Say nine o'clock or so? Good, see you then." She hung up. "You want the shower first?" The sheet fell away, down to her waist, and Tony pulled her down into his arms.

"I want to shower with you. But not just yet," he said.

Later on after they were showered and dressed, she kissed him long and lingeringly at the door. Then she wrote down her phone number on a piece of Sheraton stationary. "If I see you again this morning and there's time, I'll let you meet my folks. If not, here's my number. I won't expect anything, Tony, but if you really mean it, the ball's in your court."

"One day that phone is going to ring, Tori. I swear it." After she left he went to the phone by the bed and dialed an extension.

"Yes?" said Visconti's voice.

"Alice Silverman is in room 306," Tony told him.

***

In North Raleigh another telephone rang. "Alice Silverman is in room 306," said Karen's voice. "I saw room service going up the elevator this morning and I noticed a bottle of baby formula on the cart, and I followed. Then I saw this guy with a big moustache and a cowboy hat come out and take the tray. He had cop written all over him. He didn't spot me."

"Where's the service entrance?" asked Blanchette.

"At the back, behind the kitchens and the dumpsters. There's a basement parking garage, but it's got a bar and a booth and you have to be on a contractor list to get in. Park whatever vehicle you got around on the north side of the building and meet me there. I'll have my car out of the garage and around front in the main lot, if we have to get out that way. You can come in a side door and get on an elevator behind the front desk without too much risk of being seen. There's a security camera but I'll have it disabled by the time you get here."

"Mmm…awful lot of people gone be around. What about waiting until tonight?"

"We may not have that much time, Bob. Five O'Clock Johnny is here as well."

"How do you know?" demanded Blanchette sharply.

"I kind of ran into him last night."

"Kind of ran into him?" There was a short silence. "Oh, yeah."

"Hey Bob, you know me. I'm a real real black widow. I like to do 'em before I do 'em in," laughed Karen.

"Slideen, one of these days you gone play with fire one too many times. Never mind. We be there about twenty past nine."

✶✶✶

"Alice, there's no other way to save your life," said Matt. "You've got to go public. I understand that your career as an actress will be over, that the left-liberal establishment will never forgive you or let you work again, but once you go public they won't dare touch you or William physically. It's also barely possible that enough voters in New York might be convinced to stop Hillary from walking off with that Senate seat and then getting back into the White House in 2004, only this time with the real, official power and totally gerrymandered and cowed Congress that will rubber stamp every perversion of thought, every mockery of justice she chooses to impose on this country. It will be like life under Stalin in the 1930s. Alice, you just might be able to save what's left of America from destruction."

"I know," she sighed wearily. "Matt, I know you're right. But please, understand. I am twenty-three years old, and I have just learned that one way or the other, my life is over. I have to decide now whether I am buried in a grave or buried in that laundromat in San Jose I spoke of once. Please, don't rush me. I have to think about this. My God, don't you remember what they did to poor Monica? I think that scares me even more than the laundromat. I do this and I'm no longer an actress or an artist, I'm a dirty joke, for all time. I know what the right thing to do is, Matt, but before God, I don't know if I'm strong enough." Tears welled in her eyes.

"Look, Alice, it may not be so bad," said Heather. "I gather you're fairly well off and you'll always have at least some royalties or residuals or something coming in from your previous movies. And California isn't the whole world. Why not come here? This is a beautiful part of the world, as I have found since I came. You can sell that mansion of yours in Beverly Hills and write an 'Alice tells all' book like Monica did, and that ought to raise enough money so you can buy yourself a nice home out in Chatham County or maybe up in the Blue Ridge mountains beside a lake. There are still places around North Carolina where William can have a kind of Tom Sawyer boyhood. And you'll have friends here, us. It's a plan, of sorts."

"Thank you," she said.

"Tori said nine o'clock?" asked Matt.

"You guys go stretch your legs," said Alice. "I know this isn't something that can be delayed. I'll have an answer for you when you get back. Say hello to Tori for me, or bring her back up here. She's sweet, and I like having her around."

Down in the coffee shop Visconti told Tony, "OK, we're out of time. We got the Three Musketeers breathing down our necks and things may blow at any moment. I don't see any way to do this other than going up there and knocking on the door of that room. We need to get in and have our little talk with Miss Silverman and then get the hell out of this hotel. After that we hole up somewhere else, then we circle back in here and then try and pick them off, but right now we can't risk them getting to Silverman and killing her before we can see her. We have to move. We're going to have to muscle our way into that room, as gently as possible, if you get my drift, but muscle it is. You all packed?"

"All packed," said Tony.

"OK, go move all our stuff down to the car, our luggage and all the guns. Get your own gun and put it on. I'll take a quick patrol around the place and try and see if Blanchette or Lambert or Redmond are visible anywhere, and see if I can pinpoint the location of our Roman goddess. She's dangerous and we need to know where she is and what she's up to. Then we go up there and we insist on an interview with Miss Silverman. We flash, but we don't fire unless Redmond or one of his cops pulls down on us. When we get in let me do the talking. You may have to keep her escort at gunpoint while I do. I'll meet you in your room in ten minutes. Move."

In the lobby Tori, just back from changing in Chapel Hill, met Tony in the lobby as he was going into the elevator. "Hi," she said with a smile.

"Hi," he said. "Look, I'm gonna be kind of tied up today. I'm gonna have to pass on meeting your folks. All I can say now is I meant what I said up there. Your phone's gonna ring, Tori. I don't know when, but it's gonna ring."

"I'll be waiting," she whispered. She leaned over and kissed him unashamedly; Tony could not resist returning the kiss.

"*Ciao,*" he said with a gentle smile, turning into the elevator. Neither he nor Tori saw Matt and Heather descending the stairs from the mezzanine.

"Looks like that was quite a hot date indeed," remarked Heather dryly. "I can't help but wonder why she didn't answer the phone last night." She turned to her husband. His face was staring, ghastly, literally as white as a sheet. "*Matt!*"

"Works in the family business does he?" muttered Matt, shaking with rage. "Oh, yeah. So he does. And I know what family!"

"Matt, what is it?" demanded Heather.

"Our daughter's hot date is hot in more ways than one, Heather. That is one Anthony Stoppaglia, a soldier in the Genovese crime family. Aka Tony Stop, aka Little Blue Eyes. The grandson of the inimitable Dominic 'The Butcher' LaBrasca himself and the late Joey LaBrasca's nephew. Somehow I rather doubt he is down here to play golf. A gangster and a murderer has put his blood-stained hands on our child, Heather."

"*Oh, God, no!*" cried Heather.

"Grab Tori and get her back up to Alice's room!" rapped Matt. "I want her behind Cowboy's shotgun. Visconti may be here. For all we know the Mob may be here in force to kidnap or kill Alice and the baby. I'm going after Stoppaglia, and I am going to have a quiet word of prayer with that young man."

Matt ran down the stairs to a house phone and called room 306. "Cowboy! Heads up, *compadre,* we got company!"

"Musketeers?" asked Cowboy excitedly.

"No, it looks like the Mob is down from New York. I don't know what's going on. I'm going to try to find out now. Heather and Tori are coming up there. Let them in and get Alice and William ready to move fast, then sit tight until we get a scope on the situation. *Do not come looking for me.* I mean that, Art! Your job is to protect the lives of Alice and William Silverman."

Heather grabbed Tori and hauled her into the next elevator, jamming her finger on the third floor. "Looks like you get to be here when the action starts after all," she said in a grim voice. "Hope you enjoy the show."

"Is something going on?" asked Tori excitedly.

"Yes, something is going on." Her mother looked at her in pain and pity. "I haven't got time to break this to you gently, and in any case there isn't any way to soften the blow. Tori, Matt recognized the young man you were with just now. He's a Mafia hoodlum from New York named Tony Stoppaglia, a criminal and a killer. He is down here looking for Alice Silverman and he has obviously been using you to get at Alice and your father. Did you tell him *anything?*"

Tori looked at her and burst into tears. *"No, oh no, oh please no!"* she was sobbing as they got off and Heather led her down the thankfully empty corridor.

"Did you and he…?" asked Heather gently, terror in her voice at the anticipated answer. Tori nodded. Heather began to weep as well, hugging her daughter fiercely. "Oh, God, my poor child! If Matt doesn't kill that son of a bitch I *damned* sure will!"

"No!" cried Tori angrily. "If he is really like that, then he's a louse and I'm a fool! That's bad enough, Mom. But I don't want anything worse to come of it! Yesterday you both asked me to do you a favor as an adult. I didn't do it and this is what happened, but now I am asking you for one. You say I am an adult. Okay, let me make adult mistakes, even the really stupid and bad ones. Just leave it, Mom. That's what I'm going to do. I screwed up and…oh *God*, I screwed up bad! *I told him! I told him where Alice is!* I didn't mean to but…"

"Beat yourself to death over it later! We've got business to attend to," said Heather, knocking on the door of 306 frantically. Cowboy opened the door, hefting his 12-gauge. "Art, they know she's in this room. Never mind how. My gut isn't as good as Matt's, but I think we need to get Alice and William the hell out of here."

"What about Dad?" demanded Tori.

"He can take care of himself," said Heather. *But God, if you are listening…a little help?*

Back downstairs, it took Matt some few minutes to flash his SBI badge at the front desk, get into the hotel's registration computer, and figure out that he was looking for a Mr. Robinson and a Mr. Martin in 202 and 204 respectively, Mr. Martin being the younger gentleman in 204. During this time Tony moved all their gear down to the car and pulled it around to the staircase exit behind the hotel, then ascended the stairs and went back into the room. As he stepped inside he sensed someone behind him and whirled, but Matt caught him with a fist to the solar plexus and another to the jaw, knocking him over the bed. He was on Tony like a panther, pinning him to the floor, ripping the .44 Bulldog out of Tony's shoulder holster and shoving his own .357 Magnum under the young man's nose. "What did you do to my daughter?" Matt demanded, his voice quiet and deadly. "Were you carrying this when you were with her?" He held up the .44 and then stuck it into his back pocket.

"Fuck you," said Tony, his voice equally quiet and lethal.

"You think this is some kind of macho game, you cheap little hood?" said Matt. "You think I won't pull this trigger and splatter what passes for your brains all over this carpet, Tony? Try me! Let me hear that mouth of yours one more time!"

"And do you really think I'm gonna shit in my pants at the sight of a gun and go like boo hoo hoo for mercy?" sneered Tony. "Guns don't scare me, Pops. I seen 'em before."

"What did you do to Tori?" roared Matt, cocking back the hammer of the .357.

Tony breathed in and out, deeply. "Okay, Redmond. You don't want to play the dozens, we won't play dat. But I am not going to say anything to you while you've got a gun poked in my face. You want to talk to me about Tori, you do it man to man, standing up, and with nothing in your hand. *Capiche?"*

"Bad idea, Tony," breathed Matt. "Not recommended at all. A bullet will be quick. Me tearing you to bloody shreds with my bare hands won't be."

"One way to find out, eh, Pops?" said Tony.

"You call me Pops one more time and I will smash your fucking face in!" shouted Matt.

"You will do no such thing, Agent Redmond," said a calm voice behind him. Matt looked up and saw John Visconti standing in the doorway, the stainless steel Czech Makarov pointed unwaveringly at his head. "Tony is not only a friend of ours, he is a friend of mine. You harm him and you will be dead in the next second, I promise you. Now, why do I get the impression there is something going on here I don't know about? From what I overheard, this sounds more personal than business. Tony?"

"Uh, that girl, you know, in the coffee shop?" said Tony. "It seems she's kind of, well…"

"She is my daughter," said Matt.

Visconti was silent for a moment. "Jesus, kid, you sure can pick 'em, can't you?" he said, half in amusement and half in disgust. "Very well. Mr. Redmond, as it happens, I'd like to speak with you about something myself. Can we lose the artillery? Please remove your weapon from Tony's visage, put it away, and then I will do the same."

"How do I know you won't just shoot me?" demanded Matt.

"You don't. Alternatively, we can stand here like this for some long minutes and see what happens," said Visconti. "I don't think you want to do that, Mr. Redmond. There are other people in this hotel who are interested in room 306 besides ourselves."

"Room 306," said Redmond, looking down at Tony. "So that's what you were doing with her. You fucking little snake!"

"No," said Tony. "You're wrong."

"Mr. Redmond?" prompted Visconti. "Minutes are passing, minutes which neither of us can afford to lose at this point, I think."

Matt sighed and holstered his pistol. He stood up. Tony leaped to his feet like a young bull, his face mottled with rage and his fists balled. "Come on, punk!" snarled Matt, raising his own fists.

"*Tony!*" snapped Visconti. "*Basta!* Sit!" He pointed to a chair. Tony took a deep breath, and sat down.

"I just wanna say one thing, *padrone.* He's wrong." Tony looked at Matt. "You're wrong about me and Tori. That's not what happened."

"May I suggest we adjourn such matters until a later date?" said Visconti, putting his own weapon into his shoulder holster. "There are more urgent issues to hand."

"What did you mean just now about other people in the hotel being interested in room 306?" demanded Matt.

"The Three Musketeers are here," said Visconti.

"*Shit!*" cursed Matt.

"Exactly. The shit is going to be flying around here in very short order, I suspect. Mr. Redmond, I want to ask you a favor. If you grant it, then I will owe you a favor. Do you understand what that means?"

"I understand, and the answer is no."

Visconti ignored him. "I would like for us all to take a quiet stroll up to room 306, and I would like to speak with the lady in that room for a few minutes. That is all. I give you my word, for whatever you may think that worth, that I do not intend to harm her or her child in any way. I will not insult you by offering you money. I am offering you something far more valuable. I am offering to place myself under obligation to you. I repeat, do you understand what that means?"

"Yes, I understand. The answer is still no, but you must be very serious indeed about this," said Redmond.

"Very serious, yes."

"You two are working for Dominic LaBrasca, I take it?" suggested Matt. Visconti nodded. "And I presume you are going to kill the Three Musketeers, or try to. From what I know of them you've got your work cut out for you. After that?"

Visconti paused. "Mr. Redmond, in the city of New York there is an old man who has for my entire adult life been my friend, my protector, my employer, my teacher, and the object of my respect and admiration. What you think of him does not matter; what I think of him does. Recently this old man had to go to a funeral wherein he laid beneath the earth his last remaining child. To you, Joey LaBrasca was a thief and a criminal and a thug. To Dominic LaBrasca he is and always will be the child blowing out the five little candles on his birthday cake on the home movie, the little boy he tossed a baseball with in the back yard, the young man in the cap and gown standing by his mother and his father's side in the photograph taken on the night of his high school graduation. I know that you despise our kind. Fair enough. We on our part do not think too highly of your kind, Mr. Redmond. But we have our laws as well, unwritten though they may be. When someone harms a member of our family, then they pay the price. What you have just done here with Tony shows me that you understand that concept. You feel that Tony has dishonored your daughter and you were ready to kill him. Are we really so different?"

"Did he dishonor my daughter?" demanded Matt angrily.

"In my heart? No, Redmond. In my heart I have not dishonored Tori and I never will, so long as I live," said Tony. "Anything else is our business, not yours."

"What was done to Joey LaBrasca was not dishonor, it was death, and it will be answered with death," said Visconti. "An eye for an eye."

"Or better yet, two eyes for an eye? The law of the vendetta?" asked Matt softly.

"Better yet, two eyes for an eye," agreed Visconti. "One to punish and one to deter. I understand that to you that seems savage. We have only been here for a hundred years or so, and we lived by that iron law for a thousand years before we came to this country. It was necessary then, when the injustice of the feudal landlords and the *gabellotto* sought to grind us into the dust. It seems that it has become necessary again, in this age of Clinton, when the law is ruled by such people as Billyboy and Janet Reno. There was always a kind of balance before. It was business, not personal. You chased after us with laws and grand juries and courts and prisons, and sometimes you hurt us, but there was no outright killing on either side. We always maintained an ironclad rule against hitting cops, and on your part you stuck with your clumsy law and there were never any police death squads like the old world. That balance, that unspoken agreement between our two sides, has now been violated, and it was your side who first broke it. These people in power now have the idea that we are guinea scum who can be murdered with impunity. Of this notion they must be disabused. They have chosen to meet us on our level. So be it. They want to play our game, they play by our rules. Two eyes for an eye."

"You're going after Billyboy?" breathed Matt incredulously.

"Is Bill Clinton responsible for Joey LaBrasca's death?" demanded Visconti.

Matt shook his head slowly, a grim smile on his lips. "Christ, Visconti, favors aside, do you have any idea what kind of temptation you are subjecting me to?" he chuckled. "Do you have any idea how tempted I am to do exactly as you ask? Can you possibly understand how I long to answer the question you just asked me, and unleash you on that creature in the White House?"

"I think you just did," said Tony.

"Yeah, I guess I did," sighed Matt. "Apparently you guys don't know what's going on, but it's…well, it's filthy. It's so filthy that even one of your own kind, Eddie DeMarco, managed to exhume what remained of his conscience and couldn't do it."

"So I have assumed," said Visconti. "But I must not assume. I must *know*, and Alice Silverman can tell me what I have to know. Redmond, before God I mean her no harm! I just want to hear from her own lips what this is all about. Just ten or twenty minutes up in room 306, then we vanish and you never see us again."

"You want a favor? OK, you get a favor and I'll take mine in repayment now," said Matt. "You can come up and talk with Alice, I'll persuade her to tell you the whole vile and disgusting story. That's your favor. My favor is simple." He pointed at Tony. "This critter never goes near my daughter again. Not ever."

"Done," said Visconti.

"No," said Tony.

"What?" said Visconti, astounded. Tony stood up.

"I said no, *padrone*," said Tony. He turned to Matt. "Do you understand now? It would have been the easiest thing in the world for me to lie to you about this. But I will never, ever lie to you where Tori is concerned. I will tell you what I told her this morning. One of these days your phone is going to ring, and it is going to be me calling for Tori, and from then on I am on the scene permanently. There is only one way to stop that. You kill me now." He turned to Visconti. "I am sorry, John. I didn't mean for this to happen. It just the way it played out. But I will not renounce Tori, and I will not lie to her father. If for this you must send me home and tell my grandfather that I have failed you, then do what you gotta do."

Visconti sighed. "Jeez, kid are you sure about this?"

"Yes."

Visconti turned to Matt. "Look, those minutes are slipping away, Redmond. This is a complication I hadn't bargained on. I suspect you have an even better idea than I do what is going on here. You strike me as a man who has drawn a bad hand, otherwise why would you be skulking in this hotel? What say you throw a joker into the deck? Two jokers, me and Tony?"

Suddenly Matt laughed. "Hey, why the hell not! Okay, forget about the favors. You're right, I've been dealt a lousy hand in this, and I feel like kicking over the table. Let's go!"

They moved out into the hallway towards the elevators. Matt was about to punch the switch when he looked up and saw Andrea Weinmann to his left, pointing a 9-millimeter pistol at him. The sexy summer dress was gone; a grimly functional pants suit of blue serge had taken its place. Behind her stood a big black man dressed in FBI SWAT team gear, including Bakelite body armor, a tiny baseball cap of blue with the gold letters "FBI" balanced on his shaven skull. He held an M-16 with a 35-round banana clip. "Hobknobbing with hoodlums?" said Andrea sadly. "I'm very disappointed in you, Matt. I really am."

✷✷✷

Bob Blanchette and Luther Lambert entered the Sheraton Hotel clad in dirty white coveralls bearing the legend across the back "Carolina Heating And Cooling Services". The largest pair of overalls Bob could find barely fit Lambert; his muscles literally split the seams. They had arrived in a battered blue van bearing the same name. Both carried long red metal toolboxes containing Luther's favorite axes, as well as an arsenal of weaponry sufficient to overthrow a small Latin American government. Karen Martin met them at the door dressed in blue jeans, Adidas running shoes and a sexy white wool tank top trimmed with blue. Quickly Karen ran over the layout with them. "Bob, I think it's just Redmond and Mr. Moustache. I been all over this place and I haven't seen anyone else who might be a cop. No metal detectors or nothing like that."

"Where's Visconti?" demanded Blanchette.

"No idea, he just kind of came and went, but he's here and he obviously knows about room 306. That's why I said we gotta move now."

"Us two go up the elevator, like we're working on the air condition-ing," said Blanchette. "Slideen, you go up these stairs here and get to the third floor that way. You cover us from the stairwell in case anyone comes running when they hear the noise. Luther and me go in, we do the number on Miss Hollywood and Sweet Pea, we come out and we go back down the stairs and out to the van. Once it's done you take your rental car out of here and meet us back at the condo. Don't leave it here for that Jew FBI bitch or Redmond's *rurales* to find. No sense in leaving any loose ends." He opened his toolbox and handed her an Uzi subma-chine gun and a green canvas pack of ammunition clips. He put his hands on Lambert's shoulder. "Luther, I'm sorry, I know you was prom-ised some quality time with Miss Hollywood and your blowtorch. We thought we'd have more time than this, but it's turned into a rush job and it has to be done fast rather than artistic. We go up to the door, you bring it down, we kill everybody in there and we haul ass."

"Hey, Bob, sometimes that's the way it plays out," responded Luther with a philosophical sigh, "We cain't always git what we want. I unner-stand that. I ain't a total fool, you know. OK, fast it is. So time me. This is a movie star and I'm gone do *something* with her. I'm gone set a speed record, is what I gone do. I betcha I kin git her into six pieces inside sixty seconds from the time that door comes down. Two arms, two legs, the head and the middle."

"Uh…with the chainsaw, *maybe*," said Karen. "Once you got her caught and pinned."

"With two axes. Six pieces in sixty seconds," insisted Luther. "Starting from the time the door comes down."

"You gone take ten or fifteen seconds just to catch her, and then for the first couple of whacks you only gone be able to use one axe, because you gotta hold her down with the other hand," pointed out Karen skeptically. "Cain't be done."

"Okay, I'll take out Sweet Pea and any cops that might be in there so you don' git distracted, but you still gone be steppin' fer six pieces in sixty seconds, Luther," said Blanchette. "I don't doubt you could do it with axes in a minute if she was just laid out on a table somewhere, but this is in the field, now. Slideen's right, you gone have to chase her and pin her."

"Bet you my cut I kin do it, Karen?" teased Lambert.

"Your cut of this job against what?" demanded Karen.

"Whole case of Jolly Ranchers," said Lambert.

"Hey, Luther, it's your money. You want to throw it away..." shrugged Karen.

"Done," said Blanchette. "I'll time it from the moment the door goes down. Less go."

✶✶✶

"Move back, all of you," commanded Andrea. The huge black agent stepped in front of the elevator and covered them with the M-16. "Where is she, Matt? Tell me now. Don't lie to me. My people are all over this hotel. Come with me to wherever she is and make sure there's no trouble. We'll take her into custody and get her down to the Federal building on New Bern Avenue with a minimum of fanfare, and then as far as I am concerned this incident is closed. You two men will be placed under arrest as material witnesses, and then we'll see what else we can think of to put you away for a while," she said to Visconti and Tony.

"I gotta tell you, whoever did your nose, you got a refund coming," said Tony. "Hey, *melanza*, you point that thing away from me or I'll jam it up your black ass."

"You call me an eggplant one more time, greaseball, and yo' face gonna look like one of yo' mama mia's spicy meatballs," growled the black FBI agent.

"Put them away, gentlemen," snapped Andrea.

"But I thought you wanted to see mine?" asked Matt.

"*You bastard!*" she hissed. "Where is she?" The elevator door opened behind them, and Luther Lambert pranced out like some homicidal

River Dancer, a long red razor-sharpened fire axe in each hand. With a single backhand swipe he decapitated Special Agent Abdul Washington, sending the black man's head spinning into the air. Lambert jigged back into the elevator, the doors closed, and it resumed its upward journey. The severed head hit the floor and spun to a halt, grinning up at the stunned Andrea.

"I don't think any of us expected that," said Matt.

The black man's blood-gushing corpse began a slow slide to the floor, splattering Andrea with a torrent of crimson that made her scream in utter confusion and terror. As the body collapsed John Visconti leaped forward, snatched the M-16 out of the dead ebony fingers, and with lightning speed and precision smashed the rifle butt into Andrea's jaw, knocking her back against the wall and collapsing her onto the floor. Tony delightedly began kicking the severed head down the corridor in the manner of a soccer ball, then picked it up. "It's fourth down and ten to go in the Eggplant Bowl, Stoppaglia punts from the forty yard line!" He kicked the head and sent it sailing down the corridor, through an open door out over a piazza railing, and out of sight. "Field goal! Three points!" he cried.

"Not quite out of adolescence yet, is he?" asked Matt dryly.

"Apparently not!" snapped Visconti in exasperation. "Tony! Quit fucking around! That was Lambert and Blanchette, and they're on their way up to the third floor!"

"My wife and Tori are in that room!" shouted Matt. "Up the stairs!" Andrea Weinmann staggered to her feet, moaning. Matt grabbed up her gun and threw it after the severed head of her agent. "This will *not* look good on your resumé, you know," he said to her before pelting up the stairs after the two Mafiosi.

In the third floor corridor Blanchette and Lambert lumbered towards the door of 306. Blanchette now had his own Uzi slung over his shoulder on a strap. A Honduran bellhop pushing a room service cart with a full breakfast and a magnum of champagne on ice towards the room of a corporate vice president and his secretary took one look at the towering Lambert with his bloodstained coveralls and axes, and fled with a yell. They shoved his cart out of the way. "Why'd you cut that nigger's head off?" asked Blanchette.

"Just fer a practice swing," said Luther.

"Well, you saw that FBI jacket he wearin'? Looks like we got Janet's people on the scene as well now. There's too goddam many cooks in dis jambalaya. Less git it done and beat feet." They paused outside 306. "Bring it down and I'll start timing, but before you go in you give me five seconds to hose down the interior foist. They's gonna be some cops in there. I'll knock the five seconds off you sixty and I square dat with Slideen if you win de bet. Slideen, you hear dat?"

"I heard it," called Karen from the far stairwell. "That's OK, no need to get sloppy just for a bet. I'll give you the extra five seconds, Luther."

Lambert placed both axes side by side and gripped them with both hands, took a stance by the door, and swung them in a crushing arc that slammed into the paneled wood and knocked the door of room 306 half off its hinges. He drew back the axes for the second and final blow that would splinter the door to matchwood, but suddenly the three men from the second floor burst into the corridor. Matt fired a wild shot from his .357 Magnum that whistled by Blanchette's ear. "*Shit!*" cursed Blanchette, firing a short burst from his Uzi that made the newcomers leap behind the corners by the elevator, the bullets smashing into the walls and raising geysers of plaster. "Luther, never mind de bet, just git in there and git it done, me and Slideen will make sure you ain't interrupted!"

John Visconti snapped around the corner and fired a single round from the M-16 that blew a hole in the wall two inches from Blanchette's head; Matt noted with professional approval that he had moved the weapon's selector switch to semi-auto and was forbearing the temptation to spray his limited ammunition. At that moment, at the far end of the corridor, three more FBI agents in SWAT gear lumbered through the fire exit doors. "*It's Blanchette!*" one of them yelled. Blanchette and

Karen whirled and opened up with their Uzis; one of the FBI agents collapsed onto the floor and a second was wounded in the spray of bullets, dragged back through the exit by the third remaining agent. The air reeked of cordite and hot metal and the thin acrid vapor of smokeless powder. "Luther! We sittin' ducks out heah! Git that door down!" ordered Blanchette. Lambert swung the twin axes again and the door smashed open. Visconti and Matt leaned out, leveled their weapons, and alternately fired three evenly spaced shots each into Luther Lambert's massive torso. Lambert grunted and staggered under the impact of each bullet, then angrily hurled one of his axes in a deadly arc that would have cut Matt in two if he had not leaped back behind the sheltering corner just in time.

"He's wearing body armor!" yelled Matt. "We have to get a head shot!"

"This motherfucker's jammed!" growled Visconti, ripping off the magazine and jerking the slide on the M-16 rifle to clear the stoppage. "Shit, you'd think the fucking FBI of all people would keep their damned weapons clean!"

"Didn't you hear what he said?" yelled Tony. *"Tori's in there!"* He charged past them.

"Tony! Where the fuck is your gun?" yelled Visconti after him.

"I have it," said Matt, touching his back pocket. The abandoned room service cart with its magnum of iced champagne stood against the wall. Tony snatched the bottle from the ice bucket and leaped forward, swinging in a high arc and smashing it across Luther Lambert's face. *"I christen you the S. S. Asshole!"* he shouted. The blow stunned and blinded Lambert. He shook his head trying to clear his vision of blood and booze, swinging his remaining axe in a murderous circle like some demented, bleeding Casey at the Bat. His huge flailing form filled the corridor. Behind him Blanchette and Karen could not find an opening to shoot at Matt or Tony or Visconti, and with Tony between them Matt and Visconti couldn't get a clear shot at Lambert. Tony dodged and danced in front of the blinded giant, poking and slashing with the broken champagne bottle, trying to cut Lambert while not getting mauled by the whirling axe blade. Suddenly Luther simply turned and charged into room 306, Tony leaping after him like a panther. Blanchette pelted down the hall in the opposite direction around a far corner for some cover, and he and Karen unleashed several short bursts of 9-millimeter bullets at the other two. "Where the hell is Cowboy? I should hear a 12-gauge by now! You got that weapon clear yet?" demanded Matt, his cylinder open, reloading the smoking .357 from cartridges in his shirt pocket.

"Yeah," said Visconti.

Matt snapped the cylinder shut. "Cover me."

"We both go," said Visconti.

"Suit yourself," said Matt. He charged out into the corridor, firing at the vaguely seen form of Blanchette down the hall, while Visconti followed at a more measured pace, firing the M-16 rapidly from the hip on semi-auto. They leaped into the hotel room at almost the same time. The room was empty except for Tony Stop was staggering to his feet, his face bruised raw.

"Motherfucker got in a lucky punch!" he gasped.

"Where is he?" demanded Matt.

"Out the window." Matt and Visconti ran out onto the balcony. Luther Lambert was in the process of swinging down through a balsam pine tree two floors below like a monkey, his axe handle in his teeth, holding it as easily as an ordinary man would a knife in his mouth. He hit the sidewalk and shambled off in a loping run. Visconti flicked the selector switch, raised the M-16 and fired a sustained burst which slammed into the pavement a foot away from Lambert, sending spurts of grass and concrete leaping into the air. The bolt of the rifle locked back. "*Minchia!* Out of ammo! This goddamned thing wasn't zeroed for me! I shouldn't have missed that!"

"It was a long shot," said Matt. "Anybody could have missed it, and he's wearing a vest anyway." In the distance he saw a blue-jacketed FBI men jump forward, pointing his own M-16. Lambert's arm rose and fell so fast as to almost be invisible to the naked eye and the he shambled on out of sight, leaving the crumpled Federal agent bleeding on the sidewalk. Matt turned back into the room, trembling in fear at what he might find.

"I already checked, she's not here," said Tony. "None of them are here."

"My partner must have had sense enough to get them out of this room," breathed Matt with a sigh of relief. He looked around. "And I don't mean my SBI partner, good man though he is. I know where they've gone." On the wall of the room was written, in lipstick, a single word: CROATOAN.

"What the hell is a crow tone?" asked Tony.

"An inside joke between me and my wife." From below came the sound of more gunfire, the deadly popping corn of Uzis and the rattling of more M-16s interspersed with the occasional bark of a 9-millimeter.

"Blanchette and the Roman goddess are hauling ass, sounds like," said Tony.

"Roman goddess?" asked Matt, puzzled.

"An inside joke between John and me," replied Tony.

"Whatever. You'd better haul it yourselves, boys," said Matt. "I don't think Special Agent Andrea Weinmann's mood is going to be very sweet when she gets up here, considering the mess you made of her mouth. You'd best be elsewhere. Thanks for the assist, both of you." He tossed Tony the Charter Arms .44. "I saw what you did, or thought you were doing for my daughter, Tony. You haven't changed my mind about you and you never will, but you earned yourself and your *padrone* here a pass, at least for the time being. But Ms. Andrea doesn't honor my passes. Take off, the both of you!"

"We're outta here already," said Visconti. "There's a laundry room at the end of the hall and it has a chute going down into the basement. Come on, Tony, and no goddamn argument!"

Tony turned to Redmond before they left. "I mean it, Redmond. Your phone is going to ring one day."

Visconti and Tony made it down the laundry chute, half-sliding and half clambering. They ran down the basement corridor, shoving aside several startled housekeeping employees, and made it to the car. Tony jumped into the driver's seat and Visconti into the passenger side. "If that bar is down, smash through it," ordered Visconti as they roared through the underground parking garage. It wasn't, and Tony made it out into the parking lot. To the right, about a hundred feet away, a van disgorged more SWAT-equipped FBI men who were running for one of the doors. Tony swerved left and made it around to the front of the hotel, roaring through another clump of blue-jacketed FBI and scattering them. He made it out onto the service road when an eggshell-blue Ford LTD roared up beside them and slammed into the side of the vehicle. "What the fuck?" yelled Tony. He looked over and saw Karen Martin behind the wheel of the other car. Her passenger window rolled down automatically and she raised her right hand with the Uzi in it and let fly a short burst which shattered his window and scattered glass all over him. *"Fucking crazy bitch!"* he shouted, slamming the Nissan into her right side. A small shopping mall loomed on the left.

"Into that parking lot!" commanded Visconti, pulling the sawed-off shotgun from the back seat. "We're going to get at least one of these motherfuckers so this mess isn't a total goddamned loss!" Tony braked, got clear of Karen's car, and swerved into the mall entrance on two left wheels. Karen did a braking U-turn and followed them in. Tony ran the car up onto the sidewalk and both Mafiosi jumped out, guns at the ready. Tony leveled the Charter Arms .44 and fired at the dimly seen form of Karen behind the wheel of the oncoming LTD; the stubby, deadly pistol boomed like a thunderbolt and a visible column of flame spurted from the muzzle. Karen swerved and ran into a concrete support pillar in front of the Nature's Bounty Wholistic Health Store. She jumped out and crouched behind the open door, firing short, aimed bursts at the two Italians who dodged between parked cars while mall customers screamed and fled. Visconti tossed the Makarov to Tony. "Pin her down there!" he ordered, then he moved off among the parked cars, crouching low, the shotgun held close to his body.

Tony eased around the side of an Oldsmobile bumper and fired quick, aimed shots from the Makarov. Karen blasted back with the Uzi, blowing out the tires of the Olds and spraying Tony with debris from the asphalt and shattered taillights. Visconti leaped from the shelter of a pickup truck and ran like lightning to the other side of Karen's LTD. She saw him, she whirled and stood slightly to fire at him, and Tony hit her in the shoulder with the last bullet from the Makarov. He switched the Bulldog to his right hand, but she was stunned by the hit and staggered away from the cover of the LTD door, dropping the empty magazine from her Uzi and just managing to slap in another when Visconti leaped up, six feet away, shotgun at the shoulder. He fired the first barrel with a mighty roar that seemed to shake the very ground. The buckshot caught Karen in the belly and spun her around 360 degrees, and the second earth-shaking barrel tore off the top half of her skull. She collapsed onto the pavement. Visconti stepped forward, breaking the smoking barrels and ejecting the spent shells, which he reloaded. *"Arrividerci, bellisima,"* he whispered. Tony ran forward to Karen Martin's corpse and dipped two fingers into the spreading pool of her blood. Visconti grinned in acknowledgment of the ancient gesture, then he bent and did the same. *"Guiseppe LaBrasca, salud!"* he said.

"À salud, padrone!" said Tony, and they both licked the blood from their fingers.

"Now let's get the hell out of here," said Visconti.

✶✶✶

"He'll know we have gotten away because his car is gone," said Heather, driving Matt's Ford Taurus eastward on Interstate 40. "He'll know where we're going because I left him a message that he and only he will understand."

"Ah, yeah, but I didn't quite get that Croatoan bit. Where *are* we going, Mom?" asked Tori from the back seat. Alice Silverman sat beside her, holding the baby, her face pale.

"Your house," said Heather.

"Huh?" said Tori.

"You remember our honeymoon?" asked Heather. "The Radcliffe Inn?"

"Oh, yeah!" said Tori enthusiastically. "Mom and Dad took me on their honeymoon," she explained to Alice. "It was this neat bed and breakfast run by this old lady named Radcliffe, down on Hatteras Island."

"Their honeymoon?" asked Alice, curious. "Ah, didn't they, ah…?"

"Oh, no, they'd been shacking for a whole year before that," said Tori.

"Thank you for sharing that with the group, Tori," said Heather with a sour chuckle.

"Well, it's true, isn't it? And I really appreciated your making it a family event, so to speak. It's kind of the first time I was ever able to call Matt Dad and it was true, legally and all. Matt adopted me, you know. But why did you say it was my house, Mom?"

"Because Matt and I bought it from Mrs. Radcliffe. For you. It was going to be your wedding present, when that time came," said Heather.

Tori was quiet for a time. "I've let you both down, Mom. Maybe you better sell it."

"You have done nothing of the kind. Anyway, I keep forgetting, we do have an officer of the law here. Cowboy, is this all right with you? Hiding out down on Hatteras until things clarify?" she asked.

"Hey, I'm just along for the ride," said Garza. "Heather, don't fight it. Your hand has gone down to that dial ten times in the past five minutes. Turn the radio on."

"I'm afraid to," she said.

"Your fuel gauge is low. You need gas. Pull off at the next exit and we'll see if we hear anything. If not, then you can risk calling him on his cellular." They pulled off at Benson and turned into an Exxon station. Garza turned the radio on and then filled the tank and paid. "Let me drive," he said. They were almost out of Benson and back onto the interstate when it came. *"This is a special news update from the WQDR newsroom. There has been a multiple shooting incident at the Raleigh Durham Airport Sheraton Hotel. The shootings took place at approximately nine thirty this morning and the details are as yet unclear. At least three persons are known dead, including one law enforcement officer. Agents from the Federal Bureau of Investigation are on the scene. Stay tuned for further details."* Cowboy pulled over without being asked. "I'm going to call in. Not officially, I'm going to use Director Hightower's private cellular number." Heather got out of the car and walked toward an embankment, standing and staring out at the rushing traffic on the interstate highway below her. Tori followed her.

"If he's dead, I will go away," she told her mother. "You won't ever have to look at me again. It's the least I can do."

"How can you possibly think I could ever want any such thing?" Heather asked in agony.

"How could you bear to have me around, knowing I am responsible for you losing him forever?" cried Tori. "How can I bear to be around you, knowing what I have done?" Alice Silverman walked up to them, carrying the baby.

"You haven't done anything, Tori," she said. "I'm not sure what has happened between you two, although I can sense something has, but I tell you this. There is only one man on the face of the earth who is responsible for this unholy mess. That is William Jefferson Clinton. There are entirely too many people willing to shift the blame from Bill Clinton, take the blame for Bill Clinton, blame anybody but Bill Clinton. Don't you two join them."

Cowboy walked up behind them. "Heather, he's alive!"

Heather fainted.

✱✱✱

"Luther?" said Bob Blanchette gently, uncertain he could control the murderous giant any more without Karen. "Luther, they got Slideen. Do you unnerstand? She's dead."

"Who got her, Bob?" said Lambert, his voice deceptively soft. Blanchette shuddered.

"Don' know. Must have been them FBI. They knew my name, they knew we was gonna be there. I think we been double-crossed, Luther. It may be Doofus, may be Hillary. But I think from now on we got to assume we on de spot marked X."

Luther ran his hand through a big bowl of Jolly Ranchers, letting the brightly colored candy drip through his fingers. "These are the last ones she'll ever give me," he rumbled, real tears coursing down his cheeks over the tattooed ones, wetting his beard. "I guess I'll eat me a Big Mac or a Whopper again one day, but they won't never taste quite right. Less finish this job, Bob. The man done paid us, we do what we paid for. Thass the way it's done. Then we gone have to split up, Bob. No more Mouseketeers. It ain't gone be the same without Karen. You know it won't."

"Sure, Luther. If that's what you want," said Blanchette, secretly relieved. "What you gone do then, Luther?"

"Go home. Go back up in the hills somewhere and live in a trailer, or maybe a cave. Somewhere there's no people. People are bad, 'cept fer you and Karen. But afore I do, I'm gone go to Washington and kill Billyboy. Then I'm gone find Hillary and burn off her tits with my blowtorch."

X

Sicilian Defense

Matt ended up having to sign out a car from the SBI motor pool to go home in. He turned the key to his front door at eight o'clock that night, walked into the living room, and saw John Visconti and Tony Stop sitting in his armchairs. Visconti was reading a copy of the New York *Times* and Tony was tussling with Trumpeldor, wrestling the feisty animal all over his lap while Trumpeldor chewed on his hand and claw-kicked with his rear feet, enjoying himself immensely. Matt eyed them sourly and went to the refrigerator. Two new six packs of St. Pauli Girl that he had not purchased were sitting in the fridge, with four beers missing. Matt grabbed a fifth one and returned to the living room. "You not only bring your own brew, but I see you've been so kind as to use coasters on my coffee table," he said, pointing at their empties. "Who says you Mob guys haven't got style? The answer is no, I'm not telling you where they've gone. This is getting too hot and I want them under wraps. But I'll tell you what you want to know myself if it will get you two on your way. Although I really should be arresting you right now for wasting that Martin bitch."

"She is one less Musketeer who will be coming after your wife and your daughter and Miss Silverman," said Visconti. "I should think you'd be grateful."

"I am, but frankly I'm surprised to see you here. I thought you'd be half way back to the Big Apple by now after that fiasco at the Sheraton. Instead you seem to have headed to the nearest dry cleaner to get your silk suits cleaned of all the blood."

"These are new threads," said Tony.

"That looks like a new Saturn out front as well," said Matt.

"Our Nissan got kinda the worse for wear," said Tony.

"Yes, I gather from the witnesses Ms. Martin put a few bullet holes in it. I suppose it's crushed into a square by now? Never mind, I won't ask. But you goombahs need to ease your bodies on out of this state, chop chop. Special Agent Andrea Weinmann is on the warpath. Seems you extracted a couple of her teeth with that rifle butt, Visconti. Not to mention making her look very, very foolish and incompetent to that murdering bull dyke she works for up in D.C."

"When ladies are unladylike, they must expect the consequences," shrugged John.

"Not to mention the two remaining Musketeers."

"Ah, now, that's the problem," said Visconti. "Have you any idea where they are or what they are doing? I don't. That is not a good thing, for either of us."

"I don't think Bob Blanchette has himself listed in the Yellow Pages under Assassins," said Matt, swigging his beer.

"No, but he does have a phone number where he can be reached," said Visconti. "You see, we have not come to you empty handed. We do have something to trade, Redmond."

"Trade for what?" demanded Redmond. "Trade for one more sordid story about how Bill and Hillary Clinton committed a vile and perverted crime and are now spilling the blood of other people to cover it up? I've already told you, I'll give you that for free, just as Alice Silverman told it to me." In short, precise sentences, Matt told the two of them what Bill and Hillary Clinton had done to Alice Silverman and how Eddie Miami had come to his death. They both sat silent for a moment when Matt had finished.

"And these beasts in human form dare to look down on *us?*" said Visconti with contempt.

"That's why my uncle died?" responded Tony, his face black with rage. "Because Bill Clinton and that hag he married decided to have a little fun one night? And then expected Joey and Eddie to clean up their fucking mess? Like we was their fucking garbage men or something? They say 'Hey, guinea, here's a coupla bucks, go throw this baby in the dumpster for us'? "

Matt didn't bother to point out that Joey LaBrasca had presumably agreed to be party to the crime on promise of a sum of money significantly larger than a couple of bucks. "That's it, kid. Now I really would take it kindly if you two would vamoose. I appreciate the help you gave me back there, but we are still on opposite sides, you know, and I have no desire to get matey with you, despite the fact that you can afford better beer than I can."

"It's not quite that simple, as I think you'll understand if you think about it a bit," said Visconti. "To begin with, may I ask what spin is being put on that little fracas back at the hotel by our lords and masters?"

"Officially? The FBI and SBI were co-operating in a major drug bust that went wrong, leading to the tragic deaths of two FBI agents thus far and probably a third as well. That guy Lambert axed out on the sidewalk probably won't make it. I am not sure who they have decided to put on the spot marked X for this so-called drug bust. Most likely it will be the Musketeers, since thanks to your intervention they've got at least one dead hoodlum to show for it all, but I wouldn't be too surprised if you two as well were on the front page tomorrow. The Dixie Mafia meets the real item from the sidewalks of New York, that kind of angle. Andrea is very sore in every sense of the word tonight."

"And your people are going along with this?" asked Visconti.

"My boss is chewing nails, but he is going along with it for the time being as a personal favor to Senator Jesse Helms. He and Weinmann got into a shouting match in the Sheraton lobby and damned near tried to arrest each other on assorted state and Federal charges. But right now we all seem to want two things. First off, we want to find and neutralize

Bob Blanchette and Luther Lambert before they can inflict any more slaughter on anyone, and secondly we all want the real reason for that little bloodbath at the Sheraton kept quiet. This thing has turned into one hellacious can of worms."

"Do you want it kept quiet?" asked Visconti.

"There's something else you don't know about," said Matt. "Something extremely serious." Then he told them what he had learned from Jesse Helms that morning. "You understand that the stakes are now infinitely higher than simple vengeance for Pal Joey? That we are dealing with a madman who really can kick over the whole table if he starts losing the game? I have advised Alice Silverman to go public with the whole story at a press conference to try and save her own life and that of the child, but even that is as risky as hell. It may well drive Clinton berserk."

"More risky than even you know," said Visconti. "Five kilos worth of risky."

"Eh?" said Matt.

"Joey LaBrasca was supplying Bill Clinton with five kilos of uncut cocaine per month. The president and those in his closest circle must be high as a kite almost all the time."

"Damn!" cursed Matt. *"Damn!"* He hurled his empty beer bottle against the wall, smashing it. "Jesus Christ, I spend the best years of my life fighting that poison and the people who traffic in it, and now we're being ruled by goddamn junkies!"

"Given your DEA background, I don't have to tell you that cocaine addicts are in a constant state of paranoia, riding an emotional roller coaster that borders on madness," continued Visconti. "Clinton is entirely capable of starting a nuclear war with Red China. Or invading Canada. Or ordering some of his negro minions in the Secret Service to take your friend Mr. Helms out and have him stood up against a wall and shot, Latin American style. Or dropping his trousers and wagging his weenie at a White House press conference. He is on the way out of office and out of power. There are many sharpened knives waiting for him, and he knows it. His star is descending and that of his equally evil but far more dangerously competent wife is rising, which must be very humiliating for him. He may decide to lash out at humanity one final time, just for the hell of it, in some grotesque and bizarre way none of us can imagine. His removal now becomes a matter not just of vengeance, but of public safety, and I believe you people sometimes refer to yourselves as public safety officers. But it is not going to be easy. It will require the most careful planning and preparation of my career. Not being suicidal, I cannot do it alone, and men who can be on a grassy knoll at a certain time, do the job, and then disappear forever are not easy to find."

Matt stared at him. "So you're telling me it was...?"

"Yes. Long ago another president and his punk kid brother thought they could use us for what they wanted and then double cross us. They both learned differently, as will Clinton. But I have to be able to work on this project without Mr. Blanchette and that mountain maniac sidekick of his to worry about. You have the one bait that will draw them like flies to honey, Redmond. I am asking you to help me lure them in and dispose of them, and thus remove not only the immediate threat to Miss Silverman but also your wife and daughter, not to mention yourself. I think I know how to tip Blanchette, but I have to know what to tip him. Otherwise this little game of cat and mouse can go on for weeks or months. From what you tell me, we may not have that much time. Or do you still have legalistic scruples about such a thing?"

"My legalistic scruples, as you put it, stop where the lives of my family and the lives of an innocent woman and a baby begin," said Redmond. "But I do have scruples about endangering all of the above by calling down two world class murderers onto them."

"Do you think you can hide from them forever?" asked Visconti. "Can Alice Silverman keep on hiding without the news media picking up the story very soon? Do you think you can conceal their whereabouts from this FBI woman forever? How do you know she and Blanchette are not working in cahoots?"

"Actually, I did find out one interesting tidbit from our Federal Salomé," said Matt. "She has orders to bring her boss the heads of the Three Musketeers on her silver platter as well as John the Baptist's. My guess is that Ms. Reno is now more or less Hillary's political whore as opposed to Bill's, if she wasn't always. I have this feeling that Hillary wants to tidy up nice and neat before she goes full bore into the New York Senate campaign, with all potentially embarrassing skeletons polished up and neatly packed away in the closet. I suspect it was always part of the plan for your Uncle Joey to end up dead. As Billyboy's coke connection he was a very dangerous loose end who had to be tied up. Now the Musketeers are on the hit parade as well. Rather like the ancient pharaohs who buried their treasure, killed the slaves who did the digging, and then had the slaves who killed the slaves killed in turn to make doubly sure no one knew the secret."

"Which will make Blanchette all the more anxious to tie up his own loose ends and disappear for a good long while," said Visconti grimly. "Expunging this whole episode is now essential to his personal survival. I am offering you a chance to meet this crisis with some measure of control over the how and the when, and with Tony and myself in your corner when the main event comes. Otherwise we must both face the prospect of having these two dangerous men pop up when we least expect it. The immediate threat to your ladies is from these two men. When they are out of the picture, then Miss Silverman can re-emerge into the public view. Once she is there she will be protected to some degree. She's a star, after all. The Weinmann woman and the law can only do so much to Alice when she is surrounded by her own not inconsiderable wealth, her own entourage, and her own batteries of attorneys which her wealth can purchase. But she has to lose Blanchette and Lambert first. What is Croatoan?"

"A little bit of North Carolina history," said Matt with a chuckle. "If you ever get the chance, read the story of the Lost Colony. The first of my own ancestors who came to this land, some hundreds of years before the first Italian, I might add."

"Columbus was an Italian," Visconti reminded him gently. "A Genovese, in fact. And is not America itself named for another Italian, the mapmaker Amerigo Vespucci?"

"Ouch! Yeah, you got me there," agreed Matt with a laugh. "In any case, Croatoan is a private code word between Heather and me. We once discussed what we would do if any situation developed where we had to part company and meet up again later, as happened today. We were to meet at a place from our past. Let me see if they've made it." Matt took out his cellular phone and dialed. The phone rang and then it was answered. "Hi, Watson, it's me. Are you all right?"

"As well as could be expected with all our nails chewed down to the knuckles waiting to hear from you," said Heather from the living room of the house on Hatteras Island on North Carolina's Outer Banks. Her voice was tremulous with relief. "Are you all right yourself?"

"Oh, I'm able to sit up and take a little nourishment from time to time."

Heather sighed in relief. "Matt, what in God's name happened? We heard on the radio there was some shooting."

"Some, yes. Cowboy? Tori? Alice and the baby?" asked Matt.

"All here."

"How's Tori?" asked Matt apprehensively.

"Devastated. I don't suppose you nailed that bastard Tony?" queried Heather hopefully.

"Mmmm, kind of a long story, Watson, but no. Young Stoppaglia may yet have many a plate of linguini in his future."

"Then what the hell happened?" demanded Heather.

"Everybody converged on Room 306, and then all of a sudden Sam Peckinpah was writing the script. Damn, listen to me! Hanging around Alice is giving me a movie mindset as bad as hers. Thank God you guys had sense enough to make yourselves scarce. Luther Lambert was in top form, and my guts still turn to water when I think of what would have happened had any of you been in that room. The final score looks to be two, possibly three dead FBI agents and one dead Musketeer, Karen Martin. Plus the fact that our favorite Agent Scully got a rifle butt in the mouth that played hell with her dental work, courtesy of La Cosa Nostra. It was an appalling mess, truth to tell. How is Alice holding up?"

"She's so terrified she's on the verge of a nervous breakdown, but she's running on raw nerves and pure guts. OK, now what?"

"I'll be down there in a few hours, with some reinforcements. Then we try to persuade Alice to allow herself to be used as bait so we can do all this again and provoke another bloodbath, one where we will hopefully come out on top. Can I make a plan or what?"

"Oh Jesus, Matt! Can't Phil do anything?"

"Right now Phil and Miss Weinmann are facing off over possible Federal obstruction charges for concealing a material witness and interfering with Federal agents in the execution of their duty, blah, blah, blah. It's a Mexican standoff, because on the one hand we are in fact interfering with Federal law enforcement, and we haven't got a single legal leg to stand on by withholding Alice and William from the tender mercies of our lords and masters, but on the other hand Andrea doesn't dare bring formal proceedings and we all know it. Phil's a good man, Heather, a good cop and a friend. I'd rather not drag him down with me if I can help it."

"Then who are these reinforcements you're bringing?" asked Heather.

"I told them about your magnificent spaghetti bolognese," said Matt. "What?"

"Never mind. If I told you now you'd think I'd lost my mind, and maybe I have. I'll see you in a few hours and then you will understand to what level of sheer madness this grotesque business has descended."

"Are we going to make it out of this?" asked his wife bluntly.

"Probably not, but at least we don't have to worry about dying in some old folks' home when we're ninety-five," said Matt. "That was half humorous and half serious."

"Yes, I got that," said Heather with a laugh. "Hey. You are the wind beneath my wings."

"And you are my soul and my life. Be with you soon." He closed the phone and turned to Visconti. "They are on Hatteras Island, about five hours' drive from here. Let's go. We'll take that nice shiny new Saturn of yours, because this car I've got now is SBI and it might be traceable. On the way down we can figure out how we're going to do this."

"Was Tori asking about me?" asked Tony eagerly.

"I don't know. I do know that the hardest task we have ahead of us will be to prevent Tori's mother from putting a bullet in your brain, and the second hardest task will be to prevent me from doing the same. Tony, don't get any ideas here. This is a brief co-operative effort between us against a common enemy, and that's all. I'm not comfortable with it, and I doubt Mr. Five o'Clock here is either, but I'm kind of low on options at the moment. Let's get one thing straight from the get-go. There is no future for you and Tori. None."

"I tried to explain that to him today myself," said Visconti. "Without success. I am afraid young Anthony here has indeed been stricken by the Thunderbolt, and I would take it kindly if you would refrain from any sarcastic remarks on that topic. Among our people the Thunderbolt is very real. It is generally regarded as a curse and a misfortune. With good reason. More often than not, it has initiated unfortunate events."

"Yes, I know. I assure you I take it very seriously," said Matt. He turned to Tony. "You do not *touch* her, Tony. You so much as look at her wrong and I'll be on you. I mean it, kid. You hurt my child and it's you and me, and next time your *padrone* isn't going to be able to stop it."

"This is a business trip, Tony," said Visconti. "I told you before."

"I understand," said Tony. "This will have to be settled, but now is not the time. Both of you concentrate on what you have to do. This will wait. You may both rely on me."

"Jeez, kid," sighed Matt. "Now you've *really* got me scared." There was the sound of a car pulling into the driveway outside. Matt looked out the window. *"Damnation!* Of all the people I don't want to see right now! It's Andrea Weinmann!"

Visconti and Tony were on their feet, hands inside their jackets on their guns. "Is she alone?" asked Visconti.

"So far as I can see," said Redmond. "At least she's not crashing down the door with the whole Dynamic Response Team behind her. That's what those grunts in the blue nylon jackets with the body armor are called, by the way. They're not really FBI agents in the traditional J. Edgar Hoover sense of the word, they're basically the Bureau's gun thugs who get called in for the wet work. Somehow I don't think she wants to meet you boys right at the moment. Go out the back door and get to your car, then move it down the block until you see her leave. And take all those beer bottles with you. She sees them and she'll either think I'm a drunk, or she'll figure out I've got company." Tony grabbed up their bottles, and Visconti folded his newspaper under his arm, and they slipped out through the kitchen just as the doorbell rang.

Matt opened the door. Andrea had found time to change into a subdued brown cotton skirt with matching shoes and jacket and a white blouse with a small blue cravat, a sensible and businesslike medium between her summer dress of yesterday and her blue serge trousers of the morning. The right side of her face was black and blue still from the blow Visconti had given her. "Hello, Matt," she said. "I know I'm probably not overly welcome at the moment, but I'd like to talk to you if you can spare me a moment."

"Sure," sighed Matt. "Come on in." He led her into the living room. "Have a seat." He went to the fridge in the kitchen and pulled out a couple more St. Pauli Girls. He opened both and then went back into the living room and handed one to her.

"Thanks," she said. "Just what the doctor ordered. It's been a hell of a day, as if I needed to tell you that."

"How's the jaw?" asked Matt, genuinely solicitous.

"It's not broken, but about two hundred of my father's billable hours that he put into my orthodontist when I was thirteen and fourteen have now gone down the tubes. Don't worry, I knew when I joined the FBI that I was going to be dealing with men who don't mind smacking a woman around. I don't suppose you saw which way your friends Visconti and Stoppaglia went?"

"They're not my friends, and the last time I saw them they were beating feet down the hall in the Sheraton."

"No, I mean really. I read your statement and it's bullshit, of course, but this is off the record. I'd kind of like to meet Mr. Visconti again and return the favor. Always wanted to use my black belt, and the one time I get a chance the guinea bastard catches me by surprise."

"Somehow I don't think Johnny Vee is going to be inclined to give you ten rounds in the ring under Marquis of Queensberry rules," said Matt. "By the way, I'd like to apologize for that crack I made back there this morning, just before the Grim Reaper of the Ozarks popped out of the elevator. I don't know why, but when beautiful women point guns at me I overreact. The first one who did it was a narco muchacha down in Mexico, and I killed her. The last one who did it I ended up marrying. In your case at least I tried to strike a happy medium."

"Apology accepted. I shouldn't have come on so strong, but those two gangsters made me nervous. Visconti is a stone killer and Stoppaglia may be young, but he's got a pretty nasty rep already. Speaking of the lady you married, where is Heather?" asked Andrea.

"She's out with my daughter," said Matt.

"Out with your daughter and Alice Silverman and the baby and SBI Agent Garza," said Andrea. "Matt, I'm not a total fool. We know you were all in and out of 306 and 304. Would you please tell me what Croatoan means?"

"Well, at least you finally get to meet the mighty Trumpeldor," said Matt, ignoring her question and pointing to a huge orange furball who stalked up to Andrea and stared. "He's trying to figure out if you have cheese stashed on you somewhere." Trumpeldor leaped up onto the arm of the sofa and then onto the back of it and slid in and crouched behind Andrea's head.

"Is he going to pounce?" asked Andrea.

"I have no idea," said Matt. Andrea lifted the beer bottle to her lips and Trumpeldor swung a paw at it. Then he placed both front paws on top of Andrea's head and stood up for a long stretch. Andrea broke down and began to laugh.

"My God, I lose three agents and make a fool of myself, and now I'm being mocked by a cat!" she giggled. Matt went into the kitchen and opened the refrigerator, removed a small block of about two ounces of cheddar, held it out at arm's length into the living room and wiggled it, and was rewarded by a shriek from the cat who hurled himself off the sofa and charged, leaping into the air to try and grab the cheese. Matt grabbed the animal and threw him and the cheese into the kitchen. He came back in and sat down. "Matt, any chance you'll give me a straight answer when I ask you why you were fraternizing with two known criminals this morning?"

"I recognized Stoppaglia in the lobby from your mug shots and I tracked him and Visconti down from the hotel registrations, all of which you already know if you asked the desk clerk who was on duty this morning. Neither of them are actually wanted for a crime, and so all I could do was talk to them. They were hardly going to sit there and tell me all about who they were planning to murder, but I get the impression that Dominic LaBrasca has somehow found out it was Blanchette and his crew who murdered Joey LaBrasca and the others and they are down here hunting Musketeers, one of whom they apparently caught up with in the Pine Needle Mall. I might have learned more if you hadn't butted it, but you now know about as much about it all as I do."

"Why don't I believe one word of that?" asked Andrea. She sighed. "Matt, look, not to put too fine a point on it, I've come here to beg for mercy. I need your help. Please, tell me where Alice Silverman is! Who or what is Croatoan? That fiasco this morning is going to ruin me professionally if I can't pull this business out of the fire very, very quickly. I'm sure the rumor mill is already roaring full blast in the Hoover Building about how the incompetent affirmative action woman got three male agents killed. And that's not fair, dammit!"

"No, it isn't," agreed Matt. "What's not fair is that you are on this assignment at all, chasing poor Alice Silverman because the liberal Democratic machine is scared shitless she's going to blab about being foully violated by Bill and Hillary Clinton, when you should be hunting for Bob Blanchette and Luther Lambert. Dammit, Andrea, Alice is the *victim* here! But your whole effort seems to be aimed at catching *her*, and when the real killers in the crime you're supposedly investigating pop up unexpectedly, it's almost like they're an annoyance and a distraction to you!"

"Blanchette and Lambert will be taken care of," said Andrea. "Don't worry, they're on the agenda. Hell, maybe Johnny Vee will do if for us, waste them like he wasted that redneck slut Martin, which is fine with me. Then when we catch up with Mr. Visconti and attempt to take him into custody for assaulting a Federal officer, he will of course resist arrest and we'll be rid of him and Tony Stoppaglia as well. But we also have to take Alice Silverman into custody and make sure that she doesn't proceed with whatever bizarre blackmail plot she and Jesse Helms are planning against the President of the United States."

"That is horse shit, Andrea! You don't believe she's doing any such thing, not for one minute! Why are you a part of this? How can you possibly justify to yourself the fact that you are hunting an innocent young woman and her baby like animals?" demanded Matt.

"Because she is part of this whole vast and unprincipled right-wing conspiracy to destroy Bill and Hillary Clinton, and decent people in this country are tired of all you Clinton-haters trying to seize control of the national agenda with all this claptrap about ethics and corruption and all this Cold War paranoia about socialist China and all this disgusting voyeurism about the president's sex life, and now the First Lady's sex life as well!" cried out Andrea. "Do you understand that, Matt? Any chance you and Jesse Helms and all you other dumb *goyim* can get the message? Pat Buchanan's right, there's been a culture war going on in this country for the past fifty years and you guys *lost,* just like you lost the past two elections! Deal with it! You lost and we won, and we're not going to let some Hollywood slut who made goo-goo eyes at our president and then got her feelings hurt get away with making up some stupid fantasy and gabbling it all out on Sixty Minutes! We've had enough of that, Matt! No more of this insanity!"

"Insanity?" shouted Matt angrily. "Let me tell you about insanity, lady! This morning we both saw a maniac with an axe murder a Federal agent right in front of our eyes, a maniac who is paid to do such things by *William Jefferson Clinton!* Probably paid out of tax dollars, to add insult to injury!" He stood up in a rage, walked over to Andrea and grabbed her up by her shoulders, shaking her in his anger. "Then I go up to the third floor and I find that same maniac smashing in a door with axes which he fully intends to use to dismember Alice and her baby and my wife and my child and my friend! With him are two vicious hired killers, also in the pay of your beloved Bill Clinton, the *President of the United States,* who has sent them here to my state, my home, to commit butchery in order to cover up his own foul crimes!

"And who helps me fight these ravening beasts of the wilderness that your beloved president has unleashed on me and my family, eh, Andrea? Who steps forward when I need help and my family needs help? You? Your FBI who are supposed to uphold the law and serve the people of this country and protect Americans from fucking blood-drinking maniacs with axes and machine guns? No, you don't have time for that, you're too busy cleaning up Bill and Hillary Clinton's vomit! No, when the time comes to make a stand against this filth, this evil in the White House, who do I find standing at my side and putting their lives on the line to protect that girl and that baby and my own loved ones? I find the goddamned *Mob,* that's who! Professional criminals I once hunted and arrested and sent to prison are now the ones I have to turn to in order to salvage some kind of justice and decency out of this fucking cesspool that Bill and Hillary Clinton have made out of America! I am now under the most profound personal obligation to the very kind of men that you and I are both sworn to destroy, whom we should both be fighting against side by side, because you and others like you have become the slaves of a couple of moral degenerates and uncouth despots, in violation of your oath and in violation of every tenet of common human decency! My God, do have any idea how sick and angry it makes me that you have forced me into this situation? Can you understand the rage that fills me because I have to live in a world run by the likes of Bill and Hillary Clinton?"

"I love you," whispered Andrea, and then her arms were around him and her bruised lips crushing his. Her body was against his, lithe and soft and willing, her full breasts pressing through the cloth between them that cried to be torn away. To save his very soul, Matt could not have helped responding for a long moment, gripping her shoulders and returning her kiss and meeting her probing tongue with his own and then reaching down and sliding his hands beneath her blouse at the waist, tensing to reach upwards. She pulled him down towards the couch and ripped her own blouse open, bringing his hands up to her breasts. Matt understood that once he ended up lying down beside her it would proceed to the inevitable result, and then he would be lost forever.

He hurled her onto the couch and stood up. "No," he said, his voice steady. "No."

"She's not here!" wept Andrea softly. "Matt, for God's sake, just this once? Even if it never happens again between us? Can you not give me just this one hour, even if it is all I will ever have of you? No one will ever know!"

"I would know," replied Matt in a voice of stone.

"Please don't hate me!" she whimpered.

"I don't," he said with genuine compassion. "I just cannot possibly give you what you want. Jesus, Andrea, why me? I don't have to tell you how stunningly beautiful you are, plus everything else you've got going for you. You could pick and choose any man in Washington, from Senators and Federal judges on down. Why *me*, for God's sake?"

"Because you are the last of the ancient breed, Matt," she whispered. "You're not just a white male, you're a white *man*, the last of those dreaded and hated white men who once conquered the world. Because in my heart I know that for all my liberal beliefs, when it comes time for *me* to choose forever, as much as I admire Bill Clinton and all he has done, I don't want anyone like him as a husband and a father for my children. I don't want the kind of men that this Brave New World produces, smooth and smart and shallow and shifty, and weak as water. I want a man I know will love me and fight for me, but whom I also know won't take any crap off me, and whom I know I will never be able to push too far in the things that matter. God, what a hypocrite that makes me!"

"I'm not the last, Andrea. There are others," said Matt. "I met two of them this morning, although they are not of a kind I want in my life or in my family. Keep on looking, Andrea. Don't worry, we're out there still, and some of us aren't married." He helped her up. "That kiss must have hurt your mouth like hell."

"I'd endure ten times the pain for another one," she said. "I'm sorry. I'm making a total fool of myself, which I suppose is an appropriate way to end this horrible day."

"Now, question," asked Matt gently. "You offered me the whole nine yards and I turned you down. I have some idea of how humiliating that is for a woman, although I can never fully understand it. Are you going to be able to refrain from hating *me*?"

"I'll try," she said, buttoning up her self-torn blouse as best she could.

"One final thing," said Matt. "You understand that if you try to hurt Alice or my wife or my daughter, from then on it's death? That if one hair on Heather or Tori's head is harmed by you or any of your people,

I will kill you? Andrea, *please!* Don't do that to me! I feel horrible enough about what I have done to you already. Please, just leave it! Just walk away from it. Tell Janet Reno whatever you have to tell her, but leave Alice and the baby alone. This isn't Peyton Place or an afternoon soap opera. It's real and both of us are carrying guns. Before God, Andrea, I don't want that! Please, I am begging you, don't let it come to blood between us!"

"Matt, I have a job to do," she said in a sad voice. "You're making it impossible for me to do it, personally and professionally. Look, you've been honest with me…boy, have you ever!…and I'll be honest with you. You're tough, you're smart, and beyond that you seem to have the devil's own luck. You've bopped your way out of more hand-to-hand than anybody I've ever known or heard of and I really, really do not want to find out what's going to happen if we have to come after you locked and loaded. But you're only one man and your luck won't hold forever, and I suspect you have sense enough to know that. You are chancing not only your life but the lives of anyone with you, and if you choose to remain obstinate then you and they must bear the consequences. We live in a real world, and the real world demands that Alice Silverman and her child come in from the cold, and she makes her peace with Bill and Hillary Clinton, or else. All I can do is my job and hope that I don't have to do something which will tear me up inside more than I could ever have imagined possible a mere two weeks ago. You have my cell phone number. Right up to the last minute, I hope you'll come to your senses and dial it."

She picked up her purse and moved to the front door. "Andrea?" he called. She turned. "You know I'm right, don't you? Deep down inside? You know I'm right about it all, the Clintons and your whole Brave New World, don't you?"

She shook her head. "Matt, don't ask that of me. Not ever. My heart I have given to you already, even though you refuse it. My body you may have for the asking, whenever you want it. But my soul you may not ever touch or enter upon."

"I know. And that is why even if I were free, there could never be anything between us," said Matt sadly.

In her rented car outside Andrea leaned her head against the steering wheel and wept for a minute. Then she pulled herself together and dialed her cellular phone. "He's here at his house," she said into the phone.

"The Global Positioning Indicator that we planted yesterday says his car is on Hatteras Island," said a voice on the phone.

"Call Quantico," she told the man on the phone. "Operational Authorization Alpha One, refer AG, Eyes Only. Tell them we need the Conquistadors."

After she pulled out of the driveway Matt changed clothes, putting on jeans and a khaki work shirt and supple leather shoes with rubber soles. He checked over the contents of a large canvas pouch with a strap, tossed in several boxes of .357 ammo, put the over his shoulder, placed his fedora at a rakish angle on his head, and stepped outside. The Saturn pulled quietly into his driveway, without headlights. "I'll sit in the back, if you don't mind," he told Visconti.

"What's in the bag?" asked Tony, leaning over from the driver's side.

"It's a kind of kit I keep for these times when I need to get wild at heart and weird on top," said Matt, getting into the car. "Three years ago the contents of this bag saved the lives of myself and Heather and Tori, as well as my lunatic brother and his luscious nympho wife, when I had my entirely too well known run-in with Mr. Bennett and his buddies."

"Yeah?" said Tony. "I don't know if I like you sitting behind me with that bag. Makes me kinda jumpy, you know?"

"Good," said Matt.

✶✶✶

It was still dark when the Saturn pulled up outside a two-story Victorian gingerbread house about half a mile outside the village of Hatteras on North Carolina's Outer Banks. The yard was shaded in the daytime from the white hot sun by several lean and twisted live oaks, and there was a gallant attempt at a lawn poking up through the sand and coquino shells, as well as carefully tended flower boxes on the wide veranda. Mrs. Radcliffe now lived in a retirement home in Wilmington, but she had her son drive her up once a week so she could tend to the flowers and the small garden in the back. The front yard sloped down to a paved road, and across the road in the darkness loomed broad ghostly white sand dunes covered with high waving sea oats. Beyond the pale dunes the eternal surf rumbled in the background. Matt and Visconti and Stoppaglia got out of the car. "I'd best go in first and talk to them," said Matt. "In addition to a very angry mother there's my partner Cowboy, who is a lifelong police officer and isn't going to like the idea of teaming up with you guys." Tony spoke.

"I mean what I said. I have not dishonored her in my heart and I never will. Not ever."

"The terrible thing is that I believe you," sighed Matt. "I see unimaginable pain coming, for all of us." He walked up onto the porch and he knocked on the door, and was practically dragged inside by Heather who crushed him to her and kissed him in desperate, frightened passion. No one was asleep except baby William who lay in the center of the kitchen table entrenched in a fortress of pillows scavenged from assorted beds and armchairs around the house. "I remember that bag, and what's in it," said Heather fearfully, pointing at the canvas pouch. "I guess it really is going to get that bad again, eh?"

"Probably," said Matt. "Cowboy, how are you?"

"Better now I see you, *compadre*," said Cowboy from an armchair, raising his shotgun in salute. "You owe me big time, Matt, making me miss the big show this morning. Or yesterday morning, I guess it is now."

"I don't know whose idea it was for you all to skedaddle, but whoever it was they were right," said Matt. "If any of you had been in room 306 another ten minutes, some of you wouldn't be here this morning. Alice, are you hanging in there?"

"I don't know what to say to you," said the young actress. "If this was a real movie instead of a live one, if you get my drift, I'd have some great lines here. But how do I say thank you to someone who has done what you did so my child and I could live? I don't have the words, Matt, not for any of you."

"Tori?" asked Matt gently.

"I'll live," said his daughter with a wan smile. "You don't have to walk on eggs with me, Dad. I told them what I did. They're all being exquisitely tactful and supportive."

"They may not be supportive once they hear what *I've* done," said Matt wearily. "Gather round, campers, and let me explain to you exactly the pickle we find ourselves in. It's a dilly. First off, officially none of this is happening. The media are telling people that donnybrook at the Sheraton was a drug bust gone bad. We can try to change that, and it may be our only hope, but there is one more fix I want to try first before we burn down the hut. It is very dangerous, for all of us. I'll get into that in a minute. Right now the immediate tactical situation is that we have two very unpleasant groups of people looking for you, Alice. One consists of the two remaining Musketeers, Monsieurs Blanchette and Lambert. Milady Martin, as you may have heard, ended up with her brains blown all over the Pine Needle Mall in the RTP, courtesy of two gents of Italian-American heritage, of whom more anon. I have no way of knowing if those three human reptiles were indeed all for one and one for all, but I can tell you that Mr. Lambert has an axe with your name on it, Alice. And mine and everybody else's in this room. Monsieur Blanchette is also very keenly interested in our demise, because it seems that Lady Hillary Rodham-Macbeth has decided that his services to our lord and master Billyboy can be terminated, with extreme prejudice, and he very urgently needs to wipe this slate clean so he can disappear into the bayou for a while. Finally, we have Special Agent Andrea Weinmann of the Federal Bureau of Investigation. I spoke with her earlier this evening. Alice, she is going to kill you if she catches you. She didn't say so in so many words, but I am convinced that she holds your death warrant and it is sanctioned. Do you understand what I have just said?"

"I understood when Eddie Miami told me," said Alice steadily. "He said that Bill Clinton has sentenced me and William to death. I now know that he spoke the truth. I am in exactly the same position as if I was sitting in a prison cell watching the clock, waiting for the footsteps in the corridor outside coming to lead me down the hall to the electric chair or the gas chamber. How many minutes are left on the clock, Matt?"

"Not many," he told her honestly.

"Damn! I almost wish I *were* in a cell waiting for the chair or the rope! Bet I could beat Susan Hayward's performance in *I Want To Live!* or Nessa Redgrave in *Mary, Queen of Scots*. Instead it looks like I'm up against Jamie Lee Curtis in *Halloween*. Sorry, guys, I know I'm trivializing all this, but hey, what can I say? I'm Hollywood, I think in terms of movies."

"How do you fancy a supporting role in *The Godfather*?" asked Matt.

Suddenly Heather understood. She stood up and shouted at her husband, *"How dare you? Have you lost your fucking mind?"*

"You were grateful to Kolya Nozh," Matt reminded her. "I wouldn't exactly call him the most savory character in the world."

"Major Rozanov was a soldier and a man of honor, whatever we might think of the society and the government he served," said Heather heatedly. "This is different! These people are different, and you know it, Matt!"

"Yes, I know it! But for Christ's sake, Heather, what choice have we got? How long do you want this to go on?" demanded Matt. "How long can we skulk down here? A week? Two weeks? A month? How long before your personal leave runs out and your boss wants to know why you're not at your desk crunching numbers? How long before Alice has to get back to L. A. no matter what? How long before Tori has to start going to class again? How long before Cowboy and I get pulled off this gig and have to go back to chasing crackheads who carve up their girlfriends in the Durham projects? Do you want all this just hovering in the background all

that time?" He turned to Alice. "Alice, it's simple. We have to take down Bob Blanchette and Luther Lambert, and we have to do it now, or one day you're going to wake up in the night in your Beverly Hills mansion and the last thing you see in life will be a bearded maniac splitting your skull with an axe. I want you to agree to use yourself as bait to lure them in. Then either we kill them, or they kill us. Either way, it's over."

"Agreed," said Alice without hesitation. "When, where, and how?"

"And where are these reinforcements Heather said you were bringing?" asked Garza.

Matt sighed and stepped to the door. He opened it and beckoned. After a few moments John Visconti stepped in, followed by Tony Stoppaglia. Tony's eyes and Tori's met across the room, both stone-faced, then they turned away from each other. "Cowboy, this is John Visconti and Anthony Stoppaglia. They are here for one reason and one reason only, to help us remove the threat which exists to Alice and her baby. They are here because the law that we have both served all our lives is now powerless and in the hands of worse criminals than either of these men. They are here because no one else on earth will help us. I find this situation grotesque and bizarre and utterly distasteful, but we are drowning and when someone throws drowning people a life preserver they grab onto it. Can you handle this?"

"You guinea hoods got a problem with Texans?" demanded Garza harshly.

"You got a problem with Italians, Hopalong?" growled Tony. Visconti raised his hand.

"They say no one hates harder than brothers," he said. "We are not brothers, Mr. Garza, but we are cousins. Our languages are both descended from Latin. If I were to speak Italian to you, and you were to reply in Spanish, we could just barely understand one another."

"As it happens, the only thing Mexican about me is my name. My family are mostly Hill Country Germans from around Fredericksburg. I had one remote forebear who was a nobleman in Castile, and because I have his name I was able to get hired on here under an affirmative action quota, but I am an American, and I don't speak Spanish," said Garza. "So are you, if I recall rightly from your rap sheet."

"Yes, you are correct. I myself was born in a tenement in the Bronx. I didn't speak more than a few swear words of Italian until an old man in New York inspired me to go to Sicily when I was eighteen. I stayed until I was twenty-three, and there I learned who I was and where I came from. Whenever I have the opportunity to do so I return for a while, to refresh my links with the old land and the old ways. These things are important to know in the Age of Clinton, before the darkness that is slowly descending upon the world becomes complete and none of us can see anything but what our new masters choose to show us. Never mind. For whatever inscrutable reasons of fate, we are here to help you. Do you accept that help?"

"I accept this man's judgment," said Garza, pointing to Matt.

"*Va bene.* More importantly, Mrs. Redmond, do *you* accept our help?"

"You are scum! Both of you!" hissed Heather angrily.

"I did not ask what you thought of us, Mrs. Redmond," said Visconti. "I asked if you are willing to accept our help in the situation in which you currently find yourself?"

"Looks like we have to go ahead and settle it after all, one way or the other," sighed Tony. "She's angry with me and afraid of me, and she's got reason to be. We've all got serious business to attend to and we can't have this other distracting us. We have to get this out of the way." He stepped forward and walked up to Tori, who looked at him without expression. He took a piece of paper from his pocket. "How good are you at making snap decisions?" he asked. "Snap decisions which will determine the whole course of your future life? You got one to make now. You gave me this yesterday morning, Tori. Now you gotta decide whether to take it back."

"You're a real bastard," said Tori.

"Yeah, so they say. But that ain't what I axed you, Tori. I axed you whether you want this phone number back or not."

"Tori, before you decide, you have the right to know two truths," said Matt. "The first one I will tell you myself, however reluctantly. The second one Tony will tell you, if he's man enough."

Tony looked at him, understanding that he was being challenged. "Done," he said. "I got no idea what you're talking about, but it's done."

"My reluctant truth is this," said Matt. "Yesterday morning, I saw this man go up against a homicidal maniac armed with an axe, and two more professional assassins armed with machine guns, while he himself had nothing more in his hand than a broken bottle. He fought one of the most terrible men on earth hand to hand, and he did it for you, Tori, because he believed, as we all did, that you were still inside room 306. That bruise on his face is a badge of honor, whatever his life has been until now, because he got it trying to keep one of Bill Clinton's monsters away from you and Heather and Alice and baby William. Earlier on I had my own pistol pointed at his head and was quite ready to kill him, but rather than equivocate or promise to give you up, he defied me. When I offered these men an arrangement that entailed his agreeing never to see you again, he defied his own boss here, and in his world that is a deadly dangerous thing to do. I hate and reject everything Tony and his people are, but I will tell you this of him, that he has all the courage a man could ever want. That goes a long way with me, in this age when brave men are so rare. Whatever else he may be, Tori, his feelings for you are real."

"How could you tell her something like that?" cried Heather, upset.

"Because it is the truth. Besides, I wasn't just telling her. I was telling you. OK, Tony, you're up. You ready to tell her your truth?"

"I don't know what you mean," responded Tony truculently.

"Tell my daughter how your father died. I want to hear you tell her in your own words, your version of what happened, not just for her sake but because I've always been honestly curious as to how you people speak of these things among yourselves, how you rationalize them, what your dinner table conversation must be like. So tell her, Tony. Tell her about your father."

Tony stared at him in rage and loathing. For a moment everyone thought he was going to attack Matt, but he did not. "All right." He turned to Tori. "My father was Carmine Stoppaglia. He was a friend of ours. I remember that he gave me a guinea pig for Christmas once, and a tricycle for my birthday when I was four years old, that he drove a big gold Cadillac that always smelled like stale cigar smoke inside, and he had a blue shaven chin that scratched when he would kiss me good night. I don't remember his voice much except when he read me 'Green Eggs and Ham' and also 'The Night Before Christmas' on Christmas Eve.

"When I was six years old there was some trouble and he went away. The cops found him three weeks later in the trunk of his Cadillac, tied up with masking tape. He was beaten almost to death with a lead pipe, his throat was cut, and they fired five bullets into his back. There were four men involved, plus the boss who ordered it done. There's an old saying among Sicilians that revenge is the only dish best served cold. It is true. So we took our time, we did it right, and we took ours cold, the way my father would have wanted it, the way he would have done it himself. My grandfather killed three of the four down through the years, but he saved the fourth and last one for me until I became a man and could perform this obligation for my father's sake, and last year I killed him myself. The boss is in prison now, but when he comes out, the LaBrascas will be waiting. We never forget, and we never forgive. Your father is correct, Tori. This is a truth about me and mine that you have a right to know. Is that what you wanted to hear? Is that enough?" he asked, looking up at Redmond angrily.

"More than sufficient. You get an A plus for honesty as well as courage." Matt looked at Tori. "Congratulations, honey. You've done it. You've found a young man who loves you in his own savage way, and who is willing to take me on to prove it, should that become necessary."

"What's that old Chinese saying?" asked Tori shakily. "Be careful what you wish for, because you may get it?"

"You got it," said Matt. "Now I believe you have a decision to make regarding that piece of paper in Tony's hand?"

"I've decided you're both bastards," she said lightly, rising from her seat. She looked down at the paper. "A dramatic gesture, but meaningless. I mean, after all, we're in the telephone book." She walked out the door.

"I don't need no phone book!" Tony called after her. "I already got it off by heart!"

Visconti stepped forward and spoke to Alice. "Miss Silverman?" he asked gently. "We have come a long way to find you. You need not tell us of what you have gone through at the hands of the Clintons. Mr. Redmond has relieved you of that necessity, in order to spare you the ordeal of having to retell of such an experience to strangers, although you may yet be compelled to do so before the whole world. Do you accept our presence and our help?"

"Mmmm…God, I wish Bob DeNiro was a few years younger!" said Alice.

"I beg your pardon?" said Visconti, nonplussed.

"I'm spending my time planning the movie version of all this. The one I'm going to produce one day if I survive, which I know I won't, but it keeps me sane, even if it drives all these other guys nuts, and I warn you, it's going to drive you nuts as well. By the way, that was one hell of a scene just now between Tony and Tori. I think I've got it memorized for the scriptwriters and I'll make sure they don't totally trash it. Anyway, back to casting. I've got dibs on Kirsten Dunst. I keep trying to persuade Matt and Heather to accept Ted Danson and Mary Steenburgen, but they're too leftish for Matt. He wants Patrick Swayze or Harrison Ford, and Heather wants Kyra Sedgwick or else Sigourney Weaver. Tori wants Jennifer Aniston and Cowboy wants Nick Nolte. I haven't seen this Weinmann woman, but the others have and they're divided between Gina Gershon and Courtney Cox. The Undertaker is a shoo-in for Luther Lambert, of course, and Brett Butler is a natural for Karen Martin, although I personally would love to give Kristen Johnston a shot at it. Bob Blanchette is kind of harder to cast. I've noticed that no one can quite scope him, you know, no one quite knows who or why or how he is, if you get my drift...?"

"Perfectly," said Visconti. "That is precisely how he has been so successful in our profession. He is an invisible man, totally colorless and nondescript. That is what we must strive to be, living and working in the shadows. If you could possibly persuade John Lithgow to lose about twenty pounds, you've got him."

"Thanks, I really appreciate the input from someone who knows his stuff," said Alice enthusiastically. "Now, for yourself...you're too young for DeNiro and too young for Pacino as well, not to mention too tall. Too tall for Joe Pesci, too. Chaz Palmientieri? Mmmm..maybe? How do you feel about Chaz?"

"A fine actor, and it would be an honor," said Visconti with a smile. "But may I make a suggestion? Costas Mandylor."

"*Of course!*" cried Alice. "Brilliant! Now for your sidekick here...hmmm. Matt told me you're supposed to look like a young Sinatra and yeah, you do in a way, but we're kind of short on Sinatras in Hollywood. We could always give some young unknown a shot. Or Johnny Depp, maybe, but he's a bit old."

"The guy who played Donnie Brasco? Forget about it!" said Tony vehemently.

"Then again, Leo DiCaprio could do it—he's an asshole but he's a hell of an actor, I've got to give him that. I didn't marry him when I had the chance, so I saved him a bundle on the community property in the divorce, and so he owes me one. Plus he's Italian. You got a problem with Leo DiCaprio, Tony?"

"Hey, I'll go one better than Leo," said Tony. "You make me the right kind of offer and when the time comes, I'll play myself. I always wanted to do a love scene with Jennifer Aniston." He ignored Matt and Heather's angry stare.

"Let's hope your character doesn't end up getting killed off. Okay, how do we set up this shoot, Matt?" asked Alice. "And it sounds like you do mean shoot."

"Mr. Vee here has a number where he can leave a message for Blanchette. It's the kind of thing he picks up in the run of business. We think we've figured out a way tip him as to your whereabouts that will be credible. In any case, it's something we have to try. We lead him to believe that you're going to be in a certain place at a certain time. The time is important; we need to rush him. Then we wait for them both, and when they come we take them out. Cowboy and I are law enforcement officers and they are officially wanted criminals after that madness at the RDU Sheraton, so we can take care of the paperwork afterwards."

"Will that work?" asked Alice.

"A lot is going to depend on whether or not you're brave enough to be on the scene," admitted Matt."Visconti and I agree that Blanchette is no fool and he is unlikely to come in too close unless he has some indication that you are actually present."

"Let me be her double!" spoke up Tori, who had quietly re-entered the room. "I can wear a wig and at a distance I would look enough like Alice to..."

"*No!*" said Matt, Heather, and Tony at the same time.

"Tori, your Dad is right," said Alice. "These fish aren't going to strike at a fly, they'll need to get a sniff of the real worm. That's me. Besides, Jennifer Aniston is the love interest in this flick, remember? You never kill off the love interest."

"Tori, you do in fact have something you can do, a very important task," said Heather. "You need to take care of baby William while his mother is playing decoy. Changing diapers while the rest of us are playing tag with death may not sound glamorous, but that infant is half the reason we're all here, and somehow I don't think Mary Poppins is available for this gig."

"I understand," said Tori. "I just don't want you to leave me out any more."

"OK, Matt, when and where do I set up Alice's Bait Shop?" she asked. "Here? It seems a shame to tear up this lovely old house with bullet holes."

"I know you've probably had enough of hotels by now, Alice, but tomorrow Visconti and I need to drive up the islands to Nag's Head or Kitty Hawk and check out the Hilton or the Hampton Inn or someplace similar. This place here is simply too isolated; Blanchette will smell a rat right away. The scenario has to make *sense* to Blanchette, if you understand. The official story is that you're holding a press conference in a day or two back in Raleigh and you're about the blow the gaff on what happened to you at the Beverly Hills Hilton. In the meantime we've got you stashed down here after what went down at the Sheraton. That means he has to move fast. Damn, this picture of ours has more hotels than a Monopoly game, doesn't it?"

"It also has an illogical plot," said Alice. "Why would I be holding this press conference out here in the Carolina boondocks, no offense, rather than back in Hollywood surrounded by all my own legal and PR people?"

"Because you're being guarded by the fearless Two Gun Matt, whose badge is only good in North Carolina," said Matt.

"Not to mention the Texas Twister," chuckled Garza.

"Why don't you just take five rounds out of your .357 and play Russian roulette?" asked Heather, upset. "It would be safer."

"Heather, he's going to know I'm around anyway," explained Matt. "We're not telling him anything he can't figure out for himself in two shakes. Depending on the layout this time, we get her into as secure a situation as we find manage and then do it deliberately the way it worked out at the Sheraton, me and the goombahs roving and Cowboy sticking to Alice like glue. I want her that 12-gauge between her and the world, Art, every second of the time."

"I want some damned action this time, Matt!" said Garza. "Let Little Blue Eyes here be the bodyguard. I'll lend him the scattergun. Maybe he'll get star-struck and Tori will get jealous and come to her senses."

"Tony's not my type, Cowboy," laughed Alice. "I go for mature older men." Tony ignored them, which impressed Matt.

✶✶✶

Later, Matt and Heather lay in one another's arms on a double bed in the darkness, fully clothed. "Andrea Weinmann came to the house just before I left," he told her. "Trumpeldor walked on her head."

"I'd like to step on her head myself," said Heather.

"She made her move," said Matt.

"And?" said Heather.

"She almost connected," said Matt. "Almost. Heather, I have never been so tempted before in my life, not by any other woman. Not even you, that first time in my old apartment in Carrboro. God, she is beautiful! But I passed the test, Heather. You don't ever have to worry about my cheating on you. If it was ever going to happen, it would have happened tonight. It didn't."

"I hope Alice includes that scene in her coming picture as well. You have my blessing to tell her about it if we ever do make it through this. Matt, for the past few days I've been worried about a lot of things and very badly frightened about a lot of things. But that was never one of them. I am, however, about ready to get up and go make sure our daughter is sleeping alone, and if she isn't I may just put a bullet in that kid Stoppaglia. Matt, in God's name, what's up with that? What's going to happen there?"

"If Tony makes it, he is going to come to our door and take her from us," said Matt. "That's the natural order of things. When one has daughters, eventually young men come to the door and take them away. Unfortunately we live in a diseased and deformed society, and so this has happened. And Tori will go with him. She made her decision tonight. She equivocated instead of spitting in his face. That in itself is a kind of decision. Heather, as vitally important as this is, can we not talk about it now? Right now I want to sleep a bit and feel you near me, feel your beautiful hair under my hand, maybe a few other things as well."

Tori lay in her own room, wide awake. *Go ahead, come in here and try something,* she thought in black despair. *Try to move on me and take advantage of my weakness and my pain and my confusion to get some more while you can, scumball. Will I give it to you? Probably, because I'm a stupid slut who lets strange men pick her up in hotels. You had it last night so what the hell, why not tonight? But if you do, then when all this is over it's hasta la vista baby, or in your case arrividerci. Come on, Tony. You're not man enough to understand how I'm hurting and how I hate myself. To you I'm just a fucking block. You're not man enough to give me the respect of leaving me alone and letting me keep some kind of dignity while I make this big decision I now have to make, thanks to you. Come on, hey, it's waiting for you, get some more of the college bimbo while you can and then go back to New York and drink wine and eat spaghetti with your gangster friends and laugh at me...*

But Tony never came, and the sun rose and slowly lightened the room. Finally Tori gave in and wept. "Oh, damn you!" she sobbed bitterly into her pillow. "Why couldn't you have made this easy for me?"

✱✱✱

Heather and Tori silently made breakfast for them all of scrambled eggs and sausage and toast and oatmeal. They put the plates and bowls on the table, and the meal was eaten in quick and strained silence. "Okay, let's get to work," said Matt. "First off, what kind of firepower have we got between us?" The men cleared off the table and Visconti and Tony hauled the boxes of weapons out of the Saturn, while Matt broke out his own not inconsiderable armament from the trunk of the Taurus and from a special section he had cut out of one of the upstairs

closets. Cowboy and Tony gawked at the rising arsenal with the fascination of true gun-lovers. The women shivered, knowing what the guns
meant and what could be coming for them all. The two Mafiosi had
changed out of their Brooks Brothers ensembles and were now wearing
slacks, expensive but durable and flexible running shoes, banlon shirts,
and light windbreaker jackets. "I recognize the *lupara*. They say
Mussolini ordered all the stone walls in Sicily cut down to no more than
two feet in height so you guys couldn't hide behind them and blow each
other away with those things. Those are your throwaways, I presume?"
asked Matt, pointing to the heap of small caliber pistols.

"Yes," said Visconti. "They are not very accurate but at close range
they will serve the purpose. Each one is loaded with a full cylinder or
clip, but I have no extra ammo. Properly used, there is never any need
to reload them. Tony, I'll give you this one. It's a .32, lousy ballistics
but I've notched the tips of the slugs so they will function as dum-
dums in close quarters." Tony took the weapon in its small clip holster
and stuck in behind his back.

"Could you lend me a couple, one for me and one for Cowboy?"

"Help yourself," said Visconti, gesturing. Matt chose a .38 derringer
for himself and Cowboy a small nickel-plated .380 automatic.

"Tori, looks like you've got more than one life decision to make in all
this. I taught you to shoot properly on the police range, but now you need
to decide whether you're going to carry. This is one of my own holdouts."
Her father held up an R & G .22 caliber revolver. "John Hinckley special.
Nine shots, no recoil, long rifle hollow points that will do as much damage
as anything heavier, virtually idiot-proof, just aim dead center and pump
all nine into anyone who's coming at you. This will tickle even big Luther's
gizzard at close range, although pray God he never gets that close. But
don't take it unless you know you can use it. Otherwise you're more of a
risk to yourself and the others with it than without it." Tori held out her
hand wordlessly and put the pistol into William's large plastic baby supply
bag. "Cowboy, you've got that Remington pump and your Peacemaker

and now the .380. I hope it doesn't come to the crunch, but if it does you can have this as a backup." He handed Garza a short rifle with a deadly needle-like barrel. "Ruger Mini-14 carbine, 30 round magazine and three more clips in this ammo pouch. These magazines are now illegal thanks to Bill and Hill and Mr. Schumer. I guess they were afraid somebody might take a few shots at Federal enforcement agents, and we can't have that now, can we? Mr. Vee here has his Makarov and his Sicilian splatter-gun on the sling there, plus what, exactly, is that? Looks like an AK-47 frame, but what the hell is that barrel?"

"It is a VAL Silent Sniper," said Visconti, screwing a telescopic sight onto the rifle. "Russian manufacture. A new weapon, just in production since 1994, field tested in Chechnya with excellent performance results. It fires a heavy nine by thirty-nine millimeter bullet at subsonic velocity and can pierce any known body armor at up to 400 yards. Mr. Lambert's flak jacket will not save him again. It is also effectively silenced by this asbestos-lined barrel. The shot makes no more noise than the striking of a match." Visconti pulled a shorter weapon out of a padded gun case and handed it to Tony, as well as a leather bag full of magazines. "We may need some full auto fire. I'm giving Tony this. Beretta Model 12-S submachine gun, 9-millimeter, folding shoulder stock, ten fully loaded 40-round magazines. The Italian carabinieri use them. Now, Tony and I are rather curious to see the contents of your little bag of party favors."

Redmond opened his canvas sack and took out four OD green canister grenades of CS tear gas. "These for openers. We each get one." He handed them out. Tony and Visconti stuck theirs in their jacket pocket. Then Matt took from the bag two round pillbox-shaped cardboard tubes and withdrew several OD green hand grenades, which he put back into the bag. "I'll hang onto these, if you don't mind. Not that I don't trust you fine comrades in arms and all that, but I want to know where these are at all times and I want to be the one to decide if and when they are used." Finally he drew forth the disassembled parts of a short and heavy weapon which he rapidly assembled.

"What's that for, tanks?" demanded Tony skeptically.

"It can disable an armored personnel carrier, and we may end up facing those if Miss Andrea and the DRT decide to stick their oar in again at an inappropriate moment," said Matt seriously. "The old M-79 grenade launcher. I've got six 40-millimeter high explosive shells, two buckshot shells, one flare and one white phosphorus incendiary round for it. I'm thinking of the Feebs, of course, but I would definitely like to try chunking one of these into Luther's gut and see if he can stomach it."

"This is insane. You're going to get yourselves killed!" whispered Heather in despair.

"Where can we run to, Heather?" asked Matt. "These people are sent here by the President and the First Lady of the United States. Who will stop them, if not the people they tyrannize? We have no one else to turn to any more, Heather. There's no appeal and no referee and no rules any more. The darkness is slowly descending and the whole world is being swallowed up in this evil. We have no choice."

"You do, and you know it," said Alice. "You can walk away. There's still time. I'm the one they're after. I'll get on a plane back to L. A. and you can take William and hide in one of these beach hotels until I'm clear, and then get away yourselves. Now the time has come, and I see all these real guns, not props, and I know it's not a stupid movie. I don't want any more people to die for me, Matt!" she said, tears filling her eyes. "I don't want any of you to die for me! I've let you take it this far because I'm a coward, and I'm so afraid I am grasping at any straw to save my own wretched life. Ten days ago none of you knew me, except as a face on a video. I don't have the right to ask this of you. Save my baby, and you will have done the only good that can come of this. Just let me go and walk away from all this!"

"No can do," said Cowboy with a smile. "Ma'am, I am a police officer. I don't get paid my generous salary by the taxpayers to walk away and let people git murdered."

"Miss Silverman, you are indeed a noble lady to make such an offer, but with all due respect, you are not the only reason we are here," said Visconti. "There are larger issues. Bill Clinton is a tyrant and a bully. He is now sick in his mind and his body from the narcotics he inhales into his nose and from the putrid rottenness in his own soul. He is dangerous to everyone in the world now. He has to be stopped. He has spent his life pushing people and no one has ever pushed back, no one has ever stood up to him and punished him for the terrible injuries he has done to others. Appeasement is not the way to deal with such people; they only get worse and do more harm. Now he has laid his hands on Cosa Nostra, and neither our honor nor our self interest can allow that."

"Tyrants feed on blood, and once they taste it their thirst is never quenched and they must always have more. Today he's coming for you, Alice," said Matt. "Who will he come for tomorrow? We think we're going to be rid of him in another eighteen months, but suppose he fabricates some war with China or other crisis and assumes emergency powers and calls off the next election? Who will he come for then? If Hillary becomes president in 2004, who will she come for? Someone has to resist. Someone has to take the first step. I'm not a Bible puncher by any stretch, but this is the destiny that God seems to have handed you, handed all of us. Don't worry about your courage, just follow that destiny, and when the ultimate moment comes you will be sustained and His will shall be done. Now, do you seriously think you could *ever* persuade Ted Danson to make a speech like that?"

✳✳✳

That afternoon Matt and Visconti and Tony returned to the house in the Hatteras sand dunes. By common unspoken consent Tony had come along with them on their scouting trip in the Mafiosi's new Saturn; Matt thought it best to keep him and Tori apart, not to mention keep him away from Heather, so did Visconti, and evidently so did Tony.

"You guys go ahead with your little project," said Matt as they got out of the car. Tony carried several large brown paper bags from the Nag's Head Harris Teeter. "I rather doubt my lady will be mollified by any such peace offering, but it will certainly make a great scene in Alice's flick. They may even eat it up at the Cannes film festival, no pun intended. I'll bring Heather and Cowboy and Alice up to speed."

"After some looking around the strip along Highway 12, we've settled on the John Yancey Motor Hotel in Kill Devil Hills to set up the ambush." Matt told the others as he sipped iced tea in the living room. "It's an older place, less likelihood of Alice being recognized. We reserved three second floor rooms, one in the center of a corridor for Alice and yourself, Cowboy, one at each end which the rest of us will take turns using as guard posts, while one of us roves and watches for our boys to show up. Tori, you and Heather and William will be in one of the end rooms. We will take into that room all the baby stuff you'll need, and you will always have either me or Visconti or Cowboy in the room with you. I know you don't like Visconti, Heather, but in wartime you can't always choose who you share a foxhole with. I flashed my badge to the hotel manager and told them we were guarding a witness in an important drug case, which is true as far as it goes. That way he'll not only refrain from calling the local police on our suspicious behavior, he'll have something to leak when the dynamic duo come sniffing around. I am by no means happy about a public place like this, but we have got to pose as many obstacles as possible to these two. The more obstacles they have, the more chance they'll trip over something. Plus, there's the fact that we also have to worry about the FBI. I don't think Andrea Weinmann is sitting on her hands; she is pulling out all the stops looking for us. If they swoop in on us like they did in Raleigh I want bystanders around as witnesses so they can't get too carried away. If we stayed here they could just back off and shell the place, it's so isolated. We picked up two pairs of two-way radio handsets at Radio Shack for communications. All four of the men will have one."

"I suppose Alice's room will be more or less fortified?" asked Cowboy.

"I doubt they will try a frontal assault again. They will assume we are expecting that. My guess is that if they are a lot more stupid than I think they are, they will try to get in from the balcony, off the roof, a simple rappeling drop. The problem is that Lambert is stupid, but Blanchette isn't. Most likely they will try to lure Alice out in the open somehow, and that is where this little operation is going to get very, very tricky. I want you to tack mosquito netting over the sliding doors to the balcony, Cowboy, to slow down anyone who tries to come in that way long enough so you can get in a shot. But you also may get something heavy coming through the balcony, some kind of rifle grenade or rocket or Molotov cocktail. Maybe gas to try and smoke you out. I hope the netting will bounce it off. I've got two gas masks in my bag. You and Alice will have both of them. Tori, you need to keep some partly wet gauze handy for yourself and for the baby."

"You really think they're going to walk into something this obvious, Matt?" asked Garza skeptically. "Almost a repeat of what happened in Raleigh?"

"No, I don't. Blanchette will understand that he's being set up, but we have to hurry him, convince him he's working to a deadline so he'll risk it. He is going to stand off and try to figure out exactly why we are being so ridiculously obvious, and then he is going to try and figure out some way to extract Alice. He is going to believe the baby is in the room with her."

Alice shuddered. "Okay, Matt, when do we bait the trap?"

"No time like the present," said Matt. "You got your lines down?"

"Oh, I always was a quick study. You have that number?" she asked.

"501-239-0045," said Matt.

"I'll use my own phone," said Alice, taking it from her purse and opening it up.

"Matt, are we sure about this?" sighed Heather.

"Any last minute ideas, Watson?" asked Matt. "I mean it, Heather. If you see anything in here that I'm missing, if you can come up with any alternative even now at the eleventh hour and the fifty-ninth minute, for Christ's sake, tell me!"

Heather shook her head. "Go ahead, Alice, and pray to God we're not signing our death warrants." Alice dialed the Little Rock number and listened to the answering service's recording, a flat mechanical female voice. Then they could hear the beep.

"Hoi, Mr. Wilson!" said Alice in a snooty voice. "I'm cawling for a mutual friend of ours, you know, Mr. C? I'm afraid he's very busy and can't avail himself of the usual channels, but he would like you to take a trip to the seaside, to the John Yancey Motor Inn in Kill Devil Hills, North Carolina. One of your favorite movie stars is there and perhaps you might get her autograph. You'd better proceed with alacrity, though, because she's going to be very busy soon. We hear she's going to be holding a press conference in Raleigh day after tomorrow, and Mr. C is *very* annoyed with her, if you get my drift? Not to mention Mrs. C. We *do* hope you can fit this little excursion into your busy shed-yule. Ta ta!" She closed the phone.

"Alice, no reflection on your acting talent, but Bob Blanchette is not going to believe one word of that," said Cowboy with a sigh.

"But he will know that someone is playing games with him," said Matt. "He *has* to check it out, Cowboy. He's got no choice. This business has gotten completely out of hand from his point of view, one of his partners has been killed, and he has enough sense to understand that his employers have turned on him. He *has* to wrap this up and disappear. He'll come, but God knows when or how. We've handed the initiative to him now, which is a deadly error to make, but on our part as well, we have no choice."

"What's that smell?" asked Tori suddenly.

"Alice, you might want to check out the kitchen for your scriptwriters' reference," said Matt. "This is that scene from *The Godfather* I warned you about."

In the large kitchen of the former guesthouse, John Visconti and Tony Stop were both wearing full aprons. A large pot of water was boiling on the stove and two big packets of vermicelli lay on the counter. Visconti was stirring a second pot full of fragrant red sauce with a wooden spoon, alternating stirs with rolling meatballs between his palms and plopping them into a sizzling skillet. Tony sat at the table with a partially disassembled garlic bulb in front of him, carefully slicing several large garlic cloves into paper-thin wafers with a razor blade. The women stared at them. "You guys serious?" asked Alice with a laugh. "I thought you were the macho types."

"My grandfather is as macho as dey come, but he makes a fried scampi served on a bed of tortellini parmesan that just melts in your mouth," said Tony.

"Uh, you don't have to do that. We have garlic powder in the cupboard," said Tori, fascinated enough actually to speak to Tony.

"You only use garlic powder when you can't get the real thing," explained Tony. "You ain't careful, you'll use too much, and the garlic will kill whatever you're making. The trick is to slice the cloves really thin, like this, so that they actually melt in the pan or in the sauce. How's this, John?"

"Excellent." He took the sliced garlic from Tony on a napkin and added it into the sauce, stirring gently but thoroughly. "I am grilling the meatballs first to cook some of the grease out of them so they don't ruin the sauce. We're doing spaghetti bolognese tonight because that is stereotypically expected of us for our movie, and also because it's quick and simple, but my own specialty is *agnello Fiorenza,* which means lamb of Florence," said Visconti. "Rack of lamb marinated in a special sauce of garlic, onions, black pepper, and saffron, then slow-roasted in a low oven for about ten hours, after which it is grilled over an open flame for about ten minutes to lightly crisp it around the edges. When done right, the bones of the lamb ribs are so tender that they can actually be eaten. I understand you are from Seattle, Mrs. Redmond. If you ever go back for a visit and come to my restaurant, La Stella in Bellevue, I will be happy to prepare *agnello Fiorenza* for you and your family, but I'll need some advance notice. To answer your question, Miss Silverman, there is nothing degrading about mastering an exacting and useful craft. It is a point of pride with a true Italian man that when necessary, he can prepare a better meal than his wife can."

"Besides, when ya gotta go to the mattresses like we are now, you never know when you may have to cook for twenty guys," said Tony.

"You learned that in your family?" asked Heather.

"No, I saw *The Godfather* twelve times when I was a kid," said Tony.

"What did I tell you?" asked Matt.

"Are you married, Mr. Visconti?" asked Alice, fascinated. "You don't wear a ring."

"Yes, I am married. I don't wear a ring when I am working because like a tattoo, jewelry can be identifying and incriminating, and also because I once saw a man get his finger torn off by his wedding ring during an altercation. My wife is rather socially prominent in Seattle, the owner of one of the most prestigious art galleries on Pioneer Square. Mrs. Redmond would probably recognize her name. For obvious reasons, she retains her maiden name."

"Uh…do I dare ask how this marriage came about?" queried Heather curiously.

"In a general way, I don't mind telling you," said Visconti. "Her father is a very well known real estate developer in the Northwest, a millionaire and quite the high flying tycoon. Some years ago he got into some financial difficulties and borrowed a rather substantial sum of money from me to bail himself out of those difficulties, at the usual rate of interest, of course."

"Six for five, I believe?" put in Matt.

"Yes. He then conceived the idea that he was not obligated to pay me back."

"You didn't put a horse's head in his bed or anything, did you?" asked Alice.

"No, although that scene in the movie does have an interesting provenance. The first Black Handers in this country did have a small but thriving industry poisoning horses, or threatening to poison horses if they were not paid to refrain from doing so. In the Little Italies of the time, a threat to a teamster's or merchant's carthorse was just as serious as a threat to his family. But things with this real estate tycoon back in Seattle got a little more involved. He actually went to the police and put me through the annoyance of being indicted and arrested. Nothing came of it, of course, since the evidence and the witnesses subsequently became unavailable, and all of a sudden this gentleman seemed to understand the position in which he had placed himself. One day his daughter came to see me at one of my offices, and tried to persuade me not to proceed against her father. I was quite taken with her, and I ended up by marrying her."

"I thought you guys prided yourselves on never allowing your vengeance to be bought off, no matter what?" asked Matt.

"You don't understand, Mr. Redmond," replied Visconti with a smile as cold as the Arctic winter. "That *was* my vengeance. That cowardly dog sent his own daughter to me to try and cancel his debt with her body. He placed his own life and his wealth above her honor. So I didn't just take her body, I took her life instead, quite literally. All of it."

"Jesus!" whispered Alice with a shudder.

"Oh, it turned out all right in a way," said Visconti. "We now have two sons, one of them in sixth grade and one just entering kindergarten, and a daughter aged two. She also finds that since our marriage, no one tries to cheat her or deceive her in her own business affairs."

"And your sons? Will you bring them up to follow in your so-called family business?" asked Heather, irresistably curious.

"They will choose their own destiny when they are of an age to do so, Mrs. Redmond. Or perhaps it may be chosen for them by events, as Tony's was for him. I do not believe I am being discourteous or disrespectful to our young friend when I say that life in Our Thing was not what his father wanted for him."

"If he'd lived, then I woulda gone to an Ivy League school and been a lawyer or an architect or a legit businessman, and you wouldn't be lookin' at me like I was something to scrape off your shoe, you'd be jumping for joy when I came to your house to take Tori out and telling her what a great catch I was," Tony told Heather without bitterness. "But after what happened, I couldn't never be nothing else but a wiseguy. It would have been disrespectful to my father's memory."

"Mr. Visconti, jeez, I know I should shut up but…your wife and you, how do you…?" asked Alice, flustered, waving her hands vaguely.

"We are very, very polite with one another," said Visconti. "At all times."

Dark was just falling when they finished supper. "Visconti, you're a murderin' thug and all that, but *damn*, that was good!" said Cowboy Garza. "I sure hope them Musketeers don't show up now, because I'm so full I doubt I'd be of much use."

"I've paid three hundred dollars in Hollywood restaurants for meals that weren't as good as that!" gushed Alice. "Really! You did the garlic bread, Tony?"

"It wasn't really that good," said Tony. "Usually I do it with bread my mother or my grandmother baked an hour or so before, so it's really fresh."

"I apologize for the poor quality of the wine, but the local Harris Teeter has a rather limited selection," said Visconti. "I have yet to taste an American Chianti of any worth. The best Chianti still comes from Calabria, in my opinion, although I like mine slightly sour and some do not." Suddenly Matt Redmond's cell phone rang.

"Bet you dollars for donuts that's Andrea Weinmann," he said, taking out the instrument and turning up the volume to the max. "You other guys listen up. Hello?" he said into the phone.

"Hey dere, *mon brave*. You know who dis be?" said a Cajun voice, flat and dead yet carrying. Everyone in the room could hear it. Everyone in the room froze. "You do. I jus' callin' to tell you I got you message. Redmond, you some kind of damned eejit or what? I din' think you was de kind to play de fool, but OK, you wan' play de fool? We play de fool. Mah friend heah got somethin' he wanna say. Lissen up." From the cellular phone and into the dining room came a strange sound. *Tink tink…tink tink…chink chink…chink chink…clink clink…clink clink…*

"Okay, Bob, so Luther can bang his axe blades together," said Matt calmly. "So he's a nut, just like you're a creep. These things I know. Why, exactly, are you calling me?"

"Is she really in Kill Devil Hills?" asked Bob. "I mean, lemme see if I got dis straight. You get some bitch to leave me a stupid message because you want me and Luther to come to the John Yancey Motor Inn in Kill Devil Hills. OK, maybe we might wander on down dat way. But is she really going to be there? You tell me dat."

"And you think I'll tell you the truth?" laughed Matt. "Hey, Bob, maybe she'll be there. Then again, maybe she'll be in L. A., or Chicago, or Barcelona. Why don't you and the Missing Link just come on down here and find out? I was hoping to get this done in Raleigh, but you guys took off before we could have our little heart to heart talk. Oh, by the way, too bad about your lady friend getting greased by the FBI. I'm just *all* broke up about that!"

Suddenly Blanchette laughed. "Hot damn! She really *is* with you down there, ain't she? That means you're all alone in this, ain't you? That's what I figgered. You using her for bait because you think me and that buddy of yours in the cowboy hat can take me and Luther? Does she know that?"

Alice quietly held out her hand for the phone. Matt covered the mouthpiece. "Alice, I don't think it's a good idea…"

"Please," she said. "Trust me." Matt thought briefly, and handed her the phone.

"Mr. Blanchette?" said Alice calmly. "This is Alice Silverman speaking. Yes, I will be in the John Yancey Motor Hotel for the next two days. Come down and give it your best shot, and I do mean shot. We've got a few surprises waiting for you. It's very simple, Mr. Blanchette. I am tired of this, of all of it. So I'm going to do two things. First, after my friends kill you and that big ape of yours, I am going to dance on your dead bodies. Then I am holding a press conference which will be attended by representatives of every major news media in this country, and I am going to tell them how I danced on your dead bodies, and then I will tell them what Bill and Hillary Clinton did to me. Including how they sent three psychopaths to murder a two month old baby, and how you went berserk on that yacht down in Florida and killed nine people including a United States Congressman. I don't imagine your employers will be very happy about what I have to say. I don't care if no one believes me. I understand that my career is down the toilet from that moment on, but I just don't care any more. Everyone tells me you're supposed to be so fierce and dangerous. Well, we'll see how fierce and dangerous you are. I'm hanging my ass out for you. In fact, I'm mooning you. Think you can put a bullet in my butt?"

Blanchette's voice was almost sad. "Girl, girl, you really so tired of living?" he asked.

"Tired of living like this? Yes, I am. I don't really have much choice, do I?" she sighed. "I want this over, Mr. Blanchette. One way or another. Do you understand what's going on now?"

"I do," said Blanchette. "Look, I wanna say something to you. You understand there's nothing personal in this? It's just the way it all played out. If it means anythang under de coicumstances, I seen all your movies and I liked 'em."

"Thank you, Mr. Blanchette."

"See you soon, then." The sound came again. *Tink tink…chink chink…clink clink…*Then the telephone went dead. Alice dropped it onto her plate, buried her head in her hands, and convulsed in terror for a few moments. Heather stood up and went to her and held the wretched woman in her arms.

"I will kill him with my bare hands," said Garza, to no one in particular.

"That was an astoundingly stupid thing for him to do, and it is a very good sign for us," said Visconti quietly to the shaken group around the table. "For a man of Blanchette's normal professionalism to break down to the degree that he would make a phone call like that indicates that he is very rattled indeed. He is being rushed, and he is making stupid mistakes."

The cell phone rang again where Alice had dropped it. Matt snatched it up. "I hear those axes banging together one more time, Luther, I'll jam both of them up your ass before I blow what little brains you have out of your thick skull!" he snapped.

"Er, hey, Matt," said a male voice on the phone. "Frank Hardesty here."

"Frank! Good to hear from you, man," said Matt with a sigh of relief.

"What was that about Luther Lambert and his infamous axes?" asked Hardesty curiously.

"Nothing, just some peripheral weirdness. I think the next call I get may be some kid asking me if my refrigerator is running. I appreciate your checking in. We both know you're sticking your neck out a mile by having any contact with me at all. How's things looking for us up there in La Cesspool Grande?"

"How's the weather down there on the Outer Banks?" asked Hardesty pointedly.

Matt gasped in astonishment. "How do you know we're on the Outer Banks?" he demanded. Cowboy stood up in amazement. Every eye in the room was on Matt and the phone.

"You've got a GPI in your car, courtesy of Special Agent JAP," said Hardesty.

"*Shit!*" cursed Matt. "She really did it!"

"Yep. Matt, you got some company coming. Bad company. The call went out to Quantico a few hours ago. The Conquistadors are coming for you, in force. They're assembling at Fort Bragg even as we speak."

Matt stayed silent for a long moment. "Thank you. Frank, do me a favor. Play it smart. Don't call again."

"If I was smart I wouldn't be shuffling file folders and microfiche in a sub basement. Matt, do me a favor? Take as many of those bastards with you as you can."

"You got it."

"Adios, buddy."

"Stay frosty, Frank." Matt closed the phone. "Looks like we have a change of directors. Cecil B. DeMille is taking over the picture, and he's giving us a cast of thousands."

"I heard," said Visconti. "Who are the Conquistadors?"

"Heavies right out of central casting. You've heard of the men and the helicopters in black that right wing conspiracy buffs speak of? That's them," Matt told the group in a cold voice. "They were originally an offshoot of the Delta Force back in the 80s. Under Reagan they were a legitimate, elite anti-terrorist unit comprised of Arabs and Hispanics for use in the hot spots in the Middle East and Latin America. The Arab contingent was of some use in the Gulf War. But when the Clintons got in the Arabs were disbanded, some say liquidated at the insistence of Israel, and then when Janet Reno became AG the whole unit was transferred from the Army to the Department of Justice. They're now almost all Hispanic, mostly Colombians and Sandinista Nicaraguans, but a little bit of everything else, including some former East German Stasi and Romanian Securitate."

"A left wing death squad," said Visconti.

"Precisely. Their very existence is denied, of course. They have been used for some more or less legitimate purposes like anti-drug commando raids in Colombia and Peru and Bolivia, which I suspect is window dressing for their real purpose. That is to give the Clintons and Reno some muscle who are personally loyal to them and unaccountable to any authority, insofar as any uncorrupted authority is left in this country. Even the FBI is still in theory a legitimate police agency, and there are some jobs too sticky for them to touch. Like this one."

"How long before they strike?" demanded Visconti.

"My guess is that we've got a day at most," said Matt. "They're not going to just come charging in without a plan, they will at least use satellite surveillance to give them some idea of what's going on."

"How did they find us?" asked Heather.

"While Miss Andrea and I were discussing moral relativism on the Capitol grounds, some of her boys were planting a Global Positioning Indicator in the Taurus," said Matt. "Like a fool I believed that she was alone and I didn't look for it. As you can see, Visconti, my reputation is highly overrated. You guys had the Eye in the Sky tracking you call the way down here. But that's a plus we can turn to our advantage. We can now use the Taurus to throw them off."

"That would involve dividing our forces," said Visconti. "Plus exposing the driver of the Taurus to a very high risk."

"That will be necessary anyway. We can't fit everyone into your Saturn, although when we get back up to Nag's Head we can rent another car. I am going to need a volunteer to lead these people on a wild goose chase while we set up Blanchette and Lambert at the John Yancey. The problem is, who can we really spare? And no, Tori, don't even think about it! Visconti's right, whoever drives that Taurus is going to have several dozen heavily armed and trained killer paramilitaries stalking them. Alice has to be the bait in the trap we're setting, but we're going to need all our own firepower to handle Blanchette and Lambert when they show."

"The answer is obvious," said Heather. "You're right, you men will need every gun, even this...even Tony. I would be no good in a firefight. Yield to the logic of the situation, Matt. I'll take the Taurus and head back down to Chapel Hill, just go right home. Then I'll rent a car and come back here. If I can make it as far as Chapel Hill I should be OK. I don't think there will be a commando raid by Clinton's beaner ninjas right in the heart of the liberal empire's intellectual birthplace. It would cause talk. No offense, Art."

"Hey, I'm a Texan, I got no use for beaners myself," said Garza.

"I'll do it," said Tony quietly. "Tori and her mom need to stay together. I'll take the Taurus back up to Raleigh, dump it at the airport, rent another car and haul ass back here. I'll leave now and be back in the morning."

"OK," said Matt. "I don't like splitting the group even briefly, but our hand is being forced by Uncle Slime."

"One thing," said Alice. "Tori, there is indeed something very important you can do here, and if it satisfies your lust for adventure, this is also quite dangerous in view of that electronic thingie we now know is in the Taurus. Tony, when you leave, I would like for you to take Tori back to Raleigh-Durham airport with you. Tori and my son William. My production company has an account with American Airlines. All I have to do is to make a call, and Tori will have a first class ticket to Los Angeles waiting for her at the AA desk when you get to RDU, and some money as well. Tori, I want you to take William back to L. A. I have some very good friends whom I believe will help you despite the danger. I will call them, and they will meet you at the airport and take you and William up to a place I have in Morro Bay. Tori, please? Matt, Heather, please? It's been all I could do to keep my sanity since this whole thing began, with him here and in danger."

"Agreed," said Redmond instantly.

"Absolutely," said Visconti. "This will simplify things immensely."

"Matt!" snapped Heather.

"Oh, don't worry, she'll be safe from Latin loverboy on the trip, because you're going with her," said Matt.

"*Matt!*" she cried.

"If this goes bad and the two Musketeers get me, they'll get you and Tori as well if you're anywhere around, and if they don't then we've still got Andrea and her DRT and the Conquistadors to worry about," he said. "Yes, I know that Global Positioning Indicator will make you sitting ducks for five or six hours, but if Tony sticks to 64 and then I-40 past Benson, I don't think they'll try anything on the open highway. Too many witnesses. They'll wait to see where you're going. Tony, don't drive the Taurus directly to RDU. Drop Heather and Tori and the baby in Raleigh. Nip into town on Gorman Street and leave them in a little shopping center you'll find there, and they can get a cab to the airport from there. The watchers will pick up on that, but they may figure you've stopped for gas or a Hardee's chomp or something. Then you head back onto I-40 and go to Chapel Hill, park the car at my house and hoof it down to Franklin Street, get a cab to RDU yourself and rent a car there, then come back here. Heather, you make sure you leave your .38 in the car when Tony drops you off in Raleigh," said Matt. "Don't forget and walk into an airport with a gun in your purse. Same for you and that .22 I gave you, Tori. That's all we need is for you to get busted by airport security. When you get back to Nag's Head, Tony, call my cellular or Visconti's from someplace in town and we'll tell you where we are and what's going on."

"John?" asked Tony. Visconti nodded. "Okay, I got it."

"This makes sense, Heather," said Matt quietly. "I assume you can spring for two tickets to California, Alice?"

"Absolutely," said Alice. "Heather, I agree. It makes a lot of sense. You'll love Morro Bay, believe me."

"You promised me I could come with you!" said Heather dismally to her husband.

"Yes, I know," said Matt. "And my heart has failed me now, when the time has come and death truly threatens. Your place is with our own child and with this baby. Forgive me."

"If this goes bad and I never see you again, I don't know if I will be able to forgive you," whispered Heather.

"If this goes bad, your turn and Tori's will come soon enough," said Matt brutally. "Rest assured, they'll make a clean sweep of it."

"Mrs. Redmond, you believe us to be scum," said Visconti. "Be that as it may, I am quite good at what I do, your husband is no slouch either, Agent Garza strikes me as very capable, and though he is young, Tony is not exactly Rebecca of Sunnybrook Farm. We all owe these two men and the Federals as well a very serious debt, and we will pay it. With interest. We may die, but I promise you that if we do we will be surrounded by a large pile of Clintonista dead, and on top of them will lie the bodies of Bob Blanchette and Luther Lambert. If possible, I would also like to crown such a heap with the beauteous corpse of Agent Weinmann. She annoys me. An Italian wife would be comforted and proud at that thought."

"I'm not Italian, Mr. Visconti, but I have to admit I don't find that prospect exactly displeasing myself," admitted Heather.

"Cut!" cried Alice. "That's a wrap!"

"We have to cut the movie crap and get going," said Tony. "The clock is ticking and them black helicopters are probably on the way."

Calmly Alice picked up the wiggling baby and handed him to Tori. "You have his bottles and his formula, and I put his Pampers in the trunk of the Taurus, plus the ones you have in his bag," she said. She leaned over and kissed the tiny face and was rewarded by a smile and a drool. "Goodbye, my dearest little one." She handed Heather a folded paper. "This is the address of my parents in San Jose. Take him there as soon as it's safe, if it ever is."

"You will take him there yourself!" said Heather fiercely.

"Sure," she said.

"Heather, Tony's right," said Matt. "Events have come upon us. There's no more time. *Go!*" Without a word his wife led her daughter and the baby out to the car. Matt turned to Tony. "I would rather they were entrusted to anyone else on earth but you, but my own destiny seems in a mood for practical jokes today. Heather will try to talk you into just dropping off Tori in Raleigh and bringing her back with you. Don't let her do that. Otherwise Tori may lose both her parents, and if you really care for her you won't let that happen. Drive carefully and make sure they leave their guns in the car with you, and make sure you see them get into that cab to the airport before you get back on 40."

"You got it," said Tony. "I'll be back tomorrow morning, John. Then we give Uncle Joey another toast in the best wine of all, eh?"

"See you then, kid," said Visconti. "Redmond, we need to un-ass this place now ourselves. The Saturn can hold the four of us. We should get on up to that hotel."

The others had not been gone for ten minutes and Alice had just finished making her phone calls, when Cowboy suddenly turned his head. "I hear a helicopter," he said.

Matt drew out a pair of field glasses from the canvas bag and stepped out of the door. He scanned the twilight sky and stepped back in. "Too high to tell much, and it's almost dark, but it looks like an Apache. Black. The altitude is encouraging. If it's them, they're just looking as yet. The motion from the Taurus may have attracted them when the satellite relay picked it up. We'd better be on our way. I am acting on the presumption that once we get back up into Nag's Head, into the town and along the beach strip, there will be too many witnesses for them to get too exuberant. We may see it handed back to Andrea and her DRT squad then. At least they have blue jackets with FBI on the back; the pure unmarked black would cause comment in a populated area."

"I'm ready," said Alice. Her hair was done up into a bun and she was dressed in jeans and a white sleeveless blouse, and she carried a small suitcase with the few clothing and personal items she had been able to buy in Raleigh before going into hiding at the Sheraton. "Back to fast food and daytime TV, for a while anyway. Maybe I can catch up on the latest episode of *General Hospital.* You know, I once nearly ended up on that one as a nympho nurse? Glad I had sense enough to turn it down. Soaps are the kiss of death for serious actors. Mr. Visconti, may I put this in the trunk?" Visconti went outside with her to open it. By the light from the porch, Matt and Cowboy watched her lithe body leaning over the open trunk.

"When this is all over, Art, you really need to make your move there before we let her escape back to Tinseltown," said Matt.

The older man actually blushed. "Yeah, of course I thought about it. God, who wouldn't, being so close to her twenty-four hours a day? She's been hurt real bad, maimed in her heart and soul by those two snakes in Washington, and I got this corny longing to heal that hurt."

"That's not corny, that is noble and honorable, Art. Don't ever be ashamed of it."

"But Jesus, I'm old enough to be her father!"

"Or William's," said Matt.

Garza sighed. "Come on, Matt. Let's get real. We're from even more different worlds in a way than Tony and Tori. I ain't a total fool."

"Neither is she. That's why you just might have more of a chance than you think."

"Do you trust our new partner?" asked Cowboy, nodding at Visconti.

"If this is going to work, Cowboy, we have to stop thinking in terms of trust and just go with it. It works or we die. It's like skydiving. If you thought seriously for one minute about the rationality of jumping out of an airplane, you wouldn't do it. Problem is, the airplane we're aboard is on fire and we have to jump. We can't afford to think. I believe he does have a certain crude sense of self-image which will prevent him from shooting us in the back, if that helps."

"And you trust that punk Tony with Heather and Tori?" asked Cowboy.

"The alternative is to have them here when Luther Lambert shows up for his encore. You didn't see him cut a man's head off with a single swipe. I did. I'd hand them over to Satan himself to get them out of Lambert's way. Let's go."

⋆⋆⋆

In the darkness outside a battered mobile home in the woods near Rocky Mount, Bob Blanchette and a tall, thin man were loading a heavy crate into the back of a battered blue van. "You got the two grand?" asked the man. Blanchette wordlessly handed him a roll of bills. "Thanks, Bob. Do me a favor? I'd appreciate it if you got on down the road a bit before you let him play with it," the man went on in a low voice. "He makes me kind of nervous, know what I mean?"

Accordingly, Blanchette drove the van several miles down a single lane of paved road, his lights off, before coming to Highway 64. Lambert hunched beside him, his mammoth bulk filling the passenger side of the van. He had said nothing since the phone call to Matt, simply sucking on mouthfuls of Red Man and Jolly Ranchers in silence. "Luther, you ain't ast me what's in the box?"

"What?" rumbled Lambert.

"The box I jus' bought from Leroy back there. It's a present, for you."

"A present?" asked Lambert, perking up a bit. "Like a Christmas present or a birthday present? Nobody ever give me a present before, 'cept Karen. She din't just give me Jolly Ranchers, she give me Whoppers and Big Macs and big buckets full of the Colonel's Extra Crispy, and X-Men Avengers and Superman, and once she give a whole bag full of Spiderman. I don't really like Spiderman that much," he confided. "But I din't say nothin', so's not to hurt Karen's feelings."

"That was mighty gentlemanly of you, Luther. But that's you all over, a real gent when somebody comes to know you. Thass why I figured you was about due for a present." Blanchette pulled off the road. "Come on, you kin open it now." Lambert got out of the vehicle and lumbered to the back. Blanchette opened the rear doors of the van. "Go on, it's yours." Blanchette and Leroy had labored and sweated between them to get the wooden crate into the van, but Lambert lifted the wooden crate out like it was an empty cardboard container. Blanchette handed Lambert a small crowbar, and with a few swift slashes the box was open. Luther stared at the contents, then he looked up. "For me?" he said in wonderment. "Gee, Bob, I...I don't know what to say."

"All yours, Luther. For good and all." The giant reached in and pulled out the weapon in the box, cradling and stroking it gently. "Now, I know you ain't really into guns, Luther, everybody knows you de man wid the big axes, but since we gone be maybe running into that Jew bitch and more of her crew, and they prob'ly gone have all kinds of hot stuff they be throwin' at us, I figgered you wouldn't mind usin' this l'l darling, at least at first until we can git in close."

"You bet, Bob!" exclaimed Luther. "Ah kin be Rambo!"

"You can indeed. Dass Rambo's gun. An M-60 machine gun, 7.62 caliber, complete with extra barrel and twenty belts of three hunnert and sixty rounds each. The ammo is what they call three-off. You got three kinds of rounds alternating, one after the other, a normal copper-jacket, a teflon-coated bullet for piercing body armor, and a tracer."

"Tracers is purty," cooed Lambert, fingering the ammo belts lovingly.

"They shore is. You got an assault bag there, or you can wind them belts and drape 'em off your shoulders like Rambo in the movie if you want. There's also some asbestos steel worker's gloves in there fo' when you gots to change that hot barrel."

"Less go!" demanded Luther eagerly. "Less git on down to the beach and find them so I can shoot this! I still want to do that movie star with my choppers, though. She's mighty fine, and a beautiful body like that ought to be cut up gentle and artistic, not just shot. I mean, any asshole can pull a trigger. Blades are what a real...a real..." Luther's brain ran down.

"Craftsman?" suggested Blanchette.

"Yeah!" said Luther, brightening. "Blades are what a real craftsman uses!"

"Always did admire a man who took pride in his work," said Blanchette.

✶✶✶

"The Taurus is moving, Agent Weinmann," said Frederickson to Andrea. They were in a transport helicopter just passing over Kinston at about eight thousand feet. "It's heading up Highway 12, just passing Rodanthe. They may be going to Nag's Head or Kitty Hawk, or maybe onto Highway 64 and then west."

"Thank you, Agent Frederickson," Andrea thought quickly and hard. "The satellite photos showed another vehicle parked in the yard of that house," she said. "Has it moved?"

"I'll check." Frederickson got onto the radio and in a minute reported back. "Yes. Eagle One reports that the second vehicle is now moving north on Highway 12. They seem to have split up."

"The Taurus is a decoy," said Andrea suddenly.

"How do you know that?" demanded her companion.

"Because I am starting to have a scope on how our opponent thinks. He has somehow learned or deduced that we are tracking the Taurus."

"How?" asked Frederickson.

"I know that he does have some sources of information, possibly reactionary elements within the Bureau itself, I regret to say. After we complete this mission we need to look into that. Alice Silverman and the child are in the second vehicle, and Matt Redmond is with them, I'm sure of that. Probably Garza as well. But we have to take all of them out. Tell Hammer Two that they are to intercept the Taurus and dispose of both the vehicle and the occupants, most likely Mr. Redmond's wife and possibly his daughter. The car and the occupants are to disappear, no remains, nothing is to be found. They have a Human Remains Disposal Unit on that eighteen wheeler for the women, and there is enough swampy terrain down there to get rid of the car for good. This is to be done quickly, and quietly, in the hours of darkness. There has been too much noise already and too much PR cleanup has been necessary. Ms. Reno is not happy. Redmond himself is almost certain to put up a fight unless confronted with overwhelming force." *That's the first part of my plan,* she thought. *You will be a widower soon, Matt. Then comes the sticky part. Somehow I have to take you alive, complete my assignment while keeping you alive, and then convince you that I was not the one responsible for her disappearance. I'll have to find some way to kill two birds with one stone and blame her death on Visconti and Stoppaglia. This will take time and a hell of a lot of doing, but one day we will replay that little scene on your couch, and when it's over you will love me and not her.*

XI

Nightblood

They rode down Highway 64 for a long time, in silence, Heather in the front passenger seat, Tori in the back, occasionally cooing and tickling the baby. Tony had his Beretta submachine gun and the leather bag of magazines resting between the front seats. Just as they were passing Williamston they unknowingly met the battered blue van carrying Bob Blanchette and Luther Lambert going the other way. Finally Heather sighed. "Look, Tony, you know how I feel about it all, and that's not going to change, but I do appreciate what you're doing, and I suppose I might as well be civil to you. Plus I'm dying for a cigarette. Do you mind if I smoke?"

"Them things will kill you, you know," laughed Tony. "Sure, light up. I'll crack a window."

"Tony, I'd like a change in plan when we get to Raleigh. I want you to drop Tori off and…"

"No," said Tony. "Matt warned me you might try and talk me into letting you come back with me. I already had him shove that .357 of his up my nose once." A quarter mile behind them a number of unmarked vehicles with blue flashing lights on the top pulled across the westbound lane of Highway 64. Van doors opened and barricades were pulled out as the FBI set up a roadblock. Three miles ahead, another team of FBI was doing the same, blocking off the eastbound lanes. "No offense, Mrs. Redmond, I think you're a hell of a lady and I don't blame you for being on my case. You wouldn't be much of a mother if you weren't. But I meant it, you and Tori need to stay together. Your husband is right. Let us take care of this."

"It's man's work, is that it?" spoke up Tori from the back.

"It's *our* work," said Tony.

"I should think that the careers of Ms. Weinmann and Ms. Martin demonstrate sufficiently that women can engage in violence on both sides of the law just as well as men can," said Heather.

"It ain't a question of whether they *can*, Mrs. Redmond. It's a question of whether they *should*. It's bad enough that men do this kind of thing. If women ever start doing it then there ain't much hope for the human race. Women are supposed to give life, not take it."

"Call me Heather," she sighed. "Is that a little gem of wisdom you got from this grandfather of yours they call The Butcher?"

"Nah. When Dom was growin' up the whole question didn't even exist. I don't know as he's ever even thought about it. I do sometimes, though. It just seems true to me." They sped on through the darkness. "Traffic's kind of light tonight," he observed.

"Very light," agreed Heather. "I guess everyone's waiting until the Labor Day weekend to go to the beach. Looks like we're all alone on the highway."

"Yeah, I noticed," said Tony. "There's no headlights behind us and none coming on. You got a feeling about this? I do."

"I think we need to get off this highway," said Heather.

"Yeah. Me, too. There won't be any flights out of Raleigh-Durham to L.A. until the morning, so we got some time to take the scenic route. Take a look at the map and see if there's any place we can get off. What's that to the right of us, running parallel?"

"It's a fire road," said Heather, turning on the overhead light. "Tony, we're coming up on a little town called Robersonville. If you get off on state highway 13 South you can cut down to Greenville and get on 264, then keep on heading west to Raleigh."

"They'll still be able to follow wherever we go," said Tori. "The car is bugged, remember?"

"Yeah, but it won't hurt to zig and zag a bit," said Tony. "I don't like this empty highway."

Tori twisted around and looked behind her. "There's something coming up behind us. No lights. It's—it's in the air." Suddenly the car shook with sudden vibration and a black shape hurtled above them like a shark in the depths of the ocean beyond the sun's reach.

"That's a copter, flying with no lights," said Tony calmly. "It's them. Tori, hang on to the baby. Heather, brace yourself." Tony killed his own headlights. Then he slowed, slid evenly onto the shoulder, and wrenched the car down the embankment and onto the dirt fire road that ran parallel to 64. They hurtled along the dirt road in the darkness beside the towering Carolina pines. Tony saw a pale expanse to the right where the firebreak road branched northward. He slowed to a crawl, turned in, and drove about a hundred yards into the woods. He pulled over under a stand of pines and turned off the engine. "If they're tracking us, they'll know we've stopped. They'll send that copter back to investigate. You guys get out of the car and move off a bit into the woods."

"Why?" asked Heather.

"Because it may be a helicopter gunship and they may blast the car sky high once they realize we're onto them. Meanwhile, I'm gonna do something."

"What?" asked Heather.

"I'm going to see if I can find that damned tracking device and dump it," said Tony. "The game is up now. It will be under the car somewhere, or over one of the tires."

The women moved off into the pines, Tori clutching the bundled baby and his bag, while Tony took out a penlight and crawled under the car. For the next several minutes he scoured the axles and the tire wells and finally found a small black box with a glowing red light glued to the inside of the rear fender with a plastic, gooey substance. He ripped it out and held it up. "Bingo!" He tossed it into the woods just as a wind filled the little grove of pines and the demented whistling of a helicopter in the rather misnamed "whispered engine" mode filled the air. They could see the black hovering form sliding above them, the shark in the sunless sea once again circling for prey. Tony slid the passenger door of the Taurus open and pulled out his submachine gun. Suddenly a spotlight slashed from the side of the copter, sweeping the ground, searching for them. Tony snapped up the folding stock of the Beretta, leaned on the roof of the car, chambered a round, and aimed. The minute the searchlight hit the Taurus he squeezed off a long burst, flame spurting from the machine pistol's muzzle, and the searchlight shattered and went out, returning the lane to darkness. The copter leaped into the air and vanished. Baby William, awakened by the noise and frightened, began to howl. "Back into the car!" Tony called. "Quick!" The two women and the screaming baby jumped back into the Taurus.

"Okay, Stallone, where to now?" said Heather. "Back towards Williamston or on towards Raleigh? I figure they've got roadblocks on both lanes."

"So do I. We go for a drive in the country," said Tony. "Sooner or later we have to turn the headlights back on and that's hanging out a sign for them. We find a place to hole up and wait for daylight, then try to get back onto a paved road."

At the western roadblock down on 64, Special Agent Sammy Wong shouted out on a bullhorn to his heavily armed Dynamic Reaction Team, "Attention, K-Mart shoppers! The GPI gave off a tamper alarm so we've no more Eye in the Sky, and Eagle Three reports receiving ground fire, so we're off and running! This is now an official Fugitive Recovery Action and as legal as the day is long! They've shot at Federal agents, boys and girls, and you know what that means! Our asses are now officially covered, we have free fire zone authorization, and it's open season on white trash! Come on, boys and girls, we have three dead agents these bitches need to pay for! Let's bring Ms. Reno both ears and the tail this time, and let's show her the DRT can do the job faster and neater than our colleagues in the Conquistadors!"

"Go team!" yelled someone. Several of the female agents jumped up and down like cheerleaders, waving their M-16s in the air. "Gimme a

D!" they yelled. "Gimme an R! Gimme a T! DRT! DRT! *Yaaaaaaaay!*"

"Hammer Four, this is Hammer Two," said Wong on his radio. "Move in. Two ground units move north along the fire roads, get Eagle Three's light fixed as fast as you can, and in the meantime tell Eagle Two to sweep that area and find our targets." He switched frequencies. "Queen Bee, this is Hammer Two. Do you read, over?"

"Queen Bee, over," said Andrea's voice on the radio.

"They found the GPI and they took a pot shot at Eagle Three. We're going to hunt them down now. We'll keep it sanitized. This is isolated terrain, not many potential witnesses, and once we get them spotted from the air we'll move in. We've got a tow truck for the car and we have the HRDU with us. They'll be hamburger before morning."

"Don't fuck it up, Hammer Two," said Andrea. "My head isn't the only one on the line here, you know. I want to be able to tell Ms. Reno and the First Lady that this mission was successfully completed by the legitimate forces of law and order, and not by foreign mercenaries. Keep me posted. Queen Bee out."

Tony found a paved highway about two miles down the fire road and turned left, his lights still out. Tori had calmed the baby down and was rocking him and quietly singing to him in the back. About half a mile down the road the waning moon went behind a cloud and the road became almost pitch black. "I gotta turn the lights back on," said Tony grimly. "I know it's dangerous as hell, but so is going down this back road with no lights. Suicidal, in fact. We could run off the road into a tree, or a mack truck could come around a curve and wipe us out. We need to find somewhere to hole up until dawn. Driving with lights, like we got to, a copter could spot us from ten thousand feet. In the daytime we can blend in with other cars on the road, at least a little."

High in the sky, the observer in Eagle Two said, "I just saw headlights come on."

"Shouldn't we call Dad?" asked Tori.

"What is he going to do?" asked Heather calmly. "He and Cowboy have another life to save, and for all we know they may be in the same situation as us. If not, he'd only worry himself sick. I agree with Tony. We need to get off the road until daylight." Another half mile down the road, and a deserted, boarded up concrete block gas station loomed spectrally on the right, a weathered Sunoco sigh hanging half on its hinges from a gibbet-like post and rusted pumps in line at the front. Tony pulled into the station and around to the side, the tires crunching over old cardboard boxes and trash. He turned around and back in under the station's far wall, the front of the car pointed towards the highway, and killed the lights.

"The lights just went off," said Eagle Two's observer. "Bet you a week's pay that's our little Thelma and Louise down there."

"You girls see if you can get some sleep," said Tony, getting out of the car with his submachine gun. "Don't worry, I'll be around."

"Mom, can you take William for a bit?" asked Tori after a while. "I'd like to stretch my legs too." Her mother was silent. "Mom, I'm going to have to talk to him sooner or later." Heather held out her arms for the infant.

Tori found him sitting on a crate under a tree a little ways away, the submachine gun on his lap. The night air was warm but not oppressively hot, and air was filled with crickets and whirring cicadas. The moon was back out and so she could see him dimly. "Dad is right, isn't he? You do love me in your own savage way, as he put it?"

"Yeah," said Tony. "I don't know why. We call it the Thunderbolt. Sometimes it just happens, like a bolt of lightning. Nothing you can do about getting hit by lightning."

"The problem is, I don't know if I can handle being loved by a savage. Tony, look, I'm not trying to pick on you or anger you, but I want you to explain something to me. What, exactly, is the difference between you and that maniac who was clinking his axes at us over the phone tonight?"

"The difference between mean and crazy," said Tony. "Lambert is crazy. I'm mean. I ain't gonna lie to you, Tori. I can be real mean, although not with you. You're special, although I know you think I'm just saying that. But I ain't never mean without a reason. I get mean when somebody lies to me, or backstabs me, or tries to cheat me out of money, or hurts or insults my family."

"You kill people for money," said Tori. "How can you do that? How can you take a human life over little green pieces of paper?"

"Money is important to us, Tori, probably a lot more than in the world you grew up in. And yeah, some of us are just plain greedy. Too many, and it's destroying Our Thing. There's more important things than money, sure, money's not everything, but it is *something.* Not just so we can buy all these things like the silk suits and the caddies and the twenty-dollar cigars, but because we more than most understand that in this world, money is power. In this world if you don't have power then the ones who do will walk all over you. That's what makes us different, Tori. We don't let nobody walk on us. We reach out and we take the power into our own hands. The power of money, the power of the gun, the power of telling other people what to do and then backing it up."

"That's terrorism," said Tori.

"Not really, at least not the kind you're thinking of. Oh, gee, how the hell can I explain this? Okay, listen up, Tori, because this is the only time I am ever going to discuss any of this with you. A year ago, my grandfather called me into the basement of his house. With him around a big table were a whole bunch of other men, guys I grew up with, guys I remember coming to the house at Christmas and Easter and giving me presents, guys whose sons I played with and whose tables I'd eaten dinner at. They were my family, all of them. On the table was a gun and a knife, a long dagger from Italy. I was wearing my best suit. I understood how incredibly lucky I was to get that summons at my age. Some guys don't get straightened out until they're in their forties, and some never do. Dom stood up and spoke to me in Italian. He asked me if I was willing to do this, to become a part of This Thing of Ours, if I would come from the hospital bed of my dying son if I got a call from my boss, and I said I would. I meant it, Tori, and you need to understand that. Dom told me the rules, even though I knew them already. You never violate the wife or the daughter or the sister of any other member, you never use your hands on any other member, and you never, ever reveal the secrets of Our Thing, to anyone. I am breaking that rule for you, now. Maybe that tells you a little of how much I want you to try and understand this, how much I understand that you have to know this about me. Then he asked me which finger I shoot with. I held up my right finger and he pricked it with a pin until the blood came and dripped on a paper picture of Saint Anthony, my patron saint, and then I held the paper in my cupped hands while Dom set it on fire with a match, and told me in Italian, 'By the gun and the knife you will live, and by the gun and the knife you will die. This is the way you will burn if ever you betray the secrets of La Cosa Nostra.' Tori, on that day I became the equal of any *pezzonovante*, any big shot in America or the world, because what I swore that day wasn't just an oath, it was a statement about my life. A statement that I would live by the rules of my world, not yours, and that my destiny would be decided by myself and by my own people, not by yours."

"And what if your destiny is to end up like your father, murdered and left in the trunk of a car?" cried Tori.

"Then that's how it will play out. Tori, I chose to live this way. I still could have been that lawyer or stockbroker or architect, right up until the last minute. But I didn't choose that. Now you think all this is bad, I'm sure. You think the people with power shouldn't just appoint them-selves, they should be elected through democracy and all that crap. Yeah, well if democracy is so great, why are we running through the woods tonight? Who the hell is dis who's after us? It's your fucking democracy, dat's who! Look who democracy give us as a leader? A pig who snorts five kilos of coke a month and sends *upazzis* with axes to kill babies, who gets off on holding a gun on a woman and watching while she gives head to his own wife. And any time anybody raises too much hell about it all, he starts launching missiles and blowing things up all over the world. Sorry, I'm wandering off the subject."

"No, you sound like my Dad," laughed Tori. "I have heard him turn discussions about flower shows, mathematics, and knock-knock jokes into tirades against the Clintons." She was silent for a while. "I don't think I could ever marry you, Tony," she said. "I know you haven't asked, but I don't think I could. I can't be Diane Keaton who turns Catholic and goes to church and lights candles for your soul, knowing full well what you do all day at the office, so to speak."

"If that's the way it is, that's the way it is," said Tony. "It don't change how I feel about you. There's something else, though. I won't ask you to decide now, it's just something to think about. A lot of friends of ours have girl friends as well as wives—no, wait a minute, hear me out. Yeah, a lot of them have girl friends, sometimes a lot of girl friends. But sometimes, for some of dese guys, someone really special comes along. He ends up staying with her for thirty years, setting up a whole separate home with her, having children with her. Sometimes he's married, sometimes he's not, sometimes he can't marry this special girl for one reason or another, maybe she's already married herself, or she's from a family of cops, or she used to be a hooker, or she's Jewish or Puerto Rican. Often she leads her own separate life in many ways. But he never fools around on her, and he never marries anyone else if he's single. When he wants peace, when he wants to escape from the life we lead for a time, even if it's only for a few hours, when he's scared or confused or depressed, he turns to her. We have a name for this woman. She is called *commare,* the companion of the heart. It's not much of an offer, Tori, but if you won't marry me it's the best I can do. If you decide it ain't good enough, then that's the way it is. I'll go back to New York and try to forget you. But I never will."

"You're just determined to make this hard for me, aren't you?" she asked mournfully.

"The important stuff in life is never easy," said Tony. "*Shh!*" Tori looked up and suddenly she noticed that the crickets and cicadas had fallen silent. About two hundred yards away, down the road but concealed by the trees, they heard an engine approach and stop, and several car doors open and close softly. Tony took her hand and ran back to the Taurus. He opened the door and leaned in, grabbing up the leather bag of ammunition.

"What's wrong?" asked Heather.

"We got company," Tony told her. "Tori, take the baby, Heather, you get behind the wheel. I'm going to check things out. The very minute you hear any shooting or other noise, you start the car and haul ass out of here!"

"What about you?" asked Tori, just as the woods around them exploded into gunfire. Bullets shattered the windshield and the windows of the Taurus, showering the screaming women with glass. The muzzle flashes from M-16s and 9-millimeter pistols twinkled and flickered in the darkness all around them. Bullets exploded the tire and riddled the engine. Tony dragged Heather and the baby out by force and they ran around the corner of the old gas station. He kicked in the rotten wooden door and they tumbled into the building. Bullets whined and ricocheted off the cinderblock walls. William Silverman once again woke up and bawled his small but powerful lungs out in outrage at all the noise and disturbance.

"Hug the floor and stay there!" ordered Tony. He slung the leather bag of ammunition for the Beretta over his shoulder.

"Where are you going?" cried Tori.

"I'm going to draw them off you," he said.

"That's stupid! There are too many of them!" yelled Heather.

Tony leaned over and whispered to her, "Yeah, I know. But it's better this way. Now she won't have to choose." Then he was out the door. He leaped into the woods just as the cars and vans screeched up and the searchlights came on. Tony hit the dirt and began belly crawling further into the woods. A voice rang out on a bullhorn. "*Occupants of the 1996*

Ford Taurus! We are Federal agents! Throw your weapons out the door and come out with your hands up! You will not be harmed! This will be your only warning! Come out now with your hands in the air!"

A heavy, wheezing FBI agent came crashing through the underbrush, sweating and cursing in his flak jacket, waving his M-16, silhouetted clearly in the spotlights. Tony leveled his Beretta from the prone position and fired a short burst that shattered both the man's kneecaps. He fell to the ground with a yell, writhing. Tony leaned over and fired another short burst into the top of the agent's skull. He kicked and arched against the ground and died.

"What the hell was that?" yelled someone from behind the searchlights. Tony knelt against a pine tree, slid the barrel of his Beretta through the foliage, and fired two more short bursts that smashed two of the searchlights. "Shit, they're in the woods!" bellowed the voice. There was a flurry of motion and in the glare of the headlights and the remaining spot, Tony saw a human form stand and turn. He squeezed the trigger and emptied out the rest of the magazine in a long volley, and he saw the form jerk and heard her scream; it was a woman agent. *"Lauren!"* cried out a man in agonized horror. Over it all rang the howling cries of the baby inside the gas station. The woods exploded again in flaming gunfire as the FBI agents blasted away at Tony's muzzle flashes in the dark woods, their bullets slicing into the pines and showering him with fragments. Tony rolled, and as he did so he felt the hard canister of Matt's CS gas grenade in his pocket. He pulled out the grenade, ran forward blindly through the bushes until he was as close as he could get, then he pulled the pin and popped the spoon on the canister and hurled it, sailing high over the line of cars and vans and landing in the midst of his enemies, belching the terrible white cloud. *"Jesus shit! Gas!"* someone yelled, and half a dozen figures broke and ran, choking and gasping, fleetingly visible in the headlights. Others could be seen fumbling to pull gas masks from their cases in the smoky glare. Tony already had another magazine in his weapon and with a series of seven and eight-round bursts he cut down two more FBI, saw them drop and flop and try to crawl. He fired more bullets into their bodies until his bolt locked back again and they lay still, then slapped another magazine into the machine pistol. Some of the gas reached him, making his own eyes water and burn.

Two FBI, Special Agent in Charge Wong and Special Agent Tomchak, charged the front door of the gas station. They emptied the magazines of their M-16s into the door on full automatic, reloaded, and then kicked it in, blundering into the former garage bay area, blinded by gas and by rage. A white feminine hand slid out from behind a door and fired a single .38 bullet into the skull of Special Agent Stan Tomchak, who collapsed onto the floor like a poled ox. All Wong could hear was the screams of the baby; that sound and the dose of tear gas was driving him mad. He pulled his 9-mil automatic and fired at the sound of the baby's cries, and to his amazement he was answered by a series of small flashes and pops in the dark, each flash lighting up the face of a beautiful teenaged girl with fire in her eyes. Each flash also seemed to produce an odd sensation in his chest and stomach and neck; Wong looked down and saw that he was bleeding to death. He looked up again just in time to catch Tori's last .22 hollow point in his eye. It cored his brain like an apple and he was dead before he hit the floor. Heather ran forward, snatched up the M-16 from Tomchak's dead hands, broke a window, and emptied it into the darkness at every flicker of motion she saw.

Tony surrendered all pretense of planning or thought. For the first time he felt the power of the true *furio sangue*, the Latin equivalent of the Northmen's ancient berserk. Heedless of any danger, seeking only to kill, he charged forward and blazed away with his submachine gun. All of a sudden the Federals simply broke and ran in panic. He leaned against one of their vans and fired burst after burst into their backs as they threw down their weapons and ran into the woods. Then he leaped among the vehicles, firing, reloading, firing. More muzzle flashes were around him and he felt a white hot sear across his face as a bullet creased him, and then a blow as another bullet slammed into his right thigh, but he fired and loaded, fired and loaded until there was no more ammunition.

Then it was the Charter Arms .44 Bulldog that burst and flamed, smashing open the skulls and the bellies of one FBI agent after another. Tony pulled one cowering FBI man out from under a car, jammed the muzzle of .32 caliber Saturday Night Special Visconti had given him through his crunching teeth and pulled the trigger. Then he grabbed up an M-16 and chased down the one FBI agent who still eluded him, a small wiry black man who dodged around one of the vans, firing wildly with a pistol. Tony ripped open the door of the van; a woman's pale face looked up at him from the floor and she raised a gun. He pulled the M-16's trigger but the weapon was empty. She fired, but the bullet cut through his jacket and missed. He shoved the rifle barrel through her eye and into her brain like it was a spear, then pulled it out and went after the black man again. He leaped up into the driver's side of the van, pulled himself up onto the roof, rolled over and off the other side and onto the FBI agent. They grappled on the ground, then Tony leaped to his feet, reversed the empty rifle, and clubbed the agent to death, beating him and beating him until the M-16's brain-covered butt finally broke off. Then Tony stood up. All was silent except for the chirping crickets in the warm summer night and the crying of a very tired baby.

"*Tori!*" he called out. "Tori! Tori, for God's sake, answer me!" he croaked.

"Tony?" came a cry from inside. "Tony? Are you OK?"

"I…I think I got 'em all. Yeah," he said looking around. "Yeah! I got all the motherfuckers! Every last one! Jesus, I can't believe it! I got 'em all!" He raised the smashed rifle in the air and whooped dementedly. "Look at me, ma, I'm on top of the world!"

Heather came running out of the gas station and up to his side. "Hey, Jimmy Cagney, you're hit. You're bleeding," she said.

"They ran away!" he cackled. "The big bad FBI ran away from one guy with balls enough to stand up to them! I don't fucking believe it! They ran away!"

"Of course they did," said Heather. "They are cowards and bullies. Maybe one day the rest of America will learn that, and then we can all watch them run away." She sat him down against the tire of one of the vans and undid his belt buckle, pulling down his trousers to expose the wound in his leg. She pulled her blouse out of her waist and ripped off a long strip, which she folded and shoved down onto his wound to stop the bleeding. "Oh, Tony, your face!" she whispered.

"Hey, I was gettin' tired of that Little Blue Eyes moniker anyway," he laughed. "Now de guys can start callin' me Scarface!"

Heather stroked his hair. "You really do love her, don't you? God, why couldn't you have been someone else? Why couldn't you have been the lawyer or the architect or the stockbroker your father wanted you to be?"

"Because this is the way it's played out, and be glad. Could someone else have done this?" asked Tony, waving at the carnage around them.

"Mom, what's happening out there?" called Tori.

"I'm taking off your boyfriend's pants!" yelled Heather.

"Gimme your phone," gasped Tony.

"What? Why?" asked Heather.

"Looks like you get your change in plan after all, Heather," said Tony. "You know you ain't gonna make it to California on your own, not with this bunch after you, and now I'm out of action, damn it all! It's time we sent a message to the fort and hollered for the cavalry."

"What are you talking about?" demanded Heather.

"I'm calling New York," said Tony.

XII

The Empire Strikes Back

The sun was coming up over the Atlantic. Matt Redmond and John Visconti watched it rise together over the breaking surf from the roof of the John Yancey Motor Hotel. From the street side the first sounds of traffic were audible. Matt felt around in his pocket. "Damn! I'm out of cigars!"

"Try one of mine," said Visconti, handing him a long metal tube. "They're not your Domincans, but they're quite good."

"Di Nobili?" asked Matt. "Of course, what else would a don smoke?" He opened the tube, and Visconti lit the cigar for him as well as one of his own.

"I'm not a don, although when I go back to Sicily on a visit, all the hotel managers and waiters call me by the operatic name of Don Giovanni. But I never had any desire to get into management, so to speak. Too many headaches."

"Oddly enough, I feel the same way about my job," laughed Matt. "The day I get forced behind a desk is the day I retire." There was a burst of static from their walkie talkies. "Anything?" came Cowboy Garza's voice.

"Just the usual early morning joggers and old guys in Bermuda shorts walking their dogs," said Matt into his radio. "Hell, they may all be undercover Feds, for all we know. But no sign of the two mopes we're waiting on, no. How's our lady?"

"She's asleep. You get any shut-eye yourself, Matt?"

"A couple of hours. How about you?"

"I dozed a bit."

"Any word from the Taurus party?" asked Cowboy.

"No, which I choose to regard as good news. He should have dropped them off by now and be headed back. Heather should give me a call from the airport soon, probably mad as a wet hen because Tony wouldn't bring her back here."

As if in response, Visconti's cell phone rang. He opened it and answered it. "Yes?" He listened calmly for a while. "*Grazie.*" He closed his phone and looked up. "Some bad news, I am afraid. The Taurus was intercepted by the FBI on the highway just outside a town called Robersonville. There was a gun battle. They got away, and the two women and the baby are all right so far, but they lost the Taurus and Tony has been shot. They have commandeered some kind of government vehicle, and they are trying to make it to Virginia Beach."

"Virginia Beach?" yelled Matt. "Why? What the…who was that? Tony?"

"No, someone I know in New York. Tony decided, and I believe decided correctly, that any further attempt for the women and the child to reach California via Raleigh Durham airport was no longer feasible, and that his party needed help. We have some reliable people in Virginia Beach and Norfolk, and Dominic LaBrasca is sending some more down from New York by Lear jet, including a doctor. If they can connect successfully, they will be safe. I know you don't like the idea of escalating the involvement of Our Thing in this, but in view of the increased Federal efforts to kill us all, I think it makes sense."

Matt ripped his cell phone out of its sheath and dialed. "If they're headed back this way they may be in range." He heard Heather's phone ring. Finally he got a pickup. "Hi, you've reached the Heather house on wheels!" said his wife. "Matt?"

"Why the *hell* didn't you call me?" yelled Matt. "Where are you and what is happening?"

"I didn't call you because for all I knew they hit you at the same time and you might be dead, and if that was true I didn't want to know, because then I would go completely to pieces and I wouldn't be any good to Tori and William," snapped Heather. "I didn't call you because I was scared you would drop everything and try to come and get us, and get Alice Silverman killed in the process! Matt, they were on us not two hours out of Hatteras! They're going to be on you any minute! Get out of there, never mind Blanchette and Lambert! This is survival now."

"How's Tony doing?" asked Matt

"He has half his face torn off by a bullet, and another bullet in his hip. The bleeding is stopped and I've sterilized the wounds with alcohol from the first aid kit, but that's about all I can do. We're supposed to be meeting some kind of Mafia doctor in Virginia Beach. I think he'll make it, but he's semi-conscious now. By the by, we're both right about him. He is a scummy hoodlum, and he's also a one-man army. He fought at least a dozen of them, he killed about half and the others broke and ran into the woods like the egg-suck dogs they are. We borrowed one of the FBI's cars. We can monitor their radio transmissions and they're going berserk trying to find us, running around like chickens with their heads cut off, nationwide APB, the whole nine yards. Tori killed a man, although it hasn't hit her yet."

"He was trying to shoot the baby!" said Tori indignantly in the background.

"Matt, hang up, get that girl out of there, save her and save yourself! We're OK for now, but if they catch us we're all dead this time, and there's nothing you can do! Save Alice! By the by, how the hell do you know about it, anyway?"

"Mr. Visconti's people keep him informed as to what is going on, unlike my own wife," said Matt in exasperation. "Sorry, Watson, I'm out of line. But I still think I'm going to paddle your behind the next time I see you."

"Business before pleasure, dear. I mean it, you need to beat feet out of there, now!"

"I'll take it under advisement. OK, all the usual mushies taken as read?" Heather hung up on him. Matt closed his phone.

"You are a very lucky man to have such a woman," said Visconti.

"I know, and I pray to God I haven't thrown her life away as well as my own. Sounds like Tony's hit pretty bad. I hope he makes it. If it helps anything, your young goombah seems to have covered himself with glory. Heather says he took out half a dozen of Clinton's Finest and reduced the rest of them to a panic-stricken rout. If you'd fought that hard for Mussolini, a lot of history would have been different."

"We fight for ourselves and for our own honor. Not for strangers," said Visconti.

"My wife made a recommendation I think we need to follow, and that is to change location. This little ambush was meant for Blanchette and Lambert, not the Conquistadors. We're trying to catch a couple of snakes, not a whole serpentarium."

"I agree," said Visconti.

"Let's go down and get our girl ready to shift."

Up and down coastal road Highway 12, the roadblocks were already being set up. Over fifty FBI agents bristling with weapons, many wearing flak jackets and helmets, were massed behind the southern barricade. Snipers were taking up positions on the rooftops of motels and businesses. Andrea Weinmann was frantically directing her people here, there, everywhere, poring over a street map. She saw her executive officer moving through the press. "Frederickson! What the hell is the problem raising Hammer Two?" she shouted.

"Oh, did I forget to mention that, Special Agent Weinmann?" he sneered, anger in his eyes. "We did finally hear from Hammer Two. What the fuck is left of Hammer Two!"

"*What?*" cried Andrea.

"Those redneck bitches bopped their way out of it!" shouted Frederickson. "That Taurus wasn't a decoy, it was an ambush! That cracker bastard in there in the hotel lured the Bureau into a trap! There was some kind of goddamned commando team waiting on our people, and they were cut to pieces! It was a fucking massacre! Eight more dead agents! Sammy Wong, Stan Tomchak, Lauren Cipriani, Jimmy Withers,

Jennifer Dowling, Jaime Mendoza, Phil Brooklier, Curtis Moss, *dead!* Steve Feldstrom, Ed Gein, Fred Tarnowski, and Susan Bellmore in critical condition, and all the rest wounded in some way! "

"That's impossible!" gasped Andrea, stunned.

"There were at least a dozen of them, heavy hitters with full auto and tear gas and explosives, real pros! God knows who the hell they are or why they are involved. You sent the Conquistadors to the wrong place! Why does the phrase 'complete failure of intelligence' seem to float around in my mind here, Andrea? That and the phrase 'criminal incompetence'?"

"Let's leave the crucifixion for later, shall we, and concentrate on digging these rats out of their hole?" suggested Andrea frigidly. "Let's get done what we were sent here to do and when we get back up to Washington you can pencil-whip my ass in your report all you want."

"OK," snarled Frederickson. "Let's do it."

"I'm going to call him and direct him to surrender now," said Andrea, opening her cell phone. "And don't look at me like that. You know this is just *pro forma,* but it has to be done. We have to dot every i and cross every t." She dialed Matt's cell phone number.

Alice, dressed in jeans and running shoes and a pale green pullover sweater, was just finishing her minimal packing in the hotel room when Matt's cell phone rang. He snapped it open. "Heather?" he said anxiously.

"Matt, we've got the hotel surrounded," said Andrea Weinmann's voice. "This is it, Matt. The game is over. You and Garza come out of there, no weapons, hands in the air, and you'd better have Alice Silverman with you. It's over, Matt. You give up to us now or else we've got some gentlemen in black fatigues who will be dealing with you."

"Yes, I know. The Conquistadors. I agree, Andrea, the game is over. You sent your people to murder my wife and my daughter. I told you what would happen if you did that. Pray to whatever God you may still believe in to receive your soul, Andrea. Because if it lies within my power, today is the day you will die."

"And just who were your commando friends who were waiting for us?" demanded Andrea heatedly. "Some kind of right wing Contra death squad? Colombian narco-mercenaries? Spetznatz you managed to borrow from that Russian fascist friend of yours, Rozanov? How does one go about scraping up a private army to commit treason and rebellion these days?"

"You remember how you said you wanted one of those dreaded white men who once conquered the world, Andrea?" asked Matt. "You should have gone chasing after the Taurus. You would have found one." He closed his phone. "This is it. We run for the Saturn and try to smash our way through, and when that doesn't work we litter this shoreline with dead Federals until it looks like Omaha Beach, so that when it's all over Bill and Hillary Clinton will know that there are still a few free men left in this land."

"Lookin' forward to it," growled Cowboy Garza, jacking a 12-gauge slug into his shotgun. The Ruger Mini-14 was slung over his shoulder. Visconti was carrying his Russian sniper's rifle and had his *lupara* slung over one shoulder. Alice reached up to Garza's face, pulled it down, and gave him a passionate kiss.

"Let's go," she said.

"All units move into position," said Andrea into her radio. "As soon as you get a clear shot, open fire." *Matt! Matt! Are you insane? Why, Matt?* she screamed inside.

A battered blue van rolled up behind the long files of FBI men. "That's them," said Luther, his voice cold as a demon of the tomb. "They killed Karen."

"Yep," said Blanchette, his voice equally icy. "That's them."

One of the agents swaggered up to the driver, and another sauntered to the passenger side. "The street is closed," he said.

"I don' think so," said Bob Blanchette.

"What the fuck do you mean you don't...?" The silenced .45 in Blanchette's hand coughed and blew the FBI man's brains out.

Simultaneously a brawny tattooed arm lashed out from the passenger side of the van, seized the second FBI man by the throat, crushed his windpipe, twisted, lifted the man from the ground and shook him like a terrier shaking a rat, then threw him aside like a dead rag. Blanchette floored the accelerator and the van leaped forward.

"*Oy gevalt!*" shrieked Andrea, leaping aside just in time to avoid being run down by the van. Several of the FBI fired wildly at the van, popping out the rear windows.

Blanchette slammed on the brakes. He turned to Lambert. "Oh, hell, Luther," he said. "You ever get the urge to really let it all hang out? Know what I mean, just kind of go all *loup-garou* and kill everything that moves?"

"Yeah!" agreed Luther enthusiastically.

"Well, why the hell not?" He slapped the giant jovially. "Less have ourselfs a *ball*, Luther! Reckon Slideen would want us to! Just don't forget that bitch in the hotel, OK?"

"Oh, I won't fergit, Bob," laughed Lambert happily. They both kicked their doors open and rolled out into the street. Blanchette rolled left and came up with his own weapon of choice, simple and deadly, a bolt action Enfield .303 rifle with a telescopic sight he had zeroed to the point where he could drive nails at four hundred yards, as well as several pistols hanging from a web belt on his waist and a shoulder holster rig. Lambert was an apparition, a giant bearded ogre holding the M-60 and over four thousand rounds in the belts draped and wrapped across his back and dangling from his shoulders. On his back was slung the extra barrel for the M-60 and his two axes. He was carrying well over a hundred pounds on his body, as lightly as if the ammo and the weaponry were Styrofoam. The street full of FBI agents stared at him, stunned. He calmly took out a pack of Red Man, stuffed a wad of tobacco in his mouth, then asked in a voice that echoed even over the rumble of the surf, "Well, you assholes gonna use them guns, or jump up and down and shit snowballs?"

Then he opened fire. He sprayed the street with bullets like the machine gun was a garden hose spitting death. Frederickson hurled himself on top of Andrea and pushed her to the asphalt as the leaden scythe swept over them. They crawled under the communications van. "Thanks, Fred," said Andrea, shaken. "I owe you one."

"One what? One blow job?" asked Frederickson. "I hear you give the best in the Bureau."

"One blow job it is. Get that crazy motherfucker with the machine gun and you've got an overnighter at my place. Get the Silverman bitch for me as well, and you've got a long weekend in the Bahamas," said Andrea grimly.

"Now that's what I call management motivation!" grinned Frederickson. "'Scuse, please." He whipped out his 9-millimeter automatic and rolled out from under the van. "Jackson! Rodriguez! Axelrod! Get your asses in gear and come with me!"

Blanchette was crouched behind a dumpster, calmly chambering round after round and shooting it out with the FBI snipers on the roof. They sprayed him with full automatic fire, riddling the dumpster and popping holes in the asphalt and concrete all around him, and he fired back a single shot. One shot, one hit. FBI marksman after marksman flipped backwards under the impact of Blanchette's dum-dum bullets, bleeding out their lives on the tarpaper roofs of cheap seafood joints or plunging screaming into alleys to lie with broken bones and bullet-shattered jaws and shoulders. Luther Lambert was now behind a Volvo parked on the opposite side of the street, methodically dissecting the government's vehicles with his machine gun. One after another, they exploded into flames as the tracers in his ammo belts ignited their gasoline tanks. An alley was at his back, and Luther pretended he did not notice the line of agents slipping off to his left, trying to get behind the row of buildings and into that alley. Timing himself on pure instinct, he suddenly snatched up the M-60, quickly and expertly changed the smoking barrel, and rolled to his right to come up facing a single file of six or seven FBI trying to slide in behind him. They tried to take cover and several of them fired at him, but Lambert squeezed the trigger on a long burst that shredded them all. The teflon-coated bullets went through the Bakelite body armor of the agents like a hot knife through butter, while the tracers set their clothing and flesh on fire.

In the hotel, Matt's group was about to break out of a door at the end of the first floor corridor. Matt and Cowboy adjusted their respective unauthorized headgear at appropriate angles; Matt still had the stump of Visconti's Di Nobili in his teeth. "Alice, here's the keys to the Saturn. Can you drive like a bat out of hell?"

"Obviously you never saw *Clones*," she answered. "When I was being chased by a T-Rex the dinosaur was computer generated, but that was really me burning rubber all over Big Sur for the car footage, not a stunt driver."

"Then get ready to put the pedal to the metal. On count of three, one, two…" Then all hell seemed to break loose outside, the long rattle of a machine gun and countless other shots, the thump of exploding vehicles. "What in the name of the devil?" he exclaimed.

"Either the Conquistadors have decided to warm up by massacring the local inhabitants, which I wouldn't put past anyone working for Clinton, or else Mr. Blanchette and Mr. Lambert have made their appearance and are grappling with Ms. Weinmann's oafs," said Visconti. "My guess is that it's those two."

"Somebody's sure doing some full auto rock and roll," said Matt. "Hey, maybe Operation Chucklehead here has a better chance than we think. Okay, one, two, three, *go!*"

They burst from the door into the parking lot, Matt in the lead, and made it to their car before someone shouted through a bullhorn from across the street, *"Halt! Federal agents!"* Visconti dropped down to a kneeling position and aimed his rifle. Mat heard Visconti's weapon spit and *"Throw down your GAAAAAAH!"* An FBI agent popped around from behind a dumpster about twenty yards away, his M-16 leveled, but

Cowboy fired a blast from his 12-gauge and dropped him. The man's flak vest caught most of the buckshot, but as he staggered to his feet moaning Cowboy fired a second time, a slug, and the man fell and lay still.

"About time I got on the scoreboard!" said Garza. They leaped into the car, Alice driving and Matt in the passenger seat beside her. She started the engine and reversed out into the lot at forty miles an hour, not hitting a single car, then threw the Saturn into gear. An FBI panel truck slid into the exit in front of them and an agent leaned out of the passenger side, firing his automatic at them, holing the Saturn's windshield. Matt opened the door, slid halfway out, leveled his M-79, and fired, hitting the truck in the front grill. The vehicle exploded and blew both occupants out onto the concrete. Matt jumped back in and Alice went out the other exit in full reverse, put the Saturn back into drive and peeled off. The roadblock on the north end of the coast road was only a hundred yards in front of them. "Get down!" yelled Alice, she floored the accelerator and headed for the gap between two of the FBI cars, knocking them aside at the cost of both of the Saturn's fenders. They were hurtling northward on Highway 12 at almost eighty miles an hour. "Now where to?" she asked.

"Operation Chucklehead, Part Deux," said Matt. "The problem is, we're on an island, and the only ways off are south through downtown Beirut back there, or this way. There is a double bridge just past Kitty Hawk where we can cross over and get onto Highway 158 on the mainland, but it's simply beyond belief that they won't have that one locked down tight. We need to try and get to Virginia Beach and hook up with the Taurus group again, and that's only a short way as the crow flies, but it's going to be a nightmare doing it with these people on our tails. Highway 12 here runs out at Corolla, and after that we're in the Great Dismal Swamp. Plus we don't know where the Conquistadors are or how they have been deployed. We have two choices; find somewhere to hole up and wait until dark and see what happens, or we can run for 158 and try to bop our way through, but that bridge is almost sure to be a deathtrap."

"Better decide on something quick," said Garza. "We're flying through Kitty Hawk faster than the Wright Brothers ever did."

"If we try to run the bridge let's do it at night," said Visconti. "You two are still badge-carrying policemen in this state. Surely that will serve to get some kind of local assistance, at least a place to lie low until dark?" They were roaring down the asphalt strip, high sand dunes on the right and rows of summer beach houses alternating with convenient stores and seafood shacks on the left.

"This banged up car with bullet holes will certainly attract attention," said Matt. "Alice, pull over and let's see if we can find someplace suitable to go back to ground. Wonder how Miss Andrea and her thundering herd are doing against the Bobbsey Twins back there?"

The fleeing Saturn had not escaped the eagle eye of Bob Blanchette. "Luther! That's them! That's Redmond and the Silverman bitch!" he yelled. "Come on!" He jumped back into the driver's seat of the van. Lambert stood up just as Agents Frederickson, Jackson, Rodriguez, and Axelrod, who had gotten into one of the souvenir shops and up onto the roof, slid up over the gutters and opened fire. Lambert was creased in the neck and the left arm but he sprayed the rooftop with his M-60 and drove the four Feds down under cover again. Blanchette leaned out of the driver's side and as Agent Rodriguez peeped over the rooftop, put a .303 bullet squarely between his eyes. Then Blanchette pulled out several military issue smoke grenades, pulled the pins, and tossed them onto the street, white clouds billowing. "Let's go, Luther!" he shouted.

Lambert, quite berserk, kicked open the door and ran into the souvenir shop, raised his machine gun vertically, and fired a long burst through the roof. He calculated correctly that the armor-piercing bullets in his three-off would penetrate, and there were screams and yells from the roof as Agent Jamal Jackson received a tracer bullet up his anus, Agent Dan Axelrod leaped up in panic and was cut down by another .303 slug from Blanchette, and "Fred" Frederickson leaped off the roof in panic, breaking his ankle as he landed. The tracers set the roof on fire. *"Luther, let's GO!"* bellowed Blanchette. Lambert ran out and leaped onto the passenger side of the van, and Blanchette roared off down Highway 12 in pursuit of the Saturn, with Lambert leaning back and blasting at everything that moved with his M-60, killing one more FBI agent and a reporter for CNN who had been brought along on special assignment from Ted Turner to help with the PR angle. Andrea Weinmann stood up and surveyed the burning wreckage of her career in utter shock and horror.

Alice pulled the Saturn under a deserted beach pavilion, a long low wooden structure with a tin roof, picnic tables, and stone barbecue grills. "Another fine pickle you've gotten us into, Ollie!" she giggled. "Sorry, Matt, I'm being silly, but I really enjoyed that! Tell Kirsten Dunst I *demand* she do her own stunt driving for that scene, just like I did in *Clones.*" The stretch of beach they were on was relatively sparsely built up. About fifty yards north was a split-level beach house with a deck. No one appeared to be home. Across the road, set back by a spacious paved parking lot, was a large, ramshackle clapboard bar or nightclub of some kind called The Flying Dutchman, decorated with masts and sails and rigging on the roof and an upstairs deck with tables and umbrellas.

"A pleasant absence of curious onlookers," said Matt. "The first thing we need to do is conceal this vehicle. The garage in that house there will do nicely. I hope that place is as empty as it looks and the owners are using it for a weekend place and therefore won't be rocking up today and finding a shot-up Saturn in their carport. Then we do a little before-hours clubbing in the Flying Dutchman. Hopefully their staff won't show up until about noon and we can play it by ear from there, flash our badges and give them a tale right out of Miami Vice."

"Sounds good to me," said Cowboy.

"Cowboy, you and Alice nip across to that monument to good taste and see if you can get inside," said Matt. "Visconti and I will stash the car and then do a quick reccy of the area." Cowboy and Alice got out of the car and Matt slid over into the driver's seat. He started the car and slowly eased it back onto the road as Alice and Garza crossed, turning right and entering the driveway of the house on the beach side.

A long, lean black shape floated over the roof of the house. *"Shit!"* roared Matt. *"It's an Apache! Visconti, bail!"* Like lightning both men leaped from the car and ran up into the front porch of the house as a 20-mm cannon cracked and popped. The Saturn exploded into a ball of fire. Across the road Garza and Alice broke into a run. The Apache bobbed above the masts of the bar and lazily blasted a long burst of machine gun fire at the pair of them, but they made it to the front door of the bar. Garza picked up a potted fern and hurled it through the glass front doors, and he and Alice ran into the building. A second long black helicopter, a transport, appeared down the north side of the highway and settled down like a gigantic bumblebee onto the asphalt. The doors fell open and swarms of figures in black swirled out, at least two dozen men, scattering and taking up positions of cover. Matt could hear the officers shouting orders in Spanish. Within a matter of seconds they had the Flying Dutchman surrounded.

"You can't help them!"shouted Visconti as Matt stepped off the porch, ready to try a suicidal run for the bar. "There's more of them coming after us!" He pulled Matt back by the collar of his jacket just as a burst of bullets snapped the air where Matt would have been had he taken one more step. "Not into the house, that's a death trap! The gunship will blow it to pieces! We have to get into those sand dunes and stay mobile!" He and Matt plunged off the porch just as a sheet of machine gun fire from the hovering chopper splintered the whole front of the beach house. Visconti and Matt found a gully in the dunes and ran about thirty yards north. The gunship slid overhead. Matt dropped onto his back, braced the M-79 against his shoulder, and fired an HE grenade. It bounced and exploded against the armored underbelly of the copter but severely jolted it, and the pilot decided some altitude would be wise. The copter shot into the air and vanished.

A black figure arose over the top of a dune, an AK-47 in his hand. Visconti's Russian rifle wheezed and the figure flipped backwards. Matt loaded a buckshot shell into the M-79, whirled to his left as two more men in black, wearing ski masks concealing their faces and carrying AK-47s, staggered around a dune, their booted feet slowed by the sinking sand. The blast of the ball bearing load dropped both of them bleeding and clawing the sand. Matt loaded his third HE round as he and Visconti surmounted a dune, climbing on the rusty grating put there by the Corps of Engineers to hold the beach in place, an elevation where they had a reasonable view of the roadhouse and the highway. Visconti dropped prone amid the waving fronds of sea oats and began firing, one shot, two shots, three shots, and every time a black-clad, ant-like figure spun and dropped. Matt aimed at the open doorway of the transport and fired his grenade. The shell burst shook the copter and it rose into the air and fled, smoke billowing from the injured bird. He spotted several more of the commandos moving up the dune towards the, covering behind the ridges and wrinkles in the sand. Matt pulled out his first hand grenade, yanked the pin, and tossed it over-arm. It sailed into a depression in the sand and blew with a hollow thud; two men in black sailed backwards through the air and landed on the tarmac of Highway 12, lying still and broken.

Across the street came a hammering and a tearing like ripping cloth as the men in black fired hundreds of rounds into the Flying Dutchman, sending wood and glass fragments drifting upward in a cloud. Matt looked over and saw the Conquistadors smashing windows in the bar, firing into the building and then climbing inside. He saw that two of the assassins were crouched behind a station wagon in the parking lot of the Flying Dutchman, blasting into the building with their AKs. Matt loaded HE grenade number four, leveled his M-79, fired, and blew the gas tank on the station wagon. He could hear the screams of the burning men in black even over the other noise.

Around the two of them the black-clad killers were drawing their noose tighter, firing and running, firing and dropping down into cover in the dunes or behind billboards, moving ever closer. Matt hurled his second hand grenade, trying to get to go under a billboard advertising the Lost Colony outdoor drama in Manteo, but it bounced off and exploded harmlessly, sending a geyser of sand into the sky. He drew his .357, leveled it with both hands, and shot one of them in the throat as they closed in. AK-47 bullets splashed fountains of sand all around him. He looked over and saw Visconti calmly squeezing off shot after shot, reloading his VAL and firing again. A black form leaped slithered up the dune towards him like a snake, a pistol in his hand. Matt put a bullet into the center of the ski mask and saw blood and brains fly. He knew he had only moments left to live *"Heather!"* he cried in utter agony.

A blue van came roaring down the highway and ran down one of the commandos, sending him whirling into the air. The men in black met it with a hail of bullets. The van swerved and tore through the picnic pavilion, and crashed into the side of the empty house. Matt looked across the street and saw six or seven men in black emerging from the doorway of the Flying Dutchman. Between them they carried the kicking, screaming body of Alice Silverman. The transport copter floated down to the road, the wind from its rotor blades flattening the sea oats and sending a cloud of sand aloft, and the grenade-scorched door opened to receive them. *"They've got her!"* howled Matt in despair. Luther Lambert leaped into the roadway. In his hands the M-60 machine gun was as delicate and precise as the scalpel in the hands of the surgeon, spewing death. The party of black-clad men who had been manhandling Alice danced and leaped like demented marionettes before dropping broken to the ground, smoldering from the tracers. The copter leaped into the sky like a frightened quail, Lambert's bullets sparking and clanging as they holed the aircraft's skin. Alice staggered up from the ground, bleeding and limping, blood gushing from one leg.

She scuttled to a side door of the Flying Dutchman and wrenched at it, trying to get inside. *"Cowboy!"* she screamed in terror.

All of a sudden there came a strange lull, and a single shot split the air over the sound of the rumbling surf. It came from Bob Blanchette, who was standing on the roof of the blue van leveling his rifle. Alice Silverman arched back, dropped to the ground like a sack of potatoes, and lay still. Blanchette fired another shot into her prone body. She jerked with the hit.

"No," whispered Matt, the black pits of hell opening beneath him. "Oh, no. No. No. No no *no no no no* NO NO NO..." Then the firing began again and he was mercifully swept up again in the madness. Visconti rolled over onto his back, leveled his VAL and fired a single shot at Blanchette. He hit the .303 in Blanchette's hand, shattering the stock and knocking it off into the dunes. The transport helicopter drifted down again about four hundred yards down the road, and the remaining black-clad figures began their scuttling withdrawal. Visconti rolled back and calmly emptied his magazine. Only a handful of the decimated Hispanics made it back into the copter before it took off. Blanchette had disappeared from the roof of the van. Matt crawled forward, grabbed an AK-47 from the dead hands of one of the Conquistadors, jacked in a round and began firing blindly at anything that moved. *"I've got to try and get to Cowboy!"* he shouted.

"Past *that?*" yelled Visconti, pointing at Lambert, who was jumping up and down in the middle of the highway on the body of one of the dead men.

"I'll take care of that son of a bitch!" yelled Matt, leveling HE round number five at the giant with the machine-gun. Then a shadow moved over him. The black Apache gunship was sliding over the top of the dunes towards them. Lambert raised his weapon and blasted away, the rounds sparking and clanging off the armor plating. Like an irritated rhino, the Apache turned the nozzles of its deadly weapons toward the giant. Matt leveled his M-79. A small aperture appeared; the port by the pilot's left side was open. Matt aimed and prayed silently, *Lord of Hosts, give sharpness to mine eye and strength unto my arm to do thy justice on earth. Avenge her! Avenge her motherless child!* He fired. The 40-millimeter grenade slammed through the opening and blew the pilot's head to vapor. The helicopter flipped and exploded, shaking the ground like an earthquake. Visconti rolled over and fired at Lambert, but Lambert wasn't there any more. Nobody was there any more. The sky was filled with black smoke from the burning helicopter and the ground and highway were littered with bodies in black fatigues and ski masks, but all of a sudden there was an eerie silence. Matt grabbed up the AK, ran forward, and ripped a pouch of extra magazines off the dead Conquistador's hip. "Visconti! Cover me!" he said.

"Might as well come with you," grunted the Mafioso. "I'm out of ammunition for the rifle." He unslung the Sicilian *lupara* and stripped off the cloth sling so as not to rattle. Then he slipped forward, following Matt. They ran for the Flying Dutchman.

Matt made it to the front door of the bar. A wounded Conquistador lying in the parking lot moaned and tried to rise. Matt shot him in the head. The doors to the bar had been blown off; one of them rattled crazily in the sea breeze. Visconti and Matt kicked it aside and leaped into the long barroom-cum-restaurant together. It was a slaughterhouse inside. The long room of tables and nautical decorations was splintered and wrecked and scattered with broken glass, there were bullet holes and bloodstains on the oak paneled walls, and at least six black clad corpses lay encircled around the dead body of Arthur Garza. He lay on the steps leading up to what looked like a bandstand, the shotgun cast aside and empty, the Ruger Mini-14 in his hands. Matt recognized his friend's Stetson, but he no longer had a face. "Dear God," he whispered. "Christ, Cowboy, I am so deeply sorry!"

"He was a brave man," said Visconti.

"I've got to get to Alice," said Matt, moving forward. Visconti held him back.

"Matt, she is dead, and Blanchette and Lambert are out there waiting for you to show your face. They know you will feel compelled to try and go to her body, and they will cut you down the minute you step out that side door. We need to get up onto that deck and possibly onto the roof itself so we can spot their location." Matt sighed and drew out his .357, reloading it with a speed loader he drew from his pocket.

"Let's go," he said.

Outside, Blanchette and Lambert stood on either side of the side door. Luther had laid aside the M-60, having run out of ammunition as well as Visconti, and now held an axe in each hand. "She's mighty purty," he said admiringly, looking at the corpse of the murdered actress. "They're always purty when they're new dead. That's the best time for a woman. They cain't do all that bad stuff, but they ain't started to rot yet."

"We ain't got much time," whispered Blanchette. "Them Feebs are gonna be here any minute. That was Viscawnti who damn near blew my ass off the van. We gotta git both of 'em and git 'em quick, then beat feet outta here."

"That bad-ass Eye-tie you was talkin' about? Oh, yeah, now we gone see who got the manpower!" snarled Luther. Blanchette looked up and saw the second story deck.

"Luther, boost me up. I'm going to try to go in from above." Lambert quickly lifted Blanchette up onto his shoulders as easily as if the man were a child, and Blanchette pulled himself onto the wooden deck with the tables and chairs and umbrellas. He drew a .45 just as Matt Redmond emerged onto the deck from the stairs. Matt fired a wild shot and ducked back inside just as a slug from Blanchette's Browning plowed into the wall beside his head.

"He's on the deck!" hissed Matt to Visconti. "I go left, you go right! *Now!*" Matt charged out the doorway and tried to roll to his left, but tripped over a folding wooden chair and went sprawling instead. The fall saved his life; Blanchette turned and fired again, the bullet splinter-ing the wooden paneling right where Matt's heart would have been. The delay gave the Mafioso the extra second he needed. There was a thunder-clap and Blanchette's body doubled over. The second barrel of Visconti's *lupara* tore Blanchette's right arm off at the shoulder, and as he twirled and danced Matt fired his .357 once, twice, three times into the capering, screaming, bleeding lich before it collapsed onto the boards, flopped, and died. Visconti broke his smoking shotgun and walked over, leaned down, and dipped his two right fingers into the bloody mess. He held up the dripping fingers to Matt, his face grim. *"Guiseppe LaBrasca, salud!"* Matt walked over and plunged his own two fingers into the bubbling crimson shirtfront of the dead man, and held them up. *"Art Garza! Alice Silverman! Salud!"* he cried. Both men sucked the blood from their fingers. "One more to go," said Matt. "He's around somewhere."

"The brain is dead, the muscle won't be too hard to kill, so long as we are careful," said Visconti. The sound of sirens came screaming down Highway 12 from the direction of Kitty Hawk.

"We may not get the chance. Visconti, it's been a real slice, but I think you'd best take that van of theirs and see if you can make it across that bridge onto 158," said Matt. "I'm going to kill one more FBI agent today, but this one isn't your fight."

"Tony was in that Taurus as well. His blood was spilled," said Visconti. "It is my fight."

"Suit yourself."

Andrea Weinmann entered the Flying Dutchman cautiously, her 9-mil-limeter held in a two-handed stance, with four more FBI agents at her back, two M-16s, one Uzi and a 12-gauge shotgun at the ready. From the other end of the long barroom Matt called out, "She's dead, Andrea." He stood by Art Garza's body, his .357 held at the ready. "Your boss and his lady don't have anything to worry about. No one will ever hear from Alice Silverman's lips how Bill and Hill got high and decided to indulge in a lit-tle Tinseltown rape and sodomy one night. Their squalid little secret is safe. How many people have died now to keep that secret? I make it fifty or so, at least. You and these thugs with you will add to the tally."

"Drop your weapon and put up your hands!" commanded Andrea, leveling her pistol at him.

"Fuck you, bitch," said Matt, his voice and eyes dead and cold. "Oh, I forgot, that's what you want, isn't it? God, the thought that I once touched you in that way, even for a moment, makes me want to vomit!"

"I'll kill you for that!" hissed Andrea, her face white as a sheet.

The four agents raised their weapons, but were surprised by a sudden voice from behind them. "You four stay where you are," said John Visconti. He had risen from concealment behind the bar and he was pointing the Ruger Mini-14 at them.

"Who the hell are you?" asked one of the agents.

"Some call me Five o'Clock Johnny. Perhaps you may have heard of me. The Jew bitch is Mr. Redmond's. You are mine. I won't tell you to drop your weapons, because I want you to try something. Then I can shoot you down like the dogs you are. I think you will find me something of a more difficult target than a woman and an infant. So do it, gentlemen. Move a muscle, twitch a finger. You saw what we did outside to your big bad beaners? That's you, ten seconds from now." The staring agents had not missed the carnage outside and they were sweating, their hands shaking in fear. Then came an odd sound.

Chink chink...tink tink...tink tink...

Luther Lambert was tiptoeing down the stairs from the upper deck. He was stripped to the waist, bleeding from his wounds, wearing blood-soaked jeans and cowboy boots, the Botticelli Venus on his now shaven chest rippling, and over his head he held two axes, clinking their blades together. One of the FBI men screamed in animal panic and raised his M-16 to shoot Lambert; Visconti shot him through the head. Lambert raised his arms and in a smooth motion so fast as to be almost impossible for the naked eye to see, he hurled the axes. Both buried their heads into the skull and the chest of two of the FBI men.

Lambert leaped. From a standing position on the stairs he broke every Olympic record, hurling himself thirty feet through the air onto the remaining FBI man, crashing onto the floor and crushing the man's skull like a watermelon between his two mighty hands. Andrea turned and shot him in the jaw, and he kicked her aside like a rag doll. Lambert leaped up and found Matt Redmond leveling the M-79 grenade launcher at him. Matt fired. It was the flare shell, and it struck Luther in the belly and burrowed into the meat, burning at thousands of degrees. Lambert staggered towards Matt, roaring in untold agony, his hands clutching for Matt's throat. Matt emptied the .357 into him at point blank range while Visconti fired bullet after bullet into the dying giant. Lambert collapsed onto the floor and rose again. Matt fired his last ball-bearing shell from the grenade launcher into Lambert's face at point blank range, and Visconti trampled around the end of the bar, firing both barrels of the *lupara* into Lambert's back. The giant collapsed onto the floor, the smell of burning flesh filling the room.

"I think we can do without the little blood ritual in his case," said Matt, shuddering. "Frankly, I'm scared to go near him. The son of a bitch might get up yet."

Andrea pulled herself to her feet and raised her gun to shoot Visconti. Matt snatched up an empty beer bottle from a table, hurled it, and caught her on the elbow, knocking the gun aside as it fired. Visconti was on her like a tiger. She yelled and tried a karate kick at him. He caught her foot and twisted, snapping her ankle, making her scream in pain. He punched her in the stomach, knocking the wind out of her, and dragged her to a chair. He ripped her own handcuffs off her belt and cuffed her hands behind her back, then he tore off her belt and used it to strap her ankles to the bottom cross brace of the chair. He stripped off the belts of the dead FBI agents and in a matter of moments had the gasping Andrea bound securely to the chair. He then ripped her blouse open and shredded it until it came off her shoulders, leaving her bare to the waist except for her brassiere. Visconti tore the blouse into several long strips which he wound together. He held the impromptu ligature out, stretched between his hands. "Time for the old Italian rope trick!" he snarled.

Andrea Weinmann stared in horror. "I am an FBI agent!" she whispered, stunned. "You wouldn't *dare!*" Visconti stepped behind her and deftly wound the cloth cord around her neck. *"Matt! Matt! For the love of God, save me!"* she screamed in overwhelming terror.

"As slow as possible," said Matt to Visconti.

"No! No! Don't…!" Then her shrieks were cut off as Visconti brutally jerked the noose tight. She leaped against the bonds holding her to the chair like a fish hooked on a line. Her eyes bulged, she writhed and her tongue lolled and quivered. Just as her face began to turn blue, Visconti released the pressure and she gasped and sucked air into her lungs, moaning.

"Who ordered Joey LaBrasca killed?" whispered Visconti gently into her ear. "Who betrayed him to those three animals? Was it Bill or Hillary Clinton?"

"I'll do anything you want," she said weeping. "Please, please don't kill me! I'll suck your dick, you can fuck me in the ass, anything, please don't kill me!"

"Bill or Hillary?" asked Visconti again.

"I don't know, I swear to God I don't…" Visconti pulled the cord tight again. She thrashed and twisted, rocking the chair back and forth. A foul smell filled the room as her bowels and bladder relaxed in approaching death and voided into her underwear. Visconti released the garrotte again and once more she gasped precious air into her lungs.

"Bill or Hillary?" demanded Visconti.

"Hillary!" gabbled Andrea. "It was Hillary! Bill sent the Musketeers after Alice and the baby, but the set-up on the boat was Hillary's idea to get rid of LaBrasca too! He was her coke supplier as well as Bill's. She was scared the Mob might use the LaBrasca cocaine connection to blackmail her once she's become Senator. Bill does whatever she tells him to. Then she ordered Janet Reno to terminate the Musketeers, and Janet told me. I'll do anything you want! I'll tell the media it was Hillary,

I'll call a press conference and expose it all, just please let me live! I can't die. It can't be now, it can't…"

"Yes. Now." Andrea's eyes widened and she gave a final shriek as he pulled the garrotte tight again. She bucked like a bronco, gasping and gurgling, frantically and uselessly straining against the bonds, her chest heaving in a frantic quest for breath.

"Visconti?" said Matt softly. "As a favor?"

"Matt, this is not a human woman, this is a serpent!" he argued as he strangled her. "Compassion for serpents is the weakness of an idiot! If you let her live you will be endangering yourself and your family. She deserves this, and you know it! Can you honestly tell me that you have no desire for vengeance after what she has done?"

"I do indeed. Your kind of vengeance. Remember that very polite marriage of yours?" He gestured towards the dying woman in the chair. "Please. I'd like to explain." Visconti suddenly loosened the noose and air once again rattled into Andrea's tortured lungs. Vaguely she understood that Matt was responsible for the sudden relief.

"Thank you, Matt, thank you, oh God Matt I'm sorry I must have been out of my mind I didn't really want to hurt her…" Matt stepped up and slapped her face.

"Be quiet," he ordered. "I said to you this morning I would kill you. I have changed my mind. I am going to do worse to you. I'm not just going to kill your body, I am going to kill your soul. I am going to leave you here, surrounded by the dead bodies of yet more of Clinton's people. I am going to leave you here hog-tied like this for your colleagues to find, sitting in your own shit and piss. The men who came here with you are dead, but you will not be dead, because you are not worth killing. That is my message to them, and they will understand it and hold you in all the more contempt for it. To your personal and professional humiliation, I am going to add sexual humiliation." He pulled out a pocketknife and deftly cut her bra straps, unhooked the brassiere and tossed it away. "I have to admit, Andrea, that's a mighty fine pair of knockers. Now I have seen them, and Mr. Visconti has seen them, and the FBI who find you will see them, and know that we have seen them. You are going to become a dirty joke in the Bureau, Andrea. The FBI's answer to Monica Lewinsky. I assume you will resign, but your legend will live on, so to speak."

"*Bravissimo!*" laughed Visconti. "Redmond, are you sure you haven't got some Italian blood in you somewhere?"

"Read the history of the Scottish border clans someday," chuckled Matt. "I assure you, it will come up to your most demanding and blood-curdling standards of blood feud and revenge."

"Don't do this to me!" cried Andrea in anguish. "Matt, I was weak just now, all right, I'm a coward as well as a slut if that makes you happy, but if this is my alternative, please don't leave me here alive for them to find me like this! I couldn't bear it! Give me a bullet! I…I think I could take it, if it was quick like that, if it came from you, not him…I'll close my eyes, just put the muzzle to my head and pull the trigger and it will be over, just don't let him choke me again…please, I'm begging you, please, Matt, don't do this! I'm ready to go now if that's what you want! Yes, I sent them after the Taurus, I wanted them to kill Heather so maybe someday you and I…in God's name, don't make me go through this! *Shoot me! Shoot me!*"

"Ah, so like a woman! Always changing her mind!" sneered Visconti.

"Have a nice life, Andrea," said Matt. He leaned over and spat directly into her face, and she collapsed into convulsive weeping in her shame. "Let's get out of here. She is ugly, and I am tired of looking at ugliness."

They stepped out the side door and stood over the body of Alice Silverman. Her sightless blue eyes stared into a sky just as blue. The sea wind ruffled and lifted her golden hair. The front of her sweater was drenched with blood and she lay in a crimson puddle. Matt's eyes filled with tears and he leaned against the wall, a sob wracking his body. "Oh, dear God, why?" he whispered. "How could we do this to her? How could we have ever let these monsters rule us? That girl died for our sins, Visconti. She died because we let those unspeakable people in, not once but twice. What a contemptible people we are!"

Visconti stood over her, the shotgun in his hand. He spoke. *"Beatrice tutta ne l'etterne rote fissa con li occhi stava; e io in lei le luci fissi, di là sù rimote."*

"Dante?" asked Matt softly.

"Yes. From *Paradiso.* Upon the poet's meeting his beloved Beatrice in heaven."

"That was well said," said Matt. "She would have appreciated it." He leaned over and tenderly closed the dead woman's eyes. Visconti made the sign of the cross on his chest and raised the shotgun barrel to his lips.

"She will be avenged upon her violators and her murderers," he said. "Redmond, your part in this is over now. I'll take it from here."

"There is one more thing you can do for me, and for her," said Matt.

"It's done," said Visconti.

"Go get that car those Feebs came in and bring it around. I want you to do what you guys do best. I want you to put a body in the trunk. Alice's. I don't want to leave her here."

"And the Cowboy?" asked Visconti.

"There is no more honorable resting place for a warrior than on the battlefield, surrounded by the corpses of his slain enemies. Leave him here; whatever they do with his body, it would be okay with him. But Alice is different. I don't want her to just disappear down some Clintonian memory hole, Visconti. I don't want her to be found in some public park with a stupid story about how she committed suicide by shooting herself in the back twice with a high powered rifle, rubber-stamped by some goddamned Democratic bureaucrat. I want her laid to rest without lies and slander, to have a grave and a headstone so that someday her son will be able to come to visit her, and lay flowers on her resting place."

"How do we…?"

"You're right, I do have a copper's badge. I hope you have some of Columbus's seafaring blood in you, Visconti. How does one usually get off an island? We're going up to Corolla and I'm going to scam us a boat, and then we head for Virginia Beach."

✶✶✶

Matt and Heather Redmond stood on the balcony and watched the twilight descend on the beach below them. "This is what, the fourth hotel involved in all this, the fifth?" she asked.

"At least we've gotten some mints on our pillows," said Matt.

"What now?" she asked.

"I go back to Raleigh and face the music," said Matt. "You and Tori drop out of sight and stay out of sight until we figure out what the hell is going to come down from Washington. I'll square it with your boss at UNC. I think she's pretty well hardened to weird shit involving our marriage and extracurricular activities."

"She made an ironclad rule after Lumberton. When this kind of thing happens I have to do a long lunch with her and tell her everything that went on. She has this weird idea that I am leading some kind of exciting and adventurous double life. I wonder how I tell her that our 19 year-old daughter ended up taking up a human life this time, courtesy of Bill and Hill? God, how I hate them for doing that to our child!"

"I understand from Tori you're now in the Boys' Club yourself now, joining the exclusive company of gentleman adventurers like myself, Five o'Clock Johnny, the Emperor Nero, and Vlad the Impaler," said Matt. "Not to mention Lizzie Borden. How are you handling it, Watson?"

"Oddly enough, it doesn't bother me at all," said Heather. "I killed a man who was about to murder a two month old baby. It was simply something that had to be done, and I did it. A few years ago if I had killed someone I would have been a gibbering wreck, but I have done the very best I could to resurrect the remnants of my liberal con-science, and it seems that file has been deleted somewhere along the line. I am utterly unable to convince myself that I have anything to be

· 248 ·

ashamed of or guilty about because I took the life of the kind of human being who could fire an assault rifle at an infant. Tori did the same, but it bothers me that she did it while it doesn't bother me that I did the same thing, and I think she feels the same way about me. How strange. Now, are you ready to talk about it?"

"About the fact that a young woman came to me and asked me to save her life, and I failed, and all those dead Feebs and men in black won't alter the basic fact that Bill Clinton has won again? No. Not that there is anything much more to say. That's pretty much it. She came to the wrong man, and she died, and my incompetence also cost the life of a fine, brave man who was my friend."

"That is bullshit, but I won't push it. Matt, you spent twenty-six years carrying a cross of self-imposed guilt over Mary Jane Mears and Jeannie Arnold. In a way, that was a good thing, because finally in 1996, you went back to 1970 and you were able to give them justice. This isn't the same thing. What happened to Mary Jane and Jeannie was murder. Alice was not murdered, she was executed, and I mean that in the literal sense. Matt, face the facts. Eddie Miami was right. Alice was right. The President of the United States sentenced her to death, and in the long run there was not a damned thing that you or anyone else could do about it. Eventually her appeals ran out, the executioners came for her, and her sentence was carried out. Every one of us knew in our hearts from the very beginning that this would happen, not the least Alice herself. Mr. and Mrs. Clinton may have dispensed with the tiresome paperwork and formalities, but our society has decided to grant them that prerogative. *Volus princeps lex est.* You cannot fight that, although being the noble man of honor and courage that you are, you tried. You failed, and I am worried sick that you are going to spend the next twenty-six years crucifying yourself like you once did over Mary Jane and Jeannie. Please, Matt, don't do that. When you're ready to talk it out, you know where to find me," said Heather. "Now, any way I can possibly persuade you to refrain from joining John Visconti in assassinating the President of the United States?"

"No need," said Matt with a smile. "I've already made that decision. If I was still single I'd be Visconti's man on the grassy knoll without a second's hesitation. But I won't do that to you and Tori, and he knows it. He hasn't even asked, which I admit miffs me a little."

"I haven't asked because I already know what your answer would be," said Visconti, stepping out onto the balcony. "Otherwise you would definitely be on my short list. I've got a lot of time for any man who shoots down helicopters. Pardon me, I did not mean to eavesdrop on your private conversation. I thought you might like to know that Tony and Tori and William have arrived safely in New York, and that Tony has been checked into one of the most modern and well-equipped private clinics on Long Island. His face will be seen to by the best plastic surgeons in the country. Tori and the baby will be staying with Dominic and Teresa LaBrasca as honored guests. They are both very grateful to you all, and while you may consider that gratitude to be a fearsome thing, I promise you that you need have no concerns over her safety. However, for everyone's peace of mind, I think it would be a good idea if Mrs. Redmond joined her as soon as possible. This business may not be over yet. With a little persuasion, I think Dom might make you that scampi tortellini Tony spoke of. I assure you, it is worth the trip."

"Well, I suppose that's one way to do a food tour of the Big Apple," said Heather with a bemused giggle.

"Make sure your hosts take you to dinner at Umberto's Clam House and Sparks' Steak House," said Matt.

"Actually, that's not a bad idea. The food in both establishments is superb," said Visconti.

"Being a goodfella means never eating in a bad restaurant?" asked Heather.

"Among other perks, yes. By the by, Matt, I was listening to the radio just now. It seems there was an unfortunate incident during a live combined law enforcement and military training exercise on the North Carolina coast this morning. A helicopter crashed and a number of personnel were killed. Most regrettable. The cover-up is already beginning."

"Beautiful," said Matt in disgust. "Although I suppose that's a good omen in a way. It means that whatever else happens, they are still determined to make sure nothing goes public."

"Mrs. Redmond, I am sure you are anxious to rejoin your daughter, although again I assure you there is no cause for concern; she is as safe in Dominic's home as if she were in Fort Knox. Would you like to fly up to New York with me?" asked Visconti.

"I'll take a flight tomorrow. Please don't take offense, Mr. Visconti. It's just…"

"I understand perfectly," said Visconti, with a smile. He turned and left.

"Thanks for staying," said Matt. "I don't know how rough it's going to be down in Raleigh. I don't know how long it's going to be before I can talk my way out of this one, or even if I can."

"I have to have at least one more quiet night with you before this whole thing plays out," said Heather.

"I doubt it will be quiet," said Matt, putting his arm around her as the darkness fell onto the Atlantic shore.

XIII

The Ides of October

Matt Redmond sat on a plush lawn chair overlooking the broad blue expanse of Long Island Sound. It was a warm day, but the leaves on the trees around him were beginning to turn yellow and orange and gold and drift down to the grass. The last autumn of the second millennium had come, and here where there had been only marsh and wildlife a thousand years before stood the works of Man. He was in the private rear garden of an immense brick and plaster Dutch colonial style mansion, a landscaped vista that sloped down to the sound where boats bobbed in the water in private docks. The haze of New York City was visible lowering in the distance. Several men sat at the end of the boat dock fishing. High-powered rifles with sniper's scopes leaned beside their buckets and tackle boxes. The extensive walled grounds were scanned with close-circuit television cameras, while discreet young men in suits with bulges under their jackets stood strategically placed around the estate. Beside him sat old Dominic LaBrasca and John Visconti, also ensconced in lawn chairs. On the table before them was an antique silver espresso coffee service. "This is a hell of a view," said Redmond, impressed, sipping the superb and bitter black coffee.

"Yeah. I spend a lot of time out here these days, just looking out at the boats and the city where I did all dem tings long ago," said LaBrasca. "I gotta admit, Redmond, it's been one hell of a ride. Never thought I'd be sittin' here with a cop, though."

"This is an insane epoch, and insane things happen," said Matt.

"You got dat right," said LaBrasca. "But I'm glad we got a chance to meet Tori and Hedder, and Teresa is just crazy about dat baby. We're sorry to see dem go."

"How's Tony doing?" asked Matt.

"He's healing excellently," said Visconti. "He shouldn't limp at all, and the plastic surgery has reduced the scar on his face to something he can live with."

"Heather tells me he's doing a Michael Corleone act, and he's now off to Sicily to let the heat die down," said Matt.

"Yeah," said LaBrasca. "Besides, it's time he had some old country polish put on him. His Italian sucks." LaBrasca was silent for a bit. "Tori went to the airport with him. Redmond, look, no disrespect at all to you or Tori, she's a wunnerful girl, but ain't there nothing you can do about dat situation? They ain't right for one another. They ain't from de same woild."

"Heather and I have told her the same things that you and Visconti have no doubt told Tony," said Matt. "I don't think either them will listen. Let's just hope that it doesn't get to the point where either of them are hurt beyond repair. They grow up, Mr. LaBrasca. The time comes when you just have to let go. That's one thing I've come to talk about, but there's something more important. I owe you a lot, LaBrasca, you and Visconti here."

"It's mutual," said LaBrasca. "You know any time you need a favor…"

"In a way I do. I'd like five minutes of your time. I want to run a few things by you. It's not a request, I'd just like you to think about what I have to say," said Matt carefully. "I am not going to try and talk you out of what you're planning with Mr. Vee here. Even if I thought I could persuade you, I wouldn't try. I don't want to stop you. Bill and Hillary Clinton have a debt to pay to us all, and I'd like to see them pay it some day. I think it's grotesque and abominable that America has to rely on characters like you two to do what our own law should have done a long time ago, but better your way than never at all.

"But you Sicilians have a saying that revenge is the only dish best served cold. I'd like to suggest to you that you have the option of eating this particular serving of it cold, and that it would be better for the world if you did. You have seen what has happened in the generation since that wretched wannabe dictator John F. Kennedy got whacked. You have seen how the media and academic community has already turned one power-mad egomaniac Democrat with satyriasis into a liberal icon. If you kill Bill Clinton now, while he is in office, it will all happen again. He will become a left-wing martyr just like Kennedy. Every crime, every sickening perversion, every lie and deception, every betrayal of his, every breach of human decency Clinton has committed will be forgotten, and he will be placed on a pedestal beside Kennedy. I have only one suggestion for you: for Christ's sake, give it some time! Wait until he is out of office before you punish him for the murder of your son."

"I won't be here by then," said LaBrasca.

"Yes, I know. John told me, and believe it or not I'm sorry. You're a dinosaur, LaBrasca, one of the last of your species, and it's always sad to see a species become extinct. Even a predatory one."

"Anybody else talked to me like that, I'd punch dem in the mouth, but I know what youse is sayin'," said LaBrasca with a sigh. "Redmond, do you know who my own godfather was, at my own christening back in Sicily? Don Salvatore Maranzano. Dat name mean anything to you? God, what a woild dat was back then! Luciano, Costello, Genovese, Joe Adonis, Joe Bananas, Three-Finger Tommy Brown, even dat kill-crazy fuck Albert Anastasia. It was all our oyster. Can anyone really believe it was ever dere?" he said, gesturing towards the distant skyscrapers and smog.

"That's right, you're Castellamarese, aren't you? All right, from what I hear about Don Salvatore, he was a man capable of taking the long view. True, you won't be around to see Clinton get his if you wait too much longer, but think, what is best for your family? How much heat will taking out a sitting President generate as opposed to taking out a former President in a few years' time, especially a disgraced one?"

"A Presidential spouse," Visconti reminded them. "Remember, we are dealing with a team here. The real problem with those two has always been Hillary. Clinton is on the way out, but Hillary is on the way in. We didn't just pull Bill's beard, you know, we pulled Hillary's"

"Can't you people do anything about that?" demanded Matt. "I mean jeez, this is your home state! New York and New Jersey, anyway. Can't you stuff the ballot boxes or something so that harridan doesn't pollute the United States Senate with her presence?"

"We ain't magicians. In Joisey, maybe. Here in the city, no problem. But not statewide. Not Federal. Not if the *pezzonovante* down there on Wall Street and in the Rockefeller Center have already decided what the result is gonna be," said LaBrasca. "Remember, we don't count the votes no more, the Feds do, and they decide what the vote says. Besides, we don't exactly like Giuliani either. Now, if it were Al D'Amato…nevvah mind, I'm rambling. Look, I know what you're saying, Redmond, and I know dat whacking a sitting president is gonna cause a hell of a lot of heat. Me, I don't care, I'm headed for de boneyard, but okay, you may be right. Maybe I shouldn't leave Tony that kind of mess behind. John give him a real glowing report card, not to mention your two ladies, so I know I can leave it in his hands now, and it will eventually be done. But John is right. What about dis Hillary bitch? Is she gonna stop comin' after you and your family, and more important, is she gonna lay off Tony widdout we whack her?"

"I have an idea on that," said Matt. "I stopped off in Washington before I came up here and had a meet with an old contact of mine, Frank Hardesty. I also called in what will probably be the last of my favors down there, and I have some information that may help us send Ms. Hillary a message. If Mr. Visconti doesn't mind working with me on one more little job…?"

✳✳✳

Later on they sat in the living room of the mansion; Tori and Heather were there and Tori was holding the baby. "We have one final problem to resolve before we go home," said Matt. "What do we do with young William here? We know that Alice wanted him to go to her parents, but we have to consider whether or not that is going to be safe. My guess is that so long as the Clintons retain any vestige of power, and so long as DNA testing might reveal little Bill to be Big Bill's son, this child is going to be in danger."

"I don't suppose...?" asked Tori tentatively, looking up at her parents.

"The thought has crossed my mind as well, honey," said Heather gently. "But that can't be, if you'll think about it. I'm too old to raise another child, and you're too young. You have your whole life ahead of you. Don't worry, honey, your time will come. I haven't made any secret of the fact that I hope it won't be with Tony, as much as I have come to admire and respect him, and Mr. LaBrasca understands that. But one way or the other, it will come. You've got eventual motherhood written all over you."

"Besides, honey, a baby can't just kind of appear like we found him under a cabbage leaf," said Matt. "There are such things as birth certificates and legal custody issues."

"In this country that's true," said Visconti. "But I have a suggestion which I have already discussed with Dominic. You won't like it, but hear us out."

"In a week's time, me and Teresa are going to fly to Sicily for the winter," said Dom. "To visit Tony, of course, but also so we can both see the old country one last time. I came to America when I was six years old, after my faddah got chased out of Sicily by Mussolini, but I was born in a place called Castellamare del Golfo."

"It is one of the most beautiful and tragic and magnificent places on earth," said Visconti. "As its name suggests, it is dominated by an ancient Norman castle that looks down from a hill over the Mediterranean. High above it, in the mountains, lies the village of Corleone, which means Lion Heart, for the breed of men who are born and raised there. You are right, Redmond, in this country there are papers and social security numbers and adoption laws, but there are still places on earth where people count more than paper. Castellamare is one of them. You must decide now whether to send this child to his maternal grandparents in California, where in addition to the ever-present risk of his being murdered by the Clintons, there is the danger that he will grow up to be a silly Beavis or an evil Butthead with his cap on backwards, who has nothing in his mind except junk food and computer games. Or you can leave him here with Dominic and Teresa, who will take him to Sicily and place him with an honorable and loving family, where he will grow up herding goats and playing real games with other real children, not computers. Where he will go to Mass and listen to the old stories of the old men in the little town squares, and where he will learn not only how, but when and why to use the *lupara*."

"And where he may grow up to be a murderer and a drug dealer," said Matt.

"If that is his destiny, possibly. Or he may grow up to be a priest, or a simple farmer or fisherman, or a painter or a poet."

"I have some cousins in Castellamare," said LaBrasca. "Their name is Vitale. They have a large family but will welcome one more. Needless to say, arrangements will be made so that he never lacks for anything."

"It may not be what his mother had in mind, but he will have chance to grow up to be a man," said Visconti. "A real man. Can this society offer him that any more?"

Matt nodded to Tori miserably. She looked at Dom. "Please, Mr. LaBrasca, could you do something for me?" she asked. "Leave him one thing only from his past, the name of his father, however evil his father is and however terrible the way he came into the world. The name his mother gave him. What is the Italian version of William?"

"Guglielmo," said LaBrasca. "So he will be. Actually, in the Sicilian dialect we drawl it out to Guillamo."

Tori leaned over and kissed the small sleeping face. "Welcome to the world, little Guillamo Vitale," she whispered, tears in her eyes. "Mr. Visconti, a favor from you? I know you can't promise me this, in view of the way you live your own life, but if you can, when he is old enough to understand, either you or Tony go to him and tell him about his mother. Tell him how beautiful and brave she was. Show him her videos so he can see her young and full of life, solving mysteries and chasing a Great Dane and getting chased by dinosaurs. Then, if he thinks it is right for him, if he feels that he owes her, teach him how to use that Sicilian shotgun and bring him back here to help him finish any of this that might be left over."

"It's done," said Visconti.

✳✳✳

Andrea Weinmann stood on her balcony in the cool October air, watching the sun beginning to descend in the west over the steel and concrete canyons of Rosslyn. In the haze across the Potomac she could see the Washington Monument, the distant dome of the Capitol, and just a faint pale line that was the roof of the White House. She was wearing a bathrobe and holding a Bacardi and Coke in her hand. The booze helped to kill the pain, the very least of which was the pain of the broken ankle John Visconti had inflicted on her. Her face, although still beautiful, had grown gaunt and hollow-eyed. Officially she was on paid medical leave from the Bureau, and they had not yet demanded her badge and her gun, but she had mailed in her resignation without being asked and knew that it was being processed. There had never been any question, from the moment that Frederickson's team had found her amid the abattoir of the Flying Dutchman, that her Federal law enforcement career was at an end.

In the weeks since her disgrace she had left her darkened apartment hardly at all, having her groceries delivered as well as large quantities of liquor. She alternated lengthy hot showers with long bouts of drinking until she fell into a stupor. She tried to read but usually quit a quarter of the way through every book. Sometimes she would turn on the television, but the world around her seemed insipid and unreal and far away. She knew she was having a kind of breakdown, but she didn't care. All that obsessed her, day in and day out, were thoughts of Matt Redmond. Sometimes there would be lengthy fantasies of revenge, of his own torture and humiliation at her hands in a hundred different ways. Once she had even gotten her Lexus serviced in preparation for a trip to Raleigh, and packed a small bag containing a change of clothes and her service pistol, with vaguely formed plans of sex and violence against Matt and Heather wandering through her mind, but she did not go, for she knew that she would see again the contempt in his eyes, and that she could not bear. Sometimes there would be erotic daydreams of Matt being there with her in the apartment as her lover and her friend, all the anger and the pain vanished away. She knew she should try and figure out some way to pick up the pieces, make some plan as to what to do with the rest of her life, but she couldn't break with it all, couldn't walk away and leave it. She knew that she would never cease to look back, to live it all over again and again.

Her doorbell rang. Andrea went to the door and looked through the peephole; she saw that it was her former aide, Agent Frederickson. *Come to collect his BJ, has he?* she thought. *Fair enough. Hell, might as well give him the whole nine yards, as Matt called it. Now I can find out what's been going on over there.* She called out through the door, "Just a sec!" She ran into the bedroom, tossed off the bathrobe, took off her bra and pulled on jeans and a suitably thin t-shirt, and slipped sandals onto her feet. Then she went back and opened the door. "Hi, Fred," she said. "Thanks for stopping by. No one else has, nobody's called, but that's to be expected, I suppose. Come on in, I'm dying to find out who got my job."

"Exactly," said Frederickson, genuine sadness in his voice.

"What?" she asked, not understanding.

"Andrea, I got your job. You're my first assignment." He grabbed her and shoved her into the apartment, followed by two huge FBI agents in suits, one white, one black. Each agent grabbed her by one arm. "Janet is a real bitch to work for, right enough," said Frederickson, "But Hillary has a zero tolerance policy towards failure. Zero tolerance, Andrea. I'm sorry we won't ever make that long weekend in the Bahamas. I really am." He walked to the balcony and opened the door, and suddenly Andrea understood. She shrieked at the top of her voice, struggling and howling in the grip of the two musclemen as they carried her effortlessly across the room and out onto the balcony and sent her sailing into the air, and all the way down she screamed in a mortal agony of terror as the cruel concrete rushed up at her. Then she was staring into the sky of brass, and she saw the tiny faces on her balcony looking down at her. A single overwhelming thought filled her last flickering consciousness. *I am an evil woman. All my life I have served evil. Now I will go to hell.* Then the blackness closed over her like a sack.

*✶✶

In the small hours of the morning, Hillary Rodham Clinton arose from the double bed in the Watergate apartment. Beside her on the pillow lay the sleeping head of her partner for the evening, a light-skinned black woman with very Caucasian features and long black hair. Her husband was not the only Clinton who enjoyed the company of White House interns, but Hillary liked to feel she was the better deal. She reached into her purse, took out two hundred dollar bills and folded them beneath the bedside lamp for the girl, then she went into the bathroom and took a long, hot shower, after which she carefully combed her hair and applied a touch-up to her hair color, making sure her natural ash blond did not meld into white.

She put on a bathrobe and stepped out into the room to get dressed. The first thing she saw was that the mulatto girl was lying half in and half out of the bed, her dead eyes bulging and her tongue protruding from between her teeth, the red mark of the strangling cord around her neck, and that the room was filled with the foul odor of her urine and feces where her bowels and bladder had relaxed in death and evacuated. An iron hand clamped itself into Hillary's hair and a knee to the small of her back forced into a half-kneeling position on the bed, her head held high. The cool touch of a long, razor-sharp switchblade knife caressed her throat. Hillary eyed the body of her dead lover dispassionately. "You killed Kanesha," she said dispassionately. "Why was that necessary?"

"It was necessary to gain a few uninterrupted minutes of your time, madam," said a courteous voice behind her.

"It must be very important to you to get those few minutes, then," said Hillary. "Who are you and what do you want? And may I ask how you got in here? You're very good."

"My name is Visconti, and yes, I am very good. I am going to offer you two choices. The first choice is that I kill you. The second is that you take this cellular phone in your left hand. I will punch the redial button, and you will speak to the man on the other end of it. At the end of that conversation I will then decide whether or not to kill you anyway."

"Give me the phone," said Hillary. She held it up to her ear and heard it ring. A Southern voice answered. "Hello, this is Hillary Rodham-Clinton. I understand you have something you wish to say to me. With whom am I speaking?"

"How do!" the man on the phone said. "This is your old buddy Two Gun Matt Redmond. You may remember me from such politically incorrect débacles as the Chuck Bennett Hand Grenade Hara-kiri, Maggie Mears the Swinging Senior, the Sheraton Shambles, and last but not least, Andrea and the Conquistadors Meet Their Waterloo! Mrs. Klintoon, if you can answer the following question correctly, you can win a fabulous prize called LIFE! Yes ma'am, all it takes is the correct answer to one simple question, and Johnny Vee will NOT cut your god-damned throat and spit in your face while you bleed to death on the same bed where you have just performed unspeakable sexual perversions that would make a dog vomit! To make it even easier for you to win this FABULOUS PRIZE, we'll even offer you a multiple choice answer! Now listen carefully! The question is: if Mr. Visconti refrains from severing your jugular vein, you will: A) Scream like hell for your

Secret Service bodyguards, who will prove to be mysteriously absent? B) Send yet more FBI and Secret Service and Third World mercenary thugs after me and my family? or C) Get the message, thank your lucky stars that you are being offered a chance to walk away from this monumental fuck-up, and never so much as allow the thought of me or any member of my family to cross your mind? So what will it be, Ms. Rodham-Bitch?"

"Mr. Redmond, you know perfectly well that while Mr. Visconti has this knife at my throat I will say or do whatever I think will keep me alive, even for a few more seconds," said Hillary Clinton coolly. "You surely don't place any credence in anything I would say or promise under such circumstances. So why this rodomontade?"

"Fair enough," said Matt. "OK, it's like this. You people have tried to get me twice. Maybe you have this idea that the third time's lucky. Maybe third time you will be. But in view of your failure twice before, is that a chance you want to take? Because if you miss again, you go, Hill. So does that yellow dog, ridge-running bush ape you married, if you care for him at all, which I must admit is something of a riddle to the world. Do you understand that I will kill you if there is so much as the slightest hint that you or anyone in the Federal government is taking any further interest in me or my family? Get this message through your head now. I do not exist. My wife and my daughter do not exist. My cat does not exist. Do you understand that?"

"Very well, I understand that."

Visconti's knife pricked her throat, drawing a drop of blood. "Say it," he whispered.

"You do not exist, Mr. Redmond," said Hillary calmly. "Your wife does not exist. Your daughter does not exist. Your cat does not exist."

"CORRECT-O!" said Matt joyously. "You, Mrs. Rodham-Lesboslut, have won first prize! You have, for the moment, talked me out of killing you! Now, you get a shot at an even bigger, more fabulous prize! I am going to hang up now, and you get to see if you can talk Mr. Visconti and the LaBrasca family into not killing you! Ta-ta, and thank you for

playing I AM A FILTHY PERVERTED MARXIST HAG WHO WANTS
TO RULE THE WORLD!" Matt hung up.

"All right, the same situation applies with you, Mr. Visconti," said
Hillary Clinton. "Tell me what you want me to say and promise, and I
will do it. But I don't see the point of all this. You obviously don't intend
to kill me, or you would have done it when I stepped out of the bathroom. You know perfectly well that any promise I make under these circumstances is worthless. You must want something from me alive. An
exchange of favors, I believe that's how you people work? Something to
do with my coming post as junior Senator from New York?"

"Something to do with the fact that you're Bill Clinton's boss," said
Visconti. "There will be no war with China. Do you understand? That
option is henceforth removed from his menu."

"The irony of it is, Mr. Visconti, that you and I are in complete
agreement on that, and you have done all this and killed Kanesha for
nothing, or rather I should say for something you would have gotten
anyway. We already have this situation sorted out. Neither the State
Department nor the Joint Chiefs of Staff will do anything of the kind
without my permission. They know that I am going to be President of
the United States in four years' time and they understand which side of
their bread is buttered. Bill Clinton is the Commander in Chief of the
armed forces in name only. In fact, I am, as we saw when the decision
was made to liberate Kossovo. Those bombers flew on my orders, Mr.
Visconti, not his. I also assume you want me to promise to leave the
Mob alone. Again, you are doing all this to gain something you would
have had in any case. The LaBrasca affair was an unfortunate necessity,
but beyond that I am fully aware of the possible future necessity I
might face to come to an accommodation with Cosa Nostra. You will
find that unlike the Kennedies, if ever I should have reason to give my
word to your people on something, I will keep it. Please convey that to
your superiors, if you would be so kind. You might also remember that
my opponent in the Senate race is a former United States Attorney who

was responsible for sending a number of you to prison. Now, is there anything else?"

"You have covered it all quite adequately, madam," said Visconti. "I see that you are as courageous as you are handsome, and that worries me. It bodes ill for America. May I ask you a personal question, purely to satisfy my own curiosity? You need not answer if you don't want to."

"What is it?" asked Hillary.

"Why did you do what you did to Alice Silverman? I mean, why did you take such a risk?" He gestured towards the dead black girl. "You can obviously satisfy your own tastes pretty much wherever you desire, and it is now clear that no one in the world will interfere. So why commit such a foolish and potentially self-destructive act?"

"Because I wanted her," replied Hillary, puzzled. "Why else would I do it? I mentioned it to Bill that night, and Bill wanted her too, and so we did her. Nobody forced her to have that baby or to write that letter to the White House, Mr. Visconti. That was her choice. She called the shots. Alice Silverman brought all of this on herself and she got what she deserved, although it turned into an inexcusable mess. By the way, the woman who was responsible for all that pointless melodrama has been dealt with."

"Yes, so I have heard. Thank you for answering me, madam. It is the answer I expected. I fear I must do you the disservice of restraining you while I make my departure."

"I understand," said Hillary. Quietly she submitted to having her hands bound behind her back and her ankles taped firmly together with masking tape. Visconti was about to place a strip of tape over her mouth when she spoke again. "Mr. Visconti? May I have a few more quick words while I've got your attention?"

"Certainly," said John.

"This business has been handled with appalling ineptitude from the beginning, and it has become clear to me that I am going to need more proficient and professional assistance in these matters, certainly more than Janet Reno can provide. Your entry into these premises past the

United States Secret Service demonstrates to me that you have the kind of expertise I am looking for. I would like to offer you a job, Mr. Visconti. You have indicated that you are aware that I am going places. You can go there with me."

"I am honored, *bellissima*," said the Mafioso.

"Thank you. In fact, I am prepared to offer you your first commission now. A million dollars for your first job in my employ."

"And that would be?" asked Visconti politely.

"Kill Matt Redmond! Kill his wife! Kill his daughter! And finally, kill his goddamned cat! Bring me their heads, all four of them, and one million dollars is yours, in cash or in any bank account you name, anywhere in the world!" said Hillary fiercely.

"I see," said Visconti gravely. "Madam, there are two things you need to learn. The first thing is that there are still some genuine white men left in the world, men whom you can neither buy nor intimidate nor insult with impunity. Matthew Redmond is one of them."

"I see. And the second thing is?" asked Hillary.

"That I am another," said Visconti. He leaned forward, lifting the knife, and a moment later a scream of pain and horror shook the walls of the apartment.

Ten minutes later John Visconti stepped into an alley near the Watergate and got into the passenger seat of an automobile. Matt started the engine and slid out onto the street. Moments later they were tooling down Constitution Avenue towards the Potomac and Virginia. "How did it go?" asked Matt.

"She is fearless. Not the stupid fearlessness of a Luther Lambert, but the fearlessness of true evil. May God have mercy on us all. We may have made a terrible mistake in letting her live."

"I know what you mean," said Matt. "My father is the same way."

"She offered me a million dollars to kill you," said Visconti. They drove on in silence for a while. "Matt, it has been almost two minutes since I told you that Hillary Clinton offered me a million dollars to kill you. During that time you have kept both of your hands on the wheel, and you have not unbuttoned your jacket or made any move to get to your gun. Thank you, my friend. That is one of the greatest honors that any man has ever paid me."

"*Omertà.* You have it, you live it, and I know it. There was no need for me to unbutton my jacket," said Matt. "The thought never crossed my mind."

"*Grazie,*" said Visconti. "I brought you a souvenir." He handed Matt a small rolled up ball of paper towel. It was seeping a small amount of blood. Matt laid it on the dash, unwrapped it with one hand while he drove, and took out a small flaccid object. It was a woman's right ear. "The price of insult. Yes, it is hers. It will be amusing to us both to see how she wears her hair from now on in public, or what kind of prosthetic the best doctors in the country can make for her. You may take it home if you wish, and put it in a bottle of alcohol or formaldehyde, and whenever you look upon it, think upon the strange and wonderful and horrible and hilarious thing that is Life."

"*Grazie, amico mio,*" said Matt Redmond.

November in Carolina is a dark and brooding month, sometimes cold, sometimes warm, but almost always gray and melancholy. Matt and Heather Redmond sat on the deck of their home on Boundary Street. Tori was inside working on the Thanksgiving dinner, a variety of appetizing aromas filling the house. Tony Stoppaglia sat beside Matt and Heather, looking down over a small wooded valley into the back yards of a number of other houses in collegiate suburban Chapel Hill. "Thank you for letting me come," he told them. "This an important day for families, and I want you to know that I understand what it is costing you to let me be here today."

"Thank you for coming all the way from Italy," said Matt. "Especially in view of the situation. We still don't know what is going to happen with all this. How have you been doing?"

"The leg is as good as new. As for this?" He touched the livid white scar on his cheek that ran down to his jaw. "Hey, like I told Heather, it's cool. Scarface is a great moniker for a wiseguy."

"Tony, whatever happens, we will never forget how you got it," said Heather. "How is little William, or Guglielmo?"

"Anselmo and Giulia Vitale and all the kids damned near worship him," said Tony. "He will grow up surrounded by love, and Giulia will be a mother and a half because he's an orphan. Alice would like them and be very happy for him. Don't ever worry on that score. You did right." Tori stepped out onto the deck.

"Okay, guys," she said to her mother and father, "Almost ready. Any chance you might let me in on why we have cooked not one but two, count 'em, *two* turkeys plus one ham, and why we have enough veggies and stuffing and cranberry sauce and pumpkin pie for a small army?"

"Ah, well, we're expecting some more guests," said Matt. "The fact is that your mother and I have been writing some letters and making some phone calls to certain people out on the West Coast." The front door bell rang. "That may be them now, in fact."

"What are they up to?" asked Tony suspiciously.

"Hey, I quit trying to second-guess these two a long time ago," said Tori with a shrug. "Fact is that they're really kind of weird."

Matt answered his front door. There were airport rental cars in the driveway, and there was a group of people standing outside. Foremost among them was a tall and stunningly beautiful young woman with long blond hair, wearing an expensive but subdued dress and jacket of gray silk. She stepped forward, offering her hand. "Mr. Redmond? Hi. I'm Kirsten Dunst."

"Thank you for coming, Miss Dunst," said Matt gravely, taking her hand. "I appreciate your taking the time."

"Alice was a friend," she said. "I read her notes that you sent us, the ones she left on the screenplay and the casting. I'm honored she wanted me." The others came in behind her.

"Tommy Lee Jones," said Jones, thrusting his hand into Matt's. "I drew the short straw, Matt. I play you."

"Costas Mandylor," said Mandylor, walking up to the stunned Tony. "You must be Tony Stoppaglia, from the scar. Mr. Stoppaglia, any chance I could arrange through you to meet John Visconti, strictly on the QT? I'd like to get the best scope I can on him, for obvious reasons."

"And you must be Heather," said Kyra Sedgwick. "After dinner, could you and I talk a bit? I need to get the story from the horse's mouth, so to speak."

"Matt, when you've got a moment, I'd like to talk to you about Art Garza, what kind of man he was, how he spoke and moved, how he would have wanted this done," said Nick Nolte.

"Hi, Tori!" called Jennifer Aniston, waving from the rear of the group. She was holding Trumpeldor, who reached up and placed his paw on her nose

"Don't even *think* about it!" said Tori to Tony, a smile on her face as she waved back.

"We have The Undertaker and Kristen Johnston and John Lithgow on line for the Musketeers," said Kirsten Dunst. "Charlton Heston has agreed to a cameo as your boss Mr. Hightower, and F. Murray Abraham will appear in another cameo as Dominic LaBrasca. I'm not sure yet, but I think we've got Gina Gershon for Andrea Weinmann."

"Okay, okay, who plays *me?*" demanded Tony, gaping in astonishment. "Look, you guys, you know I was kidding about that remark I made back there on the island…?"

"Will I do?" asked Leonardo Di Caprio, stepping forward. "I know she didn't think much of me, either personally or as an actor, but I always thought a lot of good about her, in both departments. This is something I want to do for her, Tony. We don't all have our noses stuck up Bill and Hillary Clinton's asses. Our community lost a beautiful person and a great talent out there on that island. We are here to make sure she's never forgotten."

"Is this picture really going to be made?" asked Matt bluntly. "Do you dare?"

"Made, yes," said Jones. "I'm directing. We've all pooled our resources. It will be low budget, we may have to hire all the local winos on the Outer Banks to play FBI agents and all the local *illegale* migrant workers to play Conquistadors, but the script will be first rate, by two of Hollywood's best screenplay writers, based on Alice's notes that you sent Kirsten and also on the input we can get from you folks, and the production will be professionally done and edited. A lot of us are pitching in on this one, including some people who don't want their names publicly involved but who are helping out with money and facilities, special effects and technical assistance, so forth and so on. We'll have the script by Christmas, we'll do the all interior scenes by February and the external shoots here in North Carolina and Florida and the Outer Banks in the spring. Yes, Matt, the picture will be made. Released, now that's another matter."

"If it will never be seen, then what's the point?" asked Heather.

"It may not be seen now," said Jones, "In fact we probably won't be able even to get it distributed to the public for a time, at least not until after the 2000 election. The Clintons have a hell of a lot of pull in Hollywood, as you know. But it will be in the can, and we will make sure that enough copies of the picture find their way into private hands, small arts theaters, cable TV, whoever will show it, so that it can never be suppressed completely."

"What will the title of the movie be?" asked Tori excitedly.

"We've settled on kind of an artsy-fartsy title," said Kirsten Dunst. "You may not like it, but I think your Dad might. We're thinking of calling it *Sic Semper Tyrannis.*"

"Any chance we could hold the premier in Ford's Theater in Washington?" asked Matt.

"Hey, one thing I can promise youse guys for sure," said Tony earnestly. "You won't have no union problems."

X10

Slow Coming Dark

William Jefferson Blythe Clinton sat behind the big mahogany desk in the Oval Office. He sat erect in his chair, staring into the opposite wall at some object a thousand yards away. Before him on the desk, laid out on a mirror, were several long lines of white powdered cocaine. On the tip of his nose was a large daub of the white drug.

An aide quietly entered the room. "Mr. President?" he asked softly. "Mr. President?" Clinton did not answer, but continued to stare at the wall, and after a time the man went away. A fly was buzzing around Clinton's face. It landed on his nose and lapped up some of the cocaine, then it weaved off drunkenly into the air. Slowly the President of the United States began to lean forward in his chair, until his expressionless face was resting on his nose on the coke-smeared mirror.

All was silent in the Oval Office, while outside the darkness of November slowly descended over Washington. After a while the fly came back, accompanied by a number of its friends. It had evidently liked the cocaine and passed the word in the insect community. In the highest office of the land there was now darkness, and the only sound was the ticking of an ancient clock that had belonged to Andrew Jackson. That, and the buzzing of flies.

About the Author

H. A. Covington currently lives in Texas and is the author of seven novels.